MY SHOCKING MONTE CARLO CONFESSION

HEIDI RICE

A SCANDAL MADE IN LONDON

LUCY KING

MILLS & BOON

First Published in Great Britain 2020
by Mills & Boon, an imprint of HarperCollins*Publishers*
1 London Bridge Street, London, SE1 9GF

My Shocking Monte Carlo Confession © 2020 by Heidi Rice

A Scandal Made in London © 2020 by Lucy King

ISBN: 978-0-263-27812-5

MIX
Paper from
responsible sources
FSC™ C007454

This book is produced from independently certified FSC™ paper
to ensure responsible forest management.
For more information visit www.harpercollins.co.uk/green.

Printed and bound in Spain
by CPI, Barcelona

USA TODAY bestselling author **Heidi Rice** lives in London, England. She is married with two teenage sons—which gives her rather too much of an insight into the male psyche—and also works as a film journalist. She adores her job, which involves getting swept up in a world of high emotion, sensual excitement, funny and feisty women, sexy and tortured men and glamorous locations where laundry doesn't exist. Once she turns off her computer she often does chores—usually involving laundry!

Lucy King spent her adolescence lost in the glamorous and exciting world of Mills & Boon when she really ought to have been paying attention to her teachers. But, as she couldn't live in a dream world for ever, she eventually acquired a degree in languages and an eclectic collection of jobs. After a decade in southwest Spain, Lucy now lives with her young family in Wiltshire. When not writing, or trying to think up new and innovative things to do with mince, she spends her time reading, failing to finish cryptic crosswords and dreaming of the golden beaches of Andalucia.

MY SHOCKING MONTE CARLO CONFESSION

HEIDI RICE

To Teresa and Alan, the best hosts ever!

PROLOGUE

Belle

THE RIVIERA SUN blazed down as I stared into my best friend Remy Galanti's grave, but the sunshine did nothing to thaw the chill which had seeped into my bones over a week ago—ever since Remy's car had ploughed through the crash barrier at the Galanti test track in Nice and burst into flames. The horror of those moments played through my mind again, in agonising slow motion, but the tears wedged in my throat refused to fall.

I hadn't cried—for Remy, for myself, for his older brother, Alexi—because I couldn't. My body, like my mind, was numb.

The priest's voice droned on in French as I glanced across the grave to where Alexi stood.

He wore a dark linen suit and was surrounded by the local dignitaries and a host of celebrities and VIPs who had come out in force to show their respect to Monaco's—and motor racing's—foremost family at the loss of their second son. But as always Alexi looked utterly alone, his head bent and his stance rigid. A muscle in his jaw clenched and his dark hair was dishevelled, as if he had run his fingers through it a thousand times since the day we'd both watched Remy die.

His eyes, though, like mine, were dry.

Did he feel numb, the way I did? Destroyed by the loss of someone who had meant so much to us both? Remy had been my best friend ever since I had come to live in the Galanti mansion on the Côte d'Azur as a ten-year-old, when my mother had taken the job as the new housekeeper after Remy and Alexi's mother had run off to join one of her lovers.

I felt as if a part of my soul had been ripped out. But Alexi had lost a brother—the only person he had ever been close to after their mother's disappearance. Surely he had to be in as much distress as me, if not more?

But he didn't look numb as he glanced at the priest, his beautiful blue eyes sparking with impatience and contempt, he looked angry.

Not angry, furious.

Heat prickled over my skin, inappropriate but undeniable as the memories from a week ago played through my mind. The night before Remy's death the night when I'd thought every one of my dreams had come true—the night I had gone to Alexi and made love to him for the first time. I remembered the scent of salt and sweat and chlorine, the giddy rush of emotion, the glorious sensation of spending a few minutes in Alexi's strong arms and discovering what sex was all about.

Terrifyingly intimate but also fabulously exciting.

The brutal humiliation clutched at my heart as I stared at Alexi across the grave. He hadn't spoken to me since that night. I had tried to see him but he'd always been busy. Guilt pinched my ribs to go with the inappropriate heat that he always inspired in me, even at Remy's funeral.

Remy had always been there for me and now I wanted to be there for Alexi. I knew that was what Remy would have wanted. But still I felt guilty because I knew it wasn't just Remy's wishes I wanted to fulfil. But then Remy's final words to me replayed in my mind as the priest finished his graveside eulogy, the last of the words floating away on the gentle breeze scented with sea air and bougainvillea.

'My brother needs you, bellissima. *Alexi is lonely. He always has been. Just make me a promise,* bellissima. *Don't let him push you away. Okay?'*

The promise I had made to Remy rang in my head now as I watched Alexi pick up a fistful of dirt from the graveside and throw it onto the casket—his movements were stiff and lethargic, as if he had a weight on his shoulders he was struggling to bear. He looked so, so alone in that moment.

As the other mourners—many of whom had barely known Remy—lined up to drop dirt on the coffin, Alexi turned and walked towards the line of waiting limousines, ignoring the people offering their condolences.

Sending up a silent prayer for Remy as I glanced one last time at his coffin, I left the graveside and followed Alexi's retreating figure to the road out of the clifftop graveyard. For the first time since Remy's death the fog of shock and grief, the numbness, began to lift, the urgency allowing the adrenaline, the determination, to force the coldness out.

Breathless, I cried out as I saw him reach the lead car. 'Alexi, wait, please. Can we talk?'

He paused and turned, but his stance remained rigid. And, as I looked into them, his eyes were like shards of ice.

'Belle, what do you want?' The impatience shocked me, but not as much as the strident tone.

Was he angry with me? Was that why he had avoided me since Remy's death? But as soon as the thought occurred to me I dismissed it. I was being paranoid, insecure, and this was not the time. This wasn't about me, or about what we'd done seven nights ago. He wasn't angry with me. I simply didn't mean that much to him, I knew that, whatever Remy in his optimism had said about our liaison.

Alexi was angry at his brother's senseless death and probably furious with his father, who had arrived drunk at the funeral, not to mention angry at the fates who had robbed him of the last of his family—or the only part of his family who'd ever mattered to him.

He didn't want me sexually. He'd made that very clear after we'd slept together a week ago. It had been a mistake.

But that didn't mean I couldn't offer him friendship. If nothing more, I could offer him comfort in our shared grief, because I was the only other person who felt Remy's loss as keenly as he did.

'I wanted to make sure you're okay,' I said.

'Of course I'm not okay, I killed my brother.'

'Wh...? What?' The shiver at the coldness in his voice, and in his eyes, racked my whole body despite the warm day. Was he serious? How could he believe even for a moment he was to blame for Remy's death?

'You heard me,' he said, his anger slicing through my shock.

'But he wanted to be a driver, Alexi. It was his dream, his passion, for so long. You mustn't hold yourself responsible,' I said, trying to grasp the reason for his guilt.

Alexi had been managing the Galanti Super League team for two years now, ever since his father, Gustavo, had begun drinking so heavily he was no longer capable of hiding the extent of his addiction. Alexi had given Remy his chance as a test driver and had let him have his first lead this season. Was that why he blamed himself for Remy's accident?

He stared at me blankly, then his lips flattened into a

grim line. 'Don't play the innocent with me. It won't work a second time.'

'I don't... I—I don't understand,' I stammered, the cynicism in his gaze chilling.

I hadn't bled when we had made love a week ago, even though Alexi was my first lover. I'd felt the pinch, the slight soreness, when he'd thrust heavily inside me—he wasn't a small man. But the pain had been so slight, so fleeting—the pleasure overwhelming in its intensity only moments later—that I was sure he hadn't realised about my virginity. At the time, I had been grateful. I didn't want him to think of me as a child. But when he spoke again I wasn't grateful any more.

'Stop playing the innocent. Remy knew what we'd done. He pretended it didn't matter, made some joke about it at the track that day before he went out, but you were always his girl. I should never have touched you. That's why he got distracted on the track, took the turn too fast.'

'But I... I was never Remy's girl, not like that. We were just friends,' I said, suddenly understanding where Alexi's guilt came from and wanting to make it right.

His eyebrows flattened, the muscle in his jaw jumped and the cynical twist of his lips sharpened as the chill in his blue eyes darkened.

'Was it you?' he hissed. 'Did you tell him we slept together even though I told you not to?'

'Yes,' I said, blurting out the truth.

I could have lied. A part of me wanted to lie—the agonising guilt in Alexi's eyes now fired by the light of fury—but I wasn't ashamed of what we'd done. Remy had been pleased about the possibility of us dating, not upset.

Alexi didn't understand about my friendship with Remy because he didn't know his younger brother was gay.

If only I could tell him that now. The truth lingered on

the tip of my tongue, but I couldn't voice it as I saw the pain behind the guilt in Alexi's eyes.

It would only hurt him more, to know Remy had confided in me and not him—and it had always been Remy's secret to reveal. If he'd wanted Alexi to know, wouldn't he already have told him? How could I break my confidence to Remy now, simply to save myself from his brother's wrath?

'Why did you tell him?' he asked, the accusation in his voice as raw as the pain.

'Because...' I stuttered to a stop.

Because Remy was gay, because we were friends, because he knew how much I had always loved you and he wanted us to be together.

But the words got stuck in my throat, behind the huge dam of emotion forged by the disgust etched on Alexi's face.

'Don't answer that,' he said before I could get the words out. 'I think we both know why you told him. Because you thought I was the better catch, didn't you? You figured, being the older brother, I was worth more.'

I was so stunned by his accusations I couldn't even begin to defend myself.

'You little whore. I knew I shouldn't have touched you, that it was wrong, but I never realised how wrong.'

His words were like physical blows—each one more painful than the last.

How could I ever have believed he loved me, cared about me, that he knew me at all, when he could accuse me of such things?

'I want you gone,' he said curtly. 'Out of my father's house. Today.'

'But...' I couldn't speak, couldn't even protect myself, the calmness in his voice almost as devastating as the flat, impersonal look in his eyes as the guilt, the anger, the bitterness, the cynicism all melted away and became nothing.

'I'll have the lawyers pay you off. I never want to see your face again.' He turned to climb into the car and I grasped his arm.

'Please, Alexi, don't do this. Don't shut me out,' I begged. 'You're hurting, you're in pain, I understand that, but so am I. We both loved Remy very much. Neither one of us is to blame for his death. It was a freak accident. We can get through this together.'

The bitter laugh shocked me to the core.

'We didn't love him. We killed him. Now we're both going to have to live with that betrayal. If I see you at the villa when I return, I'll have you arrested. You've got two hours to get your stuff together and leave. Send a forwarding address to my lawyers and I'll wire you a severance payment.'

He yanked his sleeve free. His gaze sliced over my figure and my body shuddered in an instinctive response that shamed me to my core even now.

'Don't worry, I'll be generous. Your hot little act on Friday night was worth at least a few thousand euro.'

I stood shaking as he climbed into the car and the long, black limousine pulled away from the curb then took the cliff road out of the cemetery. He didn't look back, not once.

The numbness returned, but this time it was all-consuming. The hollow ache in my insides became a black hole as the huge loss left by Remy's death combined with the agonising evidence that the dreams I'd had about Alexi ever since I'd hit puberty had always been a foolish schoolgirl's fantasy.

He wasn't the man I had believed him to be. The man I had adored from afar.

And he wasn't the man Remy had believed him to be either.

Alexi wasn't just reserved, or lonely, or simply wary of love. He was dead inside. Much deader than Remy could ever have been.

I walked down the path away from the cemetery and hailed a taxi to take me back to the Galanti estate where I had spent so much of my childhood.

But I didn't feel like a child any more. I felt about a thousand years old as I packed my belongings. It took me less than an hour before I was on the bus to Nice. I had some savings, enough to get me out of Monaco. I wasn't going to send Alexi's lawyer a forwarding address. I didn't want his money any more than I wanted him to know where I was.

I would return to London, I decided, my mind surprisingly calm. I had a second cousin there who might put me up if I begged. Since my mother's death two years ago, she was the only family I had left.

I needed to get away from Alexi, away from the agonising memories of my best friend, Remy, and the hole that would be left in my life for ever. I needed to leave the remnants of my girlhood behind me—and the tattered remains of a dream that had never been real.

I'd loved Alexi for so long. I'd put him on a pedestal and idolised him. And when we'd finally made love I'd felt such passion, such excitement, in his arms.

But I'd never really known him. Not even while I had been clinging to his strong, powerful body and glorying in the feel of him inside me as he'd rocked us both to orgasm.

I knew him now, though. I knew his cynicism, his bitterness and his anger because I had become the target of all three.

'I'm so sorry, Remy,' I whispered as the bus made its way

out of Monaco and along the coast road towards Nice. 'I couldn't keep my promise.'

The tears I had refused to shed flowed down my cheeks as Monaco's glittering lights disappeared behind the cliffs.

I scrubbed the tears away with my fist before any of the other passengers could see them, swallowed down the choking sobs making my ribs ache and kept my gaze on the road ahead.

At last, the numbness returned.

I embraced it this time, because it protected me from the agony threatening to consume me.

The numbness gave me strength.

A strength I would need to survive Remy's death—and Alexi's brutal rejection. And to find a new home, a new job and a new life far away from the Galantis.

CHAPTER ONE

Five years later

Alexi

'SO WHO AM I looking at and what's his price?' I squinted through my sunglasses at the track and adjusted my cap—which bore my rival Renzo Camaro's team logo—to ensure the bill covered my face as I spoke to Freddie Graham. Freddie was a freelance mechanic and an old friend. He'd given me the tip off twenty minutes ago that he'd spotted a fresh new talent driving Camaro's prototype at the Barcelona track as part of their testing for the new season.

I was desperate. Galanti's reserve driver, Carlo Poncelli, had just had a cancer diagnosis. We'd managed to keep it quiet for the last few days, but as soon as the news hit the circuit that Carlo was going to be receiving chemo treatment for most of the season every agent's price would go through the roof. I wanted to find someone quickly, someone talented and as yet undiscovered who would jump at the chance of getting a reserve seat in the Super League with the top team on the circuit—and was un-agented. It was a tall order, but if anyone could spot talent it was Freddie.

'Keep your voice down,' Graham said furtively as we

watched the track together from the edge of the stands—
out of sight of Camaro and his team. 'If Camaro finds out
you're here checking out his employees, I'll get black-
listed.'

The noise of Camaro's new design drowned out the
end of Freddie's sentence as the car came shooting round
the bend and back into view. The car accelerated to two
hundred miles an hour and the back wheels shuddered,
but the driver brought it back under control with smooth,
steely efficiency. The adrenaline rush I always got from
watching a great new talent raised the hairs at my nape.

I would need to see stats and get a basic history before
making an offer, find out the guy's age and what licences
he held, but I already knew this was our man. I had a sixth
sense about this stuff. It was what I was famous for on the
circuit. Or rather, infamous for. That and having a different
supermodel or actress on my arm at every event I attended.

'Who is he? Is he actually signed to Camaro yet? And
why the hell haven't I heard of him?' I fired questions at
Freddie as the car completed the circuit and headed into
the pits.

If he was contracted to a team in one of the lower
leagues, I'd have to buy him out, which would cost me.
But I already knew I wanted him.

Camaro would probably have a cow. The guy was
known for his hard business practices and the Destiny
team had been Galanti's main rivals for three seasons. But
if Renzo was only using this kid for test driving he was
already missing a trick. I would have to act fast, though.
We were already two months into the season. And I would
need to get the new driver familiar with our car before
winter testing.

'Slow down, fella,' Freddie said in his thick Brooklyn
accent. 'Rumour on the track is she's one of Camaro's

R&D people. She's not even a driver. Story is she's Renzo's mistress and he brought her over from London when his reserve driver got the flu. He needed someone to test the car, and he knows she's a talent, but when I saw her drive…'

Freddie's voice trailed off. But most of what he'd been saying had already washed over me because my brain had snagged on one word.

She.

This kid was a woman? *Dio!*

That was…

My mind exploded. That was an incredible PR opportunity. Even if I hadn't been desperate and she wasn't as good as she appeared I would have wanted to sign her.

There were female drivers in the lower leagues and on the reserve lists. Good female drivers who, sooner or later, would break into motor sport's top flight. But a female driver *this* good who was undiscovered and wasn't even attached to a team?

Except… My excitement downgraded.

She was attached to Renzo in a personal capacity.

'You say she's Renzo's mistress?' I turned to Freddie, his hangdog expression unchanged.

'That's what one of the mechanics told me. I saw them together and Renzo's all over her. Although she's a long way from being his usual type. She's kind of a tomboy.'

I frowned. Who knew Freddie was a gossip? But right now his nosiness suited my purposes. I wanted to know more about the girl before I approached her. If she was stuck on Renzo it might be a harder sell to get her to sign for me.

My lips quirked in a cynical smile.

'Whatever her connection to Camaro, I'm sure I can make her a better offer,' I said, confident any commitment she had to my rival could be broken.

She was a woman. Women in my experience could always be bought, with either money, orgasms or both. If I had to seduce her, I would. I wasn't dating anyone at the moment and I had no problem mixing business with pleasure. It was one of the perks of being a workaholic.

'Hold your jets, Casanova,' Freddie said. 'Renzo's not your only problem. The same mechanic told me she doesn't want to be a pro driver. Apparently Renzo's been trying to sign her to his young driver programme for over a year and she's not interested.'

'What? Why?' I couldn't hide my shock. Anyone with that much natural talent would be insane not to go for the gold ring. And no one could get that good in the first place without a passion for the sport.

'Haven't a clue. But I guess she must have her reasons.'

My surprise was quickly quashed by my confidence. Whatever her reasons, I'd figure out a way to overcome them. I knew how to play women, just like I knew how to play my rivals.

Charm was easy, seduction even easier. They were both commodities I'd learned to use to my advantage, deliberately honing my image as a womanising playboy to hide the ruthlessness that had driven me ever since Remy's death.

Thoughts of Remy killed the smile playing around my lips, reminding me not just of my boyish, reckless, stupidly trusting younger brother who had died so needlessly but also of the girl—*his* girl—who had screwed with my head far too often since Remy's death.

Belle Simpson had completely disappeared after Remy's funeral and I refused to give a damn about it. I'd tortured myself enough over the thought of her—soft, fresh and artlessly seductive—during that one night we'd shared. She'd been an illusion. She was no more pure and fresh than I was, or had ever been. Just because she'd never contacted me to get the pay off I'd offered her didn't make her innocent. Maybe her conscience had eventually got the better of her too, about what we'd both done to Remy.

I cut off the thought at the fresh slice of guilt. Remy was dead. I couldn't turn back the clock and undo what I'd done to him that night when Belle's wide emerald eyes had gazed at me as if I'd been everything she could ever want. That whole night had been screwed up. My cheek had been smarting from one of my father's back-handed slaps, my head fuzzy from one too many tequila slammers. I'd had to stop beating myself up for giving into the incendiary attraction between us.

I hated that, whenever I thought of Remy, I thought of her too. And her deep-green eyes wide with distress and unshed tears.

Ruthlessly pushing thoughts of my dead brother and that fateful night to one side, I bid goodbye to Freddie with the promise of a generous gift for his help if I managed to sign this girl.

I made my way towards the drivers' lounge behind the car hangars. Driving was hard, sweaty work, particularly in Barcelona in spring—the girl would have to shower and change before she did anything else. With the Camaro team cap pulled low, no one took any notice of me as I strolled past the team of mechanics busy assessing the new car's tyres for burn-out.

I spotted Camaro at the edge of the bay, talking to his chief mechanic, but no sign of the girl driver.

My hunch had been correct. She must have headed straight for the lounge area. Now all I had to do was hope my luck held out and I could catch her alone once she'd finished changing—to make her an offer she couldn't refuse.

Adrenaline pumped through my system. I'd always been

a guy who revelled in the thrill of the chase—either in pursuit of a great new design, a talented driver or a beautiful woman. This girl could be a combination of all three.

The lounge area was empty. I noticed a makeshift sign stuck on one of the doors to the changing rooms reserved for individual drivers: *Solo Mujeres.*

Women only.

I almost laughed out loud as I sat down silently on one of the plush leather sofas.

Perfect—there was no one here. Giving me all the opportunity I needed to poach Renzo's mistress. And turn her into the driver she was meant to be. And maybe more.

I discarded the cap and the shades as I listened to the shower running in the adjoining changing room. And waited.

The shower eventually shut off and I could hear a soft British voice singing a French lullaby.

Something pricked at my consciousness. Why did the light, lilting voice sound so familiar?

Before I had a chance to register the question, the girl appeared in the doorway to the lounge, silhouetted by the bright sunlight shining through the windows behind her. She jolted and gasped, the sob of distress probably down to her surprise at finding a strange guy sitting in the lounge. I stood to introduce myself.

'Hi, Miss...' I paused, realising Freddie had never given me her name. 'I'm Alexi Galanti. I own and operate the Galanti team. We need a new reserve driver for the rest of the season and I want to offer you the position. Whatever Camaro's paying you, I'll double it.'

It was rash of me to offer her the job without talking to my legal team, getting her credentials properly checked out and giving her a probationary period. I couldn't even see her face properly and I hadn't heard her speak. Damn it, I didn't even know her name. But all my instincts were telling me to claim her, so I didn't regret the rash decision. I always trusted my instincts.

What I could see of her figure—her subtle curves seductively displayed in a pair of tomboy jeans and a white shirt and camisole—had my blood heating in my groin. Desire pumped through my veins with a visceral urgency.

Maybe it was the combination of hunger and desire combined with the knowledge of how she had handled Camaro's powerful car that was driving my determination—because I wasn't even sure what I wanted most any more. To see her in *my* car, or in my bed.

The hairs on the back of my neck prickled in time to the echo of the lullaby which still lingered in my mind as she stood silently, not speaking. I could hear her rapid, uneven breathing.

Something was wrong. Why was she so silent? So tense? Why was her stance strangely defensive, as if I'd insulted her instead of having offered her a million-dollar contract?

Then her scent invaded my nostrils—fresh, floral and disturbingly familiar, bringing back memories of the night five years ago that I had never been able to forget. Recognition struck me as she stepped into the light and her face was illuminated for the first time. The striking features—the soft, translucent skin, the sprinkle of girlish freckles across her nose, the sleepy emerald eyes and the wild shock of rich russet curls—were just as I remembered them from my dreams—and my nightmares. Grief, betrayal and longing arrowed into my gut to join the hot punch of lust that had never died.

'I don't want anything from you, Alexi,' she whispered, her voice a tortured rasp—both bold and defensive at the same time. 'I never did.'

CHAPTER TWO

Belle

IT WAS A lie. Once upon a time, I had wanted everything from Alexi Galanti. Not just his body, but his love. But as I stared at his tall, muscular body dressed in a T-shirt and worn jeans, the fabric stretched enticingly across pectoral muscles that had only become more defined in the last five years—not quite sure if he was real or a figment of my over-active imagination—I knew those desires were childish dreams borne of infatuation.

I'd locked those dreams away five years ago after the cruel banishment which had left me destitute, disillusioned and alone at nineteen.

And, as I'd discovered two months later, pregnant with his child.

I refused to let them resurface now just because he was even more handsome and compelling at thirty than he had been at twenty-five.

I was twenty-four now and I'd survived what he'd done to me. And I had a wonderful son whom I adored.

I struggled to quell the old yearning which shivered through me at the sight of him. A yearning I'd never been able to feel for any other man.

Heat careered into my cheeks as I watched him stiffen,

the knowledge of who I was hitting him as hard as it had hit me a few moments before.

Good, I was glad. I wanted him to feel as raw as I did.

But, as soon as the ungenerous thought occurred to me, another horrifying realisation hit me—bringing with it the guilt I had struggled with for five years.

Oh, no! My cousin, Jessie, was bringing Cai—my son—to meet me at the track this afternoon.

I'd known it was a risk, agreeing to come to Barcelona to test drive the car I'd helped develop in my role as Camaro's fuel-efficiency expert for their R&D department in the UK. But Renzo, my boss, had been quite insistent and I had checked to make sure the Galanti team weren't scheduled to be at the test track today.

Cai loved the cars and the trip had been a special treat for him. But I didn't want him to come face to face with his father—or vice versa.

I'd never contacted Alexi to tell him about his son. I'd been in a daze, still struggling to cope with the loss of Remy, not to mention my job and my life in Monaco, when I'd discovered I was pregnant five years ago.

I hadn't had the courage or the strength to face Alexi then and as my pregnancy had progressed I had quickly begun to justify my cowardice to myself.

Alexi had made it very clear he hated me, that he blamed me for Remy's death. He'd told me he never wanted to see me again, that he'd have me arrested if he did. He'd called me a whore and implied I was a gold-digger. He probably wouldn't even have believed the child was his, so what would have been the point?

And, in the years since Cai's birth, it had become easier and easier not to make that call. My sweet, beautiful, smiley little boy, who looked so much like his father but would always be mine, would never know the cynicism, the coldness, of the man who had sired him. Really, I was just protecting my son.

I'd seen reports of Alexi's love life in the press, in gossip columns and celebrity blogs, over the intervening years too and had convinced myself Alexi wouldn't want to be a father. That I was doing him a favour by not divulging to him he had a son. Surely he wouldn't want to be tied down, to have his rampant womanising and glamorous social life hampered by a toddler?

But, now I was faced with the possibility of him meeting Cai for the first time, all my justifications began to crumble.

The guilt combined with the inappropriate yearning in the pit of my stomach made me plummet into the black hole I remembered from the last time I'd seen him—creating a wave of pure, unadulterated panic.

I'd always told myself that one day—when Cai was older, and I had become the foremost R&D specialist in the Super League and had some serious professional clout—I would get up the guts to inform Alexi of his son's existence.

But this wasn't that day. I wasn't ready to face that reality. Not yet. And neither was Cai. I hadn't prepared Cai for this news. And I doubted Alexi would even care if he had a son.

'I need you to leave,' I said, my voice firm, even though I was shaking inside from fear and the heat that would never die as long as I was in the same room as this man.

He hadn't said anything, he'd been rooted to the spot, but he controlled himself a lot faster than I did, the naked shock on his face masked by the cynical expression I remembered from our graveside parting. Although the heat in his gaze told another story, a heat I recognised from that fateful night when we had conceived Cai.

How could we still want each other when we both hated each other so much? I wondered vaguely, as my frantic mind tried to grasp the logistics of how I was going to avert the disaster galloping towards me with each tick of the clock.

Calm down, Belle, and don't show him any weakness.

I had twenty minutes. They weren't due here till three. I had time. All I had to do was get Alexi to leave before Jessie and Cai arrived. Surely it wouldn't be that hard, now he knew who I was? After all, he had been prepared to pay thousands of euros five years ago so he'd never have to see me again.

'The offer still stands,' he said at last.

'I… What? You can't be serious,' I said, stunned. Surely he couldn't believe I would want to spend any time in his company, let alone work for him?

'I'm deadly serious. I need a reserve driver and I want you… You should be on the track, not behind it. Once you're signed with Galanti we can discuss the possibility of getting a full driver spot for you, maybe next season. I'll make it worth your while to break your attachment to Camaro…' His gaze dipped, his perusal swift but no less insulting, and the heat ignited in my cheeks as I saw the spark of desire and realised he thought Renzo and I were lovers.

I knew rumours were rife on the track and in the Camaro team that I was sleeping with the boss. Renzo had been instrumental in advancing my career, hiring me for his R&D team straight after I'd finished my masters in bio-engineering and alternative fuel technology last year. He had been remarkably flexible about my childcare commitments on the job, had befriended Cai—who idolised him—and I did sometimes wonder if he thought of me as more than an employee and a friend… But he had never stepped over that line and I certainly hadn't encouraged him.

'I'm not for sale,' I said flatly, determined not to let my hurt at Alexi's insinuations show.

I didn't need this man's approval. It had taken me five years to get over his rejection. When I'd arrived in the UK and discovered I was carrying his child, the grief for Remy and everything I'd lost the day he'd died had all but destroyed me.

My confidence, and my sense of self had been left in tatters but I'd dragged myself up off the floor, with the help of my wonderful second cousin, Jessie, and forced myself to concentrate on what mattered.

I'd had my child and dedicated myself to supporting us both with two jobs, while taking on a mountain of student debt and studying late into the night to realise a new dream that in the last year had finally started to take off.

I had been a fool to keep the news of his child from him, something about which I had become starkly aware in the last few minutes. I would have to rectify that as soon as I could manage the news in a way that wouldn't hurt Cai.

But I didn't have to defend my professional reputation to Alexi or anyone else.

'That's a shame,' Alexi said, his husky voice sending goose bumps skittering over my skin. 'Because, whatever Renzo is paying you, you're worth more. And with the talent I saw on the track ten minutes ago it's obvious you should be driving.'

'I don't want to drive, not competitively,' I said, pushing past the sexual fog threatening to envelop me, to concentrate on getting him out of here. I didn't have time for a negotiation. Or to obsess over the way he could still make me feel simply by looking at me.

Why did I have to be so affected by this man? It was

as if a spell had been cast on me as soon as I'd hit puberty and I couldn't escape the enchantment of my own body.

So not the point, Belle.

'Why the hell don't you want to drive?' Alexi shot back, his frustration only making his dark good looks and intense gaze all the more overwhelming. 'That was always your dream ever since you were a kid, wasn't it?'

I was surprised he had remembered that much about me. As a teenager, and later as a man, he had always made a point of ignoring me. Until that night.

'It was my dream *once*,' I said. 'It's not my dream any more. Now, would you please leave before I call security?' It was an empty threat, and we both knew it. No security guy in his right mind would eject Alexi Galanti from the track—the man was motor-racing royalty. But I was desperate.

Not surprisingly, he ignored the threat and, instead of leaving, stepped closer. Close enough for me to capture his intoxicating scent—spice, musk and the hint of pine soap. The aroma made my knees shake, propelling me back to that night—somewhere I *so* did not need to go ever again.

I stood my ground, though, because showing Alexi a weakness had never ended well.

'Tell me why,' he insisted, the frustration disappearing to be replaced with something much more disturbing—genuine interest in me and my life, something I'd yearned for all through my teenage years. 'Tell me why you gave up on your dream, *bella notte*,' he repeated, his voice soft, coaxing, as he used the nickname he had coined that night, no doubt to intimidate me more. 'And then I'll leave.'

I opened my mouth, determined to give him an answer, any answer that would make him leave and take this pointless yearning away again. But the only explanation I could think of was the real one.

Because I have a child, a son, who I love more than life itself. And I'm the only person he has. I can't risk leaving him alone—dying the way Remy died. So I found a way to readjust my dreams. To feed my passion for racing—while also fulfilling my obligations to my child.

But I couldn't tell him that.

As I racked my brains, trying to come up with a viable alternative reason Alexi would believe, it occurred to me I'd been hoisted by my own dishonesty.

And then the door burst open and Cai ran into the room ten minutes early, a four-year-old bundle of energy…and the black hole in the pit of my stomach imploded. For the first time in my life I was not pleased to see him.

My time had run out.

'Mummy, Mummy, I saw the car!' he cried, practically bursting with excitement as he raced towards me, oblivious to Alexi and everything else. 'Mr Renzo let me touch it.'

He ran past Alexi, who stepped back, his dark brows launching up his forehead. Cai's sturdy body barrelled into me and the love I had felt for him as soon as I'd held him in my arms after ten agonising hours of labour washed through me.

'Mr Renzo said I could sit in it if I'm good.'

Cai's arms wrapped around my legs as he peered up at me, the love in his eyes all-consuming and utterly uncomplicated. The blue of his irises was the same true, iridescent aquamarine as those of the man standing two feet away, staring at him as if he were an alien.

'Can I, Mummy? Can I?' he pleaded, completely oblivious to the tension now snapping in the room. I could almost feel Alexi's mind working as he stared at my child and calculated dates and ages. Cai was tall for a four-year-old, probably because his father was six-foot-three, but that wasn't going to help me.

With the light from the window shining onto Cai's dark, wavy hair and illuminating his face and his Galanti bone structure—which had become more defined in the last year or two as he'd grown from toddlerhood into boyhood— the resemblance to his father was all the more striking.

Alexi was not a stupid man, and as my gaze connected with his over Cai's head I watched as he figured out Cai's heritage—the stunned disbelief turning to shock before a sharp frown flattened his brows and his sensual lips pursed into a tight line of accusation.

'Can I, Mummy?'

My gaze dropped back to Cai, my thoughts in turmoil as my heart rammed my tonsils. I ruffled his silky hair, trying to stop my hand shaking. I needed to get my son out of here, away from Alexi. I didn't want Cai to witness our impending confrontation. Whatever else I knew, I knew this was not his fault.

'Of course you can, Cai-baby,' I said, using the nick-name which always made him giggle.

'I'm not a baby any more, Mummy. I'm a big boy.' The infectious laughter—so innocent, so delighted—only tightened the knots of anguish in my stomach. Whatever happened next, my only thought now had to be to protect my child from the fallout of this revelation.

I knelt down so I could hold Cai and momentarily shield myself from the accusatory frown of the man standing behind him.

'Yes, but have you been a good boy?' I asked.

Cai nodded furiously. 'Yes, Mummy. Ask Auntie Jessie, she'll tell you, I had my nap without making any fuss at all.'

'Is that true, Jess?' I asked my cousin, who had entered the lounge behind Cai and was glancing backwards and forwards between Alexi and his child.

I'd never told Jessie who Cai's father was—and she knew nothing about motor racing, so she wouldn't recognise my former employer—but it was obvious she had noticed the resemblance.

'I wouldn't say *no* fuss,' she said, letting out a nervous half-laugh. 'But certainly minimal fuss. Shall I take Cai back to the car hangar and see if he can sit in the car yet?' she added, sizing up the situation.

Thank you, Jessie. You are my life saver. Again.

I nodded. 'Great.' I cleared my throat, my voice breaking on the word, my gratitude for all this woman had done for me and Cai over the last five years choking me. 'I'll join you in a minute.'

At least whatever I had to face with Alexi now would not be faced in front of Cai.

'Yes!' Cai jumped up and punched the air, his face beaming with triumph and happiness. 'Come soon, Mummy, I want you to see me sit in the car too. And take pictures to show Imran,' he said, mentioning his best friend at pre-school.

He went to run to Jessie but stopped abruptly, noticing Alexi for the first time. 'Hello,' he said with the confidence of a four-year-old who had never learned to be intimidated by anything. 'Are you my mummy's friend?'

Alexi stared at his son without speaking, and the guilt which I had tried so hard not to acknowledge for so long all but overwhelmed me.

Had I done a terrible thing, not contacting Alexi? I wondered as I watched Alexi's gaze roam over his son's features, absorbing every detail.

'Yes,' Alexi said at last, lifting his gaze from Cai to me, his voice a rasp of emotion.

The slow-burning judgement in his eyes—judgement

I recognised from all those years ago by Remy's grave-side—made it clear that was a lie.

He wasn't my friend. He was my adversary.

Thankfully Cai didn't notice the harsh look as he rushed to join Jessie. But he stopped at the door and turned back, gifting Alexi one of his sunniest smiles. 'You can come too and see me sit in the car if you like.'

Alexi nodded. 'Okay.'

Jessie ushered Cai out of the room, sending me a concerned look. 'Take as long as you need,' she said.

It occurred to me that for ever might not be long enough as the door shut behind them. I had brought this on myself. Now I had to negotiate a way out of it. But was that even possible?

The silence descended like a shroud as I waited for the axe to fall but, when Alexi spoke, he said the last thing I had expected.

'Your son's resemblance to Remy is remarkable. Why the hell didn't you tell me you were carrying his child when I kicked you out?'

For a moment I was confused, but then I remembered the accusation Alexi had flung at me at the graveside—that I had cheated on Remy, that we both had. That Remy and I had been *more* than friends…that we had been lovers.

For another moment, I considered letting Alexi believe that misconception. If I told him Cai was Remy's child, he would have no real claim on my son. On *our* son.

But it only took a moment more for the mushroom cloud of guilt I had denied for so long to halt that line of reasoning.

There had been so many lies between us and so many omissions. I had kept Remy's sexuality a secret for five years, just like the secret of our son's existence, and it had brought us both to this point.

I had to tell Alexi the truth now, however hard. No more excuses.

'He doesn't look like Remy, Alexi. I never slept with your brother. *You* were my first lover...' *My only lover*, I almost added, but bit into my lip to stop that truth coming out.

Alexi didn't need to know no other man had ever made me feel the way he had. The way he could still make me feel if the heat pulsing deep in my abdomen was anything to go by.

I needed to tell him the truth now—but never again did I intend to make myself as vulnerable as I had been before. And my sexual history—or lack of it—was none of his business.

'Cai's not Remy's son...' I continued, because he looked suspicious now as well as confused, the brittle cynicism turning his features to stone. I took a deep breath, forcing myself to continue. 'He's not your brother's son, Alexi. He's yours.'

CHAPTER THREE

Alexi

I STARED AT Belle, stunned by her revelation.

I had known, as soon as the child had run into the room and grasped his mother's legs, that the boy was a Galanti. His round, open face, thick thatch of dark curls and sunny demeanour as he'd bombarded his mother with questions and requests had been so like Remy at the same age, it had been like seeing a ghost.

A ghost of the brother I'd lost, the brother I still missed, the only person who had ever really known me.

Shock had come first, but my surprise had quickly been overcome by the rush of an emotion I couldn't name and, more terrifyingly, couldn't control. It was sharp like the grief, loss and guilt which had dogged me for five years but was tangled up with joy—the joy of seeing that happy, uncomplicated face I'd thought I would never see again once more.

Not Remy's child, *my* child. That was what she'd said. But I didn't believe her. Or, rather, I didn't want to believe her.

How could this child be mine? I was not a father, could never be a father, did not deserve to be a father.

How did I know she wasn't lying? She said I'd been

her first, but how could that be when she and Remy had been like each other's shadows ever since her mother had first come to work for us? Remy had loved her, that much I did know. But…

The desire which had been lurking rippled through me as I recalled the intense physical connection of our one night together—the feel of soft skin, her staggered sobs as I'd entered her, the riot of pleasure cascading through me as I came…inside her.

I hadn't used a condom—hadn't been sober enough or smart enough to think about it. And the next day, when I had intended to check on her, Remy's crash, his death, had made me forget everything except my guilt at taking his girl, at using her to salve my own loneliness…

I dragged a hand through my hair and studied her face, trying to get my thoughts in order and quell the rioting pulse of emotion, the relentless desire for her, that was still there despite everything.

Did it really matter which one of us had fathered the child? If he was a Galanti I needed to protect him, give him the family name, make him my heir. And find out why she had not told me of his existence until now.

Had she ever intended to tell me?

Her face was a picture of stubborn integrity, but I could see the flicker of guilty knowledge in her eyes.

My usual cynicism returned full force. What was I thinking? Of course she hadn't told me the truth about the boy's parentage. The same reasons she had come on to me that night still applied. I had no evidence of the innocence she claimed. Had she bled? I was fairly certain she had not. Although I'd been too ashamed of my own actions, the shocking pleasure of our union, to be absolutely sure.

One thing was certain, though. She had responded to me with an intensity that had taken my breath away. I still had dreams about her soft, breathy sobs as her body had contracted around mine, forcing me to a climax so staggering that just the echo of it had woken me up on so many nights since then, sweaty and desperate, my groin aching, my erection as hard as iron.

Was that normal for a novice? How would I know? I'd never been a woman's first before. Had certainly never wanted that responsibility. And I didn't want it now. So I rejected her claims in favour of the narrative I had settled on five years ago.

'Seriously? You expect me to believe you never slept with Remy?' I said, my voice carefully devoid of the emotions churning in my stomach and tightening my ribs.

She blinked, stiffened, the flicker of distress in the green depths quickly masked but there nonetheless.

What the hell? Was she really that easy to read? Or was she simply a consummate actress?

'I'm telling you I know Cai is your son, not Remy's—whether you believe it or not is up to you.'

She went to walk past me but I grasped her arm, the emotion thundering so hard against my ribs now that the struggle to control it—to stop her from seeing it—was impossible. I couldn't stay here. I needed to get away, to think, to clear my head and decide what needed to be done now. And most importantly of all regain the emotional equilibrium that had become an integral part of who I was since my brother's death.

'There's a simple way to find out the truth. I want a DNA test done,' I said.

I needed to know. Was the boy mine or my brother's? Once I had the full facts at my fingertips, I could begin to figure out how I was going to deal with this staggering revelation.

She tugged her arm out of my grasp. I could see she

hadn't expected that demand. I could also see she wanted to refuse the request.

Satisfaction and a strange sense of regret powered through me.

I was right. I had not been her first. She didn't know if the child was mine or Remy's. Why else would she want to avoid a DNA test? Either she knew the boy was Remy's or she didn't know which of us had fathered her child.

For all I knew, she might have slept with us both that day.

The memory of her face from five years ago, so open, giving and compassionate, flashed before me. I dismissed it. Just another lie. Another act.

She blinked furiously, as if close to tears, but then her chin firmed and she stared back at me.

'Okay,' she said, surprising me with her capitulation. Clearly she had decided to gamble with the possibility I *was* the boy's father.

I wasn't sure how I felt about that, the emotions confusing me again.

Did I secretly want to be the child's father? How could that be true when I'd never intended to become a parent? When I knew Remy had always been the best of us. That it would be much better if he could claim this legacy now not me.

I shut down the foolish rush of yearning that the boy was mine.

It made no sense. And, anyway, until I had the results of the test, I did not have to deal with this confusing tangle of emotions.

'But I want it conducted discreetly,' she said. 'And I don't want my son to know what's going on until...'

She glanced down at her hands. They were clasped together, the knuckles white. 'Until I've had a chance to prepare him,' she finished, releasing her fingers and shoving her open hands into the back pocket of her jeans.

She forced her chin up to meet my gaze.

The defiant yet oddly defensive stance pressed her breasts against the soft cotton of her camisole.

I bit into my lip, determined not to let the inevitable endorphin-rush distract me. And found myself drowning in those mossy eyes when our gazes met, the way I had all those years ago.

Damn it, Galanti, snap out of it. She's an actress and a gold-digger.

But with her face devoid of make-up she looked so young, as young as she had been that night, still a teenager, and it was harder to make myself believe it. I could see the sprinkle of freckles across her nose, could remember her sweet sighs as I kissed every one of them before devouring those plump lips which had tasted of cherry cola and eagerness.

'Once you have the proof you need, what do you intend to do?' she asked.

I frowned at the direct question, the guilelessness of it disturbing me. Until I got a grip.

It's just an act. She looks artless, innocent, but she's playing you. No one is ever really honest. There's always an agenda. Once you've found out exactly what her agenda is, you'll be back on solid ground again.

Obviously it made no sense that she would keep the boy's existence a secret from me for five years, and had never contacted me for the severance cheque, if this was a simple case of extortion.

But maybe her agenda was more sophisticated than that. Was she playing a longer game, to get more? And why did I really care anyway? As long as I took control of the situation, it didn't matter what her agenda was, because my agenda was the one that would prevail.

'I don't know,' I replied, even though I knew what I wanted was likely to conflict with what she wanted.

Never show your hand until you are ready to play your cards.

It was a motto I had lived by for a long time. It had won me considerable amounts at the high-stakes game in my friend Dante Allegri's casino and had also been a guiding principle in my business and personal life.

'I wasn't expecting to find out I had a four-year-old son today,' I said.

Or that Remy had one, I added silently to myself, even though that strange yearning for the boy to be mine was still pulsing in my chest. I'd figure that out later too. 'Once I have the information, I'll be in touch.'

Whatever the outcome of the DNA test, I planned to claim the child as a Galanti. And punish her for not having told me of the boy's existence a lot sooner. I also planned to have her thoroughly investigated.

Is she sleeping with Renzo?

The question popped into my head as something wholly unfamiliar tore through my insides. Something visceral and indiscriminate. I had to curl my fingers into fists to stop me from acting on the sudden urge to capture her face in my hands and claim those lush lips with my own— driving my tongue into the recesses of her mouth until she clung to me the way she had before and I plunged deep into her....

I tensed and shoved my fists into the pockets of my jeans, shocked by the direction of my thoughts.

Dio, I needed to get laid. Clearly the shock of seeing the child, of seeing her again, had had an unpredictable effect not just on my emotional equilibrium but on my libido.

I was off-kilter, not a condition I was used to, which explained this forceful and inexplicable reaction.

She nodded, apparently taking my answer at face value.

'I… I understand,' she said.

No, you don't, but you will.

Whatever the result of the DNA test, she had kept the child's existence from me for five years. And for that she would pay.

'I should go,' she said, strangely polite. 'Cai is waiting for me. Let me know what you need and when for the test. I think it's just a swab. I can make it into a game to explain it to Cai.' She huffed out a breath to stop the babble of information, but her nervousness was visible in her trembling fingers as she pushed the shock of ruddy curls away from her face.

This was not an act. But then, if she had any idea what I was thinking, she had a lot to be nervous about.

'I'll… I'll speak to you again about Cai, when you're ready,' she said.

Walking over to the sofa, she picked up a large bag, rummaged inside and produced a card. 'This is my work number. I'll…we'll…be back in the UK by tomorrow night. And you can contact me there most week days between nine and five. Or my PA will take a message.'

She handed me the card and our fingers brushed. I managed to stifle the sudden jolt of reaction. Her, not so much.

Why did that make me want to smile, despite everything?

The tug of amusement died, though, as I read the address on her business card and recognised the location of Camaro's R&D headquarters in London.

The surge of possessiveness was as visceral as that strange pulse of jealousy and lust, but I explained it to myself as I watched her sling her purse over her shoulder.

I might be unclear at the moment about how much of a father—or an uncle—I was capable of being to this child. But he would need to live in Monaco, to understand his Galanti heritage. And that would mean his mother would have to come too.

It would be no hardship offering her a position in our R&D operation, if her credentials were as good as Freddie had suggested, and I did still need a reserve driver. That situation hadn't changed from when I'd first walked into this room. Even if everything else had.

'Goodbye, Alexi,' she said. 'I'm sorry…' She paused, her regret looking surprisingly genuine. 'I'm sorry I didn't tell you about Cai sooner. That was wrong of me. Call me when you're ready.'

I nodded as the emotion I'd been keeping so carefully at bay swelled against my ribs.

I watched her disappear back into the changing area, probably to collect her racing suit. I strode out of the lounge area. The emotion threatened to choke me as I headed towards the track's parking lot and away from the car hangars where the boy was with his babysitter.

You need to take stock, to know exactly what you're dealing with before you proceed.

But, even as the mantra ran through my head, all the conflicting emotions churned in my stomach: grief, longing, desire, anger, confusion. My fingers shook as I fished my key out of my pocket and clicked the fob.

As I climbed into the car, fired up the engine and drove away, I knew my whole life had changed in the space of one afternoon. The reality of that fact was reinforced by the tug of something vivid and inescapable—was it lust, regret, longing or grief? Who the hell knew?

But the force of it was dragging me back into the past

harder than the G-force in the driver's seat of our newest model when it hit two hundred miles per hour.

I had been running from myself, and my sins against Remy, for five years, maybe longer, and now the truth of what I'd done, what we'd both done to him, had caught up with me.

In the shape of one boisterous little boy and a woman I had never been able to forget—unlike any other, even my own mother—even though I had tried.

CHAPTER FOUR

Belle

Dear Mlle Simpson

The results of the test carried out on May 20th by The Royal Harley Street Clinic on the DNA of your son, Cai Remy Simpson, and Mr Alexi Gustavo Galanti show a 99.98 percentage probability that he is the father of your child.

As a result of this information, Mr Galanti has asked me to inform you that he has arranged for you to fly out to Monaco on his private jet on May 23rd for a meeting with him, myself and the rest of his legal team at Villa Galanti so we can outline how he plans to proceed.

I enclose details of the travel arrangements and your overnight stay at the villa.

A car will collect you at your home address at ten that morning.

Salutations distinguées,

Etienne Severo, avocat

I READ THE email from Alexi's lawyer which had arrived while I'd been busy packing Cai's lunch box and trying to cajole him into putting on his shoes that morning.

I hadn't had time to panic about it then, but I had lots

of time to panic about it now as I read it for the five-thousandth time.

I hadn't done any work this morning. My fear at the curt demand choked me. Alexi expected me to drop everything and come to Monaco to find out how *he* planned to proceed in two days' time. And to stay overnight at Villa Galanti. He'd given me virtually no time to arrange leave or child-care, and there had been little mention of Cai. While I was grateful he hadn't asked me to bring Cai, the impersonal nature of the solicitor's letter, and the laying down of battle lines contained within it, disturbed me.

I had expected Alexi's high-handed, dictatorial approach. Of course he mistrusted me. I'd kept his son's existence from him, and what evidence did he have I would ever have told him but for a chance encounter? But in the last few days I had hoped that, once Cai's parenthood was established, he would contact me personally—that his first priority would be getting to know the innocent four-year-old child at the centre of this situation.

I read the email again, scanning it for any evidence of warmth or empathy towards his son. Even if I didn't deserve any sympathy, surely Cai did? But the words remained as cold and compassionless as when I'd first read them.

A prickle of anger burned under my breastbone, which made an unfortunate bedfellow for the panic which had consumed me all morning.

Part of me wanted to refuse his demand. I didn't want to go to the Galanti mansion—there were so many memories there waiting to hijack me—and demanding I go alone and stay the night at the villa could only be a ploy to unsettle and unnerve me.

I closed the email app on my phone as the anger fizzled out.

Whatever Alexi's agenda was, and however scared I was about the outcome of this 'meeting', I couldn't keep running away from the confrontation I had avoided for so long. I had hoped Alexi would be reasonable. Clearly that wasn't going to happen, but I owed it to my son to hear what his father had to say.

I could feel Alexi's anger with me in the lawyer's words. And I had to face that in order to move forward now.

Because I'd seen how confused, how emotional, Alexi had been when I'd revealed Cai's identity to him nearly a week ago. Even though he'd tried exceptionally hard to hide it, I had blindsided him.

And I had to accept he had a right to be angry with me.

I dialled Jessie's number. My cousin picked up on the first ring.

'Hey, Belle,' she said, her warm voice already helping to release the pressure which had been strangling me ever since my fateful meeting with Alexi—a pressure which had become unbearable ever since his lawyer's email had arrived.

'Hi, Jess. I need to go to Monaco day after tomorrow and stay overnight… Could you look after Cai while I'm gone? I know it's super-short notice and I—'

'Don't be daft,' Jessie interrupted. 'You know I love to look after him. What time do you need me there?'

I rattled off the details.

Cai hadn't done anything wrong, even if I had. Cai's welfare always came first—and if Alexi's 'plans' for me and our son turned out to be not in Cai's best interests I would tell him so.

I didn't like the implication in the lawyer's email that Alexi planned to tell me how he was going to handle this situation and I would just be expected to follow his orders. But it shouldn't surprise me.

Alexi had always been pushy and, well, frankly domineering and determined to get his own way. He'd been like that ever since I'd first known him as a teenager on the rare occasions when he'd deigned to notice the housekeeper's infatuated daughter, so it was no surprise he was even more of a dictator now.

I had toyed with the idea of hiring a lawyer to accompany me to Villa Galanti but had decided against it. Why make this even more confrontational than it already was? I would not be signing anything at this meeting, and he couldn't force me to do so, because I was now the opposite of that infatuated teenager.

So I would go to Monaco, to his meeting, listen politely to what he had to say, deal with his anger, his enmity and his legal team and then, once I returned to the UK, I would hire my own lawyer to thrash out the child custody arrangements.

The anxiety thrummed under my breastbone again.

I earned a very good salary from Camaro. But I still had student loans to pay, not to mention Cai's childcare and a large mortgage for our tiny flat in west London. I wouldn't be able to afford a legal team anywhere near as fancy as Alexi's… I took a steadying breath.

Don't go getting ahead of yourself.

I didn't even know yet what he wanted to do. It was quite possible he wouldn't even want any custody. He hadn't exactly seemed overjoyed at the news he had a son. Just stunned, wary and then angry. I might well be panicking about nothing. Perhaps this meeting was simply to punish me for not telling him about his child.

'Why are you going to Monaco? Is it a work thing?' Jessie's calming voice drew me back to the present before the panic started to choke me again.

'Sort of,' I attempted to lie, but my response didn't

sound convincing even to me. I had always been a terrible liar.

'It's not to do with Alexi Galanti, then?' Jessie's question had my belly knotting.

'How do you know about him?' I rasped.

'I looked him up after he freaked you out so much in Barcelona.'

'Right,' I said. I thought I'd managed to hide that from Jessie. 'So you noticed that, huh?'

'Yes, I noticed that, Belle. I also noticed his resemblance to Cai. Is he his father?' She'd never asked me the question before, and I'd been pathetically grateful for that over the years, but I could see now that was just more evidence of what a coward I'd been. Jessie had a right to know. She'd helped me get back on my feet when I'd turned up on her doorstep pregnant, destitute and distraught.

'Yes, he is,' I said.

'And I'm assuming he knows that too, if he's an observant man.'

Alexi was certainly that. 'He insisted on a DNA test.' His mistrust still stung, but I was trying to make that not about me.

Alexi had never really trusted anyone, especially not women, not since his mother had run away and left his brother and him alone to deal with their alcoholic father.

'The results came through from his lawyer this morning,' I continued. 'He's arranged for me to fly to Monaco to talk about his plans.'

'*His* plans?' Jessie asked. 'That sounds arrogant.'

'You have no idea,' I murmured. 'I'm scared. I have no idea what he's planning to tell me, but I doubt it will be pleasant. I'm scared he's so angry with me he might try to use Cai to get back at me,' I added, finally voicing my real fear.

Alexi still believed I was a gold-digger and a whore, a woman who had cheated on his brother and lied to protect herself. Who got ahead by using men and then discarding them. A woman who had no loyalty, no honour and no morals. Given that I'd only ever slept with him, his low opinion of me would almost be funny if it weren't so damning and... I swallowed sharply, finally forced to admit something else...hurtful. It shamed me to realise Alexi's low opinion still had the power to hurt me when Cai's feelings were the only thing that mattered now.

'What makes you think he'll do that?' Jessie asked, sounding shocked and a little scared too. If she'd investigated Alexi at all she had to know how rich he was, and how powerful.

'Well, mostly the fact that he demanded to see me, but not Cai. I'm not even sure if he wants to be a father. He hardly mentions Cai in the letter.'

'Okay.' Jessie sighed, sounding relieved. 'Perhaps that's not all that surprising, though.'

'How so?' I asked.

'He's a billionaire playboy who seems to have a revolving-door policy with girlfriends.' Okay, so Jessie had *really* checked him out. 'What does he know about the needs of a four-year-old? Or being a father, for that matter? He's clearly super-arrogant but he doesn't strike me as a stupid man. Perhaps he's simply asked to see you alone first so he can get a better handle on being a dad.' She coughed. 'As well as give you hell for keeping Cai a secret for so long...' Jessie's voice trailed off into silence, but I could hear the soft note of censure. She'd never asked me about the circumstances of Cai's parentage, because I'd always made it clear to her I didn't want to discuss it, but I could hear the question in her tone now even if she hadn't asked it.

Why had I done it?

'Belle, you're not scared of him for any other reason, are you?' she asked gently. 'He didn't hurt you, did he? Force you in any way? That isn't why you ran, is it? Why you didn't want him to know about his son?'

'God, no!' I rasped as the shame cascaded through me.

'Are you sure?' she probed again.

'Yes, it wasn't like that,' I said, but the tightening in my throat made it hard for me to speak as every detail of our encounter flooded back—hot, febrile and exciting, but never frightening.

And I finally had the real answer why I was so scared to return to Villa Galanti and face Alexi alone. It wasn't just because of the hostile reception I knew I would face from him. It wasn't fear of what plans he might have for Cai's custody or even his motivations behind them. It was the harsh truth that my desire for him had never died and spending two days and one night in his company—at the location of my original downfall—had the potential to bring all those needs and wants hurtling back.

It was terrifying to realise the girl I thought had been lost long ago might still be lurking inside me somewhere, still yearning for Alexi's touch…and his affection.

As the helicopter circled Villa Galanti, the emotions rushing towards me were as strong, if not stronger, than the downdraft from the blades.

Nothing could have prepared me for the hard hit of grief as the big black machine drifted over the estate's private beach and the landscaped gardens. The marble statues and elegant follies, the enchanting water features and ancient woods, the beds overflowing with shrubs and flowers, all morphed into pirate ships, cowboy forts and haunted hideouts in my mind's eye as I imagined Remy and I running through them together as children and then teenagers.

As the helicopter flew over the fifteen-bedroomed Belle Époque mansion at the centre of the estate, and the small housekeeper's cottage behind where I had lived with my mother, the villa's swimming pool on the garden's lower terrace came into view.

My already pounding heart jumped into my throat then sunk deep into my abdomen as another memory blazed through my body. The blast of heat made my thighs tremble and my nipples pebble into hard peaks.

I had known my mind and my body would play tricks on me, but as I stared at the marble pool below, the sunshine glinting off the crystal-blue water, the whirring blades making the palm trees ruffle and bend, I knew I hadn't factored in the power of those recollections as they reared out of my subconscious and struck me like a bolt of lightning, searing and devastating…

My heartbeat accelerated as I imagined myself, aged nineteen in the green cocktail dress I had donned after I had spotted Alexi heading towards the pool terrace…and raced after him…

My heart rammed into my throat as I crept past the pool house, the sultry night air settling around me like a blanket. My gaze landed on the pool perched on the clifftop overlooking the sea. The underwater lighting gave the water a turquoise glow and illuminated the even more breathtaking figure of a man slicing through the pool in powerful, efficient strokes.

I stumbled back to shield myself, my eyes going so wide it was a wonder my eyeballs didn't pop right out of my skull.

My heart swelled, beating so hard and fast it started to gag me.

Was Alexi naked? I wondered as I spotted a pile of

clothes on one of the loungers. I studied his strong shoulders, powerful arms and tanned back ploughing through the water and tried to focus on what lay beneath the surface.

The butterflies in my stomach formed into a boulder. A hot, heavy boulder that got wedged between my thighs and made my sex beat with the same furious, erratic rhythm as my heart.

The figure powered to the end of the pool then executed a perfect backflip to thunder back towards me.

I spotted his boxer shorts clinging to the bunched muscles of his backside.

Not naked.

My galloping heartbeat slowed. A little. And my breath gushed out of constricted lungs.

But my relief was short lived when Alexi levered himself out of the pool only a few feet from where I stood.

I flattened myself against the wall, trying to be invisible as the water cascaded off his broad shoulders. He stood on the pool patio, the wet boxers clinging to the long muscles of his flanks as he scooped up a towel from the lounger. Water glistened on his tanned skin in the moonlight as he scrubbed his hair, making it stick up in tufts.

I should have left, given him his privacy. But I stood transfixed, trapped by the sensations rioting through my body as he slung the towel around his neck, slid his thumbs under the waist band of his wet shorts and bent to shove them down his legs. He kicked them off and straightened, rubbing the towel over his groin.

My heart hammered my ribs so hard it was a miracle I didn't pass out.

Alexi Galanti naked was more beautiful than anything I could ever have imagined. And I'd imagined a lot.

He stood silhouetted against the pool glow and the twinkle of lights from Monte Carlo across the bay, spotlighted like Adonis against the night.

No, not Adonis.

Poseidon.

This was not a boy. This was a man. A god-like man.

He flung down the towel and reached for his jeans, leaving him standing completely naked in front of me. I could see absolutely everything now.

Oh. My. Good. God.

My breath released in a shattered gasp.

His head shot up and he pinned me with that searing blue gaze. Heat exploded in my cheeks like a volcano, the hot lava of mortification spreading over my face and flooding across my collarbone.

He held his clothing over his groin, his dark brows drawn in a sharp frown. But he didn't look embarrassed, just annoyed.

'Belle, what the hell do you think you're doing? Go back to bed.'

My humiliation threatened to engulf me at the curt command—but, before I could mumble my way through an apology and flee, something Remy had said to me recently echoed in my skull.

Alexi wants you too. He's just better at hiding it.

And suddenly I noticed the tension in his jaw and the flicker of something dangerous in those impossibly blue eyes.

Was I imagining Alexi's response, thanks to years of adolescent fantasies and the massive sensory overload I had just endured? But, even if that was true, did it matter?

If I wanted Alexi to stop treating me like a child, I had to stop acting like one. I gathered every ounce of courage I had ever possessed and stepped out of the shadows and into the moonlight, close enough to smell the chlorine on his skin and see the ripple of tension make his pectoral muscles quiver.

'No,' I said, a little astonished by how clear my voice sounded when I was dying inside.

If he rejected me now, if he treated me like a child, if Remy had been wrong, I might never recover. But somehow I knew—just like Remy, when he pressed his foot to the floor and let the new Galanti prototype soar—that the possible reward was worth the risk.

'What do you mean, no?' Alexi replied, the dark frown arrowing down so sharply I could almost see thunderclouds forming above his head.

'I'm not going to bed.' I let my gaze glide over the planes and angles of his body, let the lava settle between my thighs. The scatter of scars from the many times his father had hurt him added to the deep well of compassion in my ragged breathing. 'I want to be here, with you. I'm not a child any more, Alexi.'

He blinked slowly, his beautiful lips, the lips I'd yearned to feel on mine so many times, firming into a thin line. A new wave of heat raged through me.

But this wasn't embarrassed heat any more. It was excited, exhilarated, triumphant heat.

For the first time ever, I'd left Alexi Galanti completely speechless. He didn't have a snarky remark, an amused comeback. He had nothing.

His gaze glided over me in return. And I felt the burn go through me like wildfire.

'So, you're a woman, are you?' I could hear the edge in his voice, but I could also see the arousal—adding a silver glint to the deep blue of his irises—and knew he was testing me. He wanted to scare me off as he had so many times before.

And suddenly I knew why he had treated me like a child

long after I had become a woman. Remy was right—he wanted me. But that gallant streak which he had always pretended didn't exist—the gallant streak which made him take his father's fists to protect his brother—had prevented him from taking what he wanted. What we both wanted.

The revelation was like a balm to my soul. And a spur to my senses. It felt how I imagined taking the chequered flag in Bahrain or Melbourne or Barcelona two seconds ahead of the field would feel like. Breathtaking and wonderful, exhilarating and life-affirming all at once.

I'd taken an enormous risk and here was my reward.

'Yes, I'm a woman,' I said, my voice clearer and more certain now. 'And I have been for a while. You've just pretended not to see it.' But he saw it now, I realised, when he put on his jeans in front of me, almost daring me to drink my fill as he tugged them on and buttoned the fly. So of course I did.

He hadn't said anything but, as he turned into the light, I noticed the bruising on his jaw.

'He hit you,' I said, lifting my hand to soothe him.

His arm shot out and he clasped my wrist in an iron grip, preventing my fingers from reaching the skin.

'Don't,' he said. The word was expelled on a tortured rasp and the subtle whiff of tequila on his breath—and my heart silently broke in two at the wary look on his face. 'I don't need your pity,' he said, but I could hear the pain.

It was so real and vivid, it made my stomach ache.

His grip loosened and then he dropped my hand and looked down. The defeated stoop of his shoulders, the exhaustion in his stance, burned away my intense anger at his father until all that was left was the grief. And the longing.

I stepped closer and cradled his cheeks in my hands. He stiffened, but made no move to stop me this time.

I stared into those beautiful blue eyes, for once unguarded, and saw the sadness there, which made me want to weep. But I could also see the desire.

The love I had always had for him—this proud, stubborn, foolishly gallant man—flowed through me and I let every ounce of it shine in my eyes.

'Damn it,' he said as he covered my hands with his but didn't move to pull them away from his jaw. 'Don't look at me like that, *bella notte*.'

The nickname sounded like an endearment as his voice came out on a husky rasp.

'Like what?' I asked.

'Like you want me,' he said. 'Because I'm screwed up enough right now to take you up on the offer and to hell with the consequences.'

Excitement and yearning leapt in my heart and I told him the truth I'd locked inside me for far too long. 'But I *do* want you, Alexi. I always have. And I don't care about the consequences.'

The helicopter touched down on the helipad, jolting me out of my reverie.

Stop it. Stop thinking about that night. About the man you thought you knew.

I rubbed my hands over my face, then gripped my bag tightly enough to score the leather as the big black machine's blades whirred to a stop.

This trip was going to be hard enough to negotiate without me reliving the painful past. I needed to control the memories and the desire that came with them.

A young man appeared from the back entrance of the house to greet me. I took careful breaths to steady my nerves and the inappropriate heat as he helped me down from the helicopter and took my bag.

'Mademoiselle Simpson, I am Pierre Dupont, Monsieur Galanti's assistant. I hope your journey was good?'

'Yes, very, thanks,' I replied, even though the memory of the journey was a blur now—the chauffeur-driven car to the airport, the flight on Team Galanti's private jet, and the subsequent helicopter ride—my mind still anchored in the past.

I shook my head, trying to jog the memories loose.

'Monsieur Galanti is awaiting your arrival with his legal team,' Pierre said as he ushered me into the house. The familiar smell hit me—a mix of lemon polish, old wood and fresh flowers reminding me, not just of my childhood, but also my mother and her titanic efforts to make the imposing, ornate property a welcoming, homely place despite the anguish that had lurked inside.

I swallowed past the choking sensation in my throat.

Time to get a grip, Belle.

I'd indulged myself enough already. This wasn't the home I'd once known. I was entering enemy territory. And Alexi wasn't my lover any more—if he ever had been— he was my adversary.

Instead of leading me to Gustavo's old office in the east wing of the house, a place where I knew Alexi had often been 'disciplined' by his father as a teenager, Pierre directed me up the stairs to a suite of bright, airy rooms on the first floor. I recognised the door leading to the sunlit terrace immediately, because no one had been allowed to enter this section of the house when I had lived in the villa's grounds as a child.

Because these rooms had belonged to Gustavo's wife, Amelie.

As Pierre opened the door to her former salon, sunshine glinted on the office's modern furniture, but it was the silhouette of the man in the far corner staring through the salon's terrace doors that got all my attention.

Dressed in an expertly tailored business suit which accentuated his tall, lean frame, Alexi had his back to me. He didn't move but tension rippled across his shoulder blades as I was introduced to the four other men in suits who sat in front of his desk.

One of them, a distinguished man in his fifties, offered his hand with a friendly smile. 'Mademoiselle Simpson, I am Etienne Severo, Monsieur Galanti's lead attorney.'

I took his hand and introduced myself, but my gaze remained glued to Alexi as he finally turned.

The sun cast his face into shadow, making it impossible to gauge his reaction. Was he bitter, angry, as wary as I was about this meeting? My heart thudded in my chest, along with the brutal heat that refused to die.

He nodded his own greeting as he walked around his desk. But, as Etienne Severo suggested we sit down so he could outline Monsieur Galanti's plans, Alexi interrupted him.

'So you came?' His voice was flat, but I didn't sense anger in the tone so much as contempt. 'I didn't think you'd have the guts.'

I blinked, taken aback by his hostility even though I had expected it. 'I want to try and make this right and help you form a relationship with your son.'

One sceptical eyebrow rose up Alexi's forehead.

'Do you really?' Disdain and mistrust dripped from his lips. 'And how exactly do you propose to do that when I have missed the formative years of his life through your actions?'

The edge of anger and judgement was rapier-sharp now. So the gloves were already off, if they had ever been on.

I could try to defend my silence or simply ignore the barb—his question after all was a rhetorical one—but this meeting was supposed to be about Cai, not me. And not our previous liaison. So I attempted to answer honestly.

'By…' I swallowed around my dry throat. 'By answering any questions you have about him. And letting you know what an incredible child he is.'

'So you've told him about me?' he asked, but it was another cynical question, his voice tense with suspicion, the anger sparkling in his eyes.

I didn't dislodge my gaze, even though I wanted to.

'I've talked in generalities with him about you. He's never asked about his father, but he's curious now, and I think he'll be ready to meet you soon.' It had only been a week since our chance encounter, but I'd already begun to prepare the ground for Cai to meet Alexi. I wanted my son to be excited about meeting his father, but I also wanted to be sure Alexi wouldn't take his anger with me out on our son.

'*How* soon?'

'I don't know, when did you have in mind?' I asked, struggling to be civil in the face of his enmity. He was baiting me. This wasn't about Cai—this was about his anger with me.

'How about I have him flown out here tomorrow?' he asked, stepping closer, his big body rippling with barely concealed rage.

'No!' I said, forcing myself to stand my ground.

'No?' he said, his voice rising. 'What gives you the right to keep my son from me a moment longer?'

'Because I'm his mother.'

'And I'm his father. A fact you chose to forget for five years.'

'You're also a stranger to him,' I pointed out.

'And who's fault is that?' he shouted, the anger unleashed.

'It's my fault,' I admitted. 'Mostly.'

I wasn't the only one to blame—maybe if he hadn't rejected me so thoroughly all those years ago, maybe if he hadn't destroyed my confidence and my self-worth, I might not have been scared to contact him. Scared he would reject Cai the way he had rejected me.

'Mostly?' The word sliced into me, harsh and unyielding.

But before I could defend myself Severo cleared his throat loudly. 'Perhaps we could sit down and outline your offer to Mademoiselle Simpson, Alexi?'

Alexi stared at him blankly for a moment, and I wondered if he had forgotten the legal team was in the room.

'Actually, I wish to speak with Mademoiselle Simpson in private.'

The other men nodded and started to gather the papers strewn across Alexi's desk, probably more than happy to leave us to it, but before any of them could leave Severo surprised me.

'Is this acceptable to you, Mademoiselle Simpson?' he asked. I had to give him credit for standing up to Alexi, his employer, on my behalf, especially as he had to sense the animosity between us.

Heat fired across my collarbone as Alexi waited for my answer, challenge as well as contempt in his expression. He was expecting me to refuse, possibly to run away again. The way I had five years ago.

And I couldn't deny the urge to do so.

Being alone in a room with him felt perilous for a number of reasons, but I knew I wasn't scared of him, or his anger. Not any more. I wasn't the naïve, easily bruised nineteen-year-old he'd rejected so cruelly five years ago, and he wasn't the grief-stricken man torn apart by guilt for his brother's death. He was the father of my child. And that meant we had to find a way through this. Somehow.

So I nodded. 'Yes, I'll talk with Monsieur Galanti alone.'

Severo nodded back before he and the other lawyers left.

'Sit down,' Alexi said, indicating a large leather arm chair as he strode across the carpet to sit behind his desk. I wondered if he needed to create distance between us as much as I did. Were the memories of our one night together as hard for him to ignore as they were for me?

Whatever his motives, the endorphins making every one of my pulse points pound relaxed as he stepped away from me.

He propped his elbows on the desk, those pure blue eyes skewering me to the spot as he studied me.

I waited for him to speak first.

'Why?' he asked at last. 'Why didn't you tell me about the boy's existence?' The words were clipped, his frustration clear, but unfortunately I didn't have a straight answer for him.

'I'm sorry,' I apologised again. 'I should have contacted you a long—'

'I don't want an apology.' He cut in. 'I want to know why. Is it because you weren't sure if I was the father?'

The hurt at his mistrust of me was like a blow. So we were back to that again. I hated that he was forcing me to admit again how vulnerable I had been that night, but I refused to be defensive.

'I told you, you were my first lover,' I replied.

'So you say, but you didn't behave like a virgin. You were so...' His gaze seared my skin, the memories pounding back to life.

'I was so what?' I said. 'So un-virgin-like?'

'So responsive, so eager.' He growled the words as if they were an insult. But my stupid body didn't take the comment as an insult. Instead the husky rasp made the fire inside me spark and spit.

'How many women have an orgasm their first time?' he added. 'Unless you faked that too?'

I leapt out of the chair. 'You bastard. I didn't fake anything. I enjoyed it. I wanted it. I wanted you. I'd wanted to find out what all the fuss about sex was for a long time,' I added quickly, in case he read too much into that bald statement. The truth was I hadn't wanted sex with anyone. I'd wanted Alexi to be my first, had dreamed about what it would be like, and he had not disappointed me. I hadn't just had one orgasm, I'd had several. But I'd be damned if I'd compliment him on his performance when he was already holding my response against me.

'If I was really your first, why didn't you tell me that?' he countered and I wanted to scream. 'Don't all women want their first lover to know?'

'Of course not,' I shot back. 'You've obviously never been a nineteen-year-old girl. The *last* thing I wanted was for you to know I'd never done it before.' *Duh.* 'You were gorgeous and sophisticated and six years older than me. I'd had a massive crush on you for as long as I could remember. I wanted you to see me as a woman. Not a little girl.'

'You didn't bleed,' he said, still interrogating me.

The anger I'd carefully held at bay ripped through me to join the riot of inappropriate hormonal responses.

'So what? I don't have to prove my virginity to you. I don't actually care whether you believe I was a virgin or not. I only told you because I wanted you to know how I knew Cai was your son.'

We were talking in circles, I realised. Pointless circles. I already knew I would never be able to break through the wall of cynicism that made him believe every woman was a cheat, an actress, a liar. And I had not come here to try.

'But what about Remy?' he said. 'You expect me to believe you didn't sleep with him when he loved you and you say you loved him?'

'It was never like that between us—we were just friends.' I wanted to say we'd been like brother and sister, but that would have been doing a disservice to our friendship. Remy and I had never fought, never argued. Unlike siblings, there had been no rivalry between us, only support and love. We had always had each other's backs, had always been there for each other. God, I wished he was here for me right now, so he could knock some sense into his brother.

'Don't make me laugh. No man would be able to love you like he did and not want to take that *friendship*...' he made sarcastic air quotes, making the anger thrum in my chest '...to its logical conclusion.'

'Unless he was a gay man,' I said.

'What?' he croaked.

Guilt ripped into me and I sat down again. I hadn't intended to tell him about Remy so cold-bloodedly... I hadn't even really considered telling him at all. Why would I reveal Remy's secret now when I had respected my friend's privacy for so long? But I hadn't expected to be subjected to an inquisition about my virginity.

Why was Alexi so hung up about that detail of our liaison?

'I'm sorry,' I said grudgingly but, as I watched the truth he had never acknowledged about his brother cross his face, the guilt blossomed under my breastbone.

I had always known this would be hard for Alexi—finding out his brother had never confided in him, discovering that their relationship had not been as close as he'd thought—but I couldn't hold on to the lies a moment longer.

'Remy was gay,' I reiterated, the anger fading and leaving me shaky and sad. 'He had his first boyfriend when he was fourteen. He never wanted me in that way because he didn't desire women.'

I sunk into the chair, suddenly exhausted. I'd got up at four that morning, left my child sleeping and been on a knife-edge of stress for days, but that wasn't what was making my bones feel so weary. It was the renewed flicker of compassion as I watched the bone-deep regret cross Alexi's face.

'But if that's true, why didn't he tell me?' he whispered. 'Did he think I would reject him? That I would love him any less? That I was some kind of narrow-minded bigot?'

I hadn't wanted to reopen this raw wound. Alexi was probably still beating himself up about Remy's death, because that was the kind of man he was, jealously guarding his pain so he didn't have to share it with anyone, or show any weakness.

'No, of course not,' I said. 'Remy *knew* you loved him, because he knew all about the abuse you took from Gustavo to protect him.'

Alexi's gaze hardened, as I knew it would. This was his private pain too. Stuff I was supposed to pretend didn't matter, hadn't affected him. But it was this secrecy which had made it impossible for Remy to confide in his brother. That needed to end now.

'What are you talking about?' he said.

'*We* knew,' I said. 'About the extent of the abuse, Alexi. The back-handed slaps, the casual violence. We could hear the shouting, the things he said to you late at night when you both thought we were in bed. We saw the bruises, the split lips, the black eyes you pretended were caused by anything else but him. Remy knew how homophobic your father was. He kept his sexuality a secret because he thought he had to, to protect you from having to protect him from your father's abuse. Again. That night...'

My breathing became ragged, the memories flowing back, the emotion, the pain, as real as the desire. 'I came to you because I'd overheard your father shouting at you again. He hit you. And you didn't hit him back, even though you could have. You were bigger and stronger than him, but you took it, the way you always did. I could see how angry you were, how humiliated, and I wanted to help, to make it better somehow.'

'What are you saying?' he demanded as he strode round the desk. 'That the night we made our son was a pity screw? That you sacrificed your virginity to make me feel better about the fact my father hated my guts?'

I stood up and tilted my head so I could look into his eyes, brutally aware of the unyielding strength of his body, the tension vibrating through him and the pulse of desire making my knees dissolve. I shook my head because I had never pitied him, only loved him.

Going with instinct, I touched his cheek. I wasn't infatuated with him any more, I could see all his weaknesses now, but a part of me still ached for that valiant young man who had always protected his brother.

The bunched muscle in his jaw clenched against my palm as he jerked his head free.

I dropped my hand. I should not have touched him. But, as I stared into his eyes, all I could see was the same rage and pain I'd wanted to soothe that night.

I didn't want to soothe it any more. Because I knew I couldn't.

'Don't touch me, Belle, or you'll be sorry again,' he said.

'I'm not sorry,' I said, the foolish urge to take away his pain getting the better of me. 'I've never been sorry. I got Cai out of it, and the best sex of my life.'

The *only* sex of my life.

He swore viciously, but then his own hands cradled my cheeks. 'Why do you tempt me still?'

I wasn't sure if it was a question meant for me or himself, but I answered it anyway. 'I can't help it,' I whispered.

His fingers threaded into my hair, sending flying the pins that I'd used to tame the red mass.

'Tell me to stop,' he said, his voice tortured as he tilted my head back.

'I can't.' I shuddered, giving him the tacit permission he sought.

The wave of need slammed into me as his lips fastened on my neck, his teeth and tongue feasting on my throat as he sucked on the pulse point. I shivered as his erection pressed into my belly and my fingers gripped his shirt to drag him closer.

His arms banded around my waist at last, his fingers roaming freely under my blouse. Pleasure blossomed inside me, tightening my nipples.

At last his mouth found mine, his tongue plunging deep—tempting, taking, conquering.

I met his demands with demands of my own. It had been so long since I'd felt this need, this desire, so long since I'd been wanted in this way. But, just as my senses surrendered to everything I knew he could do for me, a loud knock sounded at the door.

We jumped apart so fast, it was as if a water cannon had been fired at us.

Alexi rubbed his chin, swearing softly as he stared at me as if I'd grown an extra head, while I struggled to get my breathing under some semblance of control.

It would almost have been funny, like the scene from a bad sitcom, if the implications of what we'd just done.... or rather, had *almost* done...weren't so catastrophic.

What exactly had I been thinking? I'd pretty much jumped him. I was a grown woman, and a mother. I should have been able to resist the desire that had flared like a firecracker as soon as I touched him.

Alexi was still my kryptonite—that much was obvious.

But I'd paid dearly once before for letting my desire rule my head. And for thinking that sex, especially the stupendous, incendiary sex that was clearly still our MO, was a substitute for emotional engagement.

I'd been emotionally engaged when I'd made love to him the first time. And he had not been. I wouldn't get sucked into that vortex again.

'Monsieur Galanti, there is an urgent call for you from the Paris office, and Monsieur Severo would like to know if you wish to delay the negotiations with Mademoiselle Simpson until tomorrow morning.' I recognised the voice of his assistant and realised for the first time that the sun was beginning its descent in the distance. It had to be after six o'clock. Obviously Monsieur Severo and his team were keen to get the business portion of the day over with.

'I'll take the call from Paris, and tell Etienne Mademoiselle Simpson will be with them shortly,' Alexi rasped, dragging his fingers through his hair as he continued to stare at me, probably struggling to make sense of what had *almost* happened just now as much as I was.

'I should leave,' I said, the panic starting to overwhelm me. Staying the night on this estate with this man, and all the memories, was fraught with danger. I'd thought I could hack it. I was a lot less sure now. But, as I went to pick up my bag, Alexi touched my wrist.

'Don't...' He ran his fingertip up my arm. Could he

feel my instinctive shudder? Probably… But I was way past being humiliated by my response to him. 'Don't go, I want you to stay.'

'Why?' I asked.

Desire blazed in his eyes for a moment and I was almost scalded by the intensity of it. But then he lifted his fingertip from my arm and tucked his hand into his trouser pocket. 'Because there is much for my legal team to discuss with you…about our son. I have four years of back maintenance to pay, to begin with.'

I stiffened. 'Is that why you brought me here, to offer me money? I don't want your money.'

Did he still think I was a gold-digger?

'I know that,' he countered, and the clutching sensation in my stomach released. At least I wasn't still beating my head against that brick wall any more. 'But that doesn't alter the fact I owe you money,' he added. 'You and my son. I know it hasn't been easy for you both since you left Monaco. That you have student loans, a mortgage and other debts. I wish to set up a trust fund for the boy, and give you a generous allowance for his care that will be backdated.'

How did he know so much about my finances? But as soon as I'd asked the question I could guess the answer. He would have had me investigated. I'd expected as much.

But I didn't want his money. It would compromise me. I didn't want to give him any ownership of my life, and that included allowing him to pay my debts or give me maintenance. But I forced myself not to reject the suggestion out of hand.

A trust fund for Cai, I could accept. But before I did that we needed to talk about our son. That was why I was really here. And that was what I should concentrate on now. Not the heat between us that would not die.

'Your son has a name,' I said quietly.

He frowned. And I realised we had a very long way to go before I could introduce him to Cai. Was he even curious about his son? He hadn't really asked me anything personal about him yet, hadn't once referred to him by name. Jessie had been right—this was a relationship for which he wasn't remotely prepared.

'You're right, I know nothing about Cai,' he said, the deliberateness with which he made himself say his son's name making me want to weep. 'If you stay, we can work out the financial arrangements and also have a chance to talk about him. I have missed all his formative years,' he went on and, while the edge of accusation was no longer there, I could still hear it in my head.

I was the one who had denied them both that emotional connection with my silence. Whether or not Alexi was capable of being a father, how much he even wanted to be one, remained to be seen. But it was no longer for me to make those decisions for him or Cai. 'I never expected to become a father, so this is new territory for me,' he added. 'And I accept that where the boy is concerned I will need your guidance—which is precisely why I'm asking you to stay...' He paused, his stance stiff, uncomfortable and oddly defensive for a man who rarely, if ever, admitted a weakness. 'I'm not sure how much of a father I can be to him.'

He shoved both his hands into the pockets of his suit trousers.

I had the weirdest feeling he was trying to prevent himself from touching me. The thought was disturbing on one level, but oddly comforting on another. At least I wasn't the only one struggling here.

'So what is your answer?' he asked. 'Will you stay so we can continue to discuss this?'

I looked past him, out into the villa's grounds, the landscaped gardens, the pool, the beach. However hard this was for me, it was time I faced my past—and started preparing myself and my son for our future. A future with Alexi Galanti in it. And learning to rationalise and control my body's response to him was as much a part of that as anything else.

Turning back to him, I nodded. 'Okay, I'll stay.'

My stomach chose that precise moment to rumble louder than the helicopter in which I had arrived. Not all that surprising, given that I hadn't eaten today, the nerves having got the better of me on the flight over, but still mortifying.

Alexi let out a strained laugh as he watched my face ignite. 'I will arrange for some supper to be served while you meet with my legal team.'

'You're not joining us?' I asked, then wished I could pull the question back. Why had my voice sounded so eager?

'Etienne has my authority to outline my wishes. If there is anything you are not happy with, we can discuss it tomorrow.'

I nodded. 'That makes sense,' I said, trying to sound pleased and not stupidly bereft at the thought of not seeing him until tomorrow.

What was wrong with me? Speaking to Etienne and his team without Alexi there would make it much easier not to let the knot of emotion in my stomach override my reason again.

But, just as I was congratulating myself on my pragmatism, he took his hand out of his pocket and tucked a tendril of hair behind my ear.

The sizzle of reaction shot through me, as shocking as it was debilitating.

'I will see you tomorrow, *bella notte*,' he murmured, his voice as husky as my wayward thoughts. 'Sweet dreams.'

As he walked away, the yearning surged and I knew this relationship was going to be much tougher to negotiate than I had ever thought possible.

I might have grown up in the last five years, but unfortunately I hadn't grown immune to Alexi Galanti. Not even close.

And now he knew it.

CHAPTER FIVE

Alexi

As I STOOD on the balcony of my suite of rooms, I imagined Belle in the cottage where I had insisted she be accommodated after the combustible moment we'd shared before her meeting with Etienne and his team.

The guest house on the edge of the property was as far away from me as it was possible to put her. But, as I gazed down onto the pool terrace below my balcony, the site of our torrid liaison all those years ago, the night we'd made our son, I knew geographical distance was not going to control the yearning still pounding through my system.

What an arrogant fool I'd been to think she had no hold on me any more. How could I have kidded myself that my demand to bring her here—a place where I'd rarely stayed since my brother's death—was all about the boy? A clever tactic to unsettle her which would help me get the upper hand in any negotiations...

Yes, it had unsettled her. But it had also unsettled me.

So much for having control of this damn situation. I felt less in control now than I had when I'd met her again a week ago and discovered I had a son. The night was warm, but not as warm as my skin, or the pulsing ache in my groin which had refused to subside ever since our kiss in my office four hours ago.

Kiss—who was I kidding? That hadn't been a kiss, it had been an explosion of need, desire and something else. Something I definitely did not want to name, let alone think about. But how could I not, when my balcony gave me an uninterrupted view of the pool—the place where I had lost myself once before?

I wet my dry throat with a sip of the vintage Cognac I usually kept for special occasions. The liquor burned my throat as I swallowed. My skin felt tight and hot, my heart beating an erratic rhythm.

When I'd received the results of the DNA test and discovered that the boy was mine, that Remy was not the father, my feelings had been mixed. First shock, then anger that I had been denied this knowledge for so long, but underneath it all had been a strange sense of joy which I could no more explain than my incendiary reaction to Belle's touch this afternoon.

I was not parent material, had never even considered becoming a father. But my feelings towards the boy, towards becoming a father so unexpectedly, were nowhere near as volatile as my feelings for his mother.

Especially as I now knew the truth, not just about her virginity, but about Remy.

Had I always known my brother was gay? I think I had. It sickened me to realise all the signs had been there. I had spent the last few hours—ever since Belle's revelation—recalling the conversations I'd had with Remy about dating in the last few years of his life. The enquiries he'd avoided answering, the jokes he'd laughed at with a strained smile—even our final conversation when Remy had seemed so pleased about my one-night stand with his best friend which I had been determined to believe was a cover for some secret heartbreak.

Remy had been showing me the truth all along and I had failed to see it.

Was that the real reason I had been torn apart by guilt after his death—because I'd tried to blame Belle when the only person who had really betrayed Remy was me? Not by sleeping with his girl, but by refusing to see him as he really was. By avoiding that truth because it had been easier than having to deal with it—having to support him and defend him against our father's prejudices.

Maybe Belle had been a coward not to tell me about my son. But I had been an even bigger coward, not supporting Remy, not ensuring he knew he could be honest with me.

I stared down at the pool, the lights giving the water a bright-blue glow, and the knots in my stomach released. I could almost hear Remy's voice—laughing, cheeky, kind and optimistic—telling me to let go of the guilt.

Belle was right. What the hell was the point of feeling guilty now about how I had let my brother down? I couldn't go back and fix the mistakes I'd made.

We knew.

My stomach tensed again. I slugged back the rest of the Cognac.

I was not going there, or I'd only feel more confused. More angry. More humiliated. I'd kidded myself that I was protecting my brother when all the time he—and Belle, with her silence about his sexuality—had been protecting me.

I reached for the bottle to refill my glass. But then my hand paused.

Not the answer, Alexi.

Alcohol was never the answer. I, of all people, ought to know that.

I slammed down the glass and glanced back at the pool. I'd gone down there that night to cool off because I'd been so mad at my father for turning to drink, first and foremost, and at my mother for abandoning Remy and me all those years ago. But right now a cold swim felt like a better solution than sulking in my room and getting drunk.

The memories were going to haunt me anyway—there was no avoiding them. Heading down to the pool now and diving into that frigid water wasn't going to make them any worse. And it might finally kill the heat that had been messing with my head ever since I'd turned and spotted Belle standing in my mother's old parlour this afternoon— her eyes wary, intelligent and guarded.

I'd brought her here to pay her off. To pay off my responsibilities to the child, to manage the fallout from that night long ago. I'd wanted to be angry with her for her deception, wanted to believe she was guilty of everything I'd ever accused her of in my grief, guilt and loneliness, even though I'd already known before she'd arrived most of it wasn't true.

I had read the report from the private investigator whom Etienne had hired on my behalf. I knew exactly how hard it had been for her financially, especially during the early years of our son's life—after I had banished her and threatened her with arrest. I had been wrong, not just about her relationship with my brother, but about my desire for her. I had always tried to pretend it was nothing more than a one-night stand brought about by alcohol, loneliness and opportunity.

The minute she had touched my face, though, the minute she had looked into my eyes, I had seen her compassion, but also her desire, and my body's response had made me acknowledge how much I had lied to myself.

But I wasn't the only one lying.

I still wanted her—as much as, if not more than, I had five years ago—but she still wanted me. And now I needed to decide what I was going to do about that too.

Etienne had told me an hour ago Belle had refused the financial package I was offering her. But I was determined my son—and by extension his mother—would be financially secure.

Marching out of my bedroom suite, I headed down the stairs and walked out into the night. It was warm for May, the sultry breeze filling with the scent of wildflowers. But, as I crossed the villa's *terrazzo* and took the steps winding down to the pool, the memories blindsided me again. I felt tense and edgy, my skin prickling with the unrequited desire I couldn't seem to tame, but instead of struggling to hold the memories in, as I stripped off my clothes and dived into the pool, I let them flood through me again as I sunk beneath the crisp, cool water.

'But I do want you, Alexi. I always have. And I don't care about the consequences.'

As I stood on the pool terrace, my mind tried to engage with what Belle was saying to me.

Who was this girl? Because it wasn't the tomboy whose thick braids made her hair look like a couple of hunks of vibrant red rope, the kid who had trailed around after my brother, Remy, for years and got into no end of trouble with him.

I couldn't ignore the evidence of my eyes any longer. She wore the same shimmering green dress she'd worn a month ago to the Galanti summer ball. I hadn't recognised her at first that night, and after I had I'd tried to ignore her. But I'd known then I was already in big trouble. Because she didn't look like a kid any more. She looked like a woman. A beautiful woman.

And tonight she didn't just look like a beautiful woman, she looked like a goddess, wild and untamed. Her vibrant red hair—no longer pinned up in a sophisticated concoction of curls, as it had been at the ball—caught the moonlight, creating a fiery halo around her head. Those slanting eyes were the colour of rough-cut emeralds, and her high breasts pressed against the tight bodice. Barefoot, brave and unashamed, she was like some Greek water nymph—beautiful, bold and devastating to my peace of mind.

Heat throbbed and surged in my groin, stiffening my shaft and making me forget about the ache in my jaw where my father had lashed out to end our argument.

With Belle I had always felt like a person instead of a shadow. But I felt like much more than just a person now. The sweet passion and approval in those emerald pools weren't just soothing all the feelings of inadequacy which had haunted me since childhood. They were firing my soul.

What was so wrong with wanting her for myself, just this once?

Tonight I needed her so I could feel like part of the world. To take away the hollow ache in my soul that had always been there. Ever since the night my mother had left and my father had used his fists on me for the first time.

I didn't want to think about consequences, about the past or the future. I just wanted to live in the now.

Reaching out of their own accord, my palms caressed the shimmering silk.

Her breath gushed out against my lips, her arms reaching around me as her body bowed to mine.

I tasted her for the first time. She was like nectar—both sweet and spicy, both refreshing and addictive. I knew I should take things slowly. Be careful with her, be kind. How much experience did she have? But then her fingers curled into my hair, her nails scraping across my scalp, and sensation arrowed into my sex, turning my erection to iron.

Her tongue tangled with mine in fast, furious strokes as if she couldn't get enough of my taste. I knew how she felt. The hunger was consuming me as I dragged her against the thick ridge in my pants and ground it against her soft curves so she would know how much I needed her.

She didn't flinch or squeal, she matched my hunger with hunger of her own. My mind, or what was left of it, rejoiced. This was not a woman without experience, or how could she know exactly how to touch and taste me to drive me insane?

The last of my inhibitions died as I scooped her into my arms and carried her to a lounger. She lay panting, her eyes wild, her full breasts heaving against the floaty material. Material I'd wanted to rip off her the first time I'd seen her in the damn thing.

Her hair lay around her and I imagined that mermaid in the cartoon she used to love watching when she'd first come to live with us.

The thought should have had a sobering effect. But remembering her as a kid only seemed to make me more aware of how much older she was now.

Not a girl, a woman. A seductress in full charge of her sexuality.

I wanted to tear the sheer fabric, but forced myself to control the urge.

'I want you so damn much,' I admitted.

Her skin flushed, the sight breathtaking as her lips spread into a smile that consumed her whole face and left me feeling a little dazed, a lot dazzled.

'Me too,' she said on a breathless whisper so full of longing, I was surprised my head didn't explode.

I lay down beside her, forced myself to go slow. She

might know what she did to me, but that didn't mean I didn't want to cherish this moment. I couldn't offer her permanence. This would be a one-time deal. But it would be the best deal she'd ever had.

I brushed my thumb over the rigid nipple visible through her dress. The violent shiver which racked her body at the light caress made me chuckle.

'*Dio*, when did you grow into such a beautiful woman?' I said, because it still puzzled me. One minute she had been tagging around with my kid brother, climbing trees, causing trouble, and then a month ago everything had changed. She'd walked into the summer ball on Remy's arm, her curves spotlighted by the dress, her eyes connecting with mine, and all I'd wanted to do was ditch the woman on my own arm and fall to my knees in front of her.

Remy had been teasing me about my reaction ever since.

'Years ago,' she whispered.

'What about Remy?' I asked as I trailed my thumb over the pulse point in her neck—but the truth was I was finding it hard to care about my brother's claim on her. If Remy cared about her, why wasn't he here instead of heading out for the evening in Nice with a group of his friends? 'I thought you were his girl.'

She blinked and something crossed her face, but then she said, 'I'm nobody's girl. I'm a woman, and I make my own decisions.'

Blood pounded in my groin and I gave up trying to think coherently as I scooped a handful of her hair into my fist and tugged her lips back to mine. I'd always tried to protect Remy, not just from our father's anger but also our mother's neglect. But I wanted to take this one thing for myself. How could it be wrong when I needed her so much? Remy had always joked about their relationship, never staked a claim to her. Why should I care, if he didn't?

I sunk into the fragrant mass, which smelled of flowers and sea, as my mouth captured hers. She bowed back, her breasts rubbing against my chest like a cat desperate to be stroked.

I cupped the warm flesh, slipped my hand beneath the bodice. My hunger roared as I found naked flesh and her nipple swelled against my palm.

Dio! She wasn't wearing a bra.

All the fantasies I'd had about her in the last month, fantasies I had tried so hard to tame, flooded through my brain and had every last molecule of reason plummeting into my pants.

Her palm cradled me, gauging the size and weight of my erection.

I jolted. Her touch was like lightning. My palm glided up her thigh under the floaty fabric to trace the sensitive seam of flesh at the top of her leg. She shuddered and moaned, the raw thirst like a flare to my libido.

I pressed the heel of my hand against her vulva, felt the damp heat of her panties then slipped my finger inside the gusset to find the plump lips of her sex swollen and ready for me.

Grasping handfuls of the dress, I tugged it up.

'Sit up,' I ordered, and she obeyed, allowing me to drag the garment over her head. I threw it away then helped her to wriggle out of her panties.

Her naked body glowed in the moonlight, the sprinkle of freckles across her collarbone like a trail of stars leading me home.

I captured the stiff peak between hungry lips. I flicked and nuzzled the pebbled tip until she was panting with need, while my fingers explored the slick seam of her sex and found the swollen nub.

As if she had been primed and ready for me, she choked off a sob.

'Come for me, *bella notte*,' I demanded, frantic to see her shatter.

Her cry echoed in the night and drifted away on the sea breeze. Ecstasy surged through me. I wasn't a shadow, I was a man. I wasn't a nobody, I was somebody. At least, to Belle—whatever my father shouted at me.

Her emerald eyes stared at me, unfocused and dazed, her sweet skin flushed a beautiful pink.

Suddenly I was frantically releasing myself from my trousers, positioning her hips. I couldn't wait any longer. I had no protection with me. I'd never taken a woman without protection in my life, but I promised myself I would pull out before it was too late.

She wrapped her fingers around my shaft, her thumb trailing across the head, and I had to bite off a sob of my own. But I forced myself to slow down, to ask, 'Are you sure?'

'Yes,' she said, her confidence and certainty humbling me.

Notching my erection to her entrance, I pressed in slowly. I forced myself not to thrust too hard. She was tight, incredibly tight, but she didn't flinch or turn away. She lifted her hips and wrapped her legs around my waist. Welcoming me home as she clung to me, her nails dug into my shoulders, only increasing the sensory overload.

At last I was lodged deep. Our ragged breathing sounded loud in the quiet night. I felt conquered and all-conquering.

'Are you okay?' I asked. Had I ever felt this incredible inside a woman before? I didn't think so. 'You're very tight.'

She nodded. 'It feels wonderful.' She sighed. I shifted and her voice broke on a raw gasp. I had found her G-spot.

I rocked my hips, out and back, digging into that tender spot—euphoria licking at my spine and turning my limbs to jelly as she reacted like a wild thing.

I wanted to last, wanted to make this as magnificent for her as it was for me, but I could feel the orgasm crashing towards me. I held on, held back, kept pushing, kept thrusting, kept digging. Each sweet sigh, each staggered sob, added to the frenzy working through me.

At last her muscles clamped around me, massaging my length, and my climax roared through me.

I collapsed on top of her, hollowed out, spent, but as soon as the afterglow began to fade and my breathing evened out I knew I'd made a terrible mistake.

I saw Remy's face—open, joking, laughing, uncomplicated and so loyal—and disgust ripped through me. The shadows returned in a rush, chilling my body as I withdrew and felt her flinch.

Doing up my trousers, I got off the lounger and passed her the dress.

'Is everything okay, Alexi?' she asked, suddenly sounding like a little girl again, wary and unsure.

'I didn't use a condom,' I said, turning my back so she could get dressed.

I dragged unsteady fingers through my hair, appalled at my actions.

'I… I'm sorry… I think it's okay, though. I've only just finished my period.' Her voice sounded small, hesitant, embarrassed. And the shame engulfed me.

'Don't be sorry,' I said. 'Just let me know if there's a problem.'

I turned back. Thank God she had donned the dress and her panties. But she still looked… Heat pulsed. I needed to leave, to get out of here, before I took her again.

'Okay?' I said, more sharply than I had intended.

She nodded, her eyes wide. 'Yes, Alexi.'

'Are you going to the track tomorrow?' I asked, sickened with myself when she nodded.

Of course she would be there, to see Remy test the new car. He would want her there because she was his girl, not mine.

'Don't tell Remy what happened between us. It was a mistake, okay?' I said.

She looked down, her fingers clutched together, the knuckles white. Her shoulders trembled imperceptibly and I felt like a bastard. The bastard my father had always accused me of being. Was she going to cry? Damn it.

Capturing her chin, I lifted her face to mine.

'Do you understand, Belle? It was a mistake. It's not going to happen again, we're not dating,' I said, keeping my voice cool even though the heat was still thrumming through my system like a ballistic missile.

She nodded again.

'Say it,' I demanded.

'I understand, Alexi. We're not dating. It was a mistake.'

I wanted to kiss her, to apologise—she looked so forlorn—but I resisted the urge and let go of her chin. Those deep pools of green were filled with sadness, but I forced the prickle of anger to the fore. I wasn't the only one who had cheated on my brother. She had cheated on him too.

I surged out of the water, the memories of that night five years ago so strong and vivid still, I almost expected to see Belle hiding beside the pool house all over again in that devastating green dress. But tonight the pool terrace was empty, the lights from Monte Carlo blinking in the distance as I climbed out and stood on the stones. I shuddered as I grabbed a towel, but the salt-scented breeze didn't do enough to cool the heat still rioting through my body, or banish the regret.

I'd been a selfish bastard that night. She *had* been a virgin—it had been so obvious but I'd ignored all the evidence to absolve my own guilt. And she was right. What had come the day after, the devastating blow of Remy's death, had been nothing more than a tragic accident.

I'd turned on her in my grief, accused and threatened her and sent her away—not just because I felt guilty about what we'd done, devastated by Remy's death, but because I still wanted her too much. And as a result she'd been too scared to tell me I was a father. A part of me was still angry that, but for our chance meeting in Barcelona a week ago, I might never have discovered I had a son but much of that anger was now directed at myself.

According to the feedback I'd got from Etienne about her meeting with the legal team after I'd left them, she was not keen to accept any money from me for herself. And I considered that a problem. I didn't just owe my son. I also owed her.

I dried myself, took off my wet shorts and tugged back on the rest of my clothing. After dumping the towel in the bin by the pool house, I picked up my shoes.

As I walked back through the gardens towards the house in the moonlight, my bare feet warmed by the sun-heated stone, a plan formed.

I wanted Belle to accept my support. But I knew how stubborn she was and how independent.

That said, I also still needed a reserve driver, and her credentials as a fuel-efficiency expert were exemplary. Galanti's latest prototype was still in development and the R&D team was struggling to recruit engineers of her calibre.

Perhaps there was a way to satisfy both my personal responsibilities and my professional needs where Belle was concerned. But I could not risk getting close to her again until I could control the hunger.

As I walked through the silent house to my bedroom, and shucked my damp clothes to step into the shower, the heat that had pounded in my veins ever since that afternoon swelled and throbbed again...

I took the stubborn erection in hand, feeling like a teenage boy. Why could I not control this need?

I pumped my shaft in fast, efficient strokes, the steaming water cascading over my back. The orgasm ripped through me and I let out a muffled shout.

But as I stepped out of the shower and my heartbeat slowed I could feel the tension tightening the muscles at the base of my spine all over again as I imagined seeing Belle again tomorrow—and the heated negotiations that were likely to ensue.

Belle as a love-struck girl was a temptation I had been unable to ignore. Unfortunately, Belle as an independent woman was even more irresistible.

CHAPTER SIX

Belle

'YOU CAN'T BE SERIOUS? I can't possibly accept.' I stared at Alexi, concerned not just by the stubborn line of his lips but the traitorous leap in my heart.

Apparently I still yearned for his approval, despite everything that had happened in the last five years. But, what was even more disappointing, I was fairly sure it wasn't just his approval I wanted. I'd spent all night unable to sleep in the luxury surroundings of the guest cottage, obsessing about our kiss.

'Why not? I need a reserve driver and you would be an excellent addition to my development team.'

'It's too much money,' I said. The sum he'd offered to pay me for my work was ridiculous—and I suspected had more to do with what he perceived to be his financial responsibilities to Cai than to me. I had already refused a similar financial settlement offer the day before.

'Of course it's not. Your expertise is unique—the only reason you believe it is too much is because that cheapskate Camaro is paying you too little.'

'I can't be a reserve driver—I've already told you that.'

'I know you have, but you never gave me an answer as to why not. And don't lie to me and tell me your dreams have changed. No one changes that much. Being a driver was as much your dream as Remy's.'

'Which is precisely why it's not my dream any more,' I said, forcing myself not to flinch at the probing intensity in that pure blue gaze. 'Remy died pursuing his dream. I can't afford to take that risk.'

'The risk is minimal and you know it,' he shot back. 'Remy was never as talented as you are. He was too easily distracted, too confident and too addicted to the adrenaline rush of speed. If he had lived he would have learned to curtail those impulses, but you already have.'

The thrumming in my chest increased, my ribs tightening as the desire to defend Remy's impulsive behaviour was combined with the realisation that I had won Alexi's admiration at last, and it mattered, even though it shouldn't.

'I appreciate the compliment, Alexi, but I don't want to drive professionally any more because I have a son.'

He blinked, clearly surprised by this line of argument, which had my ribs squeezing my lungs. He really was clueless about the responsibilities of parenthood.

'Childcare will not be a problem. Anything you need will be made available,' he said, still not getting it. 'In fact, if you would just accept the financial package my legal team outlined yesterday you wouldn't even need to consider the boy's care a problem.'

'I don't consider Cai's care a problem. But it's not childcare that's the issue.'

'Then what is the issue?' he demanded as he paced towards me, throwing up his arms in exasperation.

'The issue is, I can't and won't risk my life to pursue a dream, however slight the risk, because that would mean leaving my child without the only parent he has.'

He stiffened as if I had slapped him. And I realised what

I'd said. Cai didn't have just one parent, he had two. But I held back the knee-jerk apology.

I still wasn't prepared to drive professionally—Alexi was a total stranger to Cai and, even if he weren't, I would never want to leave my child without a mother.

Alexi thrust his fingers through his hair and let out a deep sigh.

'You're right. I had not considered that. And I should have,' he added. 'I'll find someone else for the reserve driver position.'

I stood and placed my fingers on his arm. 'It's okay, Alexi. This is all new to you, I get that,' I said, trying to soothe the flicker of guilt.

His forearm tensed and something else, something hot and volatile, danced in his eyes.

I dropped my hand and tucked it into my pocket. Touching Alexi was not a good idea.

'It'll take a while for you to put Cai's interests first. It's an adjustment we all have to make when we become parents—and you've only effectively been a parent for a week.'

He nodded. His gaze still seared me. 'This is true, but that's not why I should have realised the implications of your decision.'

'I don't… I don't understand,' I said hesitantly, because he'd lost me, and the strange feeling of connection was only intensifying between us.

'I know what it is to be without a mother. I should not wish that on any child. And especially not my own.'

The brutal pain in his eyes shocked me, before he had a chance to mask it, but not as much as the admission of vulnerability. When had Alexi ever been willing to share his pain with me? With anyone?

'I still want you on my R&D team,' he insisted. 'The money is unchanged.'

'I can't… I'm under contract to Renzo. He's been good to me, and Cai, and he's a friend so I can't just…'

'Stop.' He pressed his thumb to my bottom lip, the flare of something hot and possessive in his gaze shocking me into silence. 'Renzo does not own you,' he said. 'And he's not the boy's father, I am.'

It was a low blow, one that he had used ruthlessly to dig into the knot of guilt cutting off my air supply. Suddenly he seemed more like a jealous lover staking a claim than an employer trying to lure talent away from a rival but, before I could voice my concern, he continued.

'I will buy out your contract with Camaro—and if he is truly a friend he will know this is a great opportunity he should not deny you.'

'I still can't accept. It seems like too much because it is. Be honest with me, Alexi, why are you really offering me this job—because you want me on your R&D team or because I refused the financial settlement your legal team offered me yesterday? And this is just a means to get me to take the money another way?'

I thought I had won the argument when his gaze dropped away, his stance wary and tense instead of possessive and domineering.

But, when he finally turned back to me, what I saw stunned me—not demand, or guilt, or even anger but brutal honesty.

'Can it not be for both those reasons?' he asked.

He walked back to me and touched my cheek. Even though I knew I shouldn't, I couldn't resist the urge to lean into the light caress. The wry smile that twisted his lips was both poignant and painful.

'I wish to get to know my son, and I can't do that if he lives miles away. The Galanti R&D department is based in Nice. I can buy you a villa there, pay for any staff you need and arrange to visit more frequently than I would be able to if you continued to live in London.'

I shifted my head back. Immediately the pang of regret echoed in my abdomen as his callused palm slipped away.

'I can't accept your charity,' I said. 'And I'm not sure upending Cai's life and mine is the right way to prepare him for this relationship. It's already going to be such a big change for him and…'

His finger touched my lips again, silencing my string of objections, some of which were genuine but some of which were borne of the same cowardice that had made me keep Cai's birth a secret for so long. Alexi had always overwhelmed me, and moving back into his orbit scared me on a visceral level I did not want to admit. What if I couldn't keep at bay the feelings I was scared I still had for him? Or the desire?

'Shh…' he murmured gently. His fingertip sent inappropriate shivers down my spine as he slid it across my mouth. 'This is not charity, Belle. You have earned this opportunity. I want to develop the Galanti X to be the best car in Super League history and the key to that is fuel efficiency. To make those innovations, I need you. But this is not just about what is good for Galanti. It is also about what is good for you and your career development. You know as well as I do the Destiny team cannot offer you the resources of Galanti, or the infrastructure. If you want to be the best, you need to be employed by the best. And that's me.'

The arrogance with which he made the comment was all Alexi, but I couldn't deny that he was right. Galanti's development centre in Nice was the best in the sport, by a long margin. Probably because the company had been at the top of motor racing ever since Alexi had taken over the reins of the operation from his father seven years ago.

I'd never considered working at Galanti because of my personal attachment to Alexi, but having that golden ring dangled in front of my nose made me realise that, while protecting myself and Cai from discovery, I had been hampering my own professional development.

Strike two to my cowardice!

I'd already gone as far as I could at Camaro—if Alexi was prepared to fund additional research....

'But I also wish to support my son in any way I can,' Alexi added.

My excitement at the new job opportunity hit a brick wall as Alexi mentioned Cai.

Yes, I wanted my son to have a chance to get to know his father, especially if Alexi was willing. But Cai's whole life was based in London. That was where his friends were, his school, the teacher he adored whose class he was due to move into full time at the end of the summer. But, even as the excuses ran through my head, I knew they were just that... Excuses.

'So, are we agreed?' he asked, tilting my chin up. 'You will take the job, and relocate to Nice, so I can get to know my son?'

My skin heated. Perhaps I was making a huge mistake, agreeing to take this job, this opportunity, agreeing to relocate—because it wasn't just Alexi's relationship with Cai that was super-complicated. But I knew I couldn't object any longer. I owed this to my son, the chance to get to know his father properly. I also owed it to Alexi after robbing him of the first four years of his son's life. And maybe I owed it to myself too. I'd worked so hard to have an opportunity like the one Alexi was offering me...

This didn't have to be about me or him. I needed to be pragmatic now. As pragmatic as Alexi had always been.

Yes, we'd kissed, and it had been phenomenal, but I

was an adult with adult responsibilities—and Alexi had not suggested that he wished to take our kiss any further. Thank goodness.

Controlling my heart, as well as my hormones, where he was concerned would not be easy, but then who said life had to be easy? The important thing was I knew the risks this time. I was going into this with my eyes open.

So I nodded. 'Okay,' I said. 'I'll take the job. And bring Cai to Nice. Thank you.'

'Excellente...' he whispered.

But then he hooked a lock of hair behind my ear—and I wondered if I had just bitten off a great deal more than I would ever be able to chew.

CHAPTER SEVEN

Belle

'Wow, WOULD YOU look at this view? It's breathtaking!' Jessie swung open the doors leading onto an elegant balcony that wrapped around the front of our new home. Nice stretched out below us: the wide arc of the beach, the promenade and the warren of streets behind, like a series of treasures waiting to be explored.

'Mummy, I can see boats and a pool!' Cai shouted gleefully, putting his small hands on the marble balustrade and lurching up onto his tiptoes to get a better view. With the city several miles away, the villa was part of the built-up area between Nice and Villefranche-sur-Mer. Perched on the cliffs, it had an enviable parcel of private land split into terraced gardens that included an outdoor patio area, a small, shallow fenced-off pool complete with a water slide and a series of steps leading down from the pool to a narrow inlet below us.

'And look, Mummy, a *beach*. Is that ours too?'
Probably.

'I don't know—we'll have to ask Pierre,' I said as I laid a hand on Cai's shoulder. 'Why don't you find him and invite him to lunch?'

Alexi's assistant had arranged everything over the past

weeks and had been in constant contact. I'd tried to veto the more extravagant places he'd suggested, but when he'd driven us here from the airport he had explained to me that Alexi had insisted on purchasing this villa for us.

I'd been prepared to refuse Alexi's extravagance—I wanted Cai to feel at home here. He wasn't used to the kind of luxury Alexi took for granted. But as soon as Cai had seen this place—and his new bedroom, which came complete with racing-car wallpaper and a bed shaped like Galanti's latest Super League prototype—I'd realised Alexi had completely outmanoeuvred me.

I wouldn't be able to tear Cai away from here with dynamite.

But as Cai ran off through the house, shouting for Pierre like a wild thing, his excitement clear, I couldn't resent his happiness. Especially as I knew my objections to living in this palace were not really to do with Cai's reaction. Cai had always been adaptable and he loved to meet new people and see new places. He would thrive in this environment.

No, my objections were all my own, because this place felt as overwhelming as all the other sudden changes in my life.

I'd been introduced to Alexi's R&D team a week before on a brief trip to France and was enthusiastic about starting my new job. I'd taken a month off after resigning my position at Camaro to settle myself and my son into our new home, but I'd already gone over the designs for the new prototype and had attended some runs at the test track. The work would be exciting, challenging and everything Alexi had said it would be in terms of my career development.

Jessie was a personal events chef, so she had arranged to take a break between contracts to join us in Nice for the summer and help ease Cai into his new childcare situation when I started my job. I couldn't have been more grateful for her presence now as she walked towards me and gave me a brief hug.

'Is it just me, or are you totally blown away by the grandeur of this place?' she said, grinning.

'It's not just you,' I said, but I couldn't muster an answering grin.

'What's wrong?'

'It's too much,' I replied.

'I know what you mean.' Jessie scanned the palatial front parlour, taking in the ornate plasterwork on the ceilings and the luxury furniture—that I wasn't sure was going to survive Cai. I had to ensure he didn't bring his felt tip pens in here, ever.

'I've never lived somewhere like this,' she said.

'Neither have I, which is why I suspect Alexi insisted on buying it,' I said.

He hadn't listened to me. In fact, he hadn't even contacted me since the afternoon I'd agreed to relocate. 'It feels like a show of strength.'

And the irony was, he didn't need to do that. I already knew how rich and powerful he was, but until this moment I had not considered how much I had put myself at his mercy by not just agreeing to this move, but also taking the job. It was a real job, with real prospects, and Alexi and I would not be working too closely together from what I could gather. But why hadn't I even considered the implications of becoming his employee—of making him my boss?

'Perhaps,' Jessie said. But her smile didn't die, it simply became thoughtful. 'Or perhaps he's trying to impress you and Cai.'

'I don't think so,' I said. 'He hasn't even been in touch

about meeting Cai since we agreed to come here.' Which I could admit now was what scared me the most. Had this ever been about establishing a relationship with his son? Or was it all some kind of power play, to let me know who was in charge? Because I felt as powerless now as I had five years ago. And I didn't like it.

Jessie grasped my hands and stroked her thumbs over my knuckles. 'Is there any reason why you can't contact him?'

The quiet question startled me with its simplicity.

Jessie was right. Why was I letting Alexi call all the shots? I'd spoken to Cai in the vaguest of terms about his father, and then waited for his father to get in touch so we could arrange some kind of plan for Cai and him to get to know each other. But no contact had been forthcoming, so I'd buried myself in finishing up my work at Camaro, organising our move, preparing Cai for his new home and new nursery school, establishing myself in the new job and waited. And waited.

No wonder I was so on edge. I still had no idea how Cai and I figured in Alexi's life, and that was my fault as much as Alexi's, because I hadn't pushed. I hadn't even asked. I'd allowed this whole thing to be managed on Alexi's timetable.

'No, there isn't,' I replied. 'Perhaps it's time I took control instead of leaving things to Alexi.'

Especially as he seemed unwilling or unable to take the initiative.

Pierre walked into the room with Cai in his arms. 'I'd love to stay for lunch, Mademoiselle Simpson. Thank you for the invitation.'

Cai giggled—he adored Pierre and the young man adored him. But it wasn't Alexi's assistant Cai had come to Nice to bond with.

As Cai and Jessie left the room to help Camille, the new housekeeper Alexi had hired for us, with the lunch preparations, I spoke to Alexi's assistant.

'Pierre, do you know where Alexi is at the moment? And how I can contact him?' As soon as I made the request, I realised exactly how much of a doormat I'd been. I didn't even have a mobile number for Alexi.

The young man's dark skin flushed even darker. 'Monsieur Galanti is coming back from Rome today. He will be at Villa Galanti tonight before he heads to London tomorrow to start preparations for the British Primo Grande Race.'

How fortunate, I thought. Just as Cai and I arrived in France, Alexi was heading to London. It was almost as if he'd planned to make it impossible to meet his son.

He wanted me here at his beck and call, but I was increasingly becoming less convinced he even wanted to meet his son.

'Do you know where I could hire a car for Cai and I to use while we're here?' I asked.

Pierre brightened. 'There is no need to hire transportation. There are three new Galanti models in the garage at the back of the house for your use, *mademoiselle*.'

'Three!' I almost choked, yet more evidence of Alexi's skill at making me feel overwhelmed. 'Why would we need three cars?'

Pierre barely blinked. 'Monsieur Galanti thought you would need a range of cars depending on your activities. He asked me to supply you with a Galanti GLQ SUV for family excursions, a new GL8 convertible for leisure driving and a hatchback from Galanti's GLTi range of city cars in case you wish to drive into Nice or Cannes.'

I nodded. 'Right.' Apparently Alexi had thought of

everything—except the most important thing, how to begin forming a relationship with his son.

Once Cai was in bed, I could leave Jessie here to babysit and drive along the coast road towards Monaco and Villa Galanti. It was less than a half-hour drive.

Surprising Alexi in person made more sense than trying to contact him.

I had uprooted my son. I wanted him finally to meet his father—and for his father to meet him. That was why we were here. And I wanted to make the arrangements with Alexi before I began work properly at Galanti's R&D centre when the ties between our professional and personal relationship would only complicate things more.

If the mountain wasn't prepared to come to Muhammad, Muhammad was going to have to be brave enough to go to the mountain—with a little help from a brand new top-of-the-range GL8 convertible.

Night had fallen by the time I drove the new convertible—which had handled beautifully—through the gates at Villa Galanti.

Would Alexi know I was here by now? Pierre had buzzed me in and would probably be informing our boss of my visit. My nerves jumped and jiggled in my belly as I braked in front of the mansion's Belle Époque façade. I ran through the speech I'd been rehearsing during the scenic drive along the Grande Corniche and tried not to recall another summer night. If the memories had been difficult to suppress the last time I'd been here, they were impossible to suppress now.

Pierre appeared to greet me. 'Mademoiselle Simpson, we did not expect you,' he said, but he looked pleased to see me. I doubted Alexi would feel the same way.

'Is Alexi here?' I asked.

'Yes, Monsieur Galanti arrived an hour ago. He has gone for a walk in the grounds. Would you like to wait while I inform him of your arrival?'

So Pierre hadn't told him yet. I could still surprise him. I wanted to surprise him. Alexi had always had the upper hand between us, just this once I wanted to be the one in charge... Or at least the one better prepared.

'Would it be okay if I went to find him? It's important I speak to him straight away.'

Pierre's expression became concerned and I knew he was assuming there was a problem with Cai. I didn't correct him.

'Yes, of course,' he said, whipping out his smart phone. 'Would you like me to text him and ask him to come to the house?'

'No, that's fine,' I said, my nerves twisting into a knot in my belly—I'd never been good at subterfuge. 'I can find him. I know the grounds well.'

Pierre nodded and stowed his phone as I hurried off.

I made my way through the dark gardens. The old paths and structures held so many more memories in the moonlight. I prayed that Alexi hadn't gone for an evening swim, the way I knew he had done once to de-stress. The last thing I needed was to find him semi-naked in the pool, but as I moved through the silent flowerbeds, the scent of jasmine and bougainvillea filling my senses, I heard the muffled splashing coming from the terrace below.

I halted, my breath catching in my lungs. I should return to the villa, confront him later, but something propelled me onwards—perhaps it was my anger with him and his avoidance of Cai and me ever since I had agreed to come to Nice. But the hum low in my abdomen which became louder and more insistent as I took the steps down to the pool terrace told a different story.

I spotted him getting out of the pool. The moonlight gilded his body, the heavy muscles and the lean sinews flexing and bunching as he grabbed a towel from a lounger. This time, I didn't wait for him to strip down further.

I was here to speak for my son, I told myself, not to satisfy the hunger that buzzed and throbbed low in my belly.

'Alexi?' My voice sounded rough as I alerted him to my presence.

His head lifted, and his gaze met mine.

If I had hoped to catch him off-guard I was sadly disappointed. He seemed as indomitable as ever and as self-assured. His gaze roamed over me—burning every inch of exposed skin it touched.

'Bella notte,' he said. 'Spying on me again?'

He threw the towel around his shoulders, giving me an unencumbered view. At thirty there was no longer even the pretence of youth or softness about him. The swimming trunks that clung to his wet thighs did nothing to disguise the hard lines and unyielding strength of his body.

'We need to talk,' I said, struggling to swallow the knot of need making my throat ache and my sex pound. 'About Cai,' I added, but the words came out on a croak.

Why did he have to be so mouth-watering?

He walked towards me, slicking his wet hair back from his forehead. The moonlight made the damp waves look so dark they were almost black. Memory stirred but the surge of heat was too real, too vivid to be merely an echo of an old desire.

Who had I been kidding? Was I really here for my son or was I here for myself? Was that the real reason I had accepted his job, his largesse, why I had uprooted my child?

'Pierre tells me the boy likes the house and his new bedroom,' he said as he approached. I was surprised by the comment. So he *had* spoken to Pierre—had he even had a hand in choosing the decor for Cai's bedroom which my son adored so much? Why had I never even considered he might have?

I caught the scent of chlorine on his wet skin. The giddy heat spiralled down to my core.

'Yes, yes he does,' I said, stumbling over the words, my gaze devouring him. 'Who chose the bed? He loves it.'

I saw the slash of colour hit his tanned cheeks and emotion swelled in my throat to go with the giddy heat.

'The designer suggested something similar,' he said. 'But I commissioned one to look like our latest prototype. I would have enjoyed such a bed as a boy. And it seemed to make sense as his mother will be working on the design.'

The thoughtfulness of the gesture made my heart thunder painfully against my ribs.

'What is the problem we need to discuss?' he said, standing so close, too close.

I knew I should step back, but the urge to feel those firm lips on mine once more was so overwhelming I felt weak with desperation. I struggled to get a grip on the conversation. To discuss his responsibilities to our son. But my reasons for being here suddenly seemed hopelessly confused. And premature. Why was I trying to force this relationship? The bed proved Alexi was thinking about his son—he wasn't ignoring him. Or avoiding him. This was as big an adjustment for him as it was for Cai. I shouldn't be here. Not when I'd clearly failed to get my hunger for him under any semblance of control.

'It doesn't matter. I should leave,' I blurted out, the flight instinct finally taking root.

But as I turned to flee he snagged my upper arm in a firm, unyielding grip.

'Don't...' The raw plea rasped across my senses, halting me in my tracks.

He tugged me round, his gaze dark with arousal as it met mine, and the hunger surged through me like a forest fire licking across my skin, and flaring deep in my sex.

'Don't go,' he said, then lifted a hand and trailed a thumb down my cheek.

I shuddered, and his pupils dilated to black.

'Tell me why you are *really* here, *bella notte*,' he said.

I was left with no choice but to tell him the truth. Or rather, the truth I had believed until I had seen him in the moonlight.

'I wanted to find out why you haven't contacted me...' I coughed, trying to release the tightness in my throat. 'Why you haven't contacted *us*,' I corrected.

His touch trailed down to my collarbone, sending the sensations surging between my thighs. He brushed his thumb across the sensitive hollow where my pulse was hammering the skin. Could he feel it too?

I knew he could when his gaze focused on mine, so hot and devastating, seeing me and only me.

'I haven't contacted you because I knew if I saw you again too soon I would not be able to keep my hands off you,' he said, his voice as hoarse and feral as mine. And I knew, with devastating clarity, that there would be no escaping this incendiary heat a second time.

There was and always had been unfinished business between us. Business I had tried not to acknowledge for five years. But I was forced to acknowledge it now as my sex swelled, the damp heat flooding into my panties.

I wore a silk summer dress, not unlike the cocktail dress I'd worn that night. Why had I changed into it from the jeans and T-shirt I'd worn on the plane? Why had I showered and put on make-up before climbing into the car tonight?

To feel strong, to feel in control, to feel as if I were a million miles away from that unsophisticated girl. That was what I'd told myself an hour ago. But I knew that for the lie it was when his fingers curled around my neck and he tugged me closer, his breath inhaling the perfume I'd dabbed at my pulse points.

'You should not have come, *bella*,' he murmured against my neck.

I know.

The thought reverberated in my head, but I couldn't seem to regret the impulses that had driven me here any more, the lies I'd told myself.

I pressed my palms to his abdominal muscles, knowing I should push him back and step away from the fire.

He didn't try to resist my touch, simply shuddered, as if waiting for me to make the choice for both of us.

But, instead of pushing him away, my head dropped back, giving him access to my pummelling pulse.

I could barely hear the harsh Italian curse because of the pulse thundering in my ears before his lips found the sensitive spot. He kissed me, sucking, nipping, devouring the sensitive flesh between my neck and my collarbone before his mouth captured mine—swallowing my sob of surrender.

The heat rioted over my body as I caressed the contours of his naked chest. Encouraging, enticing.

It was madness, but it was a madness I could no longer control.

Why couldn't I have this just once more? I'd made a child with this man, I'd loved him once, but this was just hunger, desire. Perhaps I needed to give into it one last time to escape it for good?

If this was really why I had come to Nice, why I had

driven along the coast road this evening, then maybe I owed it to myself—and my son—to get it out of my system. So we could both start concentrating on the only thing that really mattered: Cai.

Alexi's tongue delved, devouring, possessing, even more demanding than it had been the last time we'd given in to the desire. But this time I knew instinctively there would be no going back until the hunger had been sated.

He tore his mouth away, gripped my cheeks. 'Tell me you want this as much as I do.'

'Yes… I do,' I stuttered, the desire far too strong to deny.

'Bene,' he murmured, then scooped me into his arms and strode across the pool terrace.

It took me several seconds to realise what was happening, the thundering beat of my heart and the relentless heat making it hard to breathe, let alone think.

'Where are we going?' I asked.

'To my bed. I'll be damned if I take you on a lounger again,' he said, his voice harsh with frustration.

'I can walk,' I said, dazed and disorientated as he strode to the end of the terrace and up the stairs to the mansion.

'Sta'zitto.'

Shut up. *Nice*, I thought, but couldn't find the breath to say it.

All I could do was cling to him as he tightened his grip and took the steps two at a time. He carried me into the house where I had once wanted so badly to belong, and held me close as he climbed the stairs to his bedroom.

The possessiveness of his hold on me did nothing to make the riot of emotions and sensations subside.

Finally he put me down in front of the huge king-sized bed. The large room's dark upholstery and heavy furniture was intimidatingly masculine. It suited him perfectly.

'Take off the dress,' he demanded.

I obeyed, caught in the maelstrom of passion, of desire. I fumbled with the zip, let the thin silk shimmer over sensitised skin, and watched intently as he kicked off his wet swimming trunks.

His erection sprang up, hard, thick and long with a yearning he could not disguise.

'And the rest,' he murmured, nodding at my bra and panties, before grabbing a box of condoms from the bedside table.

I took off my underwear with trembling fingers, caught in the tractor beam of his gaze as he sheathed the massive erection.

The lights from Nice twinkled in the distance as I climbed onto the bed, silhouetting him through the French windows. But Nice felt like a million miles away as he joined me, cocooning us both in the unstoppable passion, the relentless desire, our ragged breathing harsh in the still night.

He pushed me back on the bed, opened my thighs and then, to my shock, moved lower to press his face between my legs.

That first slow lick as he found my clitoris with his tongue made the already out-of-control sensations sparkle and soar.

I launched off the bed, already shattering, but he held me down, drawing forth the devastating orgasm.

As my senses swelled and shattered, then rose to shatter again, the emotion I'd been trying to control gripped my chest.

'Please… I need you inside me,' I begged, shocked by my own desperation.

He rose over me, blocking out the lights, clasped my hips, notched his penis at my entrance and thrust heavily inside me.

I sobbed, the sound raw, my slick sex struggling to adjust to the all-consuming fullness, and as I gripped his thick length and clung to his wide shoulders, the pleasure swelling as he moved, I felt the emotion in my throat swell and shatter too.

CHAPTER EIGHT

Alexi

My heart expanded in my chest as I moved inside the tight clasp of Belle's body. I still had the taste of her on my lips as I established a rhythm, digging deeper, taking more. The urgency, the drive to possess her, was so strong it controlled me instead of me controlling it.

I didn't care. In that moment, all I cared about was seeing her break again for me. Her sobs echoed in my ear, her frantic breathing spurring me on. I gritted my teeth and pumped harder, faster, felt the pleasure surge, tightening around the base of my spine like a vice.

'Come for me, again, *bella*,' I commanded, desperate to have her break once more, needing her to break first.

I was the one in control this time. I had to be.

She cried out against my ear, massaging my length, and I let go at last, the climax firing through me so raw and real it seemed to surge from my very soul.

I locked my elbows to stop myself from collapsing on top of her and letting her know how completely she'd destroyed me.

It was sex—only sex.

The chemistry had always been phenomenal between us and it seemed that had not changed.

It was five years, though, since I'd felt this exhausted, this limp from a simple orgasm. And I knew it was pointless trying to deny it any longer.

Where Belle was concerned there had always been more between us than just chemistry.

It would be good if this time we could feed the desire without guilt, but as I rolled off her, covering my face with my forearm, struggling to catch my breath before I spoke, I felt her stiffen beside me and knew we could not.

Because now, instead of Remy between us, there was the boy.

She'd come here to find out what my intentions were towards the child and perhaps it was time I admitted my misgivings about fatherhood.

She shifted, ready to run again, and I gathered enough of my energy to grasp her wrist before she could escape.

'I should leave,' she whispered, her naked body shivering. 'I need to get back to Cai.'

The room was warm, the night air sultry as it flowed in through the open doors of the terrace, the terrace on which I'd stood, thinking of her every night I'd been back to the villa since seeing her again, since that damn kiss.

'Not yet. We need to talk about the boy,' I managed to say around the sickening regret in my throat.

'I can't…' Her voice broke as she twisted her wrist free of my grasp. 'I can't talk about him now, let's talk about it tomorrow.'

She scrambled off the bed, her fear almost palpable as she gathered the clothes she had taken off with such artless seduction moments before. The moon glowed on her pale skin and I became momentarily mesmerised again. As I watched her slip on her panties, hook her bra with shaking fingers, the heat swelled my shaft again.

I forced myself to climb off the bed, walk to the chest of drawers and pull out a pair of sweat pants.

The chemistry was still there, and more volatile than ever, but I was through trying to avoid it. Trying to avoid her.

Once she had shimmied back into the simple summer dress that looked more sophisticated to me than a courtesan's ball gown, she hunted around for her sandals.

I scooped them off the floor, but as she reached for them I whisked them out of her grasp.

The moonlight shone on her face as she stared at me. I could see the beginnings of beard burn on her cheeks where I had devoured her mouth before devouring so much else. The taste of her—sweet and musky, wet with need—taunted me still.

'Please, Alexi, I have to go,' she said desperately, but I could hear her struggle to keep the fear out of her voice. 'I can't...' A guilty flush burned her neck. 'This shouldn't have happened—it's not why I came here.'

We both knew on some level that was a lie. Maybe her decision hadn't been conscious, any more than mine had been to avoid the boy simply so I could avoid her too, but that cat was out of the bag now, and there would be no shoving it back in again. Even so, I needed to be careful with her.

She looked freaked out. I wondered again at her experience. How could she still seem like that young, artless girl when she was the mother of a child, *my* child?

'Maybe, but you did come here, so perhaps it is best we discuss the reason why. Do you want me to have more contact with the boy?' I asked.

'It's okay,' she said. 'I understand now why you've been avoiding us. I should have—'

'No, you don't,' I interrupted.

She'd apologised before, but she hadn't been wrong about my reasons for avoiding contact, not entirely. Perhaps it was time I took some share of the blame for my son's fatherless existence.

'Yes, I do,' she said. 'You wanted to avoid…' She gesticulated with her hands between us, in an entirely inadequate expression of the explosion of hormones and pheromones, wants and needs held in a pressure cooker for five years, that had just occurred. 'You wanted to avoid this happening again. After that kiss, I should have realised we couldn't be in the same space again without a chaperone, and yet I came up here anyway to…'

'Shh, Belle.' I pressed a thumb to her lips to silence the words and the anguish and guilt behind them. 'What happened was inevitable,' I said. 'Avoiding you and my responsibilities to the boy was never going to stop that.'

'Of course it wasn't inevitable,' she said, her face alight with panic and indignation. 'We had a choice and we took the wrong one. Again.'

I had to stifle a harsh laugh at her naivety, even though I found it strangely endearing. Surely she could not have slept with many men since me, if she didn't know how rare was the chemistry we shared?

'It wasn't the wrong choice then,' I said. 'Because it gave us our son.'

And as far as I was concerned it wasn't the wrong choice now either. I wanted her, I had wanted her for five years, and I was through trying to avoid it. Especially as I could suddenly see my avoidance had as much to do with my fear of fatherhood as it did with my fear of losing control with her.

I could see I had struck her dumb, so I continued.

'I *was* scared,' I said, forcing the words out past the lump of denial in my throat. I hated to admit a weakness, hated to admit I'd ever been afraid, but for once it made sense to let her see this was much more of a struggle than I had let on. 'Scared of being a father. That's the other reason I avoided contacting you.'

She didn't say anything, her eyes going wide and making her look even more delicious.

My erection throbbed under the loose sweats but I ignored it. We would not have a repeat performance tonight, not until she had come to terms with the idea.

If I wanted to have Belle again—and I now knew I did—I needed to get past my fear of fatherhood.

'I never intended to have a child and I'm fairly sure, given my past record, I will be incredibly bad at it.'

'Your...' She swallowed, her eyes shadowed with a grief I didn't understand. 'Your past record? You mean you have other children?'

'*Dio*, no!' I barked out a strained laugh. 'You are the only woman I have failed to protect so spectacularly,' I murmured.

You are also the only woman who has made me forget everything but the driving need to be inside you.

I bit off the admission. That would not continue to be the case once we had fed this hunger. Nothing ever lasted, especially not physical desire—it was transient, fleeting—but for us, I suspected, the intensity was increased by all the other commitments we shared, to the dead and to the living, to the past and the future.

There was no way to disentangle ourselves unless we faced the truth instead of running from it. We'd both done our fair share of that—she'd had a child and refused to tell me of his existence for five years, but I had also refused to see the truth about my own brother and refused to meet my son.

We had both been cowards about so much. The only

way forward now was to be brave. And, if that meant admitting weaknesses I did not wish to admit so I could work past them, so be it.

Facing those realities meant I would be able to feed this hunger instead of trying to deny it, which was one hell of an incentive to stop running.

'Then what past record are you talking about?' she asked.

'I failed my brother. I failed you,' I said, forcing the words past the guilt which I had deflected and denied for so long. 'I do not wish to fail the boy too…'

CHAPTER NINE

Belle

I STARED AT Alexi and blinked furiously to hold back the sting of tears at his honesty—and the hopelessness I suspected lay behind it.

Did he really believe he would be a bad father? He hadn't failed Remy, and he hadn't really failed me. He'd been cruel to me that day, but he'd been grief-stricken at the time—we both had.

But, as the emotion closed my throat, I knew I couldn't have this discussion now. My sex was still tender, my face alight with shame and shock and my pulse had accelerated to a mile a minute.

I needed to get away from him, from here, to take stock, to make sure I didn't fall into his arms again—and unleash all those destructive emotions that had tripped me up before.

I was terrified of my feelings for him—confused as they were. They felt too strong to be merely echoes of my former childish adoration.

I couldn't afford to fall in love with him again. Alexi had always been a hard man to love. I hadn't realised it as a girl, blinded by all the qualities I adored—his protectiveness, his dominance, his determination. But I could see now how destructive those qualities could be for me, as well as how attractive.

I'd never known my own father, who had died soon after I was born, and as a result I'd spent my childhood looking for male approval. The more unattainable Alexi had become, the more I'd wanted him. He was just as unattainable now. I needed to figure out how to handle discovering my body was still enthralled by him, and only him.

And I needed to figure it out quickly, before I told Cai who Alexi was.

And before I started my new job in his organisation.

We would always have a connection now, but I couldn't let it become a sexual one. I had thought I was invulnerable to his charms. I had just discovered that I was not. Managing our emotional commitments was going to be hard enough already, but adding this explosive sexual connection would turn them into a minefield.

'Being a parent isn't something you're instinctively good or bad at,' I managed at last. 'It's something you have to learn. I was terrified I'd fail Cai as soon as he was born. Even before he was born,' I admitted. 'And I still make mistakes now. In fact, I've made some humdingers. Not telling his father he existed being the most obvious one.'

'Perhaps it is time you stopped beating yourself up about that.' He shoved his fists into the pockets of his sweat pants. They hung low on his hips, only making me more aware of the muscular expanse of his bare chest.

I looked away, something releasing inside me at the offhand demand.

'Thank you for not hating me,' I said.

'You were very young,' he murmured. 'And I behaved badly towards you.'

His knuckle touched my chin, forcing my gaze to meet his.

'If you were so terrified of becoming a mother, why did you decide to keep the child?' he asked.

Because I loved you so much, too much.

The words echoed in my head. But I couldn't say them because they would make me even more vulnerable than I was already. That he would never have suspected the truth seemed to damn those feelings even more. And made me realise how futile they had always been.

'I guess I wasn't thinking much. I'm not even sure I made a conscious decision. I was too confused. Too heart-sick after Remy's death and...' *And being banished by you,* I thought but didn't add. 'And having to leave Monaco and my life here. And then, once I'd seen his tiny form on the first scan, there was only one choice that felt right for me.'

It wasn't the whole truth, but it was enough of the truth to satisfy him, because he nodded and tucked his hands back into his pockets.

'But I'm sorry I took the choice away from you,' I said, even though I wasn't sorry, because I could never be sorry for having Cai. 'Of whether or not to become a father.' I sucked in a lungful of air. I really needed to go now—this was getting awkward and too much. 'I think we should take time out. There's no pressure for you to meet Cai. It's a big adjustment for him coming to Nice and it'll take a while for him to settle. And it's obviously a big adjustment for you too. I want you both to be ready.'

It was a lie. Cai was a remarkably adaptable child and I already knew he would make himself right at home in our new palace. But I couldn't face Alexi again for a while. I needed time, space and distance. The hunger still hummed in my sex, and I couldn't seem to get any of this into per-spective.

I picked my sandals off the top of the dresser where he'd placed them and slipped them on. He was still staring at me, and I had the weirdest sensation he could see right through my show of maturity to the panicked girl beneath.

'Why don't I give you a call once Cai's properly settled, in a couple of weeks, and we can arrange some visitation—if that works for you?'

He frowned. 'A couple of weeks?'

'Well, yes,' I mumbled. 'Pierre said you're headed to the UK tomorrow to prep for the Primo Grande,' I said, suddenly desperately thankful for that piece of fortuitous timing. The British super race was several weeks away. It would give me time to get over this insistent, dangerous hunger. 'It would be much better if, when you meet him for the first time, you don't then have to then disappear for weeks.' I carried on talking as I walked backwards towards the door, scared he would try to stop me again. And even more scared that I wanted him to. 'A week to a four-year-old is an eternity. So why don't we leave it until you get back?'

He didn't answer, but I took his silence as his consent.

'Great,' I said and left.

I ran down the stairs, out the back door and climbed into the convertible. But, as the powerful car purred to life, I couldn't resist glancing over my shoulder.

My breath caught as I spotted him, standing on the veranda of his bedroom, watching me.

I accelerated into the night, swallowing down the burst of heat—and fear.

CHAPTER TEN

Alexi

AFTER RINGING THE bell the following morning at the door of the villa I had purchased for Belle and my son, I pushed my hands into my pockets and waited for her to answer.

My heart galloped into my throat and heat settled at the base of my spine as I heard footsteps inside the house and a female voice.

'Just a minute.'

The door swung open, but the tension in my gut relaxed. The woman in front of me wasn't Belle. She looked vaguely familiar, though. She had the same heart-shaped face as Belle, her hair a deep chestnut instead of the rich vibrant red of Belle's. Pretty, but not stunning. I decided the woman must be the second cousin I had met briefly in Barcelona when my life had changed for ever.

'Hi,' she said, looking surprised and then gifting me with a brilliant smile that made her look surprisingly pleased to see me and turned her pretty features into something more.

I tensed, instantly suspicious.

I had been prepared for a frosty reception from Belle and her cousin this morning, and possibly my son too. They were not expecting me, but as I'd watched the lights on Belle's car disappearing into the darkness yesterday I'd made a few important decisions. As a result, I'd spent two hours this morning rearranging my schedule for the next three weeks so I could remain most of the time in Monaco.

I was here not just to face up to my responsibilities concerning the boy but also to apprise Belle of one important fact. She could no longer keep me out of his life, or hers. I'd seen the panic in her expressive eyes the night before, and had realised her suggestion that I wait weeks more to introduce myself to my son had nothing to do with the child's welfare and everything to do with the events in my bedroom.

'It's Mr Galanti, isn't it?' the woman said, offering her hand as I stepped inside. 'My name's Jessie Burton. I'm Belle's cousin—we met in Barcelona but I doubt you'll remember me,' she added as she shook my hand in a firm grip. 'You had eyes only for Belle that day, and Cai.' She continued to beam, apparently not upset I had ignored her. 'Come through to the terrace,' she said, as she let go of my hand and led me into the house. 'Belle and Cai are having breakfast.'

As I stepped into the main living area, I spotted Belle and my son seated at the table on the *terrazza*. The panoramic view of Nice behind them was quite spectacular, and one of the reasons I had insisted on this house for them, but it wasn't the view that had the air clogging my lungs. The cousin, whose name I'd already forgotten, was still chatting about something but her words faded, my heartbeat pounding in my eardrums. I hesitated as the blast of longing blindsided me the way it had the night before….and so many other nights before that.

Spotlighted in the morning sun, Belle wore a simple pair of summer shorts and a T-shirt, her wild hair tied back in a tidy ponytail. But even in the simple, tomboyish attire she looked exquisite as she chuckled at something the boy had said.

And so young—not old enough to have a child. Not old enough to have made love to me with such unbridled passion last night.

'Belle, we have a surprise guest for breakfast,' the cousin called out as she approached the table.

The little boy's dark head whipped round and his eyes, so like Remy's, locked on mine. 'Who is he?' he said bluntly.

But it was his mother's reaction which made the heat pulse low in my abdomen.

She stiffened, clearly shocked by my appearance, and then the colour on her cheeks—devoid of make up this morning which made the sprinkle of freckles look all the more delicious—flared.

'Alexi?' she murmured, clearly not as pleased to see me as her cousin.

The boy, who had scrambled down from his chair, ran towards me.

'Who are you?' he asked as he reached me.

He stood with his small fists perched on his hips and his chin thrust out.

Wearing a pair of pyjamas, decorated with a cartoon sports car with a smiling face, the child should have looked cute but instead he looked fierce, his compact body rigid with tension, his expression wary and his stance oddly confrontational. Clearly, he didn't remember meeting me all those weeks ago.

'Why are you here?' the child demanded.

A smile creased my lips despite the tension in my own belly.

The boy was defending his mother.

'Cai, you mustn't speak to Mr Galanti so rudely.' The cousin stepped in, placing her hands on the boy's shoulders.

'Mr Galanti is…' the cousin began, and then stopped and swung her head round to Belle for guidance, who sat stiffly at the table, still struck dumb by my appearance.

Realisation dawned at the cousin's hesitation. So Belle hadn't told my son of our relationship.

Irritation gripped my insides. Was she still trying to keep him from me?

It was a struggle to keep my tone even and non-confrontational as I knelt down to introduce myself to the child.

'My name is Alexi Galanti.' I lifted my gaze to Belle who had finally got over her shock and was walking towards us.

The look on her face said it all—guilt, regret and panic.

The panic could only be from one fear—that I would introduce myself to the child as his father before he was ready.

My irritation increased. But I clamped down on it.

I should have taken charge of this situation a lot sooner.

'I am a friend of your mother's,' I told the boy, repeating what we had told him all those weeks ago in Barcelona. Perhaps it was less of a lie now than it had been then.

Although, 'friend' was far too simple and straightforward a term for what Belle and I shared.

'I would like to be your friend too,' I added.

The boy's eyes widened, but instead of replying to me he glanced at his mother. 'Mummy, you said I'm not supposed to talk to strangers. Can I talk to him?'

I had to admire his bluntness and his brutal honesty, even as part of me died inside at the word 'strangers'.

The reality of the situation hit home. This boy was my son, my own flesh and blood. His Galanti heritage was evident in every part of him—not just the dark, wavy hair, the shape of his face, the pure blue eyes so like my brother's, but also in his directness, his boldness, his bravery, his determination to stand up for his mother. The way I had once tried to stand up for mine.

And because of Belle's and my mistakes, our fears, our weaknesses, our selfishness, I could not claim him today.

Belle knelt beside the boy and banded an arm around his waist to tug him against her side. His arm wrapped around her neck, his attachment to her somehow making the regret and the longing grip my chest even harder.

In that moment, I made a promise to myself. No more running. No more hiding. For my sins, I could not claim my son today, but I would do everything in my power to make sure I could claim him soon. Very soon.

'It's okay, Cai,' Belle said softly, her voice breaking with an emotion that I could feel echoing in my own chest. 'You did the right thing to check with me first,' she said and the boy beamed, basking in his mother's praise. 'But Alexi's right, he isn't a stranger...' Her throat moved as she swallowed and I could see the sheen of moisture in her eyes. This was as hard for her as it was for me. My irritation eased a little bit. 'He *is* my friend. And I think it would be lovely if he could become your friend as well.'

The surge of possessiveness surprised me.

I wasn't the boy's friend. I was his father. And I wasn't Belle's friend either. I was her lover.

I knew I would need to hold back my fierce determination to claim the boy until I had learned a lot more about being a parent.

But I would be damned if I would pretend not to be more than a friend to Belle, especially after last night.

Our gazes met over the boy's head and the blush on her pale cheeks flared. Awareness bristled in the air between us.

'Do you have a car, Mr Alexi?' the little boy asked, forcing my attention back to him. The smile he sent me lit his whole face—and displayed a pair of captivating dimples. 'I love cars.'

The child's serious, cautious expression had disappeared. My heartbeat slowed as memories of Remy bombarded me. My son was a complete charmer, with the same sunny disposition my brother had always possessed... Sweet and uncomplicated, more than a little cocky and unfailingly optimistic. How foolish I had been to be so scared of getting to know him, when in many ways I knew him already... And had missed him terribly.

'I own several cars,' I said, an idea occurring to me. 'Do you like racing cars?' I asked, already well aware of the answer to that question after our brief meeting in Barcelona.

The boy nodded enthusiastically, his eyes widening. 'Yes, I love racing cars the best of all.'

I decided to use his enthusiasm to my advantage. So many things about this child were familiar to me, but I was not familiar to him. I wanted that to change, and soon— so why not use every weapon in my arsenal to win the boy over?

'I own some racing cars,' I said and the little boy gasped—his excitement so innocent and unfettered it was all the more endearing.

'Really?' he said.

I nodded, his awestruck expression a sop to my battered ego.

'Perhaps you and your mother would like to come to the Galanti test track today,' I said. 'And you can sit in our latest prototype?'

The boy began to jump up and down, his excitement no longer containable. 'Can we, Mummy? Can we? *Pleeeeease?*'

It was beneath me, but a part of me couldn't help being pleased that at the very least I had managed to best Camaro's offer of a month ago. I wasn't in competition with Renzo for the boy's affections, any more than I was for his mother's affections, but still I could not deny the triumphant feeling in my chest.

'Yes, of course,' Belle said. 'Jessie can go with you both. I have to stay here to...' She paused, trying to come up with a plausible excuse not to accompany us, I had no doubt.

Lifting off my knee, I stood up and held out a hand to haul her up too.

'Perhaps Jessie would like to take my...' I began, but then paused as Belle's fingers jerked in mine. I had been about to reveal my relationship to the child. 'To take Cai,' I corrected myself, 'to get dressed, and we can talk?'

'I'm not sure that's necessary...' She tugged her fingers loose, but her cousin interrupted.

'Come on, Cai,' she said, gripping the child's hand. 'Let's get you dressed so you can see the new car. And your mummy and Mr Galanti can talk,' she added pointedly.

The look that passed between the two women was not lost on me. Clearly Jessie wanted us to talk too. I decided I liked the woman a great deal.

'Can we go right now?' the child asked.

'We can go as soon as you are dressed,' I said.

'Thank you, Mr Alexi,' he said. 'I like being your friend,' he added, the innocent remark making my chest ache.

'It's just Alexi,' I called after him as he dragged Belle's cousin towards his bedroom in his rush to get changed.

As soon as Jessie and my son disappeared down the hallway, the room fell silent.

The delightful flush on Belle's cheeks had spread to engulf her collarbone. I noticed the pink rash on her neck where I'd sucked the pulse point less than ten hours ago—and driven her wild.

The heat surged back into my pants.

'I… We weren't expecting you today, but if you want to take Cai for a trip to the track I have no objections,' she said breathlessly. 'Jessie can accompany you. I've still got a ton of things to do here.'

That all sounded very reasonable, but the pulse punching her neck gave her away. She was still running, and still kidding herself we could conquer this need with denial.

I placed my hand on her neck and ignored the flash of panic. She stiffened but didn't draw away.

'Surely we discovered last night the time for cowardice is over, *bella notte*,' I said, stroking my thumb across the pulse in her collar bone, feeling it flutter uncontrollably.

'I don't know what you mean,' she said, but I could see she knew exactly what I meant. Her desire for me was the one thing she had never been able to hide.

'Then let me demonstrate,' I said as I lowered my head to hers. 'I'm not here just to claim my son,' I murmured. Her lips parted under mine with a gasp. The invitation was all the more beguiling because I was sure it was completely instinctive. 'I'm here to claim you too.'

CHAPTER ELEVEN

Belle

I'M HERE TO claim you too.

The gruff words, so sure, so dominant and so possessive, shot through me as Alexi's lips captured mine.

The dark, insistent need I had been trying to rationalise, minimise and explain all through my sleepless night leapt out of the shadows and sent glittering light cascading through my body.

My mouth opened instinctively to let him in, my fingers fisting in the soft cotton of his polo shirt as his tongue probed—demanding, relentless. He thrust deep into my mouth, exploring the recesses, tasting me again the way he had tasted me last night, but in the bright light of morning my response felt somehow more devastating, more out of control.

His hands cupped my cheeks as he angled my head for better access, his tongue delving deeper, not just claiming me but branding me.

My breathing sped up with my heart rate but my dazed mind—which was still reeling from the shock of having Alexi in my home unannounced, and seeing him engage with our son with surprising sensitivity—managed to engage.

Why was he really here? To become a father to his son,

or to reopen the Pandora's box I had tried to slam shut after last night?

I flattened my palms against his waist and managed to gather the strength to override the need and shove him back.

'Stop!' The words came out on a sob. He let me go instantly.

Perhaps he was as shocked by the incendiary nature of our physical connection as I was. But he didn't look shocked, he looked indomitable, as I stumbled back, desperate to get away from the fire still burning in my blood.

'We can't… We can't go there again.' I dragged shaking fingers through my hair, scrambling around for the right words, the right tone—calm and assured rather than weak and needy. Not easy when my heart was racing faster than the Galanti X on the final lap at the Monaco Primo Grande. I gulped down several steadying breaths.

'Why can't we, if we both want to?' he asked, his voice so assured, so reasonable, I suddenly wanted to slap him.

I shoved my fists into the pockets of my shorts to control the urge, but the switch from shock and need to anger finally helped to get my racing heartbeat past the finishing line.

'Because this…' I jerked my hand out of my pocket and flapped my palm between him and me. 'This *thing* between us isn't just about us any more.' I ground the words out, the righteous indignation for my son helping to keep the destructive desire at bay at last. 'There's a child involved. And things are confusing enough for him already. You came here this morning without consulting with me.' I'd tried to be forgiving about that, to understand. But his surprise appearance this morning was starting to look more and more like another of his power plays.

'I told you he needed more time. I haven't even had a chance to tell him who you are yet, to prepare him, and...'

'Stop it.' He grabbed my wrist and held it down, forcing my gaze to his. 'Stop pretending this is about the boy when you know it's not. You've had more than enough time to speak to him about me—four years, to be precise—but you have chosen not to. I'm not waiting any longer to get your permission to speak to my son.'

The sharp judgement in his voice, and the incontrovertible truth behind it, struck me like a blow, and the burning anger in my belly imploded, drowned by the black hole of guilt.

He let go of my wrist.

'Do you think I don't know how complicated this is?' he demanded, his voice rough now—not with judgement but with something a great deal rawer than that. 'Do you think I don't know how confusing it is—for him as well as me?'

He dragged in several breaths and I could almost feel the pain in his lungs as he did so, because mine felt the same. 'Do you think telling him I want to be his friend was easy for me, when what I want to do is tell him I'm his father?' He whispered the words, and I realised he was keeping his voice down so Cai wouldn't hear him. 'Do you think I don't know I have to earn the right to call myself that? And how hard that is going to be for me when I have no idea how to even talk to a four-year-old, let alone how to be a parent to one?'

A tear slipped over my lid—the tears I'd struggled to contain earlier when I'd watched him kneel in front of his son so he could look him in the eye, instinctively knowing how not to intimidate him. Even in that brief encounter Alexi had engaged with Cai so effortlessly—using their shared love of racing cars to start bonding with him. But

I realised now, as I should have realised ten minutes ago, that none of that encounter had been effortless, at least not for Alexi.

I scrubbed the tear away, looking down at my bare feet. So ashamed.

I'd apologised to Alexi for the years of silence, for failing to tell him about his son, and I'd meant it—but how could I ever be forgiven? How could I even forgive myself until I put his needs and Cai's needs ahead of my own?

'Actually you did very well,' I said, hitching in a breath and willing myself to hold the emotion at bay. Had a part of me even been a little jealous that Alexi had bonded with Cai so easily? I had denied my son his father for so long perhaps it was time I acknowledged one of my reasons for doing so had been my own insecurities as a mother? I'd had Cai when I had been nineteen years old. I'd been a confused, terrified child myself in many ways. I'd worked long and hard to build up my confidence. I was proud of what I'd achieved, but had a part of me been scared to test that, scared to share Cai with his father, because it might illuminate my inadequacies as a mother?

This wasn't a competition, but I had made it one.

'I suspect it helps that I own a Super League team,' he said wryly, and my heart broke more—because, beneath the irony, I could hear the insecurity.

'It doesn't hurt,' I said, forcing a smile to my lips. 'But it was more than that. The way you spoke to him was very...' I gulped, trying to shrink the boulder in my throat at his inquisitive expression. 'It was really...' I wanted to say sweet, but sweet wasn't a word you could use to describe Alexi Galanti. Even as a father. It was too ordinary, too shallow, too trite. 'It was really touching,' I managed. 'It was as if you already understood him. I think you might be a natural.'

He frowned then huffed out a bitter laugh. 'I find that unlikely, given my own upbringing.'

The remark sounded flippant, but I knew it was not— he was talking about his fractured relationship with his own father. I realised what he had said to me last night, about his fear of fatherhood, wasn't just wound up in his misplaced guilt over Remy's death but also in all the cruel things his father had said and done to him during so much of his childhood and adolescence.

All those nasty jibes, the shouted threats and criticisms, the back-handed slaps and drunken punches that Remy and I had overheard… Alexi had always dismissed them, had always seemed immune, his confidence unbowed by his father's abuse, but that treatment had taken its toll in ways of which I had been unaware until now.

'You were never like him, Alexi,' I said.

His frown deepened. The momentary flash of torment at the mention of his father was quickly masked but I knew the remark had hit home. Or at least I hoped it had, and I was glad. Because I could see now I hadn't just robbed my son of a father over the last four years, I had stopped this man from discovering how much better he was than his own father.

'I'm glad this first meeting went well,' he said. 'But I will need your help to ensure I don't make mistakes.'

I nodded. 'You have it.'

He nodded back. 'I would like to be able to tell Cai who I really am as soon as possible,' he continued. 'But I am prepared to take your lead on that, as you know him best.'

It was a huge concession. I understood that, just as I now understood the significance of him not announcing the truth as soon as he had arrived this morning. He had trusted me, and now I needed to prove to him I wasn't going to abuse that trust.

'Thank you, let's see how it goes. But Cai's actually very adaptable,' I admitted. 'He's already loving it here. And he…he's always craved male attention,' I added, thinking of how quickly he'd attached himself to Renzo and Pierre.

Why had I never noticed that before for what it was? Especially as I had yearned for a father myself through so much of my childhood.

'He's already thrilled to bits that I'm working for you… because apparently Galanti make "the bestest racing cars ever",' I added with a smile, quoting our son.

'He's a smart boy.' Alexi's eyes sparkled with amusement. 'And handsome and exceptionally self-assured. He reminds me so much of Remy at that age, it is almost uncanny.' He sobered, the frown reappearing between his brows. 'You have my word, Belle, that I will do everything in my power not to hurt him.'

My heart galloped into my throat at the sincerity in his voice.

And two things occurred to me at once: that although he was unaware of it Alexi, who guarded his heart so fiercely, had already lost it to his son and how selfish and immature I had been to believe even for a minute, let alone five years, that Alexi would not be a good father to our child when he had been such a good brother to Remy.

'I know,' I said, realising the only way I could undo the damage I had caused by keeping my secret was to support and encourage Alexi as much as I could now.

'But now we must talk of the other elephant in the room,' Alexi said.

He cupped my cheek and the buzz in my stomach ignited all over again. His thumb trailed across my lips, lips still tender from his kiss.

'What elephant?' I asked, my voice husky enough to sandpaper one of the luxury yachts anchored in the bay.

Alexi's lips quirked into a sensual smile. And I knew he could hear the husky invitation in my voice too. 'I still want you, Belle, and you want me. And I see no reason for us not to satisfy this burning hunger for each other while I learn how to be a father to our son.'

'We…we can't.' I stepped back, desperate to break the spell he could so easily weave around me. His hand dropped away but I could still feel the warmth of his palm, the roughness of the callused skin against my cheek.

'You said this before, but you didn't give me an answer. Why can't we?' he asked. There was no aggression, only mild curiosity, as if he were dealing with a skittish mare who needed to be handled gently but firmly.

'I did give you an answer. We can't, because it would be too confusing for Cai.'

'Why would it be confusing for him? We have already told him we're friends. It is not as if we would be making love in front of him,' he said.

'He's only just met you. I don't think…' I began, but he silenced me with a touch.

'You must trust me, Belle. I will not neglect him. When I am with him, my focus will be on him. My relationship with him is not dependent on my relationship with you.'

I already knew this to be true from his impassioned response a moment ago.

'Okay, but I still think it'll be too much having him know we're a couple…'

'Why will it?' he persisted. 'Surely you must have taken other men to your bed in the last four years? How did you explain them to our son?' I heard the distinct edge in his voice but ignored it. How could he possibly be jealous when he was the one who had discarded me? And, anyway, there was nothing to be jealous of. I had never taken any other men to my bed.

'I… I didn't,' I said. 'I mean, Cai never met any of them,' I added, hating the need to lie. But how could I tell Alexi he was the only man I had ever slept with when he was already behaving like a cave man? 'I always kept my sex life separate from our home life, precisely so he wouldn't get confused. I didn't want him becoming attached to someone as a father figure who would not be a permanent part of my life.'

'That does not apply here, though, does it?' he said, and I suddenly realised my lie had allowed him neatly to outmanoeuvre me. 'I am not a father *figure*—I am his father. I will always have an attachment to him, no matter whether we are sleeping together or not, so there's no reason to keep our liaison a secret from him. Or for us not to pursue this hunger in the hours we have alone together.'

'What—what hours?' I said, stammering as he pressed his palm to my cheek again. I could not hide the shudder of reaction. 'You're a busy man, and I need to be focused on getting Cai settled here before I start a demanding new job in three weeks' time…' I was babbling now, his touch making my heartbeat race and my pulse sink deep into my sex as he stroked my cheek. His hand strayed to my neck, his thumb rubbing the thundering pulse in my collar bone.

'I have cleared my schedule for the next few weeks—let's see what happens,' he murmured, before placing a possessive kiss on my lips.

My breath shuddered out, my mouth opening to accept so much more, my surrender complete. But he drew back at the sound of Cai's footsteps running back down the corridor.

'I'm ready!' Cai shouted as he appeared. But then he stopped and tilted his head to one side. 'Mummy, your face is all red,' he announced in the way children have of stating the obvious. 'Why?'

I pressed my hands to my cheeks, my face igniting even more at Alexi's smile. His large hand settled on the small of my back, making me feel owned, before he pressed a kiss to my temple.

'I just kissed your mummy,' he said. 'I hope you don't mind,' he added, asking my son's permission in a way that made my heart squeeze painfully in my chest.

'Yuck, I hate kissing,' Cai replied. 'It's so boring.'

I found myself choking out a laugh alongside Alexi's deep chuckle.

'You may change your mind about that when you're older,' Alexi announced, recovering his cool a lot quicker than I could. 'But enough talk of boring stuff,' he added, folding his son's small hand in his. 'Let's go check out the new Galanti X.'

Jessie appeared with Cai's coat and a bag full of toys just in case he got bored during the trip, something I suspected was unlikely, as he stared at his father with something akin to hero worship in his eyes.

As they made their way to the door, Jessie excused herself, neatly manoeuvring me into going with Alexi instead. A part of me still wanted to object, but Alexi sent me a look that clearly said he had no intention of letting me retreat behind my 'it's too confusing for Cai' shell again.

And I realised the only way to convince him I wasn't running any more was to go with them both today.

No man had ever staked a claim on me in front of my son.

And, even if they had, I doubt they would have been able to do it in such a way that made Cai feel more secure instead of less so.

The decision as to whether we took this 'thing' between

us further was still mine. But I couldn't use Cai as a cover any more. As well as not being an answer, avoidance was no longer an option.

Alexi wouldn't allow it to be an option. So I pulled on my big girl panties and took my son's other hand as we made our way out of the house to Alexi's car.

Cai swung between us. As his sturdy little body lifted into the air, my heart swooped and swung with him, and my gaze met Alexi's.

This day would be a new experience for all three of us. We weren't a family, but we were both Cai's parents, and that was all that mattered today.

CHAPTER TWELVE

Alexi

I BRAKED THE car in front of Belle and Cai's villa as the sun dipped towards the horizon. Swinging my head round, I spotted Belle in the back seat, her head propped against the window, her eyes shut. Our son sat in the car seat beside her, his small head lolling to one side.

A smile spread up my chest to my lips at the sight of them both fast asleep. It had been an exhausting day. But I had discovered several important lessons about being a father, or even simply being a friend to a four-year-old. Their energy seemed to operate on a scale of ten or zero—full-on or fast asleep—and there was no in between. The questions never ended and could be repeated on a loop. I'd answered everything, from what was my favourite animal to why I liked racing cars, not once but approximately four hundred times.

The other thing I had discovered was that Belle was a magnificent mother. All her attention had been focused on the boy today, checking that he was okay, answering the questions I could not, directing him in everything from manners to personal safety with an ease that was always thoughtful, patient and never unkind.

The car's engine purred to a stop as I turned off the ignition.

Belle's eyelids fluttered open, the rich emerald instantly alert. 'We're here. I'm sorry. I must have drifted off,' she murmured, her voice thick with sleep. Would she sound like that when she awoke in the morning? The pheromones that were never silent buzzed back to life. I ignored them, as I had done all day.

'It's been a tiring day,' I said.

'It must have been a baptism of fire for you,' she said, sending me a rare unguarded smile. My heart skipped at the thought of how much I had missed that smile. I'd seen it several times today whenever Cai had done something funny, silly or simply enthusiastic—and every time it had had the same effect on my heart rate—but this was the first time it had been directed at me.

'Cai's pretty full-on,' she added. 'Especially when he's excited. But you were wonderful with him. I hope you know he hero worships you now?'

Her praise was as genuine and unguarded as her smile.

'I'm sure it's normal for any active four-year-old,' I murmured, at least one thing I could now say with some authority.

'Thank you,' she said, then stretched her arms up in a yawn. It made her T-shirt stretch over her full breasts. The spike of heat hit me hard. 'For making today so fun for him…' she finished.

The spike of heat was followed by a spike of irritation.

'I'm his father—why wouldn't I?' I asked.

'Of course,' she said, the guilt shadowing her eyes again.

I wanted to snatch the words back. 'Now it's my turn to be sorry,' I said.

'Why?' she asked, those mossy eyes widening. 'You have every right to be angry with me for creating this situation.'

'No, I don't,' I said firmly. 'And, anyway, that's not why I snapped at you.'

'Why did you, then?' she asked, with that artlessness which still confused me.

I let my gaze roam down to her breasts and immediately felt the sexual tension snap between us before lifting my gaze. 'Because being this close to you all day and not being able to touch you has been an exercise in frustration.'

The blush flooded her face, reddening her pale skin and illuminating her freckles in the half-light from the setting sun. She chewed her lip. 'Oh,' she said in that husky tone of voice which told me I wasn't the only one who had been frustrated.

'But that is my cross to bear,' I added, just in case she assumed I was blaming her for not being able to control my own libido. 'Not yours.'

I climbed out of the car and opened the passenger door on Cai's side. As I unhooked the harness on his child seat, she appeared beside me. She was still flushed, but when she spoke she didn't sound so wary, which I considered a good thing.

'I can carry him,' she said.

'I would like to,' I replied.

She drew back and I could see she was torn, as she had been on occasion all through the day. Giving me a piece of our son's care was hard for her, I realised. But I didn't resent her reluctance any more. He was precious cargo, and she was only protecting him, like a mother bear. The last four years or so must have been hard for her. Caring for a child was not easy.

'I swear I will not drop him,' I added, forcing a smile to my lips.

She smiled back. 'I know.'

As I lifted his slumbering body out of the car seat, a

strange emotion washed over me. Protective, possessive but also filled with a strength of feeling I had never had before.

I had picked him up a few times during the day—lifting him into the Galanti X model we had come to see at the test track, later at the restaurant we had gone to for lunch and at the beach, where he had run for hours, letting me chase him as he'd shrieked. But this time was somehow different, as he lifted tired arms around my neck and snuggled into my embrace. I held him against my chest as the feeling spread and felt the sting of something in my eyes…

Could it be tears? Surely that was ludicrous? I never cried—even as a child, when my father had taken a belt to me, when my mother had left my brother and me, or as a man when I had stood over my brother's grave…

I could feel Belle's eyes on me, so I gently shut the car door and swallowed down the rush of strange emotions. But I couldn't seem to stop myself from folding my arms securely around the boy's sturdy body and breathing in his childish scent of sweat, sea salt and the chocolate ice-cream that stained the front of his T-shirt.

As we walked together into the house, Belle rushing to open the door in front of me, the boy's head finally stirred. He lifted his eyes to mine as I stepped into their new home.

'Hello, Mr Alexi,' he said sleepily.

'Hello,' I replied, impossibly moved by the fact his arms only tightened around my neck. He wasn't scared of me. He felt safe, secure. Even after only a day in my company, he trusted me. I swore to myself never to abuse that trust. 'It's just Alexi,' I added, for about the fiftieth time that day.

'You smell different to my mummy,' he murmured.

I let out a hoarse chuckle at the sleepy observation. 'I

know,' I said as Belle directed me through the house towards the boy's bedroom.

'I like your smell,' he said, then rested his head on my shoulder, his fingers threading into the short hairs on my neck, and dropped back to sleep.

The simple statement had the rush of emotion surging through me so strongly, I had to lock my knees as Belle opened the door to his bedroom and turned on a night light beside his bed.

I stood holding my son, *our* son, for a few moments as she pulled back the duvet, my hands cradling his body, feeling his breath against my neck and inhaling his sweet scent. I knew in that moment I never wanted to let him go even as I forced myself to place him on his bed.

'Why don't you go into the living room and pour yourself a drink?' she whispered as she began to strip the sleeping child, her movements fast and efficient.

I nodded and walked out of the room, trying to control the emotion in my chest that was making it hard for me to breathe.

I walked through the living room and onto the balcony, and took a few steadying breaths of the sea air. But as I stared at the lights of Nice in the distance, just starting to illuminate the coastline, one devastating truth occurred to me. I would never again be able to dismiss the emotion this small boy stirred in me—because he was mine.

What surprised me more, though, was the realisation that I did not want to.

CHAPTER THIRTEEN

Belle

AFTER TUCKING CAI into bed, I made my way downstairs to the house's large living area.

Where was Jessie? I needed her here as a buffer.

I had seen the rush of emotion on Alexi's face as he'd held Cai so carefully, so gently, as if he were the most precious thing in the world.

He had been wonderful with my son... I swallowed heavily...with *our* son all day. He'd answered all Cai's questions, talking to him in a way that acknowledged he was a child while also acknowledging he was an individual. A difficult balancing act few people instinctively knew how to do. But Alexi did.

Watching Alexi with Cai had brought back bittersweet yet beautiful memories of his close relationship with Remy.

Alexi, underneath the caution, the control, the commanding personality, had always been a supportive and kind brother, and it seemed he would be exactly the same as a father.

The joy of watching the two of them begin to form a bond—as they'd chatted about cars or had chased each other in a wild game of tag on the beach—had been intense at

times, but it had also brought with it regret, confusion…
and fear.

I needed to be careful. Alexi's relationship with his son
did not change his relationship with me.

But as I walked into the living room and glimpsed Alexi
standing alone on the balcony, his pensive expression lit by
the lights of the city and the gold of the sunset, I felt the reaction I had struggled to ignore all day ripple over my skin.

The chemistry was still there and still unbearably intense—last night had not dimmed it in the slightest. That
one searing look he had given me in the car had proved
that beyond a doubt.

'Would you like a drink?' I asked.

Alexi turned and shook his head.

I trembled, blaming the breeze that drifted in from the
balcony, even though the evening was warm.

I should go and join him, talk to him, thank him again
for the wonderful day he had given Cai…and myself. But
I knew I couldn't talk without babbling, and the balcony
felt too intimate, my thoughts too volatile, to allow me to
get that close to him. So I detoured to the sideboard, planning to pour myself a drink. And spotted a note in Jessie's
handwriting propped on the dining table, addressed to me.

I picked it up and flicked it open.

Hey Cuz,
I hope you and Alexi and Cai had a fabulous day
together. I've decided to take a last-minute trip to
Paris and finally see the City of Lights, like I've been
promising myself for ever!
    I'll make sure I'm back before you start work—
just text me if you need me in the meantime.
    Alexi seems like a good guy—he's also super-hot!

*I'm sure the last thing you need right now is your old
maid cousin cramping your style.*

    You can thank me later.

Jess xx

I screwed up the note with shaking hands.

Oh, Jess, what have you done?

My cousin wasn't an old maid—she was younger than
me, having taken me in when she was still in catering col-
lege. And she wouldn't have cramped my style. If anything she would have been an important safety valve. One
I desperately needed as I stole another glance at Alexi's
silhouette standing in the sunset looking proud, indomitable and... Yup, super-hot.

My cousin had deserted me in my hour of need. In fact,
she'd gone over to the dark side—encouraging rather than
curtailing the madness that had overtaken my senses the
night before. Unfortunately, the same madness was coursing through my veins once more.

As I struggled to control the wave of excitement and
need, the weird mix of panic and validation at Jessie's desertion—and attempted to make a sensible decision about
what to do without our chaperone in residence—Alexi
turned, almost as if he'd sensed my struggle and decided
to intervene.

I could feel his gaze rake over me as it had in the car,
igniting every inch of exposed skin.

'Stop hiding, Belle, and come here,' he said, his expression full of the same intensity I had seen on his face
as he'd lifted Cai out of his car seat and held him close.
But this time his expression wasn't stunned—it was raw
and turbulent.

The need throbbed and ached at my core, but I couldn't
seem to stop myself from crossing the room towards him.

When I reached him, he cradled my cheek, the rough calluses of his palm stroking the sensitive skin.

'Where is your cousin?' he asked.

So he'd noticed Jessie's absence too. He had to know how much more volatile the situation between us would become without her here.

'She...she left a note,' I babbled, the burning sensation becoming overwhelming as his head lowered to mine.

'What does it say?' he coaxed, before his warm lips settled on my neck, licking and nibbling the pulse point.

I gasped, sobbed, as he rubbed his mouth against my collar bone in an erotic rhythm that blurred my already dazed senses.

'She's...she decided to go to Paris for a while,' I managed to choke out around the lump of need and desire throbbing in my throat.

His head lifted, his gaze fixing on mine. He framed my face in his hands, his fingers threading into my hair.

'Good,' he rasped, before covering my mouth with his.

The kiss was harsh, searing, demanding, leaving me breathless and limp when he reared back. He gripped me under my arms and lifted me against him.

'Wrap your legs around my waist,' he commanded. I did as he told me, unable to deny the need surging through me like a tsunami.

It still scared me, still shocked me, how quickly, how undeniable, the need was with him. How it seemed to daze all my senses and destroy all my objections. But as he marched through the living room and down the corridor, to the stairs leading to the bedrooms on the floor above, I could do nothing but cling to him and let the riot of sensations surge through me.

'Which door is yours?' he asked, his voice hoarse with need as we reached the first-floor balcony.

I signalled to my bedroom, my voice having deserted me, the need so strong I knew nothing on earth would stop me from feeling that thick length inside me again.

He shouldered open the door and kicked it shut, then placed me on my feet.

My breath shuddered out as he dragged my T-shirt over my head, unhooked my bra and pulled it off. He filled his hands with my breasts, the tender flesh aching as he caressed me, then leaned down to capture one swollen peak with his lips.

I cried out, the sound echoing round the ornate furnishings and into the night through the open terrace doors.

I heard the zip on my shorts releasing, the sound loud in the quiet room, almost as loud as our laboured breathing.

He dragged off my shorts, and I heard the rip of fabric as he tore away my panties.

'I can't wait. I need to be inside you,' he said. For the first time I heard the tremble of uncertainty, the note of desperation in his voice.

It was like a spur to my already overwrought senses. 'I need you too,' I whispered.

He clasped my hips in large hands then turned me, bending me over the bed. I could hear fumbling, several curse words in Italian as he stripped off his own clothing, then his wallet landed on the bed beside my head. The rip of foil told me he was sheathing himself.

His large hands returned to my hips to steady me. My legs quivered, my senses so attuned to his I could feel the staggered rasps of his breathing beating in my sex.

His fingers slid through the slick folds, testing my readiness. I bucked, sobbed, as his touch glided over my swollen clitoris, tightening the coil in my abdomen, the pleasure already beginning to ripple and pulse.

'Grazie Dio,' he murmured against my neck, his perfect English deserting him, his tone as tortured as I felt.

He covered my aching breasts with his hands, caressing the nipples, making sensation arrow down to my already molten sex. Then he held me steady as the huge head of his erection notched at my entrance and slid deep in one relentless thrust. My slick folds adjusted to take the full measure of him, the muscles clamping down as the pleasure surged anew.

'No,' he demanded, withdrawing sharply. My breath shuddered out as the pleasure dimmed and the torture increased.

'Don't come, *bella*,' he rasped. 'Wait for me.'

'I can't,' I sobbed, the pleasure on a knife edge, so close and yet so far away as I yearned to feel him deep inside me again.

'Yes, you can,' he said, tweaking my nipples, making them throb and ache.

I tried to focus as he slowly thrust back in, filling me up to the hilt again. I struggled to hold back the inexorable wave, my whole body shuddering, shaking with the effort as he began to move—out and back, thrusting deeper and deeper—forcing me to take every hard, thick inch.

My mind reeled, my senses sparking along every nerve ending, throbbing in every pulse point, but I clung to that high ledge as his thrusts became harder, faster, slicing through more of my control.

Sweat slicked my skin, my sex pounding in time with the punishing, relentless thrusts, until all I could focus on was the heavy weight possessing me, overwhelming me. Then he shifted, nudging that spot deep inside only he knew was there. The merciless stroke ignited the inferno and I could cling on no more, flying over as the coil released in a rush, the blast of heat incinerating me as the pleasure exploded.

My sobs turned to keening cries as the waves engulfed me. I heard his shout as the orgasm shattering me powered through him, destroying everything in its path. He grew even larger, harder, as the devastation gripped us both.

He collapsed on top of me eventually, rolling so as not to crush me. His palms caressed my tender breasts as his arms tightened around me.

We lay like that for an eternity, cocooned together, the sweat drying on our skin, his heartbeat punching my back, the musky scent of sex filling the air, his breath harsh against the damp tendrils on my nape. My own heart pummelled my ribs so hard I was surprised it didn't burst out of my chest. The tears of emotion I had hoped to control stung my eyes.

The sob seemed to come from nowhere as he held me in the darkness. I dug my teeth into my bottom lip to hold it back, tasting blood. I mustn't fall apart. Mustn't make this mean more than it did. I didn't want him to know how weak I was, how needy.

His lips nuzzled my nape and his arms tightened, making the ache in my throat worse.

'Non piangere, bella,' he whispered.

Don't weep.

I blinked rapidly, glad he couldn't see my face and the struggle to hold the overwhelming emotions at bay.

'I'm not crying,' I said, willing it to be true.

'Bene,' he murmured, then he gave me one last squeeze and let me go.

Lifting off the bed, he dragged the quilt up to cover my naked body.

I gathered the quilt around me to stave off the sudden chill as he headed for the *en suite* bathroom.

I fixated on the glorious sight of his naked buttocks, limned by moonlight, to stop the emotions overwhelming me.

And tried to tell myself the instinct to make love to Alexi wasn't an emotional one, it was purely physical. A basic, animalistic urge I had never been able to control.

He returned a few moments later but, instead of picking up his clothing and getting dressed, he climbed into the bed beside me. He wrapped an arm around my shoulders and tucked me against his side.

The tears threatened again, so I swallowed them down. What was the matter with me? Why was I falling apart at the smallest show of affection?

Just because I'd expected him to leave, just because he'd never held me like this before.

I shifted, peering up at him in the darkness. His gaze was fixed on the horizon but his expression was impossible to read. I wondered what he was thinking. Then tried not to. Why did it matter? Despite his relationship to Cai, he had made no promises to me. And I didn't need him to.

'It's probably better if you don't stay,' I murmured before I could get too comfortable having him with me. His gaze shifted to mine.

His thumb stroked my cheek. 'Why?'

I breathed. There were so many answers I could give him.

That I hadn't agreed to become his lover.

That as far as I was concerned this was just another one-off brought about by an emotionally and physically exhausting day.

But I knew he'd see through those excuses to the truth beneath—that I was terrified I'd become too dependent on his care and support.

I had surrendered again, as he had known I would. All

I could do now was learn how to manage the hunger, and not entertain any unrealistic hopes, until the chemistry between us died. As it inevitably would for him, if not for me.

Alexi had never had a long-term relationship to my knowledge. Our chemistry probably wasn't anything out of the ordinary for him, the way it was for me. He'd had lots of sex with lots of women, according to the gossip columns and blogs I'd scoured over the last five years while pretending not to.

I had to make sure I didn't become dependent on the sex or, worse, the attention. Which meant not reading too much into a simple post-coital hug. So I kept my voice even when I replied.

'Cai usually runs in to wake me up at the crack of dawn every morning. It could get awkward if he finds you here tomorrow.'

He let out a gruff chuckle. 'So our son is an early riser,' he murmured, hooking a tendril of hair behind my ear. 'Why does that not surprise me?'

I smiled, even though my heart swelled against my ribs, making it hard for me to draw a breath. Why did he have to look so much more breathtaking when he talked about our son?

I knew it was dangerous to enjoy this moment too much while my sex was still humming from that titanic orgasm. But as his thumb stroked my cheek, his gaze both protective and possessive, I couldn't seem to stop myself from basking in his approval. Just a little bit.

He pressed a kiss to my forehead. 'Go to sleep, *bella notte*. I'll make sure I leave before he wakes up in the morning, but I want to hold you tonight.'

'Why?' I rasped, then wanted to snatch the question back. Did it sound as needy and hopeful to him as it did to me?

His lips spread in a sensual smile. 'Because you gave me a beautiful son, Belle, and it's way past time I thanked you for him.'

I blushed at the sincerity in his voice and the fierce gratitude in his eyes.

I tucked my head under his chin, hiding my face as I blinked rapidly to hold back the tears.

'It was my pleasure,' I murmured, toying with the dark curls of hair on his chest. 'Cai is the best thing to ever happen to me, so I should probably thank you too,' I added, my voice breaking.

He pressed his palm over my hand to stop my fidgeting, then tucked a knuckle under my chin. He lifted my face until I was staring into those pure blue eyes, filled with so much heat, I shivered.

'I will leave before the boy wakes this time, but I wish to spend more nights in your bed and I see no reason to keep it a secret from him. As you say, he is a bright child and adaptable and I will always be a part of his life. Plus, we have a rare chemistry, which we would be foolish not to indulge while it lasts.'

While it lasts...

My heart stumbled over the end of his statement—Alexi was already putting an end date on this affair, something I needed to do too. But still it made me feel unbearably sad.

'Do you not agree?' he asked gently in his usual confident, pragmatic tone.

He was asking me to sanction our affair, to welcome him into my bed and my life—for a limited time only—as well as my son's life. The fear clawed at my throat for a moment. Could I really do this—jump into a relationship with him, knowing it would not last? Knowing that, when he tired of me, I would be discarded and replaced like all the other women? Knowing I would have to spend the rest of my life as we brought up our son together, seeing him and no longer being able to touch him, to taste him, to feel him inside me as I could still feel the imprint of him now?

But as he waited patiently for my answer, his thumb stroking my upper arm while he held me, I could see the determination in his eyes, how much he wanted me to say yes, and the fear clawing at my throat loosened its grip a fraction, and then a fraction more. The raw ache of desire flooded in to replace it.

He was the only man I had ever loved, the only man I'd ever wanted, the only man to whom I'd ever made love. He was the father of my son and the brother of my best friend, whom I still missed.

I had lost Alexi once and survived, and I was so much stronger now than I had been then.

Perhaps there was still a chance for us. Who knew? But one thing I did know was that I wanted him in my bed, and I wanted the chance to become an intimate part of his life, to get to know the man I had never really known before. If for no other reason than he would always be a part of my life now, and Cai's, whether we were sleeping together or not.

So I threaded my fingers back into the hair on his chest and said, 'Yes, I want that too.'

His quick grin dazzled me, the low chuckle of relief, as if he had been unsure of my answer, a sop to my ego as he lowered his mouth to mine and kissed me.

He drew back first, the sensual smile spreading across his lips. *'Mille grazie, bella notte,'* he said, the rough, sexy tone scraping across my nerve-endings.

I settled into his embrace and waited for the flush of pleasure to subside as I listened to his heart thud steadily beneath my ear.

As long as I didn't make the mistake of becoming infatuated with this man again, everything would be absolutely fine, I assured myself as I drifted into a deep, blissful and exceptionally erotic sleep.

CHAPTER FOURTEEN

Alexi

'THE BOY IS your son, Alexi, is this not so?'

I turned to my friend, Dante Allegri, and frowned, annoyed by the perceptive question, even though I had expected as much as soon as I had arrived at the Allegris' annual summer barbeque at Villa Paradis with Belle and Cai.

'You are an observant man, Dante,' I murmured as the knot in my gut tightened.

To distract myself and him, I smiled at his toddler daughter Celeste, who was perched on his hip and was staring at me with wide tawny-green eyes.

The child reminded me so much of her mother, Edie Trouvé—or, rather, Edie Allegri, as she had become two summers ago at my friend's lavish wedding. The knot in my gut took a new twist, a twist that felt suspiciously like envy.

An envy I did not understand.

It was true, once upon a time I had wanted Dante's wife for myself. In fact, I had flirted mercilessly with her three years ago at the high stakes poker game in Dante's casino in Monaco when both Dante and I had met Edie for the first time. When she had rejected my attempts to seduce her at that game, having had eyes only for my friend, I had got over it quickly—so quickly, I had taken another woman home to my bed that night. A woman whose name—and face—I couldn't even remember three years later.

My gaze tracked to Belle, who stood beside Dante's wife on the Villa Paradis lawn. She had Cai's hand gripped firmly in hers as he showed another boy his age the toy car I had given him that morning.

I forced my gaze off Belle, and back to Edie, trying to understand the stab of envy. Dante's wife looked beautiful in an elegant blue dress, even more beautiful than she had looked the night I had first met her—and wanted her. Today she looked composed, graceful, happy, carrying the baby bump of her second pregnancy—which Dante had announced earlier—with all the poise of a woman who had somehow managed to have it all.

But I didn't want Edie any more. If I ever really had. She, like so many of the women I had dated, had been nothing more than a passing fancy. Unlike the woman who stood beside her. My gaze returned to Belle, and the heat surged as it always did when I looked at her.

After three weeks of sex whenever we could fit it in around our commitments as Cai's parents, why hadn't the hunger for her dimmed, at all?

I devoured the sight of her slender curves in the fitted designer dress, emblazoned with poppies to match her vibrant hair, the way I had when I had picked Cai and her up for the drive to Monaco an hour ago.

This was our last outing together before Belle started work and I would have to travel to England for the Primo Grande race—and I was already feeling agitated at the thought.

Unlike Edie's, Belle's stomach was flat. I remembered kissing it the night before when we had retired to her bedroom after tucking Cai into bed together. Remembered exploring the soft flesh around her belly button with my tongue, then drifting lower to capture the sweet taste of her arousal, which I had become addicted to. The heat rushed through me all over again as I recalled her broken sobs as she'd bucked and cried out against my hold.

I shook my head, trying to dismiss the memory. *Dio!* What was wrong with me? Why would this need not die? And why did it feel like so much more than just a physical hunger?

'If the child is your son, why have you not claimed him?' I registered Dante's question, tinged with incredulity and no small amount of judgement.

The accusatory look on my friend's face said it all. I bristled, but couldn't ignore the tinge of guilt. Dante was right. It had been several months now since I had discovered the boy was mine. And my relationship with Cai was going well.

I enjoyed spending time with him. I had taken him swimming and go-karting and tended to live at their villa when I was not forced to return to mine to catch up on work. The boy never stopped talking but I found his conversation fascinating. He still reminded me a great deal of Remy, but Cai was an individual too, his quirks and passions, his cheeky smile and sweet manner very much his own.

It was way past time I told him who I really was. I knew Belle would not object. In fact, I suspected she was becoming impatient for me to do so.

But, where once I had been keen to claim Cai as my son, now I hesitated. And I knew it had nothing to do with the child and everything to do with his mother.

'It's not as simple as that,' I said in answer to Dante's question. My friend frowned, not looking convinced. But then Dante had always been far too intuitive—it was one of the qualities that made him impossible to beat at the poker table.

'When did you discover he was yours?' he demanded, clearly affronted by my failure to claim my son.

'How do you know I did not always know and chose to ignore him?' I asked.

'Because I know you better than you think, Alexi,' he said, his eyes narrowing. 'You pretend to have no morals, but you are not a man to ignore his own flesh and blood.' He glanced to where Belle and his wife stood together, still deep in conversation. 'And the way you look at the boy's mother suggests she is much more to you than one of your casual conquests.'

The statement struck me square in the solar plexus because it was a truth I had been determined not to acknowledge until this moment. And it explained perfectly why I had been reluctant to claim the boy.

Fear.

Fear that claiming my son would only increase my need for his mother.

My hunger for Belle had not dimmed, and the more time we spent together, both as parents and lovers, the more it seemed to strengthen the bond—and only increase the chemistry that made me constantly want her.

And I hated that need.

After my brother's death—hell, even before it—with every woman but Belle I had been able to shut off my emotions. To keep them under lock and key.

I had no desire to do that with my son. He was a part of me, a part of Remy, and he could be better than both of us, with none of the scars we had borne from our own upbringing, if I made the effort. And with Belle's help I knew I could be a good father to him.

But with Belle? I didn't want to need her in any way other than the physical. It made me feel vulnerable and insecure, exposed and weak in a way I hadn't felt since I'd been a boy…and I had watched my mother climb into her lover's convertible and disappear into the night without a backward glance.

'You're right,' I murmured.

Why was I giving Belle this kind of power over me? Claiming the boy had no bearing on my relationship with her. We'd already established that before we'd embarked on this affair. I'd made her no promises, nor had she asked me for any.

The strange spurt of envy returned, still making no sense. I didn't want her to ask me for more than I was willing to give. Why the hell would I?

'I am?' Dante said, obviously surprised by my capitulation.

Ignoring him, I strode across the lawn towards Belle and my son. The boy let go of his mother's hand and ran into my arms. I hoisted him up and his small fingers gripped my neck.

'Mr Alexi, I showed Jean-Claude the Galanti X,' he said, shoving the model under my nose. 'He said it was cool.'

'Of course he did,' I said, catching Belle's eye. 'Belle, could I talk to you—and Cai—alone for a minute?'

Her face flushed and Edie grinned. 'I told you so,' Dante's wife murmured as a knowing glance passed between the two women.

I had no idea what had been said, but I suspected I had been the subject when Belle's face heated even more.

'Yes, of course,' she said.

'If you need some privacy,' Edie said, her grin spreading, 'there are some steps leading down to a private cove

behind the Japanese pagoda. Dante and I always go there
when we need some alone time...'

I nodded and gripped Belle's hand, giving her no time to
change her mind. Cai was excited at the sight of the beach,
and after I had carried him down the steps I put him down
and took off his shoes so he could paddle in the water.

'Only get your toes wet, Cai,' I told him. 'It's dangerous to go in too deep without me, okay?'

He nodded. 'Yes, Mr Alexi,' he said as he sped off. I
sighed.

'What is it, Alexi, is something wrong?' Belle asked,
her concern clear even though she had been careful not to
show it in front of Cai.

'There is nothing wrong. I simply wish to get your permission to tell Cai who I really am.' I smiled, trying to
hide my own nerves. 'I'm tired of being called Mr Alexi.'

'Okay,' she said. 'I think he'd be thrilled,' she added. Although, she didn't look thrilled. 'But why now?' she asked.

*Because I've been a coward. Because it's way past time.
Because I'll have to let you go soon. And before I do I must
take this next step.*

But I couldn't say any of that without exposing myself. So I settled for telling her the one truth I could acknowledge.

'Because I'm tired of not being able to kiss you and
touch you in front of him,' I murmured, and before she
could evade me I dragged her into my arms, desperate to
feel her surrender.

She gasped but her lips softened against mine as I covered her mouth. The kiss became hungry and seeking instantly, as it always did.

'Why are you kissing my mummy?'

I ripped my mouth away first to see Cai standing in
front of us, having returned from the water's edge.

He tilted his head, more curious than accusatory.

Belle's face lit up like a Christmas tree and she crouched down to talk to him eye to eye. 'Cai, it's okay, you don't have to be afraid. Alexi and I are...'

'Shh, Belle, let me explain.' I touched her shoulder to halt the guilty tangle of words. 'Come here,' I said to Cai. The boy slung his arm around my shoulders as I knelt beside him in the sand, the way I had once seen him do with his mother. 'I kissed your mother because I like kissing her,' I said.

His nose wrinkled at that. 'Why?'

'Because she is special to me,' I said, the fear returning as I realised the truth of those words.

'Why?' the boy asked again.

There were so many answers I could give to that question, but there was only one I could allow myself to acknowledge. 'Because she is the mother of my son.'

The boy's brow furrowed, and although I felt choked at admitting the truth to my son for the first time I could see I'd been too cryptic for a four-year-old to understand.

'You are my son, Cai—and I am your father. I am sorry I haven't been in your life before now, but I would like to be in it for a very long time to come.'

'You're my daddy?' The boy's eyes widened as he caught on, and then his gaze shifted to Belle. She nodded, and then sniffed, and I realised she was struggling to keep her emotions at bay.

'Yes, I am,' I said as the boy's gaze shifted back to me.

'Can I call you Daddy?' he asked.

'Of course,' I said and he grinned.

'Can I tell Imran?' he asked. 'His daddy doesn't own racing cars,' he added, the proud, sweet smile making my heart expand in my chest. I had been accepted, and all I had had to do was ask.

'Yes, you can tell Imran. We will tell everyone together,' I said. I gathered him close and hugged his small body to mine, but as I drew back he put his hands on my shoulders, a serious expression on his face, and asked, 'Can you kiss my mummy more, so you can make me a baby brother, like Imran's mummy made him?'

I coughed, shocked not just by the innocent request but the surge of heat it brought with it—at the thought of making more children with Belle. The sudden urge to see her belly round with my child, the way Edie's was with Dante's, brought the surge of envy I hadn't understood earlier into sharp, too sharp, focus.

What I felt for Belle wasn't just sex. It had never been just sex. I knew that. But suddenly the amount I did feel for her—the visceral desire to make another child with her—terrified me even more.

My ties to my son, and before him to my brother, I understood. They were my flesh, my blood. I owed them my honour, my loyalty and what was left of my heart that I still had to give.

But binding myself to a woman—wanting to make my relationship with Belle any more permanent than it already was—that could not happen. I could not allow it to happen. Because the only woman who had ever had such a tie to me had broken it at her earliest convenience. And almost broken me at the same time.

The panic tightened around my ribs. I couldn't need Belle this much. I didn't want to need her this much.

'Cai, stop being so cheeky,' Belle said, looking flustered.

'Why is it cheeky? Imran said that's what happens when his mummy and daddy kiss too much.'

I choked out a strained laugh at the child's precocious explanation. But the claws digging into my chest were of fear. A fear I recognised from long ago, when my mother had deserted Remy and me after I had begged her to stay.

'It's cheeky because you shouldn't keep asking Alexi for things,' Belle said.

Cai leaned into me, his arms wrapping around my neck in a possessive gesture. 'But he's not Mr Alexi any more,' he said. 'He's my daddy.'

I chuckled, attempting to let the surge of love for this bright, cheeky child overwhelm the rush of panic as I gathered him close and stood up. 'Yes, but you should still always do what your mother tells you,' I murmured.

We made our way up the steep steps from the beach back to the barbeque and I announced my relationship to Cai to the party guests. The surge of pride I felt at finally announcing our relationship was tempered by deep unease. And a desperate loneliness that only made the panic more acute.

We could never be a real family. We would never fulfil Cai's wish for a baby brother or sister. Because I could not expose myself again to the same devastating betrayal I had suffered as a child.

Which brought me to only one conclusion. I would have to cut this tie to my son's mother tonight, before it got the chance to cut me.

CHAPTER FIFTEEN

Belle

I GRINNED ACROSS the console at Alexi as he parked the Galanti GL8 in the garage under the house. Something wonderful, something immense, had happened today at the Allegris' summer barbeque. Something I hadn't expected but still felt so exciting, so new—unleashing all the feelings I had held in my heart for Alexi, not just for the last three weeks, but for the last five years.

When he'd announced to Cai that he was his father, with such tenderness, such humour and such understanding, it had felt as if the last bit of the wall between us was finally beginning to crumble.

But what had finally shattered it was the look he'd given me as he'd announced to everyone there that Cai was his son.

I hadn't really realised how desperate I had been for him to make this final move in the last few weeks—weeks of awesome sex and even more awesome family outings—until he had finally said the words out loud to all the people who mattered to him.

Edie Allegri, with whom I had bonded instantly the minute I had met her, had been the first to congratulate me. And something she had said to me earlier—just before

Alexi had stalked across the lawn to ask to talk to Cai and me privately—had been ringing in my head ever since.

'Isn't it odd?' she had said with a knowing look in her eye that at the time had made me feel more than a little inadequate. Edie Allegri was a stunningly beautiful and an extremely confident woman. Not just confident in her career and her abilities as a mother but, from the way Dante looked at her, also one hundred percent confident in his love for her. 'I've always thought of Alexi as handsome, charming and amusing, but also careless and shallow. I never could figure out how he had become so successful in the Super League when he didn't seem to take anything seriously.'

'Alexi takes the business of racing very seriously,' I had said, jumping to his defence, but also confused by her description of him. I didn't recognise it at all. Not only was he a brilliant businessman, but I'd always found him to be the opposite of careless and shallow. Our relationship in the last few weeks had been so intense, but even as a younger man he had always been serious. I knew he had a reputation as a playboy, but it had never really occurred to me what that might mean.

Before I'd had a moment to process the thought, Edie had smiled at me and added, 'He also takes *you* very seriously, much more seriously than any of the other women he has introduced us to. He certainly seems to have bonded with your son.'

I had murmured some platitude about him being a good man, sick that I was still having to lie publicly about his real relationship with Cai.

But as I sat opposite him in the car now—after everything else that had happened since my conversation with Edie—the hope that I might be different from all the other women in his life came back. But this time it didn't feel ludicrous or misplaced any more.

He had acknowledged Cai this afternoon, but by doing so it felt as if he had also acknowledged me. Intimacy had been growing between us these last few weeks—every time he touched me with such passion, every time he spoke to me with such respect, every time he strengthened his relationship with our son, while being sure to include me.

And the moment Cai had innocently mentioned getting us to 'make him' a baby brother I had seen the same flash of intense yearning in his eyes, when they had met mine, that was echoing in my heart.

Was it possible he wanted to make us a real family as much as I did?

I hadn't dared hope for that. I'd been trying in these last weeks not to expect too much from him. Not to let all the old fantasies devour me again. But we had turned an important corner tonight and I was tired of being a coward.

I reached across the console to rest a hand on his arm as he turned off the ignition.

'Thank you for today, it's been…' I laughed, so full of hope for the future I thought I might burst. 'Pretty special for me and Cai.'

'Good,' he said, sounding oddly perfunctory.

I dismissed the flicker of concern. Alexi was a serious, intense guy. He'd never done gushing, or light-hearted, or certainly not with me.

He glanced back at our son fast asleep in his car seat with the toy car Alexi had given him that morning still clutched in his fist.

'Let's get him to bed,' he said.

Need prickled over my skin and joy echoed in my heart as we exited the car together and Alexi lifted his newly acknowledged son out of his child seat.

We'd been through this ritual nearly every day for the last three weeks—putting Cai to bed together then retiring to my bedroom, where Alexi would invariably rip my clothes off in his urgency to feed the hunger which had been stoked to fever pitch as we'd avoided touching during the day.

Perhaps we wouldn't do that so much any more, not now that Alexi had kissed me in front of Cai and explained the situation to him. I wondered vaguely if I'd miss that urgency.

I grinned at the silly direction of my thoughts as we closed the door on Cai's bedroom after tucking him into bed and kissing him goodnight, the electric attraction buzzing in the air between us. Our hunger would always be volatile, exciting and full of heat—no amount of PDAs was going to defuse that.

But as I pressed myself against Alexi's body and flung my arms over his shoulders—planning to take the initiative tonight—he jerked back and caught my forearms.

'Don't, Belle,' he said, drawing my arms down to my sides. 'We can't, not tonight.'

'Why not?' I asked, shocked by the rigid expression on his face, especially as I could see the heat in his eyes and I had felt the beginnings of an impressive erection.

He gave my wrists a gentle squeeze, then let me go. He took a step back and raked his fingers through his hair. But he didn't meet my eyes when he spoke. 'I need to leave. I've got an early flight to London in the morning. And you're starting work at Galanti tomorrow.'

'Oh, I see.' Although I really didn't see. He had to leave early most mornings to avoid Cai finding us in bed together. My heart kicked into overdrive again at the joyful thought we wouldn't have to hide that from our son any more because it was totally normal for children to know that their parents shared a bed. I grinned at him, despite my disappointment. 'I'll take a rain-check, then,' I said, trying out the flirtatiousness I was still learning. 'And I appreciate you being so thoughtful about my new job. I'd hate my boss to think I was slacking on my first day after spending all night in bed with him.'

But as I leaned up on tiptoes to give him a teasing kiss, which I hoped would make him regret his decision, he pulled away again, his eyes strangely guarded.

'I don't think you understand, Belle,' he said, his expression cold now, as well as rigid. He was starting to scare me. Why did he seem so distant all of a sudden? 'There'll be no rain-check. This is the end of our affair.'

'What?' I gave my head a shake, sure I must have heard that wrong. Had he just said…?

'You're going to be working for me, Belle, and I don't screw around with my employees.' His gaze raked over my figure—the heat in it somehow insulting. 'However tempting.'

'But…'

But I'm not just an employee. I'm the mother of your son, and I love you.

The admission exploded in my heart. It was the first time I had ever been brave enough to truly acknowledge it, even to myself. But it wouldn't come out of my mouth, because right alongside it was the fear that had always stopped me from articulating it in the past. The fear that he would reject my love the way he had before. And that fear was real, raw and vivid now. As was the memory of the long-ago rejection I had struggled to recover from once before. I had thought it could never hurt as much again. I realised how wrong I had been as my heart shattered in my chest.

'But what?' he asked. 'I thought you understood we

were simply scratching an itch here. You're not a child any more. You've slept with other men—you know how this works.'

But I haven't slept with any other men and I don't want to know how it works for you with other women. I thought I was different. I thought I was more.

The pleas died inside me, frozen out by the chill creeping through my body, the humiliation almost as excruciating as the pain. A pain I had to hide as best I could, or I would be reduced to nothing again, the way I had been once before. A nothingness I couldn't afford to inhabit again because I had a son.

We had a son.

I tried to cling on to that as I nodded and closed off the aching pain in the pit of my stomach.

The sting of the tears I was holding back felt like acid burning my eyeballs. I blinked rapidly and nodded again, forcing what I hoped was an approximation of a smile to my face.

Don't let him see you break. Pride is all you have now.

Thank God I had never told him the truth about my so-called other lovers or I would have been even more reduced now, even more vulnerable.

'Okay,' I said in a brittle voice which I could not let break. 'Well, let me know when you next want custody of Cai. We should probably arrange proper visitation rights.'

'I'll get Etienne on it,' he said, his gaze searing into my soul. But I forced the hurt down, desperate to keep it hidden just a little longer. 'I'll give you both a call when I get back from London to make arrangements.' He nudged a shoulder towards the stairs. 'I'll see myself out.'

'Okay,' I whispered again. But he had already walked past me.

It seemed to take no more than a second for his footsteps to pad down the hallway and for the front door to slam shut.

It took longer than an eternity, though, for me to control the painful sobs that consumed me once I had watched his brake lights disappear around the bend in the coast road from the balcony of the room we had once shared.

CHAPTER SIXTEEN

One month later

Alexi

CAI GIGGLED DELIGHTEDLY as we were both sprayed with champagne by Team Galanti's drivers—Rene Galoise and Ludovic Seveny—who had just taken the top two positions at the Italian Primo Grande Race. Cai bounced in my arms, adoring the attention—and the chance to join me next to the winners' podium after the race—as Rene and Ludovic high-fived him. I should be celebrating too, but I couldn't help searching the crowd for his mother.

Where the hell was she? It was her job to be here. I could have her fired if she didn't show.

I had insisted all my R&D staff attend the race today and the celebration event afterwards in Milan. But I had known, as soon as I'd had Pierre send out the emails a week ago, there was only one person I really wanted to see here. *Belle.*

'Daddy, Daddy, can I go to the party tonight?' Cai placed his hands on my cheeks to turn my gaze back to him. 'Rene said I could.'

'I am afraid not,' I said. 'You will have to stay at the hotel tonight with Carly,' I added, naming the nanny I had employed for when I had care of him. Cai usually adored spending time with her in the evenings, on the rare occasions when I had to attend events without him, but even so his bottom lip quivered.

'But, Daddy, I want to,' he said.

I steeled myself against the adorable pout, which I had discovered in the last month my son was a master of applying, and the tantrum I had no doubt was coming. Cai had been at the track all day with me, eating junk food and getting everything he desired, because I was always tempted to spoil him when he was with me. But there was usually a price to pay for that.

Tonight, though, was an adults-only affair. An adult affair that his mother was supposed to be attending. His mother whom I had not seen for over a month. Not since the night I had walked away from her.

Ever since I had returned from London, she had endeavoured never to be at the villa in Nice when I came to pick up Cai or drop him off. And at work I had made a point of avoiding her.

I hadn't lied completely about not wanting to complicate our working relationship. But that was going to stop. Tonight.

Because I missed her—much more than I had thought possible. Not just her passion, her hot, responsive body and the time we spent together with Cai—she certainly was much more skilled at dealing with that pout than I was—but also her smile, her wit, her tenderness, her intelligence and that captivating sparkle in her eyes whenever she'd been testing out her flirtation skills on me. I even missed her blushes, those vibrant flashes of red that made her freckles light up her face.

I wanted her back in my bed again. In my life. But I'd had to steal myself against approaching her at work. I didn't want to step over that line, compromise her, myself or the incredible job she was doing on the new prototype, according to my R&D manager, Ben Allison. But I had been forced to break even that embargo a week ago when I had composed that email.

I had ended our affair too soon. I wasn't over her yet, not completely. I'd allowed my fear to drive my actions, which was pathetic and beneath me. Why should we not continue our affair in private while co-parenting our son? How else was I going to get rid of this grinding sense of loss whenever I thought about her, which was far too often?

But despite that I did not want to make the first move. I had made a decision to get her to attend the race, assuming she would come to find her son—and me—as soon as she arrived. But I hadn't seen her at all.

Agitated and frustrated, I tapped out a text to Pierre on my phone.

Did Belle Simpson get on the Galanti jet with the rest of the R&D staff, this morning?

The reply popped up on my phone.

Yes, Alexi, she is here… Somewhere. I think I saw her chatting to Renzo Camaro and one of his technicians earlier.

I frowned. Why was she talking to Camaro? She didn't work for him any more, she worked for me.

I stifled my temper and shoved the phone in my back pocket. Didn't matter. The point was, even if she hadn't come to find Cai and me today, she would be at the event tonight. I had arranged for Carly to stay with our son until the morning, giving me ample time to seduce his mother.

Cai started to cry as I calmly and firmly explained to him again that he would not be going to the party.

He rubbed his eyes, so I hugged him a little closer. He was tired and cranky. I needed to get him back to the hotel and into bed.

But as I headed through the crowd towards the car park, still searching for a glimpse of Belle, a thought occurred to me.

Was Belle avoiding me deliberately?

Warmth and regret flooded through me. Why hadn't I seen the obvious before now? Of course she was avoiding me. I had rejected her. And her pride had forced her to hide the hurt I'd caused.

I promised myself that tonight I would correct that mistake. I would show Belle how much I respected her, and her work, and tell her I wanted her back.

I was the one who had ended our affair too soon. So I was the one who needed to make this first move.

The surge of passion and possessiveness was joined by the visceral need that had terrified me a month ago but didn't scare me so much any more.

I'd proved I could live without Belle for a month, but why live without her any longer if I didn't have to?

CHAPTER SEVENTEEN

Belle

'YOU LOOK EXQUISITE TONIGHT, Belle.' Renzo's smile was full of appreciation and just a hint of more. If I wanted it.

A part of me wished I did.

Dressed in a tailored grey designer suit, Renzo looked impossibly handsome tonight—tall, dark and Italian. Even the scar on his cheek only added to his rugged masculine beauty. He had always been kind to me both as an employer and now as a friend. But unfortunately he didn't make my heartbeat accelerate whenever he was near me. And nothing about him made me yearn for his touch. His taste. His approval.

Even so, I forced what I hoped was a flirtatious smile to my lips. Tonight I was determined to try.

It had been a month since Alexi had walked away from me, and I had spent more than enough time grieving the loss. And beating myself up about how foolish I had been ever to believe we could have had more than a quick fling.

He had devastated me again. But this time I had let him by investing much more in that relationship than had ever been there. Alexi would be here tonight to celebrate another triumph for the Galanti team, no doubt with a new supermodel on his arm, and I wanted to be able to greet him without giving him even a hint of how destroyed I had been by his desertion.

I'd cried pitifully that night, but had picked myself up the next morning to be a mother. The first few days had been exceptionally tough as I started my new job—terrified that Alexi would appear, but thankfully he never had. And eventually the work, and Cai, had saved me from sinking further into the pit. I knew it would probably be a very long time before I would ever want another man the way I had wanted Alexi, but I had to stop hiding.

It wasn't good for Cai and it wasn't good for me either.

I refused to let Alexi have that power over me. He'd been callous and unkind, but he was still my boss, and I didn't want to jeopardise my career with Galanti over something that had always been doomed to failure.

Alexi wasn't capable of trusting women. In the back of my mind, I had always known that.

'Are you absolutely sure I can't tempt you away from Galanti?' Renzo carried on talking as he whisked a glass of champagne off a passing tray and handed it to me. 'I'm still annoyed he managed to tempt you away from me in the first place.'

I sipped the champagne.

'I'm afraid not, Renzo, but I'm happy to let you keep trying,' I teased, from the marble balcony where we'd positioned ourselves as my gaze darted once again to the entrance of the Grande Palazzo Hotel's elegant ballroom.

My heart thrummed in my chest.

Cai was staying in the hotel with Alexi and his entourage. I'd seen the two of them together earlier in the day at the track on the winners' podium from my seat in the stand. That I hadn't been able to get up the courage to approach them both afterwards, to congratulate Alexi on the team's win and check on my son, had made me realise I had to get over the last of my feelings for Alexi and close for ever that deep well of sadness—and unrequited yearning—that still overwhelmed me every time I thought of him.

It wasn't healthy, and it wasn't fair on our son. I'd been a coward once before and Cai had suffered. I wasn't going to do that again.

So stop looking for him like a lovelorn little girl. You're over him.

I forced my gaze back to Renzo and the fanciful spires of the Duomo di Milano, lit by the setting sun in the distance. And willed my fingers to relax their grip on the champagne flute as Renzo continued to flirt with me.

When Alexi finally showed I would be professional and impersonal. I would show him that I had survived, that I wasn't enthralled by him any longer and that he hadn't broken my heart. Because he really hadn't. All he'd done was bruise it a little. My heart was strong, because it had had to be. But as Renzo and I began to chat about the latest Galanti X model—with Renzo gently probing for information I had no intention of giving him—I could still feel the pulse of sadness that had never really gone away since Remy's death.

I took another gulp of champagne and dismissed it, as I had a million times before.

I was strong. I was a survivor. If Remy's death hadn't broken me, nothing ever could. Not even losing Alexi.

Alexi

As I entered the ballroom, I scanned the crowd, keeping a lid on my frustration as friends and acquaintances accosted me to offer their congratulations.

At last my gaze snagged on the open doors across the

ballroom. And the longing that had been gripping my chest for weeks sunk deep into my abdomen, twisting my guts into tight knots of need… And fury.

The mother of my son, the woman who I had come here to get back, stood on the balcony with Camaro. A wispy dress of summer green hugged her slender curves, displaying her cleavage like an offering, her russet hair lit to gold by the sunset.

Abruptly cutting off the latest congratulations, I marched through the crowd, never taking my eyes off her.

How dared Camaro talk to her, flirt with her? What secrets was he trying to prise out of her? The crowd parted to let me pass, probably sensing my foul mood, but then I saw her smile at him and a knife lanced into my gut.

Were they sleeping together?

I gritted my teeth as I stepped onto the terrace. My fury was only fuelled by the pain knifing into my stomach.

What the hell had I been thinking? Why had I let her go?

Renzo saw me first, his brows launching up his forehead, but then he smiled—the sensual, assured smile of a man who was in control—and the last thread on my own control snapped.

The wispy curls of Belle's up-do clung to her nape and my mouth dried to parchment, the urge to kiss her there, to make her sigh, sob and ache, and to drag her back into my arms—where she had always belonged—making my voice crack.

'Belle, we have to talk.'

She swung round, startled, and the champagne in her glass splashed over her fingers. The intense desire to lick it off turned the mix of pain, fury and bone-deep regret in my gut to something much more volatile.

'Alexi, is—is something wrong?' she stammered, her

gaze shadowed. For a moment I thought I saw hurt there. But I couldn't be sure.

What was I doing here, behaving like a jealous lunatic?

What if I had been wrong about her needing me as much as I needed her? What if she didn't care for me at all—any more than my mother had?

'Yes, Alexi,' Camaro said, the smile turning to a grin. 'What's the problem?' he asked, but I could see he knew exactly what the problem was, and he was deliberately making it worse.

Bastardo.

Another time, I would not have risen to the bait. But tonight my usual humour, my usual charm, my usual control, had deserted me.

He was standing too damn close to her.

I swore at him in Italian, gutter words I knew he would understand, because he came from the gutter, and that was where he belonged.

I grabbed the front of Camaro's suit and yanked him towards me. Belle gasped.

'Leave, now,' I growled in Italian. 'And never dare to touch her again.'

He only laughed, disengaging my hands, and brushed down the front of his suit. 'If you wanted her, perhaps you should have staked a claim,' he said to me, also in Italian, words he knew Belle would not understand.

But then he turned to her and bowed. 'Belle, I will leave you with your boss,' he said, lifting her hand and buzzing a kiss across her knuckles. I imagined knocking out his teeth. 'But remember, the offer still stands. *Ciao.*'

Saluting me, he strolled away.

'Come,' I said, grasping her hand, barely able to speak now round my fear. I forced my fury to the fore—with

Camaro, with myself—to try and stem the terrible feeling of *déjà vu*.

Belle didn't care for me, because no one could. Only Remy had. And I had lost him long ago—without ever really deserving him. Any more than I deserved Belle.

But Renzo was right. I should have staked a claim to her. Bound her to me with sex. She was the mother of my son. Surely that gave me a right to have her? A right to want her by my side?

I marched to the opposite end of the balcony that wrapped around the ballroom, heading for the entrance to the main lobby, clasping her wrist too tightly, but unable to loosen my grip.

I had seen the flash of need in her eyes when she had first laid eyes on me. She wasn't immune. There was still desire there, a desire I could exploit. A desire I *would* exploit. If sex was the only way I could make her return to me, I would use it. And be grateful.

But as we reached the end of the terrace, she tugged her hand out of my grasp.

'Alexi, stop, where are you taking me?'

I turned back to her and cradled her cheek, no longer able to stem the urge to touch that soft skin. 'To my suite, where else?' I said as she shuddered, the spark of desire in her wide eyes both gratifying and torturous.

How had I ever let her go? *Why* had I? I couldn't seem to make sense of any of my decisions any more. My mind was a blur of long-ago fears and much more current ones. Why had it never occurred to me until this very moment that I could not live without this woman in my life? And it had nothing to do with the beautiful son she had given me. Or even the insane sexual chemistry we shared.

The pain twisted and sharpened in my gut as she jerked away from my touch and the spark of desire, the shadow of hurt in her eyes, died, replaced by something blank, shuttered and guarded.

Was she scared of me? The thought horrified me and humbled me.

Her whole body trembled, making me desperate to gather her in my arms and soothe her, promise her I would do anything to get her back. But the words got lodged in my throat, my own fear so huge now it consumed me. What if it wasn't fear I saw, but indifference? The same indifference I had seen flash in my mother's eyes when I had pleaded with her not to leave and she had simply laughed and left anyway.

But when Belle's gaze locked on mine and she spoke, she didn't sound scared or indifferent, she sounded brave... and indomitable. 'Whatever you have to say to me, we can talk here.'

'I don't want to talk, the time for talk is over,' I managed, frantic now, because I knew there was nothing I could say to make her stay. All I had now was our sexual connection. The cruel irony of that didn't escape me as I reached for her hand again, desperate to get her alone so I could touch her and tempt her, taste her and tease her, until she came apart in my arms as she had so often before...

Then I would never have to voice these terrible needs, never have to endure her rejection...

But she yanked her hand from my grasp.

'Don't touch me, Alexi, you have no right,' she said, her voice low and shaky but somehow unyielding.

It was too much.

The red mist that had descended when I had first spotted her smiling at Camaro returned. But this time I welcomed it to smother my fear.

'And Camaro does?' I snapped. 'Our bed is barely cold and you are already sleeping in his?'

CHAPTER EIGHTEEN

Belle

MY HAND WHIPPED UP of its own accord, Alexi's snarled words wounding me so deeply the anger surged from no-where before I could stop it. But as his head reared back in an instinctive reaction to avoid the slap—a reaction I knew he had learned as a boy—my hand dropped back to my side.

I had never hit another human being in my life. And I had almost hit him. The horror of that was almost too much to bear. But as he watched me, his eyes guarded, the fortifying anger returned.

'You bastard,' I whispered. 'You were my first lover and you are my *only* lover, Alexi.'

His expression changed, going from anger to aston-ishment, tinged with stunned disbelief. The pain ground into my gut.

Why had I kept my innocence a secret? Why had I ever been ashamed of my lack of experience? Suddenly I didn't care how vulnerable it made me for him to know he was the only man I had ever wanted... Ever loved.

I had owned the mistakes I'd made—not telling him of Cai's existence—but he had never owned his. Because I'd never told him the truth. But, if I never did, he would always have this power over me. I would always be less than him. Why shouldn't I own my feelings, own the love I had for him? If he didn't want my love, he could reject me again, but I'd be damned if I'd let him ride in and claim my body, make this all about sex when for me if had always been so much more.

'I've never slept with another man,' I said, gritting the words out. 'Only you. I've never felt for any other man what I feel for you. But that doesn't mean you own me, not any more.'

I could still see the staggered incredulity in his eyes and my heart shattered in my chest, just as it had a month ago. Just as it had five years ago. For so long I'd despised that foolish girl for her wayward emotions but, as I stared back at him, I didn't despise her any more. I had been right to feel what I did. The mistake I had made was never to admit it.

Hiding my feelings to protect myself from hurt had only allowed him to hide his too...

'I've just told you I love you, Alexi. That I've always loved you. Don't you have anything to say to me?'

He blinked but then his face became the mask I'd seen so many times before. The mask that kept him safe. I knew that mask, because I'd worn it myself.

'How can you love me?' he finally said, sounding shocked now as well as incredulous.

'Really, that's all you have to say?' I said.

When he didn't speak, I huffed out a sad laugh that tasted bitter on my tongue. I hadn't expected a return declaration of undying love. But I had hoped for something, despite everything. One burning tear slipped over my lid and trickled down my cheek, his gaze tracking it as I brushed it away. 'Then I guess there's nothing more to talk about,' I murmured.

He didn't believe me. He didn't trust me. And now I knew he never would.

I turned to go, keeping my back straight and my legs as steady as I could. But as I took a step away I heard a choked cry.

'Wait! Stop...'

He grasped my wrist, but this time he didn't drag me back, only held on to me.

'Per favore, non andare,' he rasped. *'Per favore, non lasciarmi.'*

My Italian wasn't fluent, but I understood him.

Please don't go. Please don't leave me.

As I turned, to my shock he dropped to his knees and pressed his forehead against the back of my hand. It was an act of supplication, of penitence so real, so powerful, so naked that the hope I had thought was dead surged back to life, firing through my heart like a phoenix rising from the ashes.

His shoulders shuddered, and for one terrible moment I thought he might be crying. I wasn't looking at the man any more, I realised, I was looking at the boy, who had been abandoned all those years ago by a woman who should have loved him but hadn't loved him enough.

I sunk to my knees too, the marble cold against my shins as I gripped his face. His hard jaw flexed against my fingers as I lifted his head, the sheen of moisture in his eyes piercing my heart.

'It's okay, Alexi, I won't leave you,' I said. 'If you need me to stay.'

His breath shuddered out on a rasp of relief and he gathered me close, squeezing my ribs, my heart pummelling my chest so hard I was sure he could feel it.

'I do... I need you so much,' he whispered, his voice

raw as he spread kisses over my cheeks, my lips, my neck, worshipping me with his mouth. 'I always have. Forgive me for never admitting it,' he said as he drew back, cradling my face to stare into my eyes, all the love in my heart reflected in the warm blue depths of his. He sighed, the shudder of breath reverberating through my body as he gathered me close, stroked my hair and held me to his heart as if he would never let me go.

'I was so scared to love you,' he said, his voice breaking. 'So scared that if I did I would lose you, the way I lost my mother. The way I lost Remy. The way I lost you when I turned you away. Can you ever forgive me?'

I pulled out of his embrace, the tears streaming down my cheeks now unbidden. But they were no longer tears of sadness, of heartache, they were tears of love. 'There is nothing to forgive,' I said, my voice thick with the happy tears.

A small drop escaped his own eye, but even as he scrubbed it away with his fist the emotion behind it pierced my heart.

It was a tear for us both, of sadness for all that we had suffered, for all that we had lost. And a tear of joy, for all that we had gained and would continue to gain. Together.

'There is *much* to forgive,' he said, but the wry smile that lifted his lips only intensified the joy. 'But I intend to spend the rest of my life making it up to you.'

Standing up, he offered me his hand. I took it and let him haul me off the cold stone and into his arms. The insistent heat rose to match the warm glow in my heart.

'If you will let me?' he asked, his hands settling on my waist as his gaze searched my face, still a little unsure, still so naked with need.

Love spread through me like wildfire—for this damaged, determined, indomitable man.

'Of course I will,' I said as I flung my arms over his broad shoulders and let his soft laugh wrap around my heart.

EPILOGUE

Three months later

Alexi

THE WINTER SUN warmed my face as I stood beside my brother's grave with Belle's hand gripped tightly in mine and our son perched on my hip. I had never had the courage to return to this place until today, scared the immense sadness—and the terrible guilt over Remy's death that had crippled me for so long—would return.

The deep, aching loss was still there, of course, as I knew it always would be, but I didn't feel hollow and empty any more. The hole in my heart was tempered by joy. Not just the remembered joy of being Remy's brother, but the new joy of being Cai's father and the all-consuming joy of becoming, as of an hour ago, Belle's husband.

I still missed my brother, I always would, and I knew Belle would too. Her slender body in the seductive white velvet wedding gown she had worn in the chapel as she'd pledged herself to me did nothing to stem the shudder of emotion running through her as her green eyes met mine. Her hand squeezed my fingers tight. Sweetly reassuring but also life-affirming.

'Who are we meeting here, Daddy?' Cai asked, his inquisitive blue eyes and that dimpled smile making my heart skip a beat. 'I can't see anyone.'

'We can't meet him, Cai,' I said, my voice rough as the sense of loss sharpened. I cleared my throat, determined finally to introduce my son to his uncle, the way I should have done months ago.

I knelt beside the grave, placing Cai gently on his feet to point out the grave stone. 'Because sadly Remy, my brother and your uncle, isn't here with us any more. But this is where he is buried. I thought we could come to his grave and say hello to him. Today is a very special day for us all because you and your mummy became Galantis.'

The surge of pride that had hit me earlier, when Belle had said, 'I do,' and Cai had leapt into my arms after our kiss, made my chest ache all over again. 'And Remy is a Galanti too.'

'Remy is my extra name,' Cai said, looking thoughtful.

'I know,' I replied. 'Your mummy gave you that name because she loved Remy too, just like I did.'

'Where did he go, Daddy?'

I heard Belle cough and sniff, and guessed the emotion was probably choking her the way it was choking me. But I sent her a smile and squeezed her fingers back.

'I've got this,' I mouthed at her.

'He went to Heaven,' I said to our son. 'But I know he would have loved to meet you.'

Cai wrapped his small arm around my neck and stared at the grave stone. 'Did he like racing cars, like I do?'

I let out a raw chuckle, the feel of his sturdy body beside mine—so trusting, so affectionate—making the emotion thicken my throat again. 'He liked racing cars the best of all, *just* like you do.'

'Will he come back? So I can show him my racing cars?' Cai asked.

I shook my head, not quite able to speak. 'No,' I managed at last. 'He can't come back. But he's here.' I pressed a hand to my heart. 'Always, just like you and Mummy are. Because I loved him very much, just the way I love you two.'

I scrubbed away the tear that slipped over my lid, but then I heard Belle stifle a sob.

Cai's head whipped around. 'Why are you crying, Mummy?' he asked. 'Are you sad?'

Belle shook her head, wiping her tears away with the heel of her hand as she sent us both a radiant smile. My heart expanded even more than it had an hour ago when she had walked down the aisle towards me in the stunning dress and Cai had skipped behind her, throwing petals around as if they were grenades.

'I'm sad and happy at the same time,' she said.

Cai giggled. 'That's silly, Mummy.'

'I know,' she said. Her eyes connected with mine over our son's head, the teary smile becoming tender. 'I'm sad that Remy isn't here, but happy that he'll always be with us in our hearts. And I know he would be so happy that we have each other...' She pressed a hand to her stomach, the way I'd noticed her do several times in the past week. 'And that we're going to have a new Galanti baby to join us in eight months' time.'

'*What...?*' I croaked, the joy and shock blindsiding me as Cai began to dance with excitement.

'You made me a baby brother with all your kissing!' Cai shouted. 'Just like Imran's mummy and daddy.'

Belle

'Yes, we did, Cai-baby, although we don't know yet if it's a brother or a sister,' I said to our son, who looked ecstatic as I grinned at Alexi's look of shock and awe.

I hadn't intended to tell Cai or him today. I'd only taken the test this morning to confirm my suspicions, and I was still reeling from the news myself.

The wedding preparations had been insane in the last few months after Alexi had insisted in Milan we marry as soon as possible. It must have happened during one of the many stolen moments we'd shared—in the shower, on the balcony, by the pool at night, and even one memorable moment at the test track in Nice after the rest of the staff had left for the evening—while frantically juggling our careers, family commitments and the wedding preparations.

We must have jumped the gun before the contraception I had started taking had become fully safe. We hadn't planned this, hadn't spoken about having another child, *yet*. But we *had* spoken about having another child eventually. Alexi was such a brilliant father, and we had both agreed we didn't want Cai to be an only child.

But hearing Alexi speak about Remy, standing over his grave, had just made it seem like the right moment to share the news. Why was I keeping it a secret? I'd married the man of my dreams today, and while I'd said my vows to my husband I'd felt Remy's presence by my side and had heard his voice in my head, laughing and saying, *It's about damn time you finally kept your promise to me,* bellisima.

'If I have a sister, can she play racing cars with me?' Cai asked, swivelling his head between the two of us.

'Of course she can,' Alexi said as he rose to his feet—still looking a little shell-shocked. But then he leaned close, gripping my cheeks with his usual confidence while sandwiching our son between us.

The broad smile that spread across Alexi's impossibly handsome features made my chest feel tight as Cai wriggled furiously and started to giggle.

'Galanti girls like racing cars too,' Alexi said to our son as he wriggled free. 'And I've got the bestest Galanti girl of all,' Alexi whispered against my mouth, before wrapping his arms around me and lifting me off my feet.

He swung me around, to Cai's delight—and a spontaneous laugh burst out of my mouth to match the joy I could no longer contain bursting in my heart.

* * * * *

A SCANDAL
MADE IN LONDON

LUCY KING

For Flo, for all the support and encouragement.

CHAPTER ONE

WHAT ON *EARTH*...?

From behind his desk, situated on the top floor of the forty-four-storey building that housed the Knox Group, Theo Knox stared at the web page that filled the screen of the iPad that his head of security had just brought in and placed in front of him.

It appeared to be a table of information.

Harmony was the heading; below that came the details.

Geographical location: London
Age: 26
Height: 6' 1"
Vital statistics: 38-28-38
Hair: blonde
Eyes: blue
Tattoos: one
Interests: travel, books, music
Sexual experience: none

And the website? Belle's Angels, according to the elaborate logo involving entwined vines that shimmered in the top right corner. *'Matches made in heaven'*, apparently.

Which was all well and good, but of what use was any of this to him? And why did Antonio Scarlatto, a valued employee he'd previously considered competent and level-headed, think it would be?

Theo had absolutely no interest in dating sites, or in any kind of dating at all, since the occasional one-night stand when the need arose suited him fine. And even if he did, he had no time for it. As owner and CEO of a company that spanned the globe, employed thousands and was worth billions, he had a multitude of issues clamouring for his attention, the principle one of which currently was figuring out how he was going to persuade the ridiculously sentimental owner of the business he badly wanted to sell it to him.

'Why are you wasting my time by showing me this?' Theo demanded, lifting his gaze from the screen and levelling it at the man standing on the other side of the desk, who was way out of line if he thought Theo needed Harmony in his life.

'It relates to a current member of your staff,' said Antonio, not batting an eyelid in response to the dark look and arctic tone that usually had people quaking in their boots. 'She's registered on the site and this is her page. She tried to log in from her work computer twenty minutes ago. Our firewall flagged it up. As it's against company policy to access sites like this, I need to know what action to take.'

'It's a dating site,' Theo said flatly.

'It's not just a dating site,' Antonio countered. 'I wouldn't have disturbed you if it was. Scroll down.'

Mentally having to concede that point, Theo shoved a lid on his exasperation and switched his attention back to the tablet. He briefly ran his gaze over the table again, automatically registering and dismissing the information, then swiped up.

And froze.

Because to accompany Harmony's description were half a dozen photos. Of the woman in question in various outfits in various eye-popping poses. In the first four pictures, she was at least wearing clothes—short and tight and pretty revealing, but clothes nevertheless. In the last two, however, she wasn't wearing very much at all. Technically she had on a negligee, he saw, but she might as well not have bothered. It was so diaphanous it hid nothing that wasn't concealed under a few scraps of strategically placed lace beneath. Not her curves. Not the length of her limbs. Nothing.

And her face…

He knew that face.

It was Kate Cassidy.

Harmony, with her luscious body and dazzlingly striking looks, was Kate Cassidy.

The realisation hit Theo like a blow to the gut and he reeled.

What the hell was she up to?

Steeling himself, he scrolled down and read the text that accompanied the photos, and his blood turned to ice. Antonio had been right. Belle's Angels wasn't just any dating site and Kate wasn't after any kind of normal date *at all*.

As the implications of what he'd read and seen sank in, questions ricocheted around his head. What on earth was she thinking? Did she have *any* idea of the danger she could be putting herself in? More importantly, now he knew what she had planned, what was he going to do about it?

Because he'd definitely be doing *something*, he thought grimly as he clicked around the site, his horror growing with every passing second. Kate clearly needed looking out for. In fact, he should have been keeping an eye on her and her younger sister ever since their older brother Mike's death nine months ago. Discreetly. From afar. But nonetheless making sure they were as okay as they could be, because the debt he owed him was huge, because Mike had died because of something *he* could have prevented, and finally because they had no one else.

So why *hadn't* he done anything? Why hadn't he even been aware Kate was working for him? Guilt? Denial? The fact that these days he only seemed to function through sheer force of will?

Well, whatever it was, it stopped now because she, at least, was not okay. She'd evidently lost her tiny little mind.

Furthermore, by signing herself up to this particular website she'd put herself at considerable risk, and that was unacceptable. The potential consequences didn't bear thinking about, and a person hurt—or worse—because he hadn't done enough to stop it simply could not happen again. Twice in one lifetime was more than enough.

'What action do you want me to take?' asked Antonio, cutting off Theo's thoughts before they could scythe through the fog of Mike's death and hurtle down memory lane to his own turbulent teenage years.

'Shut the site down,' Theo said as he pushed the tablet in Antonio's direction and slammed a mental door on Harmony's bio and the photos. 'Whatever it takes, however much it costs, shut it down.'

The head of security acknowledged the order with a brief nod of his head. 'And with regards to the employee in question?'

'I'll deal with her.'

Not once in the five and a half months she'd been working at the Knox Group had Kate been summoned to the hallowed top floor of the central London building that housed it, and that was fine with her. Her position as a middle-ranking accountant didn't merit the dubious honour, and, quite frankly, the less she had to do with the horrible Theo Knox, the better.

Not that they knew each other well, thank God. He might have been supposed 'friends' with her brother—although she struggled with the concept that her uptight, aloof *über* boss could ever do anything as human as *friends*—but she'd only met him once. At Mike's funeral nine months ago, in fact. And since that had hardly been a cordial encounter, she hadn't expected him to be in touch.

He was the man, after all, who'd coldly told her he wasn't interested and then turned his back on her when she'd made the monumental mistake of asking him for his support. All she'd wanted was a quick drink after the wake. To talk. Nothing more. Everyone else had left and she'd been distraught, feeling so horribly alone she'd simply wanted to prolong the afternoon by talking about her brother with someone who presumably had known him well. High and mighty Theo Knox, however, had evidently interpreted her suggestion as an invitation, and had treated it with the disdain and contempt he obviously felt it deserved before spinning on his heel and stalking off.

Kate had stood there staring at his retreating figure, open-mouthed and dumbstruck, unsure whether to laugh or cry because had he *really* thought she was coming on to him? At her brother's *funeral*? How inappropriate, how downright absurd, *was* that? His arrogance had been breathtaking. She'd never encountered self-absorption like it. Even worse was the lousy way his unwarranted rejection had made her feel. She shouldn't have cared what he thought of her since he meant absolutely nothing to her, yet his response had pulverised what little self-esteem she had, and for one blazing moment she'd never hated anyone more.

So if she'd been in any position to turn down the offer of a job at his company that had come her way shortly after, she'd have done so. However, she had bills to pay and the salary she'd been offered had been too generous to refuse. Not generous enough, of course, to cover the stratospheric sums of money her sister's residential care facility required, nor the repayment of the ever-increasing debt her brother had accrued to cover it, but definitely generous enough to make her want to pass her probationary period. And that was why, when she'd received the call from Theo's assistant requesting her presence on the top floor at precisely six p.m., the time she should have been leaving for home, she'd obeyed instead of telling him where to stick his imperious demand.

The lift she was travelling in slowed until it came to a smooth stop, and the doors opened with a soft swoosh. Automatically reminding herself not to slouch, Kate lifted her chin and crossed the plush white carpet that covered the floor with a long-legged stride.

When she arrived at the reception desk, she was waved in the direction of a pair of vast wooden doors, and headed towards them. Taking a deep breath, she knocked, and didn't have to wait long before a deep masculine voice barked, 'Come in.'

Kate braced herself and did as he'd commanded. The minute she walked through the door her attention instantly zoomed in on the man sitting behind the oak monolith of a desk, the man who was looking at her with a dark intensity and a stillness that radiated powerful authority and suggested complete and utter control.

Of her surroundings—the sleek white office so vast her entire flat would fit in it, the crystal-clear wall-to-wall windows that allowed the early evening late spring sunshine to flood in, the luxurious furnishings and the colourful pops of modern art on the walls—she was only dimly aware. All she was conscious of was her boss, the rude, condescending, hurtful jerk, and the memory of the intense loathing he'd once aroused in her.

'Shut the door.'

She did so, then walked towards him, the office becoming increasingly hot and claustrophobic with every step she took. Which, given the state-of-the-art temperature control the building had, was odd, and not a little disturbing.

As was the automatic way in which she seemed to be taking a mental inventory of his looks. At Mike's funeral she'd been in too great a state to register much about any of the guests, least of all him. Now, though, she had to grudgingly admit that the gossip columns, which lauded his appearance as much as they lamented his enigmatic elusiveness, were right. With his short dark hair, obsidian eyes and chiselled features he was easily the best-looking man she'd ever seen. The shoulders beneath the suit were impressively broad and they were matched by an equally impressive height, which she knew to be true because even though he was now sitting down, she'd just had a brief flash of memory of how she'd been in the unusual position of having to look up at him when she'd suggested a drink that afternoon.

He was also immaculate, she thought resentfully, taking in the perfection of his appearance as she advanced. Did he *ever* shove his hands through his hair in frustration? Ever permit even the *hint* of a five o'clock shadow? She doubted it. And had he ever been paralysed by self-doubt or plagued by rock-bottom self-esteem as she continually was? Even more unlikely. The man was a machine. A high-performing, single-minded, ruthlessly brilliant one, if the business press was to be believed, but a machine nevertheless.

Well.

Whatever.

What he was and how he looked were immaterial. So he was staggeringly handsome, in enviable control of himself and a good three or four inches taller than her. He was still a deeply unpleasant human being.

Coming to a halt a foot from the desk, Kate pulled herself together and reminded herself to stay calm, since it wouldn't do to reveal either how little she thought of him or how vulnerable she could be if she kept remembering how wretched he'd once made her feel. 'Mr Knox,' she said coolly. 'You wanted to see me?'

Something flickered in the depths of his dark eyes, something that flashed and burned and swiftly disappeared but nevertheless made her pulse skip a beat and her blood heat. 'I did,' he said with a brief nod in the direction of the two modern armchairs on her side of the desk. 'Theo will do. Sit down.'

'Thank you.'

Deliberately taking her time, Kate folded her six-foot-one frame into a chair and then spent a couple of vital seconds tugging her jacket down and smoothing her skirt. She needed to settle herself. This pulse-skipping, blood-heating business was ridiculous, as was the strange restlessness that churned around inside her. Nerves, most probably, because she had no idea why she'd been summoned and despite what she thought of him he *was* a bit intimidating. Or dread perhaps, the kind that came from knowing that one false move and the many plates she had spinning would crash to the ground. But still, either way, it was absurd.

'How are you?'

She stilled for a second and fought back a frown. What? *Now* he wanted pleasantries? Well, okay, she could do that. She could forget how they'd met for now. She couldn't imagine *he* remembered in any case. He certainly didn't appear to recognise her. 'Fine,' she said brightly, as if she weren't wrung out with stress and exhaustion. 'You?'

'Fine. Coffee?'

She gave her head a quick shake. 'No, thank you.'

'Tea?'

'No.'

'Anything?'

'I'm fine.'

'How's the job going?'

Hah. Which one? As well as being an accountant, she now worked in a bar five nights a week and dog-walked at the weekend. What little time she had left when she wasn't visiting her sister, she dedicated to the freelance bookkeeping work she'd also started to take on. 'Extremely well,' she said with a beaming smile, determined not to think about how close she was to the edge or how terrifying that was. 'I'm enjoying it very much.'

'Good,' he said, leaning forwards in a way that for some bizarre reason made her breath catch and her pulse skip a beat all over again. 'So. Kate. Tell me about Belle's Angels.'

And just like that—*bang!*—there went her composure. Talk about being lulled into a false sense of security, she thought, her smile fading as the churning started up again in her stomach. What did Theo Knox know about Belle's Angels? And how? Surely he couldn't be a member. He'd have no trouble getting a date. But had he visited the site? Had he seen her page? She had no idea why when her profile had racked up over a thousand views since she'd rashly stuck it up last night but the thought of *him* looking at her photos made her feel quite weak.

'What about it?' she said carefully, since his expression was giving absolutely nothing away.

'You're on it.'

Ah. Right. Busted.

Since Mr Knox—*Theo*—was allegedly insanely sharp, Kate didn't see the point in trying to come up with an excuse. 'I am,' she said, reminding herself that she had nothing to apologise for and nothing to be embarrassed about. What did it matter if he *had* seen her page? The photos were good. Empowering. Or something like that. At least she'd come up with a solution to the traumatic situation that had been robbing her of what little sleep she did get, even if it *had* had unexpected and rather unsettling consequences.

'You tried to access it while at work.'

Indeed she had. Earlier this afternoon. Her profile had attracted a great deal of interest, her alluded-to virginity in particular, and she'd been inundated with emails, some merely curious, some a bit odd, some downright creepy. Not having a clue what to do about any of it and wanting

the deluge to stop, she'd decided to alter her account set-
tings while she figured it out. 'I did.'

'Which is an infringement of company policy.'

At that Kate went very still, her heart giving a great
lurch.

Oh.

Oh, dear.

That hadn't occurred to her. But it should have done
because of *course* it would be. Belle's Angels, registered
in Germany and possibly skirting the boundaries of legal-
ity in the UK, was just the sort of website that would be
blocked by a firewall. Which was undoubtedly why it hadn't
opened. She hadn't thought to reflect upon that. She'd just
wanted to switch off the interminable stream of responses.
But clearly she'd been an idiot. More than an idiot, actually.
She could very well have put herself out of a job.

'That was a mistake,' she said as the potential ramifica-
tions raced through her head and a sweat broke out all over
her skin. 'A one-off. It won't happen again.'

'You're right,' he said flatly, his eyes dark and inscrutable. 'It won't.'

A ball lodged in her throat and she swallowed it down
with difficulty. 'Are you firing me?' she asked, the rising
panic making her voice tight.

She needed this job, she needed *all* her jobs, but if she
lost *this* one, she'd be in even more serious trouble than
she already was. Fired accountants weren't exactly desirable potential employees and who knew how long it would
be before she got another job? The bills were mounting up
daily and the correspondence from the debt agency was
growing increasingly threatening, not that her salary was
anywhere *near* enough to cover the repayments or the cost
of her sister's care, but Milly depended on her and *only* her
since there was no one else now Mike had died, and if she

had to leave Fairview she'd be devastated, and, oh, she *really* should have thought this whole crazy plan through.

'I'm not firing you.'

Phew.

'Then what do you mean?' she said as her racing heart slowed and the jumble of panicky thoughts faded.

'I had the site shut down.'

What? The tension that had ebbed a moment ago shot straight back.

No.

No.

This was *not* good.

'You can't do that,' she breathed, appalled, as it dawned on her that if what Theo was saying was true then he'd scuppered what, as far as she could see, was her only chance of making some serious, much-needed money fast.

'I can,' he said grimly. 'And I have.'

'How?'

'It wasn't hard.'

No, it wouldn't be to a man of his considerable influence and power, but— 'You had no right.'

'Probably not.'

'So why?'

His eyebrows shot up, the only sign of expression she'd seen in him since she'd walked in. *'Why?'*

'Yes, why?' What was it to him? Even if he *did* know who she was, which was doubtful, why would he care all of a sudden?

'You signed up to an escort agency, Kate.'

His tone was brutal and icily condemning but she refused to be intimidated. It was all very well for him and his billions in the bank. Lesser mortals had to think more creatively if they didn't want to firstly destroy the happiness and security of their vulnerable younger sister, secondly lose the home they'd once shared with their adored, much-missed brother and lastly be declared bankrupt and never work in the field they loved again.

'And so what?' she said, resisting the urge to lift her chin since a punchy show of defiance could well make him re-assess his decision not to fire her.

'How could you be so reckless?'

Reckless? She wasn't reckless. Desperate and exhausted and all out of options, yes, but reckless, no. 'I'm not. I did my research.'

'So did I,' he said ominously.

'Well, then.'

'Belle's Angels is basically an online brothel.'

'Possibly,' she had to admit, since there *was* that aspect to it, 'but it's a very high-class one.'

A tiny muscle began to tic in his jaw. 'That is utterly irrelevant.'

'No,' she said. 'It isn't. Because *this* one has different levels of service agreement, and I only signed up to level one.'

He looked at her as if she'd grown two heads. 'Did you honestly think someone was going to pay you a thousand pounds an hour for *conversation*?'

'Why not?' she said. 'My conversational skills are first class.'

'I have no doubt they are. However, believe me, your… *clients*…would have been expecting far more.'

'Yes, well, you obviously have more experience of such sites than I do.'

In response to her demure yet pointed little dig Theo's face darkened and the look he gave her was hard and for-bidding. 'I've heard stories,' he said flatly. 'None of them good. Do you have *any* idea of how dangerous it could have been?'

Kate opened her mouth to reply and then closed it be-cause he might have a point there. Truth be told, she hadn't exactly been thinking entirely rationally when she'd signed up to the site late last night. Another exorbitant bill had just come through from Fairview on top of a none-too-friendly email from the loan company Mike had used *and* a letter from her mortgage company informing her that she'd missed a payment, as if she needed reminding.

She'd had a couple of glasses of wine to dull the resulting anxiety, but they hadn't worked; they'd just made her feel even sicker. A documentary about webcamming had been on TV in the background, and in the midst of her despair it had suddenly struck her that sex sold. Extremely well, apparently. And while she wasn't desperate enough—yet—to perform for the camera, she'd figured there had to be other less extreme options.

It had been remarkably easy to find an appropriate site and register. When she remembered the stash of normal-sized clothes she'd bought over the years because it made her feel dainty and feminine just to know she owned them even though none of them actually fitted, it had seemed as though the stars had aligned. In fact, the most challenging aspect of the whole exercise had been mastering the self-timer on her phone.

Of course she'd considered the possible consequences of her plan—she wasn't a *complete* fool—but she'd been at her wits' end and as a result her assessment had been brief. Conveniently, the pros had vastly outweighed the cons. What cons there were—mainly concerning the sort of people who might use such a site—she'd presumed would be neutralised by the application of filters and a robust screening process.

Clearly, however, there'd been little of that because some of the creepier emails she'd received had been downright disturbing. The staggering sums of money she'd been offered for her virginity, not to mention the many ways it could apparently be relieved, had been even more alarm-

ing. And, actually, even the more moderate correspondence
had hinted at something other than conversation, so maybe
Theo also had a point about her would-be clients' expectations.

Perhaps, then, in hindsight, she'd had a lucky escape,
even if it did mean that her only hope had vanished and she
was now back at a terrifying square one. Because if she was
being brutally honest, the reality of what the site offered
was far seedier than in her naivety she'd imagined, and,
regardless of the amount of money on offer, the thought of
actually having to go through with some of the more lurid
scenarios described made her want to throw up.

'It is absolutely *none* of your business,' she said, not in-
clined to admit that Theo could be right and give him the
upper hand.

'That's not strictly true.'

No. Well. There was the small issue of pesky company
policy, but still. He had no right to meddle in her affairs
in this way. In *any* way. 'I don't need rescuing, Theo,' she
said steadily. 'I'm twenty-six. I'm eminently sensible and
perfectly capable of making my own choices.' Not that she
had many at this precise moment.

'It doesn't look like it from where I'm sitting.'

Ooh, he was insufferable. 'Why do you even *care*?'

He stared at her silently for a moment, as if he couldn't
work it out either, and the hard intensity of his gaze cou-
pled with the way he seemed to be trying to see into her
soul was sending a strange sluggish heat oozing through
her blood, detonating tiny sparks along her veins and electrifying her nerves.

To her consternation she found she couldn't look away.
She could hardly breathe. All of a sudden she wanted to
get up, clamber over his desk and plaster herself against
him. And then she wanted to—well, she wasn't quite sure
what she wanted to do next since she had little experience

of such things, but she wanted to find out. So badly she was ablaze with it.

Appalled at and bewildered by her reaction, she shifted in an attempt to alleviate the fizzing of her stomach and the prickling of her heated skin, but all that did was inch her skirt up her thighs, at which point Theo's darkening gaze dropped to her legs and lingered there a while, which sent the heat buzzing through her shooting straight down to the spot where she suddenly, *alarmingly*, burned.

Maybe she moved again, maybe she let out an audibly breathy gasp. She didn't know. But Theo jerked his gaze back up, his expression once again cold and inscrutable, and the tension snapped.

'I take it you need the money,' he said bluntly, and all she could think was money? What money?

Ah.

Well, of course she needed the money, she thought, tugging her skirt back down with annoyingly shaky fingers as the reminder of her precarious financial state obliterated the bizarre heat and dizziness and refocused her attention. Why else would she do it? She wasn't *that* desperate for a date. 'I do.'

'How much?'

'A lump sum of a hundred thousand, plus around five thousand a month on an on-going basis for the next sixty, possibly seventy, years.'

Up shot his eyebrows. 'That's a lot of money.'

Really?

'I am aware of that,' she said coolly. And now, thanks to him and his high-handed ways, it was a lot of money she still had to somehow find because, quite apart from the distressing threat of homelessness, she was *not* having Milly moved when she was so happy and secure where she was.

'It's a concern,' he said.

'You're telling me.'

'It's *my* concern.'

'How?'

'You're an accountant,' he said. 'You're about to finish your probation, at which point you will have access to certain aspects of the company's bank accounts. Fraud is a risk.'

What the—?

Kate blinked at him, for a moment completely lost for words. Was he being serious? 'Are you suggesting I might indulge in a little light embezzlement in order to pay my bills?'

'It's a possibility.'

'It is *not* a possibility because I am *not* a criminal,' she said heatedly.

'What do you need it for?'

Kate took a deep breath to soothe the outrage surging through her. 'I have a younger sister,' she said. 'Milly. She was in the car accident that killed our parents ten years ago.' She swallowed hard but made herself continue. 'She survived but she suffered catastrophic brain injuries. She can't live on her own. She needs twenty-four-hour care. The insurance pay-out only covers the most basic of facilities, which just aren't good enough.'

For a few long moments, Theo said nothing, just frowned. And then he nodded, as if something in his head had slotted into place. 'Your brother used to fund the rest.'

Ah. So he *did* know who she was.

Well.

'He did,' she said, steeling herself against the surge of grief that still sometimes shot out of nowhere and walloped her in the chest. 'And there was some money from his estate, but it's run out.'

'His flat?'

'Rented. A few months before his death he gave it up and moved in with me.'

'Life insurance?'

'He didn't have any.' If only. 'Believe me, if there was any money anywhere I'd have found it. After he died I discovered that he'd been taking out high-interest loans. They need repaying, like, yesterday.'

'I see.'

Did he? she wondered, swallowing down the tight ball of emotion that had lodged in her throat. She doubted it. The gut-wrenching combination of despair, guilt, anger, grief and dread she'd felt when she'd found out what Mike had done had to be unique. Besides, had Theo ever needed money so badly he'd do anything to get it? Unlikely. He'd made his first million by the age of seventeen and his fortune had rocketed year on year since.

'You'll have it.'

She stared at him in bewilderment. What was he talking about? Have it? Have what? 'I'm sorry?'

'Give me the details and I'll pay off the debt and set up a trust fund to pay for whatever your sister needs for however long she needs it.'

What?

Oh.

Right.

Wow.

'Are you serious?' she asked in stunned disbelief.

'Yes.'

'Why would you do that?'

His eyes clouded and she caught a glimpse of what bizarrely looked like…what? Guilt? Anguish? Regret? As if. By all accounts he didn't do emotion any more than he did friends, so who knew? It was most likely irritation that he'd had to interrupt his no doubt busy schedule to deal with what he perceived to be a problem. 'Because I can,' he said eventually.

That was undeniably true. He was one of the ten richest

men in the world according to one newspaper article she'd read. What she needed might amount to millions but to him it was a rounding error. Nevertheless, what ultra-successful reportedly ruthless businessman did something like that?

'Do you really expect me to believe you're that altruistic?' she asked, unable to keep the scepticism from her tone.

'I don't particularly care what you believe.'

Nice. 'Well, thank you,' she said primly. 'But I can't accept it.'

'Why not?'

Hmm. Where to start? Because she didn't like him and the thought of being indebted to a man she loathed was abhorrent? Because any man who could single-handedly close down a large, foreign website was to be treated with caution and she didn't trust him an inch? She could hardly tell him any of that. He was still her boss.

'It's too much,' she said instead.

'Not from my perspective.'

'Still no.'

'Where else are you going to get the money?'

'I'll think of something.' Hadn't her brief foray into the shady world of online escorts proved that? Surely she'd be able to come up with a workable solution, one that didn't involve seedy sex or overbearing men.

'It sounds like you'd better think of it quickly.'

Well, yes, there was that. She was running out of time. Fast. How much longer did she have? How much more could she take? She was *so* tired of worrying about the money. About the debt and the reduced quality of life her sister might have if she had to move because she—Kate—had failed. About losing her home and the precious memories she had of her brother. The responsibilities she now had, which landed entirely on her shoulders, were crushing, bewildering, overwhelming. Sometimes she wished she could just go to bed for a month and cry.

'Just out of interest, what would you want in return?' she asked, because even if she had been considering it, which she wasn't, surely that amount of money would come with strings.

'Nothing.'

She stared at him. 'Nothing?'

He gave a brief nod. 'That's right.'

'Why not?'

'Do I need a reason?'

'*I* would. You're in the business of deal-making. No one ever gets something for nothing. Even I know that.'

'You have my word.'

'I don't know what your word is worth.' What if hypothetically she agreed and he suddenly decided that his money gave him the right to influence Milly's future? What if at some point he decided to stop?

'I'll have a contract drawn up,' he said, clearly able to read the scepticism that must have been written all over her face. 'You can state the terms. I won't challenge them.'

'Things that sound too good to be true generally are.'

His jaw tightened. 'Just accept my offer, Kate. It's the only one on the table.'

True. But— 'I'd never be able to repay you.'

'There'd be no need.'

'I'd feel a need.'

'Then I suggest you get over it,' he said tersely, 'because you should know that I will be doing this, with or without your consent. Your agreement will merely speed things up.'

And quite suddenly, in the face of such intransigence, what remained of Kate's resistance suddenly crumbled. Why was she still fighting this? She was running on fumes and at her wits' end. What Theo was proposing would obliterate all her worries and stresses overnight. So if he could afford it and wanted to help, why shouldn't she let him? Maybe he *did* feel something after all. Maybe he and Mike *had* been good friends. Ultimately, did it even matter? She didn't need to like him, and his motivations were none of her concern. He was offering her a 'no strings attached' deal, which would get the debt collectors off her back and, more importantly, ensure Milly's comfort for the rest of her life as well as the best treatments available. So despite feeling as though she might be making a deal with the devil, she couldn't *not* accept his help. She just couldn't.

'Okay, fine,' she said with a brief nod. 'You win.'

CHAPTER TWO

HE'D WON, HAD HE?

Hmm…

Theo wasn't so sure. He might have achieved the outcome he'd been intent on getting, but in reality, given the massive debt he owed Mike, the provision of financial support for Kate and her sister was long overdue and it certainly didn't lessen the crushing omnipresent guilt he felt over the part he'd played in their brother's death. If anything, it made it worse because he hadn't known about the loans and he should have.

And then there was the battle for his self-control, which he'd started waging the moment Kate had walked into his office and detonated a savagely fierce and wholly unexpected reaction inside him. Was he winning that? By the skin of his teeth, and only then because he had years of practice.

He had not been prepared for her effect on him. The first and last time they'd met—at her brother's funeral, an insanely tough and gruelling experience for a number of reasons—had certainly given no indication. This evening, however, she'd come through that door and for some unfathomable reason every sense he possessed had instantly sprung to high alert. The way she'd moved—languidly and sinuously graceful—had mesmerised him, and as she'd approached his desk, that web page she'd set up had slammed back into his head. So much for thinking he'd successfully excised it from his memory. Clearly he'd merely drawn a veil across it, a veil that her appearance in his space had instantly swept back.

With every step she took towards him, his blood had

begun to heat and questions had started ricocheting around his head. Forget her vital statistics and her hobbies, he'd thought, his pulse thudding heavily and his body hardening. What he'd like to know more about was the tattoo. Where was it, and what was it of?

Then there was the tiny yet somehow momentous detail regarding her sexual experience. The 'none' of it implied that she was still a virgin, but regardless of its meaning, it shouldn't have been of the slightest interest. However, infuriatingly, he seemed to find it fascinating because all he could think was, why? She was twenty-six and it couldn't be from lack of opportunity. She looked like a goddess. Not, perhaps, conventionally beautiful, but certainly breathtakingly striking with her long blonde hair and big blue eyes and above average height.

And last, but by no means least, there were the photos, the last two in particular, which once seen could not unfortunately be unseen and were now indelibly etched into his memory. Those had had him instinctively thinking about the suite adjoining his office, the oversized bed he had in there, and her sprawled across it wearing nothing but that negligee.

Such a savage and unexpected assault on his senses had decimated his self-control and his body had responded—and was still responding—in the inevitable way, hence the subsequent battle.

However, he was concealing the attraction scorching through his blood effectively enough and he was well used to conducting a conversation that bore no reality to what was going on inside him. He might have been momentarily distracted when she'd shifted and the movement had exposed even more lovely long leg that he'd suddenly, *appallingly*, wanted to touch, but their discussion had remained—and would continue to remain—firmly on track. Kate would never have any idea of the fierce need pounding away inside him. It was purely physical and of zero importance anyway, and nothing she could do or say would ever entice him to yield to it. Not the blush on her cheeks, not the darkening of her irises, not the soft breathy gasp.

'Is there anything else you need?' he said coolly, his voice bearing not even a hint of the inner turmoil he was experiencing.

'No. Thank you. I have everything else under control.'

Lucky her. 'Let me know if that changes.'

'Of course,' she said, about to move again before clearly thinking the better of it, thank *God*, and adding, 'And, actually, thank you for your offer of help. That "you win" of mine was churlish.'

'It was.'

'Although, to be fair, you *had* just ridden roughshod over my plans without any consideration for my feelings.'

She had a point, just not one he could bring himself to apologise for. 'Perhaps.'

'Nevertheless, that's no excuse,' she continued. 'I apologise. My parents were particularly hot on manners. They'd be spinning in their graves at my lack of them…' She tailed off for a moment, a flash of sorrow flitting across her expression, but then gave herself a quick shake. 'Anyway,' she said briskly, 'I really am grateful for your offer. And since this seems to be the moment for it, I suppose I also ought to thank you for closing down that website.'

Sitting back and ignoring the desire to respond to that moment of grief because he didn't do emotion and it was no business of his anyway, Theo rested his elbows on the arms of his chair. 'Oh?' he said, arching an eyebrow since only five minutes ago she'd been outraged by what he'd done. 'Why?'

'There were emails,' she said with a shudder. 'Disturbing ones. There are some very sick people out there.'

'What did you expect?' he said, not even wanting to *think* about the offers she might have received.

'I'm not entirely sure,' she said with a naivety he envied because he'd give everything he had not to know the depths people could sink to. 'A few emails perhaps, maybe resulting in one or two regular clients with more money than sense. Certainly not *that* kind of a response. To be honest, it never occurred to me that my virginity would cause such a furore.'

He'd never have imagined taking such an interest in it either. He still couldn't work out why he did. 'You are pretty unique.'

Her eyebrows lifted and another blush tinged her cheeks. 'Am I?'

'In this day and age a twenty-six-year-old virgin is unusual.'

She appeared to deflate for a moment, but then rallied. 'I suppose so,' she said with a shrug.

'What's the issue?'

'It's none of your business.'

'True.'

She tilted her head. 'Why would you want to know anyway?'

Good question. He barely knew her. He didn't do personal and didn't need to know. He certainly had no intention of helping her out with it, and where the hell had that idea even *come* from? Nonetheless, he could tell himself all he liked that it was important to be in full possession of all the facts so he could stop her embarking on any further acts of recklessness, but the plain truth was that for some reason he just wanted to know. 'I'm curious.'

'It's hardly an appropriate topic for a boss/employee conversation,' she countered. 'And besides, I'm still on probation.'

No problem there. He'd spoken to her line manager in

the accounts department earlier just in case she did need firing. Fortunately, she didn't. Her work was superb and she was a reliable, valued member of the team.

'You're excellent at your job,' he said. 'You'll pass it. And we crossed the boss/employee line the minute you tried to access the Belle's Angels site from a computer I own.'

'Nevertheless, no.'

'Okay, fine,' he said, annoyed with himself for pushing it. He wasn't *that* curious, dammit. If she didn't want to tell him, so what? In fact, it was a good thing, because she ought to go. The battle he was having to keep his eyes off her legs and his mind off the rest of her was taking more effort than he'd anticipated. Their business was concluded and, frankly, the sooner he could get back to work, back to *normal*, the better. 'You can see yourself out.'

Kate watched Theo nod in the direction of the door and then turn his attention to whatever was on his computer screen, and thought that if that wasn't a cue to leave, she didn't know what was. As dismissals went it was unambiguous. She'd refused to play ball and he'd lost interest. Which was fine. There was no way she was going to share the issues surrounding her non-existent sex-life with her boss, of all people. Imagine the humiliation. It didn't bear thinking about.

Therefore his cue was one she was going to take. Right now. She was going to get up, waltz out and go home, where she could ponder at length this evening's whole surreal conversation and, when it came to her money troubles, pinch herself hard.

So why wasn't she moving? Why did her bottom appear to be glued to the chair? Why was her heart hammering at such a rate it might crack a rib and why was a cold sweat breaking out all over her skin? She couldn't actually be thinking of telling him what he wanted to know, could she?

No. It was out of the question. Theo Knox was the very *last* man she ought to want to confide in, although her brother had obviously had time for the guy and he *was* prepared to come through for Milly so maybe he wasn't all bad. But that was irrelevant. Spilling her innermost thoughts and fears to him would be insane. Complete and utter professional suicide. Not to mention epically mortifying. Besides, why would she even *want* to? She shouldn't. She *didn't*.

And yet, to her horror, it was growing increasingly tempting to think to hell with it and throw caution to the wind. She could feel the pressure to do exactly that building unbearably inside her, and the words were on the tip of her tongue, piling up one on top of the other, clamouring for release.

What was going on? she wondered in mounting panic, clamping her lips together as horror thundered through her. Had the stress of everything that had happened lately finally broken her down? Had Theo cunningly deployed some sort of reverse psychology that suddenly had her desperate to share every tiny detail? Or was it simply that now she'd experienced a smidgeon of his interest she wanted more?

Impossible, she told herself as she took a deep breath through her nose and willed the dizziness to subside. That would be utterly ridiculous. She wasn't that pathetic. She certainly wasn't so starved of attention that she'd forfeit her dignity and fall on any crumb dropped at her feet.

But when *was* the last time a man had expressed any interest in her? Ever? Okay, so Theo had made it perfectly clear at Mike's funeral he wasn't interested in her like *that*, and that was fine because it wasn't as if she wanted him to do anything about her little problem, was it? Heaven forbid. When she did finally get around to losing her virginity she didn't want him anywhere near her. He was rude, high-handed and unpleasant and made her bristle with loathing, although, come to think of it, it wasn't loathing she'd been bristling with for the last quarter of an hour. She wasn't entirely sure what it was, any more than she understood what that charged moment when he'd looked at her legs had been about. The blessed relief that her money worries were over, most probably.

It couldn't be anything else. It certainly couldn't be attraction. What a waste of time and energy *that* would be. Even if she *had* liked him, Theo Knox was so far out of her league he was on another planet. He was a staggeringly handsome, enormously successful billionaire. She was an inexperienced ordinary woman of significantly above average height, who managed to look passable on a good day in the right clothes, of which, truth be told, she had few since it was expensive to clothe well a body like hers. She was moderately good at her job and reasonably intelligent, but she wasn't beautiful. She wasn't special. In fact, she was the very opposite of special.

But regardless of her non-specialness, *something* about what she'd done had caught his attention enough to summon her up here and grill her when he could have just had her fired. And that was more appealing than it ought to be.

And so it seemed that—oh, dear—she *was* that pitiful and she *was* that starved of attention, because whatever the cost to her pride she wanted Theo's interest back. She wanted to matter to someone. It was undoubtedly stupid and she definitely didn't want to think about what it said about her, but the longer she sat there, the more inevitable it became, the more powerful was the urge to share, and she suddenly didn't have the strength to resist.

'Well, if you *really* want to know,' she said, vaguely wondering if she hadn't completely lost the plot, 'mainly it's my height.'

'What?' Theo snapped as he whipped his head round,

his deep scowl clearly indicating his displeasure at her continued presence.

'It's my height.'

'What the hell does that have to do with anything?'

'Everything.'

'Why? Lying down—or in most other positions, for that matter—height makes absolutely no difference.'

What?

Okay...

'Well, naturally I don't know much about that,' she said, hoping she wasn't blushing quite as madly as she suspected and wishing she had stronger willpower. 'But I hit six foot some time around my fifteenth birthday. I was lanky and clumsy and towered over the boys in my class at school. When it came to adolescent hook-ups they gave me a wide berth. There were plenty of other more normal girls to choose from.'

'There is nothing abnormal about you,' he said darkly, his gaze roaming all over her and setting her skin on fire.

'Others might beg to differ,' she said, determinedly ignoring it. 'It was a difficult time anyway. My parents had just died and my twelve-year-old sister was in hospital, fighting for survival. Life as I knew it had shattered. Most people were kind and full of sympathy. Others, not so much. Some didn't know how to handle it, well, me, really, and teenagers can be cruel, can't they?'

His eyes narrowed. 'What did they do?'

'It was more a case of what they *said*,' she said, her throat tightening as she recalled the grief, pain and confusion that had dominated her emotions during that time. 'There were a lot of stupid, nasty rumours going round. A few bitchy comments. On one particularly memorable occasion a boy came up to me and said that my parents must have deliberately crashed because death was preferable to the embarrassment of having such a freak for a daughter.'

There was a pause, during which Theo's jaw clenched imperceptibly and his entire body seemed to tense. 'I literally have no words,' he said eventually.

'No, well, that wasn't pleasant. It took me a while to get over it all, the loss of my parents, the new reality my sister faced, the bullying and then the guilt that my brother had been forced to leave university to come and look after me. And then when I did—which was no mean feat, I can tell you, not least because part of me was convinced that it wasn't fair of me to live my life when Milly's had been so devastatingly curtailed—it was to discover that even grown men are put off by my height. Apparently it's emasculating. Not to mention intimidating.'

A tiny muscle began to hammer in Theo's cheek. 'That's pathetic,' he said grimly.

'I know,' she said with a casual 'what can you do?' kind of shrug, as if the years of bullying and rejection that had crippled her self-esteem and destroyed her sense of self-worth meant nothing. 'But, well, it was what it was and on the upside, all that time my classmates and fellow uni students were dating I spent studying. I got a first-class degree and now have a career I love.'

'I find your height neither emasculating nor intimidating,' said Theo, his eyes not leaving hers for a second.

'Why would you?' she said as a tiny shiver raced down her spine. 'You're a hugely successful businessman with the world at his fingertips. I doubt you're intimidated by anything.' Or emasculated. He oozed such virile masculinity it simply wasn't possible.

'You'd be surprised.'

As his mouth curved into a faint smile, Kate thought that this was another of those occasions she wanted to look away. More than she wanted to know what intimidated him, which was saying something. The intensity of his gaze was making her skin feel all hot and prickly and yet again she was finding it oddly hard to breathe. She felt trapped. On fire. And suddenly, quite out of the blue, acutely aware of him.

Inexplicably, the tiniest of details began to register. The minute scar that bisected his right eyebrow. The slight bump on the bridge of his nose. And was that a silvery grey hair she could see at his left temple in amongst all the ebony? She rather thought it was.

And it wasn't only the physical details that she now noticed. She could sense the tension radiating off him and the power he was keeping tightly leashed. The non-verbal signals he was emanating gave her the impression he was furious. On her behalf. And although she had no idea why that would be the case it made her go all warm and fuzzy.

What would it have been like to have had someone like him on her side when she'd been at school? she couldn't help wondering as the silence stretching between them thickened. What would it feel like now?

Come to think of it, what would *he* feel like? He'd be hard and muscled, she was sure. All over. He wasn't the type to tolerate softness. Except maybe where his lips were concerned. Those looked nice and velvety. And what about the sprinkling of dark hair she could see on the backs of his hands? Would it be rough to the touch or silky? And where else might he have it? She had no way of knowing, and now, bizarrely, that, as well as the realisation she'd never find out how soft his lips actually were, seemed a shame.

'Anyway,' she said, baffled by the unexpectedly carnal turn of her thoughts and suddenly really rather keen to lighten the weirdly tense atmosphere, 'your experience of height has probably been far different from mine.'

Theo started, as if she'd jerked him out of deep thought, and his brows snapped together. 'Has it?'

'Has anyone asked you what the weather's like up there?'

'No.'

'Suggested a career in basketball?'

'No.'

'I bet you haven't ever had to put up with tiny little aeroplane seats and bashed knees.'

'I have a private jet.'

Of course he did. 'I always wanted a little zippy convertible,' she said with a whimsical sigh. He nodded and she thought for a nanosecond that maybe he did understand after all. 'Being hugged is a problem.'

'Is it?'

'Yes,' she said with a nod, although it wouldn't be a problem if it was Theo doing the hugging, would it? Her head would tuck into his neck perfectly. Her body would fit against his beautifully. And then she'd know exactly how hard and muscled he was...

'Doorways.'

What? Oh. 'Pendant lights.'

'Hotel showers.'

Not helping. But what was going on? Why was she so flustered by the thought of Theo in the shower? Why was she even *thinking* about Theo in the shower? And why did she get the impression he was thinking about her in the shower? Unanswerable questions all of them, so she put them out of her mind and focused. 'Much of the world is structurally tallist, don't you think?' she said, thankfully sounding more in control than she felt.

'It is,' he said with the glimmer of a smile so fleeting the minute it was gone she thought she must have imagined it.

'Sleeves?'

'My clothes are tailor-made.' Naturally. 'Shoes?'

'Nightmare,' she said. 'I'm a size nine. And I never wear heels. You?'

'Heels have never been my thing,' he said, that faint smile back again.

Kate nearly fell off her chair because, good heavens, was that a *joke*? Crikey.

'It's hard to be inconspicuous.'

He arched an eyebrow. 'Is that a negative?'

It was for her. She'd been taller than her contemporaries since the moment she'd learned to walk. Throughout her childhood barely a week had passed without someone commenting on it. She couldn't remember a time she hadn't felt different, and not in a good way. No amount of positive parental input had helped. She'd just wanted to be the same as everyone else. To fit in. Subsequently she'd spent so much of her childhood and teenage years hunching her shoulders and trying to appear shorter than she was her posture was abysmal. 'I imagine that depends who you are.'

'You command attention.'

Obviously he was using the 'you' in the general sense, not referring to her in particular, but nevertheless she weirdly found herself sitting up a bit straighter. 'Possibly,' she hedged.

'And statistically, taller people tend to earn a higher salary.'

Her eyebrows lifted. 'Really?' That *was* interesting.

'So I once read.'

'I must remember that at my next performance review.'

'I would.' He paused, then said, 'Light bulbs.'

'Maxi-dresses,' she batted back.

'You never have a problem reaching for something from a high shelf.'

'And you can always spot friends in a crowd.'

'Quite,' he said. 'Definite pluses.'

His words were spoken evenly enough, but something flickered across his expression and the smile faded, and it suddenly occurred to her that while she'd assumed he was too uptight and aloof to do friends, maybe it wasn't just that. Maybe it was more that it was lonely at the top. And so maybe he was as lonely as she was…

Or not.

The strangely electric heat surging through her dissipated and she went cold, because what planet was she *on*? A man like Theo would never be lonely. He certainly wouldn't lack for female companionship. Just because nothing appeared about him in the gossip columns didn't mean he was a monk. And a moment or two of banter did not make him a kindred spirit. She must have been mad to imagine he ever could be. And to think she'd even harboured the vague hope that he might have some advice for her about how to deal with an excess of centimetres. Of course he wouldn't. He clearly had no hang-ups about anything at all, and why would he? He was a god and she was about as far from goddess-ness as it was possible to get. She and Theo were poles apart in virtually every way. She had to be even more starved of attention than she realised if she was deluding herself with the idea that they somehow shared something unique. And as for the inappropriate little fantasies about hugging and showers, what had she been *thinking*?

The setting sun was casting an oddly seductive golden glow across his office and the sense of intimacy it created was messing with her head. That was the trouble. It spun a sort of web that rendered reality all blurry. That was why she found it so easy to talk to him. Why she'd been all of a flutter when he'd so casually mentioned the many sexual positions he'd obviously experienced.

The sooner she could get out of here, the better. If she stayed, who knew what else she might reveal? She'd already humiliated herself quite enough. Once she'd started talking she hadn't shut up. Besides, what with the rolling of her stomach and the bizarre way she kept going hot and cold at the same time, she was beginning to feel very peculiar indeed.

'So, anyway,' she said with a feebly bright smile. 'There you are. The reasons why I'm still a virgin. Basically no one wants me. And on that pretty mortifying note I should definitely go. I'm sure you have plenty to be getting on with and I've taken up more than enough of your time. So, sorry for the firewall breach thing and, uh, thanks for everything… I'd best be off. Unless, of course, there's anything else?'

CHAPTER THREE

ANYTHING ELSE?

Anything else?

God.

There was so much going on in Theo's head he didn't know how to even *begin* to unravel it. How he was managing to keep a grip on things he had no idea. If he'd known what chaos Kate was going to unleash by not leaving when he'd told her to, he'd have picked her up and carried her out instead of ignoring his better judgement and like an idiot encouraging her to continue.

When she'd been talking about everything she'd been through his entire body had started to churn. When she'd mentioned the short-sighted fools who'd rejected her over the years he'd had an irrational urge to demand a list of names. When she'd revealed that she'd been bullied and how, his hands had curled into fists and he'd wanted to hit something for the first time in fourteen years, six months and ten days. As they'd batted back and forth the pros and cons of being tall, for the briefest of moments he'd forgotten where and who he was and had found himself actually enjoying the conversation, until she'd mentioned friends and he'd crashed back down to earth with a bump.

And then there was the want, the searing, clawing, deeply inappropriate need to show her what the soft gasps and blushes meant and what her body was capable of. Of what they'd be capable of together, because when she'd looked him as if she was somehow imagining him naked he'd nearly combusted.

The strength of his reaction to this woman didn't make any sense. She was by no means the most beautiful woman he'd ever met and he'd always preferred sophisticated experience over naivety. He had absolutely no reason to behave and feel the way he did around her. It was too visceral, too dramatic, and wholly unacceptable.

Why did he even care about her issues anyway? And why had he taken such umbrage to her registration to that site in the first place? As she'd repeatedly told him, none of it was any of his business. She was obviously perfectly capable of taking care of herself. He wasn't responsible for her in any way. Yet hammering away inside him was the conviction that for some unfathomable reason it *was* his business and she *did* need his protection.

He'd never felt anything like it before, he thought grimly as she uncrossed her impossibly long bare legs and put her hands on the arms of the chair. He certainly didn't *want* to feel anything like it. In fact, he'd spent the majority of his adult life avoiding precisely this kind of thing. He'd experienced enough horror, confusion and unpredictability growing up to like his life now controlled, ordered and sterile.

The way he responded to Kate threatened that. It screwed with his head and made a mockery of everything he considered vital. So he ought to just let her go. She wasn't even making it difficult. By getting to her feet, smoothing her clothes and turning to head for the door, clearly taking his silence for acquiescence, she was actually facilitating the best outcome he could have hoped for this evening.

And yet, it wasn't the outcome he wanted. Not by a long shot. He wanted her horizontal and beneath him. He wanted to spend the evening running his hands over every glorious inch of her to see if she felt as silky smooth as she looked. He wanted to find out what sounds she made when she came, and with a primal instinct he'd never have dreamt he possessed, he wanted to be the first man to make her make those sounds.

The battle for control was one he was losing with increasing momentum. The desire thundering through him had grown too powerful to ignore. With every step she took away from him his self-restraint slipped that bit more and he found himself caring that bit less. By the time she reached the door, a hair's breadth from walking out of his life for ever, which should have been perfectly fine but wasn't, all reason had fled. His blood pounded in his ears and his body ached unbearably, and all he could think was, so what if he did respond to her with an unfathomable intensity? Was he really going to let her walk out of here with her self-esteem needlessly non-existent, thinking no one wanted her when someone very definitely did?

Was he hell.

'Stop,' he said roughly, pushing back from his desk and standing up barely before he knew what he was doing.

At the door, her hand on the handle, Kate froze, then turned, and he saw a combination of wariness and surprise filling her expression as she watched him stride across the carpet towards her. 'What is it?'

He came to an abrupt halt a foot in front of her, close enough to see the rapid rise and fall of her chest and hear the breath hitch in her throat. Close enough to reach for her.

'There is one more thing,' he said, jamming his hands into his pockets before he could act on the instinct hammering away inside him.

'Oh?'

'You're wrong.'

She stared at him, bewilderment flickering in the shimmering cobalt depths of her eyes. 'You *don't* have a lot to be getting on with?'

'About your desirability.'

The pulse at the base of her neck began to flutter wildly. 'What?'

'Those boys were fools.'

'In what way?'

'You are very, *very* desirable.'

Her eyes widened for a moment and then she frowned. 'And you are very, *very* funny,' she said. 'Or not at all funny, actually.'

'You think I'm joking?' said Theo darkly, gripped once again by an irrational desire to locate everyone who'd ever decimated her self-esteem and string them up. 'I am *not* joking.'

'Nevertheless,' she said dryly, 'experience would suggest otherwise.'

'You have no experience.'

'Which kind of proves my point.'

'And I can prove *my* point.'

'Oh, yes?' she asked, lifting her chin an inch and arching an eyebrow. 'How?'

Now was the time to retreat, yelled the little voice of reason banging away in his head, demanding to be heard. *Now.* He'd achieved what he'd set out to do when he'd told her to stop. He'd corrected her misconceptions. His work was done. He should take a step back and reinstate some desperately needed distance.

Yet he couldn't move. Her wide-eyed innocence and intoxicating scent were drowning out that voice in his head. The tilt of her face and the challenge in her voice were tugging at a viscerally primitive part of him deep inside. And then he noticed that her breathing was rapid, shallow, that she was staring at his mouth, and now, heaven help him, she was actually leaning towards him, and as a strange feeling of fate enveloped him what little remained of his control simply evaporated.

'Like this,' he muttered, and with one quick step forwards, he took her face in his hands and slammed his mouth down on hers.

* * *

Theo moved so fast, so unexpectedly, that for a nanosecond Kate had no idea what was going on. She was too busy trying to process the seismic shift she'd experienced when he'd demanded she wait and she'd turned to see him striding towards her with the intensity and focus of a heat-seeking missile. The set of his jaw, the hot look in his eye and the gruffness of his voice had made her shiver from head to toe. When he'd stopped just in front of her, the tension emanating from him palpable, something deep inside her had flared to life and rushed through her blood, making her head spin. And then his words. Her? Desirable? Yeah, right.

She didn't know what had made her demand proof of it and she had no idea what she'd expected, but now he was touching her, holding her, *kissing* her, seemingly as if his life depended on it, and she reeled first with the shock of it and then with the electrifying notion that maybe she'd been a bit too quick to dismiss his claims about her appeal. There certainly didn't seem anything half-hearted about the searing pressure of his lips on hers and he really didn't seem the sort of man who would do anything he didn't want to do.

Maybe though, just to check that he hadn't been lying when he said he wasn't joking, she ought to stop just standing there like a flake and start kissing him back. Then she'd know.

Before her courage could fail her or her hang-ups get the better of her, Kate closed her eyes and leaned into him. She put her hands on his waist and took advantage of his sharp intake of breath to part her lips and then crush them back to his. And in that instant the chemistry that she'd been too ignorant to identify before ignited. The second their tongues touched, Theo groaned and immediately deepened the kiss, pulling her closer, sliding his tongue into her mouth and blowing her mind with his breathtaking skill.

As she kissed him back with equal intensity but significantly less skill, she was sure, liquid heat rocketed through her veins and pooled between her legs. Instinctively, she moved her hands further round his back and he tilted his hips, and when she felt the huge rock-hard length of his erection pressing into her abdomen, she suddenly wanted it inside her with a clenching, gnawing, relentless ache that obliterated what remained of her wits.

All rational thought evaporated, and as her head emptied her senses took over with stunning ferocity. She was aware of nothing but Theo, the solidity of his broad chest hard up against the softness of hers, his heady masculine scent and the intoxicating taste of his mouth. The heat emanating from his body fired the flames in hers, turning her insides to molten lava and setting off so many tiny fireworks that her knees went weak.

It was as if some sort of devastatingly powerful tropical weather system had taken up residence inside her, she thought dizzily. And incredibly, it seemed as if Theo were caught up in it too because, in response to the sensory onslaught and the increasingly incendiary kiss, Kate gave a helpless little moan and suddenly he was pushing her back against the door and trapping her there with his big hard body.

And she wasn't complaining. Why would she when she felt so alive, so on fire? When, for the first time ever, it seemed that someone desired her? She was not going to look this gift horse in the mouth, so when Theo removed his hands from her face and clamped them to her waist she granted him better access by arching her back slightly and winding her arms around his neck.

In response, with one hand he shoved her skirt up just enough to jam one hard muscled thigh between hers and with the other he undid the button of her jacket and then tugged her shirt from the waistband of her skirt. And all the while he continued with the drugging, soul-shattering kisses.

As white-hot desire pounded through her, Kate instinctively shifted her hips to grind herself against his thigh and alleviate the burning ache, and then he was sliding his hand beneath her top and up, singeing her sensitised skin, then cupping her breast and rubbing a thumb over her agonisingly tight nipple. The lace of her bra might as well not have been there because she felt the heat of his hand like a brand. The friction was unbearable yet she wanted more. So she pressed herself closer, ground her hips that little bit harder and the hot sparks of electric pleasure jolting through her were so thrilling, so exquisitely powerful that she instinctively tensed and gasped—

And the spell that wild, desperate need had been weaving around them shattered.

As if doused with a bucket of iced water, Theo instantly froze. His hands sprang off her, and with a rough curse he jerked back. He looked stunned. His eyes were black and his breathing was laboured. And as he raked his hands through the hair that only moments ago she'd been threading her fingers through, somewhere in the midst of the hazy desire and intense disappointment that he'd stopped, it occurred to Kate that, yes, he *could* look dishevelled, he *could* be thrown off balance, and oddly enough it was something of a relief.

'That was not meant to happen,' he said roughly, clearly as poleaxed by the strength of the chemistry that flared between them as she was.

No, well, obviously not, she thought, righting her clothes with shaking hands, hugely glad that the door was behind her for support since she wasn't sure her legs were up to the job. 'I'm sorry.'

His gaze shot to hers and his brows snapped together. 'What?' he growled, rubbing his hands over his face and shaking his head. 'No. You have nothing to be sorry about. I do. I overstepped the line. I apologise.'

Oh. Right. 'I thought there was no line.'

'There's a line.' His dark eyes glittered and she shivered. 'And you should go.'

'Or what?' she challenged rashly, responding to the warning she could hear in his tone before she could reflect on the wisdom of her question.

He let out a quick, humourless laugh. 'You do not want to know.'

Oh, but she *did*. 'I do.'

'No.'

'Yes.'

'Fine,' he bit out. 'If you don't go, we cross that line together and your virginity becomes history.'

For a moment his words hovered in the space between them, charging the air with electricity and tension, and then Kate swallowed hard, her heart thundering and the blood drumming her ears. Dear God. What was he saying? Did he want her that much? Or was he merely teasing?

'Are you serious?' she said hoarsely.

'Deadly.'

'You want to have sex with me?'

His eyes drilled into hers as he thrust his hands in his pockets. 'Yes.'

'Why?'

'*Why?*'

'Well, is this a pity thing?' she asked, accepting the mortification that surged through her because she had to make sure. 'You know, help the poor orphan virgin with her pathetic self-esteem issues? Are you still trying to prove a point?'

His jaw clenched and he looked as if he wanted to hit something. 'No,' he grated, evidently hanging onto his control by a thread. 'You were right. I am not that altruistic. And believe me, pity is the last thing I am feeling at this precise moment.'

'I see,' she said, although really she was too bewildered, too stunned, to see anything.

'Good,' he snapped, taking a step back. 'So, for your own sake, Kate, I suggest you leave. Now.'

It was excellent advice. There was no doubt about that. The evening had taken an unexpectedly dramatic turn. Kate was so out of her depth she was in danger of drowning. With the way her head was spinning and her body was ablaze she ought to be feeling for the handle, yanking open the door and legging it to the lift, to *safety*, as fast as her trembling legs could carry her.

But she didn't want to leave. She didn't want safety. She wanted more of those wild kisses, more of the magnetic darkness and thrilling passion she could sense in him, and she wanted it all with an urgency that was breathtaking.

The strength of her feelings ought to have made her wary. Instead they were electrifying. She'd been hoping to offload her virginity for years. As unbelievable as it was, Theo appeared to be a hair's breadth from taking it, and she desperately wanted him to have it, because that attraction she'd so blithely dismissed as impossible earlier? Blazing.

So to hell with the consequences. So what if he was who he was and she was significantly less? It wasn't as if she were going to bump into him again. They quite literally operated on entirely different levels. Besides, recent events had taught her that life was short, and in all honesty she'd rather regret something she *had* done than something she hadn't.

She took a deep breath, licked her suddenly dry lips and opened her mouth to speak.

'Kate,' Theo cut in tersely, as if he was able to read her mind and found her thoughts deeply ill-advised.

'Yes?' she replied, knowing it was far too late for warnings when the decision was already made.

'Think very carefully.'

'I have.'

'Don't be a fool.'

'I know what I want.'

'I make no promises.'

'I don't want any.' Reality had no place here. 'Once is enough.'

He took a step towards her, his gaze cleaved to hers, and her entire body began to tremble with desire, excitement and anticipation.

'Last chance, Kate,' he said, his voice so low and gravelly it scraped along her nerve-endings.

'I'm going nowhere.'

And it was at that precise moment that Theo's patience, already stretched paper thin, snapped. He'd tried to warn Kate off—repeatedly—and he'd given her every opportunity to leave. If she chose to defy him then she was just going to have to face the consequences. She was an adult. As she'd told him earlier, she was perfectly capable of making her own decisions. He was only human, as much at the mercy of scorching desire as the next man, and so, really, there was nothing else to be done.

'Yes, you are,' he muttered, grabbing her hand and peeling her off the door as he inexorably caved in to the raging need he'd been holding at bay for the last five minutes.

'Not here?' she said with a little gasp of surprise.

Up against a door? Her first time? Not a chance. 'Not here.'

'Then where? The sofa? Your desk?'

'My bed,' he said, leading her straight past all the furniture and towards the door cleverly built into the wall and disguised as a bookcase.

'What—?' she started, pulling back a little, instinctively resisting the idea of walking into a wall, until he pushed the section he'd had constructed, the door opened and he led her through.

'Oh, wow,' she breathed, looking around the white minimalist room that was bathed in the soft light of the setting sun. 'You have a suite.'

He kicked the door shut, let go of her hand and strode past her towards the bed. 'I do.'

'It's incredible.'

'It's convenient,' he said, loosening the knot of his tie and pulling the whole thing off.

'For seducing the odd virgin who comes along?'

He looked at her. 'You're the first and you're not odd.'

'You're funny.'

'You're still talking.'

'I may be a bit nervous,' she said. 'Your bed is huge.'

Theo tossed his tie onto the armchair that sat in the corner of the room and undid the top two buttons of his shirt. 'If you change your mind—at *any* point—we'll stop.' It might well kill him, but he would.

Kate gave her head a quick shake and the relief that flooded through him was so fierce he didn't want to analyse it ever. 'I won't want to stop,' she said, staring at the wedge of his chest that was now exposed with a hunger he doubted she was even aware of. 'Especially not if you make it good.'

Good? *Good?* 'With chemistry like ours,' he said tautly, 'I won't even need to *try.*'

'Nonetheless, I'm expecting great things.'

'You don't know what to expect.'

Her lips quirked into a quick smile that for some reason stabbed him right in the chest. 'Ah, but that's where you're wrong, Theo. I've had orgasms. Good ones. However, I want more. I want fireworks.'

'Demanding,' he muttered, his pulse racing as his head

filled with images of how she might have gone about achieving all those good orgasms.

'Long-suffering and impatient and *extremely* ready to get on with it.'

'Then stop talking.'

'Tell me what to do.'

'Come here.'

She walked—no, *sashayed* towards him, pulling the band out of her hair so that it flowed around her shoulders like liquid gold, and it was all he could do not to stalk over to her, pick her up and tumble her straight down onto the bed before whipping the desire into a frenzy and then sinking into her. Instead, he drummed up a modicum of control to merely pull her into his arms and capture her mouth with another kiss that blew his mind.

There was nothing mere about her response, though. It was as fierce as it had been when he'd first taken her in his arms and they'd shared the kiss that had been utterly unplanned, deeply unwise and yet stunningly hot.

Now as they devoured each other, she wound her arms around his neck and pressed herself against him, every inch of her seeming to fit to him perfectly, and the desire beating through his blood erupted.

Somewhere deep in the recesses of his mind he was aware he shouldn't be doing this, that if he knew what was good for him he would stop and put as much distance between himself and Kate as was humanly possible. He was no Prince Charming and it wasn't his job to help with her issues. God knew he had plenty of his own to fix. Besides, one touch of her and he turned into a man he didn't recognise and liked even less, a man driven by the basest of instincts, a man without control.

Yet he couldn't have stopped now even if someone had been holding a gun to his head. He wanted her with a hunger it was impossible to ignore, a hunger that had had him pinning her up against a door and forgetting his name.

He could tell himself all he liked that if it wasn't him relieving her of her virginity it would be someone else—a notion that was so distasteful it made him want to retch—or that it was just because it had been a while since he'd taken a woman to bed, but in truth…well, in truth there was no reason beyond clawing need and a desire that demanded to be assuaged.

And it would be fine, he assured himself, his muscles tightening as she slid her hands beneath the lapels of his jacket and pushed up. Kate might be innocent when it came to sex but she wasn't stupid. She knew the score. His conscience was clear on that front at least. Once it was over that would be that. He'd put her in a cab and out of his mind, and the entire evening would be consigned to history. He'd lock up the memories and throw away the key. He'd have no need for them. In the meantime, however, he was going to focus on her, on *them*, and on getting naked as soon as was humanly possible.

Breaking off the kiss, he shrugged his jacket off and it fell to the floor. 'Anyone would think you'd done this before,' he muttered thickly as she moved her hands to his shirt and started tackling the buttons while he set to work on getting her out of her skirt.

'I did once get to second base,' she murmured, her breathing all ragged and shallow. 'But that was only because of a bet.'

What? A bet? Somewhere in the recesses of his mind Theo was aware that little bombshell needed processing, but there was no way it was happening now. Not when all his blood was rushing from his brain to a different part of his anatomy entirely.

'Doesn't matter.' Kate frowned and bit her lower lip. 'This isn't working,' she said with a little growl of frustration that had him leaning away to tug on the back of his shirt and pull it over his head and off.

He let it drop on top of his jacket and a moment later her clothes and his trousers had joined the growing heap on the floor. He ran his gaze over her, taking in every incredible inch of her, her skin golden and glowing in the setting sun and, aha, there it was. The tattoo. What looked like an upside-down bird the size of a two-pound coin at her hipbone. He'd wondered. Now he knew. He did not need to know what it represented. That was not what this was about. Instead he focused on the expensive cream lace of her bra and knickers and the intriguing contrast it made with the shapeless navy suit she'd been wearing.

'This is sexy,' he said gruffly, touching her hip and tracing the lace there with his fingertips.

He heard and saw her breath hitch in her throat and the knowledge that she was turned on so easily had the blood thundering in his ears.

'Underwear is about the only thing that fits me properly,' she said raggedly. 'I like to buy the good stuff.'

She had excellent taste, but— 'Lose it.'

'Help me,' she breathed. 'I'm all fingers and thumbs.'

Gritting his teeth against the pounding desire, Theo put his hands on her shoulders and turned her around. He unclipped her bra and he slid it off her, then swept her hair to one side and pressed his mouth to the spot where her neck met her shoulder. She shivered. Dropped her head against his shoulder and leaned back, and the sigh she let out hit him right in the chest.

He closed his eyes, the scent of her filling his head, and almost of their own accord his hands moved slowly down her back and then round, beneath her arms, to cup her breasts. As he took the heavy weight in his palms, she gasped softly and arched her back, which pushed her breasts further into his hands and her bottom into the hard, aching length of his erection, and it took everything he had to stay where he was instead of where he wanted to be.

He swore, low and guttural, the word smothered by her skin, as desire surged to an almost agonising level. While he continued to tease her breast and nipple with one hand, he stroked the other down the smooth silky planes of her torso, her abdomen, until he slipped it beneath the lace of her knickers and reached the soft curls at the juncture of her thighs. At the intimacy of his touch she tensed for a second, and he stilled.

'Want me to stop?' he murmured, hoping to God she didn't.

'Don't you dare,' she breathed, backing up her words by opening her legs and gripping his forearm.

He parted her with his fingers and stroked, and she was so wet, so hot, it nearly unravelled him. But she hadn't done this before, at least not with anyone else. He had to go slowly, be gentle and give her time to adjust, however much it killed him. He would not be that man who lost control and shoved her up against a door.

Abandoning her breast, he took her chin and turned her head slightly and kissed her, while lower he slipped first one finger into her slippery heat and then another. Slowly he rubbed and stroked, feeling her tremble, hearing her sigh and gasp, and automatically registered her responses. When she moaned into his mouth, then whimpered, however, the sound of it blitzed his brain and he couldn't help moving his fingers that little bit faster, that little bit harder.

One of her hands shot up to the back of his head and her kisses grew frantic. Her other hand covered his, urging him on, moving him exactly where she wanted him. Her hips twisted, minutely at first, then more frenziedly and suddenly she was wrenching her mouth from his, crying out and clenching around his fingers and it was so sexy, so intense, that Theo nearly came right along with her.

CHAPTER FOUR

KATE WAS STILL tumbling down from her first orgasm given to her by someone else when her legs were whipped from beneath her and she was picked up as if she weighed nothing. Her head was still spinning. Her entire body was still quivering, and little darts of ebbing pleasure kept shooting through her, and they hadn't even got round to the actual virginity-taking part of the evening yet.

But as Theo deposited her on the bed and then turned his attention to the drawer of the bedside table, the heat dissipated and the fireworks faded. With every second that ticked by she became aware that she was lying there naked and exposed and vulnerable, and the insecurities that had been nowhere to be seen moments ago kicked in.

It wasn't that she was ashamed of the wild, desperate abandon with which she'd responded to him. She wasn't. At least, not much. It was more that she'd been so caught up in the way he'd made her feel she hadn't given her body a moment's thought beyond the pleasure it was experiencing. And then there was the fact that from the moment she'd started shedding her clothing at no point had Theo been able to look at her properly. To judge.

But with her sprawled across his bed like this, he could now, and she couldn't help wonder what he would think. There was just so much of her. She might have the height of a supermodel but she did not have the frame. She had padding. What if there was too much? Best not to let him see, she decided, scooting beneath the sheets and clutching them to her chest, then watching him take a foil packet out of the drawer and rip it open.

Of course, in terms of surface area there was way more

of Theo, but in his case that wasn't a negative because he was quite the sight for sore eyes. She'd been right in her assessment of how hard he'd be. He had muscles everywhere. They rippled across the breadth of his shoulders and flexed in his strong powerful thighs. And she didn't have to wonder about where else he might have a smattering of hair any longer. She could see it sprinkled across the lean planes of his chest, then narrowing down to the erection onto which he was now rolling the condom with what looked like impressive efficiency although what did she know?

Moments ago, all that hardness and strength had been rubbing up against her back, the friction driving her wild. With any luck it would be soon rubbing up against her front, driving her even wilder. Assuming he didn't change his mind about the whole virginity-taking thing, of course. Which was a possibility because really he was out of her league in every single way. He might well take one proper look at her, wonder what on earth he was doing and leave her there feeling like a fool. And quite honestly, she wouldn't blame him.

'Stop it,' Theo muttered, his voice low and rough.

Jerked out of her madly oscillating thoughts, Kate lifted her gaze to his and saw that he was looking at her, his eyes dark and his face tense. 'Stop what?'

'Whatever it is you're thinking.'

Flushing, she bit her lip and glanced across at the curtainless windows. 'Is there some way of shutting out the light?'

'No.'

Right. 'Would you mind closing your eyes, then?'

'Yes. I would.'

'In that case, I'll just have to close mine.'

He stood there before her, enviably unselfconscious, and regarded her thoughtfully. 'You have no idea how much I want you, do you?'

'Well, I guess…that…is some sort of indication,' she said, waving a hand in the direction of his erection and vaguely wondering how on earth something of that length and girth was supposed to fit, 'but seeing as I have nothing to compare it with, no, not really.'

'You will.'

He leaned down, putting one knee on the mattress, and as he came down beside her he tugged the sheet down to her waist. When she tried to grab it back he took her wrists and held them to the bed. He ran his gaze over her for one long slow moment and a rush of heat surged through her. Her nipples tightened and a fresh ribbon of desire began to unfurl deep inside her.

'You are stunning,' he murmured and she wished she could believe it. At least he hadn't called her beautiful. If he'd done that she'd have known he was lying. 'And I am extraordinarily attracted to you,' he added gruffly, 'so stop worrying.'

Easier said than done. But the physical responses he aroused in her body did seem to obliterate her self-consciousness and whitewash her mind, so maybe she ought to trust it would work again. 'Make me,' she breathed, and he didn't need asking a second time.

Bending his head, Theo kissed her long and hard, and as she'd hoped, as before, her insecurities faded, and rational thought gave way to something primal, instinctive and way beyond her control.

As he continued his devastating assault on her mouth she softened inside with renewed need. He lowered himself, twisting slightly so he lay half on top of her, and the deliciously heavy weight of him pressed her down. So much strength and power, she thought giddily. So contained. And as for his scent, that was a dizzying combination of spice and wood and something she couldn't identify but tugged at a spot deep inside her.

Swept up in a maelstrom of desire and heat, and feeling slight and feminine for the first time in her life, Kate moaned as she kissed him back and writhed against him in a desperate, instinctive effort to get closer.

With a harsh groan, Theo tore his mouth from hers and moved it to her breast, and if she thought the sensations had been stunning when he'd touched her there earlier they were nothing compared to the electricity that zinged through her at the heat and feel of his mouth.

She clamped a hand to the back of his head and let out a strangled gasp as her stomach liquefied. He turned his attention to her other breast and as the desire rocketed through her with ever-increasing intensity, the need to touch him back became overwhelming.

She wanted to explore him. Everywhere and at length. With her hands and her mouth. She wanted to learn the texture of his skin and the strength of his muscles. She wanted to see if she could drive him as crazy as he was driving her. She'd read books. She'd seen films. She had a fairly good idea of what to do.

But what if she did it wrong? niggled the tiny voice in her head that managed to penetrate the chaos. He'd implied he wanted her a lot, and it certainly seemed that way, but what if her clumsy, naïve attempts put him off? What if he *laughed*? She couldn't risk it. And besides, she was getting impatient. Theo's kisses and caresses were divine but wanted more. She *needed* more. Deep inside she actually ached.

The sheet that before had acted as a shield was now just in the way. It was stopping her from feeling the whole length of his body against hers, and she wanted it gone. She wanted nothing between them, not even air. So beneath him she wriggled and struggled, kicking at the fine white cotton, and Theo froze.

'What's wrong?' he said sharply, instantly lifting himself off her, and staring down at her, his eyes blazing. 'Do you want to stop?'

'Stop?' Kate muttered with a frown. 'Why would I want to stop?' Nothing short of Armageddon would make her want to stop now. Maybe not even that.

'Then what's the matter?'

'The sheet. I'm trying to get rid of it.'

'Are you sure?'

'Never been more so.'

'Thank God for that,' he breathed, yanking it off her and tossing it to one side.

Finally free, Kate bent her leg and, turning slightly, pressed her pelvis to his, her body clearly knowing how to ask for what it wanted. And Theo seemed to get it because he put a knee between her thighs and nudged her legs apart, and then he was between them, looming over her, his jaw clenched and his face dark and tight.

She could feel him at her entrance and she caught her breath, her pulse racing. It was about to happen, she thought, her entire body trembling and her heart swelling with a giant tangle of emotions she couldn't begin to unravel even if she wanted to. It was finally about to happen. After all these years. After everything…

She let her knees drop, parting her legs even wider, and then he was sliding into her, inch by incredible inch, giving her time to adjust to the strange feeling of being stretched and filled.

'Oh, my God,' she breathed, when he was embedded in her, deep and hard and strange.

'Are you all right?' he muttered harshly.

She took a moment to think about it. It might feel odd, but it hadn't hurt. She was getting used to it, and the promise of what he could do to her, how he could make her feel, bloomed inside her. 'Extremely all right,' she said, the desire and excitement building all over again at the thought of the pleasure to come. 'You?'

'Fine.'

Fine? Just *fine*? Oh, well. He had done this before. It was only momentous for her. Nevertheless, she sighed deeply and he grimaced.

'Don't move,' he said roughly.

'Why not?'

'Because if you do this will be over before it's begun.'

Oh. 'It was just a sigh.'

'That's all it'll take.'

He really wanted her that much? Perhaps he did. She could feel him pulsating deep within her. She could see the tension in his face and straining of his muscles. He looked as though it was taking every drop of his control to hold back, and it wasn't what she wanted. It wasn't what she needed.

'What if I can't help it?' she said, the ache spreading through her body demanding release with an insistence that was impossible to ignore.

'Try.'

'Impossible. Sorry.' It was too much. The need gnawing away inside her was too strong to control. Her hips shifted of their own accord, and Theo groaned.

'Heaven help me,' he said through gritted teeth before lowering his head and kissing her fiercely as he slowly withdrew, dragging along all her nerve endings, sending new thrills of desire coursing through her, and then plunged back into her.

The rhythmic pull and push of his movements stoked the flames inside her, melting her bones and boiling her blood. Her hands somehow found their way to his shoulders and she could feel his muscles shift beneath her palms with every strong powerful thrust of his body.

He was blowing her mind, and within minutes her breath

was coming in short sharp pants, her heart was thundering so hard it could well escape and all she could think about was racing towards a finishing line that was simultaneously rushing towards her.

Stifling a sob of desperation, Kate wrapped her arms round Theo's neck and her legs round his waist, and it must have been the right thing to do because suddenly he was moving faster and harder, pounding into her over and over again, pushing her higher and higher, until the unbearable tension within her snapped and, with a cry, she shattered.

White-hot pulses of pleasure, stronger and more powerful than anything she'd ever experienced, barrelled through her body. Stars exploded behind her eyelids and lit up her nerve-endings. She felt as if she were falling apart, and it was so intensely incredible that she barely registered Theo letting out a tortured groan, thrusting one last time and then burying himself deep and pumping into her over and over again.

As he collapsed on top of her and they lay there for a moment, all ragged breath, pounding hearts and long sweaty tangled limbs, Kate reeled with the intensity and magnificence of it all.

She'd done it, she thought, feeling weak, limp and completely wrung out. She'd actually done it. She wasn't frigid. She wasn't undesirable. All those years of disappointment and rejection, wiped right out. All those horrible mean comments, wrong.

The enormity of everything that had happened this evening suddenly struck and emotion welled up inside her, a swirling mix of relief and triumph, inexplicably tinged with guilt and sorrow, so massive, so overwhelming that she felt a tear escape and trickle down her temple.

But this really wasn't the time or the place to dissolve into a puddle, she told herself, choking off a sob and blinking frantically as Theo carefully levered himself off her and rolled onto his back. She'd save that for the privacy of home. Right now she needed to act as if everything was fine. Deep breaths and composure. That was what was called for here.

'So that exceeded my expectations,' she said huskily, with a nonchalance that sounded almost genuine.

'Good.'

'Thank you.'

'You're welcome.'

She thought she detected a note of aloofness in his voice that was at odds with the gruff impatience that had dominated his tone for the last half an hour, and glanced over. He was staring at the ceiling, and gone was the raw passion and the fevered tension, she saw. His expression didn't bear even the hint of a reaction to what had just happened. He certainly wasn't about to collapse into a quivering heap as she was. He was back in control, and this whole mad little interlude was over.

'So...ah... I should probably, really, go now,' she said, keen to leave before the situation could get any more awkward but unsure of the etiquette.

'You should,' he said, pushing himself up off the bed and, with barely a backwards glance, heading in the direction of what she presumed was the bathroom. 'Get dressed and I'll call you a cab.'

Kate spent much of the following forty-eight hours either breathlessly reliving the earth-shattering encounter with Theo in his office in gloriously vivid Technicolor or being battered by the emotions she'd managed to stave off when lying there in his bed.

At home, there was no one to witness the moments she drifted off into a sizzling daydream from which she generally emerged hot, flushed and trembling. Or the occasions when muscles she never knew she had twanged and she suddenly felt so vulnerable, so raw, it brought a lump to her throat and tears to her eyes. Alone, safely cocooned within her own four walls, she had no need for defences, which was just as well because any she might have mounted would have been crushed within seconds. The enormity of what had happened—not to mention the speed and unexpectedness of it—was simply too overwhelming.

She couldn't stop thinking about what it meant. She was no longer a virgin, was the bewildering, incredible realisation that kept ricocheting around her mind while she pottered about her flat achieving very little. She was no longer unusual. Well, not on *that* front, at least. She was still a great, unwieldy giant, and the boost that Theo's rampant need had given her would no doubt fade, but losing one's virginity was a rite of passage others took for granted and she'd finally made it.

And now she had, it was as if a light had suddenly switched on in her head, illuminating the shadows and making sense of things that deep down she'd always found baffling. Such as why she'd never found anyone willing to date her when out of a potential population of millions *surely* there would have been someone somewhere. It wasn't even as if she were particularly fussy, so how come she'd never met a single man who'd been up for it?

Maybe she just hadn't looked hard enough, she thought now. In fact, maybe she hadn't looked at all. Maybe it had been easier, safer, to resign herself to the status quo. Maybe she'd even become accepting of it. *Happy* with it.

And when she asked herself why that might be, it began to dawn on her that when she'd told Theo about the relationship between her height and her virginity she hadn't furnished him with the whole truth. What she hadn't revealed, what she hadn't even *known* at the time, was that for years she'd been scared. Of sex. Scared of doing it wrong and making even more of a fool of herself than she already felt.

It was so obvious now she could see it from the other

side. When she forced herself to look back to her troubled adolescence, to the time when her school friends had started losing their virginity and talked about it in great detail, she remembered she'd been fascinated and so excited about her turn, so desperate to be normal and fit in.

But when her turn never materialised, when it became apparent that she would always be on the outside, always rejected, she'd become quieter and had hidden her embarrassment and shame behind an air of mystery. Over the years that embarrassment and shame had escalated and had eventually turned into fear, which had put her off even more, creating a vicious circle that she hadn't even been aware of and which had possibly spread to other areas of her personal life, preventing her from trying new things in case they didn't work out and she made even more of an idiot of herself in the process.

But she'd had nothing to fear. Sex with Theo had been incredible. And momentous. And not only because she'd finally got rid of her virginity at the grand old age of twenty-six. Didn't it also prove that even though she would probably never be normal and would most likely never fit in, she might just *not* make a fool of herself? Theo certainly hadn't laughed at her, and he'd seen her stripped of not just her clothes but also of the protective shield she'd always kept wrapped round her.

So what was she going to do going forward? Was she really going to spend the rest of her life not trying things, just in case? Didn't that seem a bit of a waste? And hadn't there already been too much waste of life in the Cassidy family?

Surely she owed to it to herself, to her parents and her siblings, to make the most of what she had. To live life to the max. She'd allowed her virginity to hold her back by tethering her to a time of her life dominated by painful memories and teenage angst for too long.

Well, no more.

Now she'd recognised her fears she was going to confront them and let them go. So there'd be no more hiding. No more slouching. No more trepidation about the unknown. She was going to pull her shoulders back and hold her head up high as she sallied forth. She was going to be brave and bold and fabulous, and nothing was going to stop her.

CHAPTER FIVE

A MONTH LATER, Kate made herself a mint tea and took it into the sitting room to sit cross-legged on the sofa. It was one thing deciding to hold your head up and your shoulders back while you blazed a trail, she thought wretchedly, quite another to put it into practice. Because not only had it become apparent that decade-old deep-seated issues couldn't be wiped out quite as effortlessly as she'd assumed, but also life really did have the habit of suddenly walloping you about the head when you least expected it.

And to think that everything had been going so well. Theo, clearly a man of his word as well as action, had wasted no time in instructing his lawyers, and in the aftermath of a flurry of correspondence between her and his legal team, the monstrous debt her brother had accrued had been paid off and the fund Theo had promised for her sister had been set up.

As she'd hoped, the worries that had been hanging over her like the sword of Damocles disappeared in an instant and the relief was indescribable. Her home was safe and she'd been able to give up her extra jobs, and she had no regrets. Every time she visited her sister and saw how happy and settled she was, she knew she'd done the right thing, even if her visit the first Sunday after That Friday had momentarily shaken that conviction.

'Those are pretty,' she'd said to Milly, spying the huge bouquet of yellow roses sitting on the windowsill having dumped her bag on a chair and given her sister a hug.

'They're my favourite.'

'I know. But where did they come from?'

'Theo.'

At the mention of his name her pulse had leapt and questions had spun around her head but her smile hadn't faltered. 'That's nice.'

Milly had grinned. 'He's very good-looking, isn't he? He said he was a friend of Mike's. I liked him.'

And then her smile *had* faltered. 'He came here?'

'Yes.'

'When?'

'Yesterday.'

'What did he want?'

'To find out what my favourite flowers were.'

'Anything else?'

'I don't think so. I don't remember.'

The conversation had turned to the series Milly was watching on Netflix but Kate hadn't been able to focus. She'd been too concerned about why Theo had really shown up. When she'd questioned the staff, however, they'd reassured her that the only instruction Theo had issued was that Milly was to have whatever she needed. Kate had been sceptical, but gradually she'd come to accept it in much the same way she'd come to accept the flush of heat she experienced every time she looked at the fresh flowers that arrived weekly and reminded her of that Friday evening.

From the man himself she'd heard nothing, nor had she expected to. He'd been very clear about what he was offering and she had no reason to doubt that, which was fine because there was no future to be had with him. Apart from above average height and intense chemistry they had nothing remotely in common, and she'd neither seen nor heard any evidence to suggest he did relationships even if they had.

She hadn't bumped into him at work, thank God. As she'd suspected they trod completely different paths, so there'd been no awkward moments in a lift and no darting into nearby cupboards in an effort to avoid him. She kept her head down and worked hard, passing her probation and being given the pay rise she'd brazenly asked for after recalling what he'd said about tall people earning more.

So far, so fabulous.

But now…

Well…

Who knew what happened now?

Taking a sip of her tea to settle her churning stomach, Kate thought of the small pile of pink and white sticks on the vanity unit in the bathroom and felt her throat tighten and her head spin.

She was pregnant.

Not sick with a stomach bug as she'd assumed two days ago when she'd rung up and told her line manager she was too ill to come in.

Pregnant.

And there was no doubt about it. Because while one test might be faulty, all ten were unlikely to be, damn them and their over ninety-nine per cent accuracy.

But how could it have happened? she wondered for the billionth time since the breakfast she'd thrown up, when her brain had finally connected the random dots of early morning nausea, a missed period and recent sex. It didn't make any sense. She was no expert but she and Theo had only done it the once and he'd used protection. She'd even watched him rolling the condom on. They were supposed to be pretty infallible, weren't they, so how? Had he done it wrong? Had he ripped it? Had it somehow been *her*?

More importantly, more *relevantly*, since it was a little late to be worrying about the hows and the whys, what was she going to do? Because she couldn't have a baby. Still riddled with issues despite her best efforts to get over them, she was a mess. She was not equipped to bring up a child. She had no support network. None of her friends had children and her sister wasn't capable of understanding her situation. She had no mother to lean on and from whom to seek advice. She didn't even have grandmothers or aunts. And what about the baby's father? She couldn't imagine Theo wanting to be involved. She couldn't imagine *what* he'd think. She couldn't even *go* there right now.

And then there was the pregnancy itself. If she thought she was large and ungainly now, imagine how she'd look in nine months' time. Whales and ships in full sail sprang to mind, and, oh, the comments she'd get, the looks... How would she stand it all?

Yet the longing she felt... The *yearning* that filled every single inch of her to bursting... She'd only known about the baby for a handful of hours, but right down to her bones she wanted it. Desperately. Her heart and mind ached with it. She was so lonely and she had so much love to give. And an even greater capacity to receive it. A baby would never judge her and find her lacking. The love they'd share would be unconditional, and the mere thought of it was so intoxicating, so powerful that it shook her to the core.

There'd already been such loss in her life, she thought, her chest squeezing as she glanced at the photo on the bookshelf, the one taken of her, her parents and her siblings at the beach twelve years ago, all beaming carefree smiles and simple happiness. Such sorrow and grief. Such heartbreak. Here was her chance to rebuild the family she'd lost. To rediscover that happiness. To love and be loved. How could she *not* take it?

And so what if she did have issues? Who didn't? She could do it. Of course she could. Thousands of women had children in challenging circumstances and, really, how challenging were hers? Now she was debt-free and Milly was taken care of she could build her resources back up. And as for help and advice, there was always the Internet. It wouldn't be easy, but if she took things one step at a time and kept her head, surely she'd be able to muddle through.

And who knew? Maybe she wouldn't even have to do it on her own. There was only one way to find *that* out. Besides, Theo had the right to know about the baby, of that she was certain. And so while he'd had no reason whatsoever to contact her, she now had a very good one to contact him.

For the last four weeks Theo had found himself flat out, with a workload of Everest-like proportions.

The acquisition of the company he'd been pursuing for months was not going according to plan. Despite putting the best brains he had on it, including his own, he still hadn't come up with a way to clear the obstacles blocking the path.

Unlike every other deal he'd done, where the other side put up the semblance of a fight but inevitably collapsed during the negotiations, this one was proving trickier. Unusually, money wasn't the issue. The offer his corporate finance team had put together was the best on the table. The problem was that the current owner, a man with solidly traditional values and an extraordinary belief that ruthlessness wasn't a necessary ingredient for success, had more than enough money and was instead primarily concerned with the personality and integrity of the potential new owner. Incredibly, he appeared to have doubts about him, Theo, in this role.

Theo wanted to acquire Double X Enterprises with a hunger that gnawed away at him ceaselessly. It would be his biggest deal to date, the biggest the world had ever seen, and when he got it, it would be enough. He'd at last be satisfied. He'd have secured his place at the top, and the restlessness and the worthlessness that had dogged him for so long would be vanquished.

So he was *not* going to let it slip through his fingers simply because Daniel Bridgeman had an issue with him personally. He might be ruthless when the situation called for it but his integrity was without question. As for his personality, the aloofness and steel that the business press attributed to him suited him just fine. He was more than comfortable with being described as an ice-cool automaton. It was entirely accurate. Emotions were dangerous. They put a person at risk in so many ways just the thought of what could happen, what had *already* happened, made him break out into a cold sweat. He'd kept a lid on his for so long he doubted he had any of the damn things left anyway.

Regardless of the obstacles, though, he'd find a way to persuade Daniel Bridgeman to give him what he wanted. The man would fold eventually. Everyone did. He just had to identify his weak spot and drive a knife through it.

And in truth, the immense workload was welcome, especially today, the anniversary of his mother's death, which still hit him with the force of a sledgehammer no matter how major the distraction. He was no stranger to twenty-hour days. He'd been working all hours since he was fourteen, when he'd figured the only way he and his mother could escape his father's brutality was by being financially independent. He'd wheeled and dealed, buying low, creating value and selling high, grafting every spare minute he had with the sole aim of making enough to set them free, his relentless drive and grim determination to succeed surging with every muffled thud, every desperate cry, every sickening silence.

No one apart from himself had expected him to have such a knack for it. He'd shown little talent for anything at school apart from truancy and brawling. Yet he'd never forget the day he'd turned sixteen and told his mother that he'd amassed one hundred thousand pounds and that they should pack their bags.

He'd never forget her reaction either. The profound relief and gratitude and the maternal pride he'd been expecting were nowhere to be seen. Instead, once she'd recovered from her shock, she'd been appalled. To his bewilderment she'd refused to leave, and no amount of pleading on his part had moved her. Stunned, unable to comprehend it and devastated by her rejection and betrayal, Theo had left alone and had barely looked back.

It had been eight years since his mother died of a brain haemorrhage that he was convinced had been caused by his father although nothing could ever be proven, but the effects of how his sixteenth birthday had played out were deep-rooted and long-lasting. He'd never understand his mother's reasons for choosing to stay with a man who hit her instead of fleeing with a son who needed her, and he doubted he'd ever be free of the irrational guilt that he'd left instead of staying and trying harder to protect her despite her rejection.

And then there was the stomach-curdling knowledge that he bore his father's genes. As a kid he'd picked fights. As a sixteen-year-old he'd swung one proper punch that had had a devastating impact. Patterns by definition repeated themselves, and the risk that he might turn out like his father was sickeningly real.

But at least the cycle of abuse ended with him. He'd vowed never to marry, never to have children, and to never *ever* let anyone close enough to tempt him to break those vows. Even if there *was* no pattern, he couldn't be a part of anyone else's life. At least, not anyone he might be foolish enough to allow himself to care about. The consequences were too severe. He couldn't be relied upon. He let people down. And if he'd ever wished it could be any other way, well, he'd stamped out that kernel of hope and yearning many years ago before it had a chance to take root. Because in the long run everyone was better off if he remained alone.

But God, he didn't want to be alone right now, he thought, his jaw tight as he stared unseeingly at the city stretched out far below his penthouse, grey and wet beneath heavy clouds and relentless rain. Not with the darkness of his adolescence, the regrets and the guilt closing in on him on all sides. His entire body ached. His head throbbed. The emotions he preferred to deny he had were bubbling fiercely beneath an increasingly fragile surface, and the effort of suppressing them was pushing his formidable will to its limit.

Right now, he wanted to forget who he was and what he could never have. He wanted to forget everything. He wanted to lose himself in the oblivion of a warm body, long limbs and soft sighs. But not just anyone. He wanted Kate.

For weeks he'd buried the memories of the evening she'd spent in his bed. He'd put her in that taxi, set his lawyers to work, and that had been that: funding in place, desire assuaged, problem solved, the details shoved away in a corner of his brain and left to gather dust.

Today, however, with his iron-clad defences suffering a battering and the string of sleepless nights catching up with him, the memories were pushing through the cracks and invading his thoughts in scorching, vivid detail. He kept remembering the silk of her skin and the sounds she'd made. The taste of her mouth and the heat of her body. Her courage, her loyalty and her vulnerability and, most of all, the way that when they'd been talking she'd briefly made him forget who he was.

And he wanted it all again. He wanted *her* again. With a clawing ache that had his body as hard as stone and was becoming increasingly unbearable.

However, he was just going to *have* to bear it because while he could want all he liked, there was no way he was going to actually seek Kate out. He would not be that weak. One night was all he ever allowed himself. Two with the same woman represented the kind of risky behaviour he'd always spurned. He would not indulge it. Nor would he ever again put himself in a position that demolished his control, because without control, what was he? He didn't want to know.

The grim turmoil of today would pass. It always did. He just had to get through what was left of it. Tomorrow he'd be back on track and unassailable for another three hundred and sixty-four days. In the meantime, he'd find solace in work. While many who'd grown up in similar circumstances to his had found oblivion in drugs and alcohol, he'd always found it in the pursuit of success. It had worked for him for the past sixteen years. It would work for him now.

Setting his jaw, Theo swivelled his chair round. In the drawer of his desk he found a packet of painkillers, popped the two that were left and made a mental note to buy more. He turned to one of the three screens on his desk, and was in the process of opening his inbox when his mobile rang.

'Yes?' he muttered, forcing his attention to the latest email from the head of his corporate finance team, which came with a stark lack of suggestions for how he might push through the Bridgeman deal.

'I have a Miss Kate Cassidy in the lobby,' said Bob, the concierge who manned the desk twenty-three floors below. 'She wishes to see you.'

As the information hit his brain, Theo froze. His heart slammed against his ribs and his gut clenched. His concerns about the deal evaporated and his head emptied of everything but the knowledge that Kate was downstairs, bulldozing the boundaries he'd established and breaching his space, as if in his dangerously febrile need he'd somehow conjured her up.

But he could not see her. He was too on edge, his mood too dark. Her effect on him was too unpredictable, and the last thing he wanted was to be blindsided again. So he ought to instruct Bob to send her away and keep her away.

Yet what if she *was* in trouble? What if he had her thrown out and something happened? Could his conscience bear any more guilt? No. It couldn't. So he'd find out what she wanted, deal with it, and then get rid of her. And it would be fine. She was just one woman. He'd faced far worse. He might have once temporarily lost his mind with her, but he wouldn't lose it again. Weakness of will led to unpredictability, which led to damage and destruction, and that was unacceptable. So this time he would be prepared. This time he would be resolute and unflinching. This time would be different.

'Thank you,' he said curtly. 'Five minutes, then send her up.'

How much longer was she going to have to wait? Kate wondered as she perched on the edge of the sofa in the vast lobby of Theo's apartment building and rubbed her damp palms against her jean-clad thighs. It had already been four minutes and fifteen seconds since the concierge had told her to wait, and her nerves were shredded. Deciding to confront Theo and tell him about the pregnancy was all well in theory, but in practice it was lip-bitingly, heart-thumpingly terrifying.

How would he respond? What would he say? She'd had twenty-four hours to get used to the idea, but it was going to come as one massive shock to him. Would he be pleased? Would he be horrified? She didn't have a clue, and it was impossibly tempting to get up, spin on her heel, go home and leave it for another day.

But she wasn't going to do that, she told herself, sitting on her hands to save her nails. It went wholly against her recent resolution to be bold and brave. Besides, she had to tell him at some point, and the sooner she got it over and done with, the better. She might even be pleasantly surprised. And who knew when she'd get another chance? Just because she'd struck lucky with him being home today—a Saturday—didn't mean she would again, and it was hardly the sort of conversation she wanted to have with him at work.

So she'd wait for however long it took and try to refrain from chewing on her already raw lip. She'd admire her lavish surroundings instead. The giant dazzling chandelier that hung from the ceiling cast sparkling light across the polished marble floor and mirrored walls. The furnishings were tastefully leather and quite possibly cost more than her flat. The difference between the worlds that she and Theo inhabited could not be more marked.

What *was* he going to think?

'Miss Cassidy?' said the concierge a moment later, his voice bouncing off the walls and making her jump. 'Mr Knox will see you now.'

Finally.

'The lift on the right will take you directly to the penthouse.'

'Thank you,' she said, mustering up a quick smile as she got to her feet and headed for said lift on legs that felt like jelly.

The doors closed behind her and she used the smooth ten-second ascent to try and calm her fluttering stomach and slow her heart-rate. It would be fine. She and Theo were both civilised adults. They might be chalk and cheese, but they could handle this. What was the worst that could happen? It wasn't as if she was expecting anything from him. She just had a message to deliver. It would be fine.

But when the lift doors opened and she stepped out, all thoughts of civility and messages shot from her head because all she could focus on was Theo.

He was standing at the far end of the wide hall, with his back to a huge floor-to-ceiling window, feet apart, arms crossed over his chest. The interminable rain of the morning had stopped and sunshine had broken through the thick cloud. It flooded in through the window, making a silhouette of him, emphasising his imposing height and the powerful breadth of the shoulders. Although clothed in jeans and a white shirt, he looked like some sort of god, in total control, master of all he surveyed, and she couldn't help thinking that if he'd been going for maximum impact, maximum intimidation, he'd nailed it.

Swallowing down the nerves tangling in her throat, Kate started walking towards him, her hand tightening on the strap of her cross-body bag that she wore like a shield. His gaze was on her as she approached, his expression unreadable. He didn't move a muscle. His jaw was set and he exuded chilly distance, which didn't bode well for what was to come, but then nor did the heat suddenly shooting along her veins and the desire surging through her body. That kind of head-scrambling reaction she could do without. She didn't need to remember how he'd made her feel when he'd held her, kissed her, been inside her. She needed to focus.

'Hi,' she said as she drew closer, his irresistible magnetism tugging her forwards even as she wanted to flee.

'What are you doing here?'

The ice-cold tone of his voice stopped her in her tracks a couple of feet away, obliterating the heat, and she inwardly flinched. So that was the way this was going to go. No 'How are you? Let me take your jacket. Would you like a drink?' He wasn't pleased to see her. He wasn't pleased at all.

Okay.

'We need to talk,' she said, beginning to regret her decision to deliver this information in person. With hindsight, maybe an email would have sufficed.

'There's nothing to talk about.'

'I'm afraid there is.'

His dark brows snapped together. 'Your sister?'

'She's fine,' she said. 'Thank you for what you did for her.'

'You're welcome.'

'Did you get my note?' Shortly after he'd fixed her finances she'd sent him a letter of thanks. It had seemed the least she could do. She hadn't had a response.

He gave a brief nod. 'Yes.'

'She loves the flowers.'

'Good.'

'It was thoughtful.'

'It was nothing.'

Right. Beneath the force of his unwavering gaze and impenetrable demeanour Kate quailed for a moment and was summoning up the courage to continue when he spoke.

'Are you in trouble?' he asked sharply.

'That's one way of putting it.'

'What?'

'Sorry, bad joke,' she said with a weak laugh although there was nothing remotely funny about any of this.

'Get to the point, Kate,' he snapped. 'I'm busy.'

Right. Yes. Good plan. She pulled her shoulders back and lifted her chin. 'There's no easy way to say this, Theo,' she said, sounding far calmer than she felt, 'so here goes. There's been a…*consequence*…to our…evening together.'

A muscle ticced in his jaw. 'What kind of consequence?'

'The nine-month kind.'

There was a moment of thundering silence, during which Kate's heart hammered while Theo seemed to freeze and pale. 'What exactly are you saying?' he said, his voice tight and low and utterly devoid of expression.

'I'm pregnant.'

The words hung there, oddly loud and blatantly unequivocal, charging the space between them with electrifying tension, and Kate wished there'd been a less impactful way of saying it because something that looked a lot like terror flared briefly in the black depths of Theo's eyes, and it made her shiver from head to toe.

'Is it mine?'

'Yes.'

'Impossible.'

'Apparently not,' she said. 'Apparently it happens.'

'How?'

'I could ask you the same question.' He did, after all, have vastly more experience than she did.

'It makes no sense.'

'I know.'

His eyes narrowed. 'Are you *sure* it's mine?'

Ouch. 'Quite sure,' she said, choosing to forgive him for his scepticism since he was clearly in a state of shock. 'I saw a doctor this morning. I'm six weeks along and I haven't had sex with anyone other than you. I could arrange a paternity test if you need proof.'

He gave his head a quick shake, although whether it was to dismiss the need for proof or to clear his thoughts she had no idea. 'Are you going to keep it?'

'Yes,' she said with a firm nod, just in case he was thinking about persuading her otherwise. 'I am.'

'I see,' he said vaguely, and she got the impression that he'd gone to another place entirely.

'I don't expect anything from you, Theo,' she said. 'I thought you had a right to know, but that's it. It's entirely up to you how involved you would like to be. I can do this with or without you.' And it looked as if it was going to be without him because he was obviously *not* happy about it. Which was fine. 'Anyway, that's all I came to say,' she added. 'I get that it's a shock. So, take your time. Have a think about it and let me know.'

And with that, she turned on her heel and left the way she'd come.

CHAPTER SIX

HAVE A THINK?

Have a think?

How was that even possible when his safe, steady world had just been blown to smithereens? When his biggest nightmare, his greatest fear, the one he'd taken the utmost care to avoid for the whole of his adult life, had shockingly, horrifyingly materialised?

Only dimly aware of Kate's departure, Theo stood there, reeling. He couldn't move. He felt as if he were imploding. As if someone had punched in him the solar plexus and followed it up with a lead pipe to the backs of his knees. His chest was tight. His lungs ached. Dizziness descended and his vision blurred.

Breathe.

He had to breathe.

Before he passed out.

Pulling himself together, he dragged in a shaky breath and released it, and the minute the lift door closed behind Kate, he staggered back and sagged against the window.

How the hell could it have happened? he wondered numbly as he dragged shaking hands through his hair and swallowed down the nausea that surged up from his stomach. What warped twist of fate was this?

That Kate was telling the truth he didn't doubt. She'd been so calm. So matter of fact. He, on the other hand, felt as if he'd been swept up by a tornado, tossed about, and hurled back to the ground. He didn't need proof of what she claimed. He needed a drink. A damn time machine would be better. One that took him back to that evening so he could throw her out of his office instead of recklessly caving in to inexplicable desire and carting her off to his bed.

As for his involvement, well, that was a no-brainer. He wouldn't be involved at all. He couldn't. He was no good. It was highly probable he'd turn out to be worse than that. He could not be part of Kate's pregnancy or the raising of a child. Under any circumstances. He wouldn't even know how. To him the word 'father' didn't conjure up images of fishing trips and football games in the park. It represented fear and pain and desolation. He had no experience of anything different. None of the other kids he'd hung out with, kicking around the streets and causing trouble in order to avoid having to go home, had had positive father figures in their lives. He couldn't provide what a child needed. Hell, he didn't even know what that was.

All he did know was that he could not claim his child. The risks were too great. It would be in the child's best, *safest*, interests if he stayed far, far away. Emotionally. Physically. In every way that he could think of. He would not allow himself to give even a nanosecond's thought to what could be if he weren't so terrified of history repeating itself. He couldn't. The child deserved to live a life without fear.

So he would wipe Kate and the baby and the last fifteen minutes of his life from his head, and get back to the problems he *could* understand. If he focused on work and nothing else, the tightness in his chest would ease. The swirling blackness would clear. *Something* would come to him.

Although…

Hang on…

What if this latest development wasn't quite the horrendous disaster it appeared to be? What if it could, in fact, be the answer to the issue that had been plaguing him for months?

The questions slammed into his head, burying the chaos and turmoil with the cold clear logic that had rescued him from such situations many a time, and he instinctively clung onto them like a lifeline.

Were Kate and this pregnancy to become public knowledge, he thought, strength flooding back to his limbs as his brain started to teem with possibilities, it would definitely make him more palatable to Double X Enterprises' recalcitrant CEO. Especially if he stood by her. Daniel Bridgeman had been married to the same woman for fifty years. They'd had no children, but his wife was an integral part of his business. She was on the board of directors and appeared by his side at functions. He cited her as being behind every major decision he'd ever taken.

All of the above clearly indicated that the man valued such a partnership highly, so what if Theo presented one of his own? One he had ready-made. Surely that would allay any concerns the other man might have about his so-called ruthlessness and his less than acceptable personality? How much more touchy-feely could you get than a partner and an imminent baby?

So what if manipulating situations and faking a relationship *did* seem to smack of the ruthlessness and the lack of integrity he was aiming to disprove? The end more than justified the means. For the deal of a lifetime, a deal he'd *needed* to push through, he could—and would—do anything.

He foresaw no problem implementing this strategy. It wasn't as if any of it were for real. Once he'd achieved his goal he'd let Kate go and they'd be done. Should she put up any resistance, he had an arsenal of weapons with which to persuade her otherwise. And presenting to the world a facade he wanted it to see was second nature to him. He'd been doing it for years, ever since he'd learned at the tender age of seven to explain away the bruises and fractures and convince anyone who asked that everything at home was absolutely fine.

It was the best, the *only*, option on the table, so, ignoring the tiny voice in his head demanding to know what the hell he thought he was doing, Theo hauled his mobile out of his back pocket, hit the dial button and strode towards the lift.

'Kate Cassidy,' he said curtly when Bob answered. 'Stop her.'

Kate had got as far as the enormous slowly revolving glass door when the concierge caught up with her. Her thoughts on the scene that had just gone down up in the penthouse were mixed. On the one hand she was relieved that she'd accomplished her mission and had escaped unscathed, yet on the other she was gutted. She wasn't sure why. It wasn't as if she'd been expecting Theo to break open the champagne. She hadn't been expecting anything. So the disappointment didn't make any sense, which was yet another entry in the ever-growing canon of things about herself she didn't understand.

'Miss Cassidy,' called the man, puffing a little as he reached her.

'Yes?'

'Mr Knox requests that you wait.'

Kate stilled, her heart irrationally giving a little leap. He wanted her to wait? Why? What could that mean? Had he changed his mind? Did he want to be involved? *What?*

Well, she was about to find out, she thought, adrenaline surging and her pulse racing as her gaze shifted to the man striding across the lobby towards her. He seemed so energised, so full of purpose now that she found it hard to reconcile this version of him with the rigidly monosyllabic one she'd left up there in his penthouse. It had only been two minutes. What could possibly have happened in the interim?

'Thank you, Bob,' said Theo to the concierge before

switching his attention to her and virtually lasering her to the spot with the force of his gaze. 'Come with me.'

Before she could respond, he'd taken her elbow and was wheeling her in the direction of a room off the lobby. He led her into what was clearly a private meeting room, judging by the antique breakfast table and half a dozen dining chairs, and let her go.

'Are you all right?' she asked with a frown as she watched him close the door and then turn back to her.

'Couldn't be better.'

'I don't understand.'

'Marry me.'

Kate froze and stared at him, her jaw practically hitting the floor while her head spun. 'I—I'm sorry?' she stammered.

'You heard,' he said, something about the gleam in his eyes making shivers race up and down her spine. 'Marry me.'

'Don't be ridiculous.'

'I'm not being ridiculous.'

Her eyes widened. 'You're being *serious*?'

'Yes.'

Kate studied him closely for a moment and thought, no, well, he did look intense and steely and he wasn't the type to joke. But *marrying*? Her and *Theo*? What alternative universe was this? 'Why?'

'You're pregnant with my child.'

Okay, so there was that, but it didn't seem a likely motive in this day and age. There had to be something else behind it. But what? What could possibly have had Theo dramatically haring after her and issuing a proposal? He couldn't have suddenly realised he'd developed *feelings* for her, could he? No. That was impossible. He'd shown no sign of wanting her at any stage since he'd hustled her out of his office suite and bundled her into a taxi. Although presumably stranger things had happened. Somewhere and at some point…

Had her news jolted him into some kind of epiphany or something? He *had* been in a state of shock earlier. And he did have a reputation for knowing what he wanted, going for it and not giving up until he got it. So had she, however improbable it might seem, fallen into that category of being something he wanted?

Doubtful.

And yet…

What if this was her rock-bottom self-esteem making her assume the worst again? Just because no one had ever wanted to marry her before—or even date her, for that matter—didn't mean that no one ever would. So could Theo actually want her? For real? She had to allow that it was a possibility, for personal growth purposes, if nothing else. He *was* looking at her in a spine-tinglingly fierce kind of way. And he *had* just asked her to marry him, which he would not have done if he hadn't meant it.

So.

Maybe the circumstances were a bit of a surprise but people had married for less. Maybe she and Theo could work. Somehow. They already did on a carnal level, and imagine a lifetime of sex like that…

Hmm.

Perhaps it was best not to do that. Or get too carried away. Already excitement and a longing for what could be were drumming through her and scrambling her brain. She had to remain calm.

'Right,' she said, forcing herself to proceed with caution and fervently trying to keep the familiar fuzzy image of a cosy family unit at bay. 'I see. Well. This is rather unexpected.'

'Tell me about it,' he said, his eyes dark and his expression unreadable. 'I should clarify.'

Clarify? Yes. Good idea. 'Please do.'

'What I am about to tell you is highly confidential.'

A shiver ran down her spine as her heart thumped. Could this be because relationships between personnel at his company were discouraged? How thrilling. 'I understand.'

'I am pursuing the acquisition of Double X Enterprises.'

What? Oh. Right. Back to business. Odd. But never mind. His brain was famously nimble and at least it would give her fevered thoughts a respite. 'I'd heard.'

'It's not going as smoothly as I'd hoped,' he said, and she could hear a hint of frustration in his voice. 'To gain a competitive edge I need to acquire something I lack. To put it bluntly, a partner.'

Kate frowned. What on earth was he talking about? Why would he need a partner to seal the deal? From what she knew about him he was a lone wolf all the way. He didn't do partners. Besides, how could *she* help? She was way down the corporate food chain. And although she supposed it was flattering that he considered her a sounding board, what did any of this have to do with her and the pregnancy and his absurd yet intriguing offer of marriage?

'Would you like me to help you find one?' she asked, more than slightly bewildered.

'What? No. As I said, I want you to fill the role.'

She stared at him, still none the wiser. 'I'm afraid you've lost me.'

'I need a partner, preferably a fiancée,' he said flatly, his patience obviously stretched to the limit by her complete inability to grasp what he was getting at. 'Someone to accompany me to dinner from time to time. The odd gala or party. Lunch. Drinks.'

Huh?

'Daniel Bridgeman, the CEO of Double X Enterprises, values such a relationship so I need to provide him with one. For appearances' sake. Temporarily. Until he signs on the dotted line.'

Oh.

Oh.

As the true meaning of what he was after sank in Kate felt as if she'd been thumped in the gut. Her throat tightened and her ears began to buzz and a hot flush rocketed through her.

'Your company is all I require, Kate,' Theo continued, evidently unaware of the devastation he was beginning to wreak on her. 'Your time and your acting skills. Nothing more. Apart from complete discretion, naturally. I anticipate it'll take a fortnight. A month at the most. I'll supply you with the necessary wardrobe and a campaign plan. All you have to do is turn up when and where I tell you, pat your abdomen and smile.'

He stopped and looked at her, clearly waiting for a response, but Kate couldn't speak for the pounding of her head and the blurring of her vision. Oh, she was an idiot, she thought, swallowing hard to dislodge the knot that had formed there and turning away to blink back the sudden sting in her eyes. Why on earth would someone like Theo be interested in marrying someone like her for real? What had she been thinking? How deluded could she still *be*? They hardly knew each other. All they'd had was a one-time thing. He hadn't changed his mind about her. Why would he?

Of course, it would have saved her a whole lot of trouble if he'd started with the business angle to the marriage proposal in the first place, but obviously it hadn't occurred to him that he needed to. Why would it have when the notion was so laughably inconceivable?

That she'd got the wrong idea was entirely her fault, and it wasn't even the first time. There'd been the occasion that evening in his office when he'd told her she was unique.

For the briefest, headiest of moments she'd thought he'd been paying her a compliment, but all he'd meant was her situation—her virginity. Then, as now, she'd been stupidly filled with a hope that had been swiftly dashed, and she had nobody but herself to blame.

But while she might be naïve and hopeless, one thing was very clear. She was *not* going to be steamrollered into a fake engagement, marriage, whatever, just because it suited him. Self-esteem issues or no self-esteem issues, even she was not going to be used in that way, and there was no way she'd allow their unborn child to become a pawn in its unfortunate father's shady business deals. So she swallowed hard and stamped down on the emotions swirling around inside her.

'It's an interesting proposal,' she said, with a strength that interestingly she didn't even have to dig very deep for.

'A necessary one,' he countered.

'I see.'

'Excellent,' he said, with the flicker of a satisfied smile. 'I'll email you the details in the morning and—'

'No.'

The word was like the crack of a whip and for a moment it hovered in the silence between them.

Theo looked at her, his eyebrows lifting a fraction. 'What do you mean, no?' he said, sounding faintly taken aback, as if he was unused to hearing the word, which, she supposed, he was.

'I'm not going to do it.'

'Why not?'

She stared at him. *Why not?* She didn't know where to begin. 'Well, for one thing,' she said, opting for the least complicated reason, 'it wouldn't work. No one would ever believe it.'

'Of course they would,' he said, failure obviously a concept he was as familiar with as defiance. 'People do not tend to question me.'

Right. 'It's unethical.'

A flicker of irritation flitted across his face at that. 'It's business.'

'So find someone else.'

'I don't want someone else. I want you.'

'Because it's convenient.'

A muscle ticced in his jaw. 'Why else?'

At least he didn't bother denying it. 'Still no.'

His eyes narrowed minutely and the hairs at the back of her neck jumped up. 'Think very carefully, Kate.'

'I am,' she said, determined not to be put off by her body's infuriating response to him. 'Do you honestly believe you can basically say you want to use me and our baby for your own selfish ends, and I'd be all, sure, why not?'

'Yes.'

'Well, you're wrong.'

His jaw tightened. 'You will be handsomely compensated for your efforts.'

'I don't want your money.'

'You were happy enough to take it a month ago.'

At that, Kate went very still, her blood chilling and her heart thudding. Why would he mention that now? 'What are you suggesting?' she asked as a ribbon of trepidation wound through her.

'Nothing,' he said, not taking his eyes off her for a second. 'Merely stating a fact.'

'Then why bring it up?'

'Why not?'

'Because it sounds like a threat.'

'How you interpret it is up to you,' he said smoothly. 'However, there is also your career to consider.'

Her stomach clenched. What did that have to do with

anything? 'My career?' she echoed, the apprehension growing.

'The ICA may take a dim view of what you get up to online, don't you think?'

'But then again, they may not.'

'I imagine it would depend on who filed the complaint and how many favours they were owed.'

'There's no need for anyone else to know.'

'I couldn't agree more.'

And there it was.

The threat she'd heard earlier.

Now not even *thinly* veiled.

As the truth of what he was saying struck her like a blow to the head Kate went from icy cold to boiling hot, numb incredulity giving way to a burning deluge of emotion.

The *bastard*.

The complete and utter rat.

How could she ever have thought he wasn't all bad? He was just as cold and heartless as she'd originally believed. She'd heard he'd go to any lengths to get what he wanted, but there was clearly no line he wouldn't cross and no weapon he wouldn't use. He'd taken everything she'd told him that evening in his office, all those deeply personal issues of hers, her troubled adolescence and her worries about her sister, the money, and turned them against her.

How could he *do* that? she wondered, her entire body shaking as the silence thundered between them. How could he stoop so low? Oh, she was *such* a fool to have shared. She should have known she'd come to regret it. If only she hadn't taken his money. If only she'd been stronger. But how could he have insisted she'd owe him nothing and then demand repayment? Had he *no* integrity?

Something inside her withered and died, and she ruthlessly squashed down the surge of disappointment and hurt and who knew what else.

'You bastard,' she said, her voice hoarse with suppressed emotion.

His mouth twisted. 'If only.'

'What you're suggesting is blackmail.'

'That's an ugly word.'

'It's an ugly concept.'

'How this plays out is entirely up to you, Kate,' he said. 'The choice is yours.'

'It's no choice at all and you know it.'

'So we have a deal?'

He made it sound like a question, but it wasn't. He had her in the palm of his hand. She so badly wanted to tell him to go to hell but there was too much at stake. While she might be willing to forfeit her career and even her home to retain the moral high ground and never have anything to do with him ever again, she was *not* risking her sister's well-being. If she didn't comply with his wishes, Theo would withdraw his funding. She was sure of it. Because his word clearly meant nothing.

So fine. She'd accompany him to the odd social event if that was what he wanted. She could dangle off his arm and smile nicely for a month. Now she'd seen a glimpse of the man behind the mask she wouldn't be taken in again. Her guard would remain well and truly up and she would never forget what a low-life jerk he really was.

'We have a deal.'

CHAPTER SEVEN

THE FOLLOWING EVENING, Kate sat at her dressing table, peering into the tiny mirror while she fastened hoops to her earlobes and wishing she were somewhere else. Like Mars. Outwardly, dressed in a gown of green satin, all made up with her hair done, she looked a picture of sophisticated serenity. Inside, she seethed.

Theo had wasted no time in putting his diabolical plan into action. This morning she'd received a brief text informing her that tonight they would be going out to a black-tie function. Half an hour later she'd been summoned to an exclusive store in Knightsbridge that catered for the exceptionally tall, where a personal shopper had revamped her entire wardrobe. She'd then been whisked to a salon and had emerged three hours later with a sleek up-do and a face full of make-up that was way more than she usually wore but at least did a good job of disguising the effects of a sleepless night and continued morning sickness.

While she'd been sitting in the chair with people flitting around and dancing attendance on her it had occurred to her that what the makeover suggested was the height of insult but then she'd expect nothing less from a man who'd coldly and calculatingly used her honesty and her hang-ups to blackmail her.

Twenty-four hours after Theo had delivered his ultimatum she still reeled with the shoddiness of it. For some reason she'd thought he was somehow *more* than his reputation would have her believe. Foolishly, she'd allowed herself to change her mind about him. She didn't know why. The evidence had been flimsy at best, and, with the benefit of hindsight, granting him attributes he clearly didn't have had been a mistake of epic proportions. She couldn't have been more wrong about any of it, and the worst thing was it was her own fault because, while he might have manipulated her, he hadn't exactly tricked her. So not only was the disillusionment hitting her hard, she also felt stupid and naïve and unable to trust her own judgement. Again.

The buzzer sounded, shattering the quiet, and Kate jumped, the simmering anger and resentment she continued to feel towards Theo flaring up deep inside her. It was show-time—but, oh, how tempted she was to lift the window, lean out and tell him to get lost. But she didn't dare risk it. She didn't trust him one little bit. Not now.

There was no need to hurry, though, was there? Keeping him waiting another five minutes might be petty, but it would also be deeply, *deeply* satisfying. So Kate calmly redid her lipstick and gave her neck another squirt of scent. When the buzzer went again, she ignored it in favour of checking her phone for messages and emails before popping it in her bag.

It was only after the third, longer, more jabbing buzz that she figured if she didn't want him storming up here and dragging her out she'd better get going. So she slipped on her shoes, locked up and went downstairs. At the end of the hall, she took a deep breath and pulled her shoulders back, and opened the front door to see Theo leaning against a car, his hands thrust into the pockets of his trousers, looking decidedly unimpressed. Which was extremely pleasing and, frankly, only fair given his lousy treatment of her.

What *wasn't* fair, though, she thought, the sharp stab of triumph fading beneath an unwelcome surge of heat and an unforgivable thump of desire as she walked towards him, was how he could look so devastatingly handsome when he was so horribly, mercilessly *awful*. His tuxedo fitted him as if he'd been stitched into it. The snowy white of his shirt highlighted the strength of his jaw and the chiselled perfection of his features. Smouldering and dangerous were the adjectives that sprang to mind and, oh, great, now she was being bombarded with images of all the things he'd once done to her.

'You're late,' he said curtly, pushing himself off the car and turning to open the rear passenger door.

Kate snapped out of her trance and inwardly bristled at the icy annoyance in his tone. 'I nearly didn't come down at all.'

'We have a deal.'

'I know,' she said before adding pointedly, 'and I, for one, don't go back on my word.'

Wrenching her gaze from his, which was annoyingly harder than it ought to be, she slid into the car with as much elegance as she could manage and settled back against the soft leather seat. A minute later Theo joined her, closing the door behind him with a soft thud, and instantly it felt as if all the oxygen had been sucked out of the air. To her horror, her breath caught in her throat and her entire body hummed with a dizzying sort of awareness. Her dress, which had fitted perfectly a moment ago, suddenly seemed impossibly tight. As he shifted on the seat she realised he was too big, too near, and he smelled too good. She wanted to climb into his lap and get all up close and personal, and see if she couldn't do something about the tired lines that fanned out from his eyes and bracketed his mouth, which was simply insane when she loathed him with every ounce of her being.

Channelling the outrage that had dominated her emotions recently, Kate kept to her side and made herself look out of her window, but it didn't block the heat of his gaze on her or the corresponding flip of her stomach.

'You look stunning.'

'Thank you,' she said, refusing to acknowledge the brief stab of pleasure she felt at his compliment.

'How have you been?'

'Busy.'

'Shopping?'

'Among other things.'

'You maxed out my credit card.'

'This body costs a lot to clothe well,' she said, 'and all this,' she added, shooting him a quick glance and waving a hand around her face and hair, 'comes at a price.'

'It was worth every penny.'

She was *not* going to respond to that. 'Yes, well, you did say the budget was unlimited,' she said. 'And given how I ended up in this particular situation, it seemed the least you could do to make amends.'

'Did it work?'

'No.'

'Unusual.'

'In what way?'

'Money tends to fix most problems.'

'But not all?'

A pause. A flash of bleakness in his eyes. 'No,' he said with a faint frown. 'Not all.'

He was obviously thinking of the deal and the obstructive Mr Bridgeman, and Kate mentally high-fived the man she'd never met but who had to be the only person on the planet to defy him.

'So what's this evening about, then?' she asked, abandoning the view of the heavy traffic of central London through which they were inching, and shifting to bestow on him her iciest glare.

'It's a fundraiser.'

'What for?'

'A charity that helps young entrepreneurs who haven't had the easiest start in life.'

'Like you?'

'How would that be like me?'

The look that accompanied his response was dark and

forbidding, and she would have wondered what had caused the sudden tension radiating off him had she been remotely interested in digging deeper. 'Well, you started in business at a young age, didn't you? No handy trust fund or Oxbridge education.'

The tension eased. 'Yes.'

'A worthy cause.'

'Very.'

'Who's going to be there?'

'Business acquaintances mainly.'

But no friends. *How* unsurprising. 'The CEO you're trying to sweeten?'

'No. He's away.'

Oh. 'Doesn't that rather defeat the object of the exercise?'

'Not at all. Tonight is about building a narrative and spreading your news.'

Her news, she noted. Not *their* news. Right now she was useful to him, the means to an end, but once it was done she'd be on her own and she must never forget it. 'Why are you so keen to impress him?'

'I want his business.'

'I know, but why doesn't he want to sell it to you?'

'He has concerns.'

'About what?'

'My personality,' he said with a faint grimace that she found enormously satisfying. 'My integrity.'

Really? Hah. There were clearly no flies on this Mr Bridgeman. 'He knows you well.'

'We've never met.'

'Then he disapproves of your reputation.'

'Apparently so,' he said, as if he found it impossible to believe that anyone would dare.

'Astounding.'

'Quite.'

'Don't you think faking an engagement to facilitate a business deal falls somewhat short of the integrity you're keen on showing him you have?'

His jaw tightened and his expression hardened. 'Once the papers are signed it won't matter.'

Did he really mean that? He must. After all, she had direct experience how single-minded and immovable he could be when he wanted something, didn't she? 'How long do you think it's going to take?'

'As long as is necessary.'

'What if the deal never comes off?'

'That's not going to happen.'

Hmm. 'Yes, well, while your confidence is impressive,' she said, managing to inject a pleasing note of disdain into her voice, 'I'd be happier if we put a time limit on things.'

He arched one dark eyebrow. 'Conditions, Kate?'

'It's a fair one, you have to admit.'

'You're in no position to negotiate.'

Damn. He had her there. 'So that's a no?'

'That's very much a no.'

Then she'd better put her back into this ridiculous farce so that Daniel Bridgeman sold Theo his company asap and she could get on with her life. 'I have another one,' she said coolly. 'One that's not as easy to dismiss.'

'Oh?'

'I might have agreed to this little charade, fake engagement, whatever, but I do not consent to kissing or inappropriate touching or anything else like it.'

For a moment Theo didn't respond. Instead, his gaze dropped to her mouth and for some reason the temperature inside the car rocketed. Her head spun and her mouth went dry and an unforgivable punch of lust hit her in the gut.

'I wasn't aware I'd asked you to,' he said, sounding so in control, so uninterested, she envied him.

'Just making sure.'

'I'll keep it in mind.'

And she ought to keep in mind the reason she was here—the blackmail. 'So my job is to enhance your personality and show Mr Bridgeman your softer side?' she said, pulling herself together and focusing.

'Yes.'

'A Herculean task when you don't have one.'

'I have no doubt you are up to the challenge.'

'Aren't you concerned I might muck it up?'

'Why would you do that?'

'I've never had a boyfriend, let alone a fiancé.'

'You're a quick learner,' he said, something about his tone heating her blood and melting her stomach despite her resolve to remain cool and aloof. 'You'll soon pick it up.'

Kate thought of glaciers and straightened her spine. 'How do you know I'm not planning to sabotage things in revenge for the way you blackmailed me into this?'

'Are you?'

'I might be.'

'I wouldn't,' he said mildly, although she could hear his warning loud and clear.

'If only I still had my virginity to sell,' she said wistfully, half meaning it.

'Regrets?'

'Do you care either way?'

Something flitted across his expression, but it was gone before she could even try and identify it. 'No.'

'No, well, why would you?' she said, feeling the tiniest bit stung despite herself. 'When you own the world, I guess you don't need to worry so much about other people's feelings.'

'I guess not,' he agreed impassively.

'So brusque,' she said with a shake of her head. 'So serious. So *steely*.'

'Is that a problem?'

'Not particularly, although I guess it depends on your perspective. It seems to me, though, that a real girlfriend might expect the occasional smile. A fiancée definitely would, I should think.'

'How would you know?'

Ooh, that was harsh. But fair, she grudgingly had to admit. 'Well, what do *you* think?'

'Me? I have no idea.'

She stared at him, surprise momentarily nudging everything else out of the way. 'None?'

'None.'

'But you must have had a girlfriend.'

'Must I?'

'Haven't you? *Ever?*'

'I don't have the time.'

Oh, dear.

She'd assumed at least Theo would know what he was doing, but it now seemed as though it was a case of the blind leading the blind. How had he thought this approach would ever work? Was he nuts?

'Right,' she said, resenting him even more for putting her in this position. 'Well. Let's hope I'm not the only one who's a quick learner.'

Four hours later, having escaped to the bathroom after interminable drinks, a sumptuous six-course dinner and an auction of promises during which the extravagant luxury of the lots and preposterous figures whizzing around had blown her mind, Kate was exhausted. Keeping a smile fixed to her face and gazing at Theo in adoration when all she wanted was to stab him with a hairpin was draining.

He was not playing fair. Having no intention of giving him any reason to think she wasn't doing her best and therefore renege on his side of the bargain, she had thrown herself into her role. Theo, on the other hand, had not. He'd introduced her as his pregnant fiancée, and remained by her side, but that was pretty much it. He hadn't smiled at her. He'd barely even looked at her. She'd had to do all the work, and once tonight was over they were very definitely going to be having words.

Unexpectedly, however, there had been *some* positives to the evening. After the initial flurry of interest, Kate had become pretty much invisible, which was a novelty. Everyone was far more interested in the man at her side. His appearance in public was apparently something of a rarity, and, despite his giving off such chilly vibes he could cause frostbite, people couldn't get enough of him. The awe he was held in and the resultant fawning she witnessed made her stomach turn, but at least it meant she could observe instead of being observed for once.

And then there was the fact that he stood nearly a head above her. She had no need to slouch or try and make herself smaller. She could pull her shoulders back and hold herself straight and amazingly she still only just reached his chin. She might tower over everyone else but at Theo's side, for the first time ever, she felt normal. So normal, in fact, that next time they went out she might even wear a pair of the heels she hadn't been able to resist adding to the pile of new clothing she'd accumulated this morning.

Of course there'd also been some negatives, because unfortunately her body still hadn't got the memo about what a despicable human being Theo was. Her body kept wanting to take advantage of the fake engagement and, well, *snuggle*. So much so that she found herself actually regretting the no kissing and no contact condition of hers, which was wrong on practically every level there was.

At least the evening was coming to an end. She couldn't wait to get home and collapse into bed. She had the feeling that the continued attraction she felt, so obviously now one-sided, was going to become increasingly hard to handle, and she could only hope that Daniel Bridgeman got wind of the 'engagement', was fooled into thinking Theo's unfortunate personality had undergone a one-hundred-and-eighty-degree change, and announced his plan to go ahead with the deal just as soon as was humanly possible.

What she *couldn't* do was stay in here, much as she wouldn't mind taking a quick nap, because the door to the bathroom had just opened and people had come in, no doubt wishing to use the stall she was occupying.

Fighting a yawn and rolling her head to ease the kinks in her neck, Kate pulled herself together. She stood up and smoothed her dress, and was just about to slide the lock when something about the conversation on the other side of the door made her go very still.

'Yes, but who *is* she?' she heard one woman ask, the incredulity in her voice as clear as a bell.

'Apparently she works for him.'

'Theo Knox dipping his nib in the company ink? That doesn't sound like him.'

'I agree. But, well, it wouldn't be the first time a woman has trapped a man into marriage by getting pregnant, would it?'

'I guess not.'

'So, Miss Cassidy, what was it about gorgeous billionaire Theo Knox that first caught your eye?'

'Why, his sparkling personality, of course.'

Catty laughter.

A pause.

What sounded like a rummage in a handbag.

Then, 'No ring, I noticed.'

'I noticed that, too.'

'And he's not exactly *doting*, is he?'

'Well, would you be? Have you seen the size of her? She's huge.'

'I *know*.'

'Do you really think the baby's his?'

'No idea. Pass me a tissue, would you?'

The conversation stopped and then came the vague sounds of make-up being reapplied but Kate barely registered any of it. Her head was spinning, her heart was racing and she was trembling from head to toe. Every word had slammed into her, leaving her battered and bruised and sore. She didn't know why. Logically, they should not affect her. Her engagement to Theo was fake. She wasn't a gold-digger. She most certainly didn't want him to dote.

But they did. For some reason, they did. They sliced right through her and ripped her open, brutally exposing her innermost vulnerabilities and stabbing straight at them. When would she stop being a freak show? When would someone want her for real? What had she ever done to deserve any of this?

Her eyes stung and her throat tightened—blasted hormones—but she summoned up strength from somewhere deep inside and took a long, steadying breath, because *she* knew the truth. The gossip and these women meant nothing. And yes, she was abnormally tall, but there wasn't anything she could do about it, so she could either crumple in a heap of self-pity or let it go, and, frankly, this dress was too gorgeous to ruin.

Mind made up, she briefly looked up at the ceiling and blinked rapidly to dispel the threat of tears, then pulled her shoulders back and set her jaw. Clinging onto her courage as if her life depended on it, she opened the door, walked to a basin to wash her hands and, with a wide beam at the two bitchy women who stared at her in dawning shock and horror, sailed out.

CHAPTER EIGHT

BACK AT THE table that Kate had left fifteen minutes ago, Theo rolled a tumbler of thirty-year-old single malt between his fingers and tuned out of the conversation going on around him to run a quick assessment of the evening. Socialising was not his forte. He loathed small talk and sycophancy as much as he abhorred the idea of the press poking into his background and his personal life. However, things had gone well tonight, and he had no doubt that the news of his newly altered civil status would soon reach the right ears.

Despite her vague threat to sabotage his plans, Kate had embraced the role of fiancée admirably, although he could have done with fewer of her dazzling smiles and the occasional touches to his arm. Each of the former momentarily blinded him and each of the latter sent stabs of electricity shooting through him.

His irritatingly intense response to her was the only fly in tonight's ointment, and would have been a whole lot easier to ignore if he weren't so constantly aware of her. When she'd emerged from her building earlier, wrapped in green satin and looking so spectacularly sexy he'd gone as hard as granite, his gut instinct had been to grab her hand and take her back upstairs. In the car, which he'd always considered roomy, he'd had to fight for air. Her understandable spikiness, which ought to have doused the desire rocketing through him, had only intensified it.

But he'd held it together then and he was holding it together now. No one had any inkling of the battle that had been raging inside him all evening, and it would stay that way. Even if Kate hadn't imposed that no kissing, no inappropriate touching condition on their relationship, which now, perversely, was all he could think about, there was too much at stake to crack. He could not, and would not, concede even a millimetre of ground to anyone, let alone a woman who had once rendered him so unacceptably weak. Nevertheless, the tension gripping him was draining, and the minute Kate returned they'd leave. He'd drop her home and initiate the next step in the plan because, now, this evening, their work was done.

And here she was, he thought with a familiar bolt of heat, his gaze instinctively finding her as she wove sinuously between the tables towards him. Beneath the low, warm light of the chandeliers, she shimmered. Her hair gleamed and her skin glowed and the overall effect was irritatingly dazzling. But as she drew nearer, something struck him as wrong. The rest of her might be glowing but her face was pale. Her smile was too tight and no amount of smoky eye make-up could mask the fact that her eyes were overly bright.

Without even thinking to question why any of this was relevant, Theo abandoned his drink and got to his feet. He strode over to intercept her and took her elbow to draw her to one side, leading her through the French doors that opened onto the torch-lit terrace and into the warm jasmine-scented shadows. To his alarm, she didn't protest.

'What's the matter?' he said, noting the taut rigidity of her body and wondering whether it had anything to do with the pregnancy he was finding unexpectedly difficult to ignore.

She swallowed hard and stared at the ground an inch to his right. 'Are we done here?' she said, her voice strangely hoarse. 'Because I'd like to leave.'

Theo frowned and thrust his hands in the pockets of his trousers. 'Are you all right?'

'Of course.'

'Tired?'

'I'm always tired.'

'So what's different?'

'It's not important.'

Frustration speared through him. How could he help if he didn't know what was wrong? 'Anything that might affect what I'm trying to achieve here is important.'

'Ah, yes,' she said with a bitterness he found he didn't like. 'It wouldn't do to forget that.'

'What happened?'

'Nothing happened.'

'Tell me.'

'Okay, fine,' she said, sighing in exasperation as she *finally* looked at him. 'We're fooling no one with this whole fake engagement thing, Theo.'

'Oh?' he said, the hurt in her eyes that she was trying so hard to hide hitting him in the gut and for some reason knocking him for six.

'Apparently I'm a gold-digger who's played the oldest trick in the book and trapped you into marriage by deliberately getting pregnant.'

What the hell? 'According to who?'

'Some women I overheard in the bathroom.'

'I see.'

'There's no other possible explanation because someone like you would never see anything in someone like me.'

Wouldn't he?

'I did warn you,' she added. 'And they do have a point.'

No, they didn't. 'What are you talking about?'

'The glowering, Theo.'

He frowned. 'The what?'

'You've been glowering at me all evening. I've been working my socks off and you just, well, *haven't*. Aren't you supposed to at least be *pretending* you're interested in me?'

Pretending was the trouble, he thought grimly. He was

too interested. If he smiled at her, if he touched her anywhere other than the elbow, he might not be able to stop and, quite apart from the unacceptable lack of control that would incur, he would *not* breach her no kissing, no contact rule.

'If you're not going to meet me at least halfway,' she continued, 'you could do the decent thing and release me from this deal. There has to be another way. You could just let me go.'

There wasn't another way. And let her go? For myriad reasons he didn't care to analyse, that was not an option. But neither was this state of affairs because, despite her attempts to brush off what she'd heard in the bathroom, it had clearly upset her and he wasn't having that.

'I have a better idea,' he muttered, taking her elbow again, wheeling her around and marching her back into the ballroom before she could protest. He came to a halt in the middle of the room, amidst the well-heeled, well-oiled guests milling about, and let her go. 'Where are they?'

'Where are who?'

'The women you overheard.'

'Oh.'

With a slight frown of concentration Kate scanned the room while Theo felt his displeasure rapidly morphing into anger.

'The woman in purple sitting over there,' she said after a moment, nodding in the direction of a table in the far corner, 'and the woman in red next to her.'

He knew both and he'd have expected better. Too bad. He strode across the room and stopped at table twelve. 'Samantha,' he said icily, looking down at the owner of the PR company he used.

'Theo,' Samantha simpered while batting her eyelashes up at him. 'So lovely to see you out. I was wondering if we might get together at some point to discuss—'

'The Knox Group no longer requires your services.'

In the moment of silence that followed, Samantha's eyes widened and her smile faltered. 'I'm sorry,' she said, giving her head a quick shake as if she'd misheard. 'What did you say?'

'Your contract expires at the end of the month,' he continued icily. 'It will not be renewed.'

'Oh, but—' she spluttered, turning pink. 'I mean… You can't do that.'

'I can.' He snapped his gaze to the brunette in the red dress who was sitting open-mouthed beside her. 'And you— Rebecca, isn't it? Stand down as chair or I'll find another charity to support.'

'Wh-what?' managed Rebecca, who, now he thought about it, was about as effective in her role as a wet dishcloth.

'You heard,' he said brutally. 'Do it. By nine a.m. tomorrow. And the next time either of you feels like gossiping about my fiancée, don't.'

If only Theo hadn't leapt to her defence like that, thought Kate, tossing and turning in bed that night as the memory of it circled around in her head and an unwelcome, unshakeable fuzzy warmth enveloped her.

She couldn't remember the last time someone had stood up for her, and the way he'd gone about it… The energy that had suddenly poured off him, the take-no-prisoners attitude of his and the sense of protectiveness… It was dangerously attractive and all too appealing to a certain someone who was starved of attention and achingly lonely. So appealing, in fact, that when they'd pulled up outside her building after a tautly silent journey, she'd inexplicably found herself wanting to ask him in for coffee, and maybe even more than that, which would have been unwise to say the least.

The trouble was, what he'd done made him so much harder to hate, and she needed to hate him because if she didn't, she could well end up liking him, and then where would she be? At the top of a very slippery slope that plummeted from the dizzying heights of excitement and hope to the miserable depths of disappointment and heartbreak, that was where.

But she had no intention of venturing anywhere near that slide so she could not allow his brief moment of chivalry detract from the rest of his lousy personality. She had to focus on the blackmail and the ruthlessness and not the feel of his hand on her elbow that burned her like a brand and the mesmerising eyes, dark with seething outrage and grim determination on her behalf.

She also had to accept that realistically there'd be many more naysayers like Samantha and Rebecca out there. Who knew what the press would make of the engagement? Of her? And then there were her colleagues. Her sister. How were they going to react?

She had no idea about any of it, but one thing was certain. If she had any hope at all of surviving the next few weeks, with whatever Theo or circumstances threw at her, ice-cool control and steely self-possession were the way to do it.

By lunchtime the following day, Theo had fielded more messages of congratulations than his limited patience could take, and the anger that had led to the instant dismissal of two significant business partners had swelled to fury.

How dared they? was the thought that kept ricocheting around his head during the three meetings he'd already held and wouldn't go away. How dared *anyone* attack what was his? Even temporarily his. So far the press had reported the facts without opinion, but if he ever heard *anything* in the way of sly accusation and measly insinuation again more heads would roll. Big heads. The biggest there were, in fact.

That he hadn't exactly behaved in an exemplary fashion himself was not on his conscience. Coercing Kate into a fake engagement by firing threats at her wasn't the most ruthless thing he'd done in pursuit of a goal, and what was at stake outweighed everything else.

What *did* trouble his conscience, however, was that she'd been right about his lack of input last night. He could have done better at playing the besotted lover despite having zero experience in the field, and if he hadn't been so wrapped up in frustration, he would have. It infuriated him now that he'd allowed himself to get so distracted, to lose sight of what was important.

However, it wasn't too late to rectify the situation. News of their engagement was out and in need of consolidation and that was precisely what he was going to do. In fact, he'd already taken steps, and by the time he was done no one would have any doubt whatsoever about its veracity.

Picking up the phone, Theo dialled the extension for the accounts department. 'Put me through to Kate Cassidy,' he snapped when his call was answered.

'I'm sorry, sir, she no longer works here.'

He scowled. What the hell? 'Why not?'

'She resigned this morning and was put on immediate gardening leave.'

'Where did she go?'

'Home, I believe, sir.'

'Thank you.'

Theo hung up, grabbed his keys, wallet, phone and the box he'd picked up this morning, and stalked out. As the lift whizzed him down to the garage he rang her mobile but the call went straight to voicemail. He left a curt message and got in his car, irritation pummelling through him as he negotiated his way through heavy London traffic. Without warning, Kate had gone off script and he didn't like it. Unpredictability led to confusion, which led to chaos, and he was not having his plans derailed by anyone or anything.

Half an hour later, he parked outside Kate's building, leapt up the five steps to her front door and pressed the buzzer for her flat.

'Hello?' came the tinny response an exasperating thirty seconds later.

'Kate, it's Theo. Let me in.'

There was a moment's silence and he thought grimly that she'd better not be deliberately keeping him waiting as she had done last night, because this afternoon he was in no mood for games.

'First floor on the right,' she said eventually and he let out the breath he hadn't even realised he'd been holding.

The door clicked and in he went. He took the stairs two at a time and swung to the right and there she was, standing in the doorway to her flat, still in her work clothes although barefoot. Was she pleased to see him? Surprised? Annoyed? He couldn't tell. Her expression was giving him nothing, which was fine because what she thought of him turning up like this was of zero importance. He just wanted her back in line.

'What are you doing here?' she asked coolly, as if totally unaware of the disruption she'd caused.

'What are *you* doing here?' he countered.

'I resigned.'

'I heard.'

She raised her eyebrows. 'So?'

'May I come in?'

She frowned for a second, as if debating whether to let him into her space, and then shrugged, as if it didn't matter either way. 'Sure,' she said, turning her back on him and padding into her flat.

Ignoring the inexplicable irritation he felt at her indifference, he followed, automatically assessing the space as he did so. Bathroom on the left. Two bedrooms on the right. Compact open-plan kitchen, dining, living room at the end, flooded with light that poured in through two huge sash windows.

'Nice place,' he muttered. But on the small side. How was that going to work when the baby came along? he wondered before reminding himself sharply that it was none of his business and he couldn't care less.

'Thanks.' She walked into the kitchen and shot him a glance over her shoulder. 'Tea?'

'No.'

'So what do you want, Theo?' she asked as she filled the kettle with water and switched it on.

'I want to know why you resigned.'

'My situation was…untenable.'

Damn, he knew it. He flexed his hands. 'What did they say?'

'What did who say?'

'Anyone. Give me names.'

'No one said anything. It just felt awkward what with you and me and—' she waved a hand in the direction of her abdomen '—this. You own the company. Beyond congratulations, my colleagues didn't know what to say. And in all honesty I couldn't see it getting easier. So I resigned.'

His jaw clenched. 'I see,' he said, dismissing the jab at his conscience when the sacrifices she was having to make because of him inconveniently struck. 'Do you want another job?'

'At some point.'

'I have contacts. If you want one, you'll have one.'

'Thank you,' she said with a chilly smile that didn't reach her eyes. 'But so do I.'

Of course she did, he thought as the kettle pinged and she poured the water into a mug and stirred it. She didn't need his help. But she'd have it anyway. 'Whatever decision you choose to make,' he said, 'I will ensure that you're financially secure. Both of you.' That much he could do. 'I'll set up a fund.'

'That won't be necessary.'

Too bad. 'Nevertheless, it'll be there.'

'But you won't.'

'No.'

'Just out of curiosity, why not?'

Well, *that* was a question he wasn't going to answer with the truth. 'There is no space in my life for a child,' he said, instantly crushing the brief, sudden surge of denial.

'You could make some.'

'No. I couldn't.'

'That's a shame.'

Not a shame. A necessity. 'That's reality.'

'Right,' she said, taking a sip of tea and setting the mug back down on the counter. 'So was there anything else?'

'There was one more thing.' He dug around in his pocket and pulled out the small blue velvet box he'd brought with him. 'This should help dispel any doubts people may have about us.'

For a moment she just looked at the box in silence. And then she stepped towards him and took it from him, her fingers brushing his and her proximity doing odd things to his equilibrium.

When she opened it, her eyes went wide and she let out a soft gasp that would have instantly transported him back to that evening in his office if he let it. 'Wow.'

'Do you like it?'

'Who wouldn't? Is it real?'

'Yes.'

She frowned. 'Borrowed?'

'No.'

'It's too much,' she said with a faint shake of her head as she closed the box and handed it back.

Theo felt the faint sting of something undefinable and

ignored it. 'Just wear it,' he said sharply. 'It's important. For the narrative.'

'Okay, fine,' she said with a careless shrug that some-how stung even more. 'But only when we're out together.'

'I don't mind what you do when you're on your own,' he said. 'As long as you remember your role when we're out in public.'

'I'm unlikely to forget with this on my finger.'

As was he. Which was, after all, the point. 'And speak-ing of which,' he said, dismissing as ridiculous the inexpli-cable urge to demand she put it on now, 'tomorrow night we're going to the opening of a new wing at the National Gallery that my company has funded. And this time, Kate, don't keep me waiting.'

A fortnight later, Kate eased off her shoes after yet another function, and with a grateful sigh flopped onto her bed.

To call the last two weeks a whirlwind of activity was an understatement. She'd attended eight events, one ante-natal appointment and a hospital scan. She'd been to see her sister to explain the engagement and the pregnancy as best she could without going into detail, and had been relieved when Milly had accepted without question that she was going to be an aunt. In fact, her sister had been delighted, had immediately announced that she was going to take up knitting. Their WhatsApp chat channel was now filled with pictures of tiny bootees, hats and cardigans in various stages of progress and Kate's heart squeezed at every one.

She'd also been getting used to not going into work. Being at home on a weekday felt very odd; however, she hadn't really had any option. Once the news of her engage-ment had broken, her astonished colleagues had initially swooned but then backed off, as if any office gossip might reach Theo's ears at which point they could all well be fired.

She'd come to the swift conclusion that things would only get worse and had promptly handed in her notice, after which her entire floor had seemed to breathe a sigh of relief.

What she'd do about work in the future she had no idea. Discriminatory or not, she couldn't see a prospective employer jumping for joy about her condition. The hole in her bank account was still pretty big and any maternity benefit she might receive would hardly fill it. But she'd figure something out, maybe by reigniting the freelance bookkeeping she'd started, because she had no intention of ever touching Theo's money.

That he was going to set up a fund as he'd promised she had no doubt. Not so long ago he'd told her that there was barely a problem that couldn't be solved by throwing money at it and he clearly considered both her and their baby just such a problem.

As she sat up, it struck Kate once again that the way Theo had no interest in their child was strange. Weren't men, especially the alpha males among them, pre-programmed to instantly claim possession of their offspring, as a sign of their supremacy or virility or continuation of the bloodline or something? Wasn't it in some way evolutionary?

Well, Theo was as alpha and male as they came, yet he appeared to buck the trend. It was as if he was determined to distance himself from the very idea of it, and she couldn't help wondering why. Was it simply inconvenient? An obstacle en route to global domination? Was he really just too busy? Or did he genuinely not want a baby? She remembered thinking at one point, when she'd first delivered the news, that she'd caught a glimpse of pure terror in his eyes, but she must have been mistaken because she'd never met anyone less afraid of anything, so what was it?

However much it intrigued her, she could hardly ask. She'd already tried once, the afternoon he'd pitched up at her flat and filled her space with his dominating, disturbing presence, and had been firmly shut down. He didn't do personal and he didn't share anything other than the most superficial of information. The conversations they'd had over the last fortnight through necessity had been desultory at best, and, really, she didn't need to know.

To her surprise, though, he *had* taken on board her comments about his lack of participation when it came to faking their engagement. At the events they'd recently attended, he'd left no one in any doubt about his supposed intentions towards her. He no longer glowered in her direction. He even managed the occasional smile that flipped her stomach every time he bestowed it on her. He focused wholly on her, which was heady stuff, and ensured the ring he'd given her did not go unnoticed. And even though she knew it was all for show, that she shouldn't feel a million dollars when she was with him, her poor battered self-esteem lapped it up.

But she had to remember that this whole thing was nothing more than an elaborate charade, that the attention Theo paid her wasn't real, she told herself for the billionth time as she levered herself off the bed and unzipped her dress. He continued to show no remorse, no regret for the way he'd blackmailed her, and she couldn't fall again into the trap of crediting him with traits he didn't have. She had to stop drifting off into daydreams where every touch, every smile, was real. And she had to stop secretly putting the ring on at home, turning her hand this way and that so the beautiful stone caught the light and cast dancing sparkles on her walls, and pretending she had a man who loved her. The wave of longing she felt every time she succumbed to temptation did her no good at all.

Oh, how she wished she'd insisted on a time limit. There'd still been no word for Daniel Bridgeman and she didn't know how much longer she could keep it up. The pressure was immense. The battle between her head and her body was exhausting. And what was taking so long anyway? Their appearances in public had been noted, although thankfully with considerably less vitriol than experience had warned her to fear, and their performance had been entirely credible.

What if Mr Bridgeman had no intention of ever signing? Would she be locked into this absurd charade until Theo decided to release her? How would she bear it? She should never have agreed to it in the first place. She should have been tougher. She should have called his bluff and—

Her phone buzzed and she turned from the wardrobe where she was hanging the dress to reach down to fish it out of the evening bag that lay on the bed.

A message flashed up on the screen. From Theo.

Where was she to be paraded next? A charity ball? Business drinks?

No.

Italy, according to the text. On Friday. For the weekend. Because Daniel Bridgeman had finally, at long flipping last, been in touch.

CHAPTER NINE

'I CAN SEE why you like to travel by private jet,' said Kate, yanking Theo's attention from the document he'd been perusing for the past ten minutes with zero idea of its contents. 'I haven't bashed my knees once. It's heavenly.'

No, he thought grimly, watching her settle on the sofa as the plane climbed to thirty thousand feet and stretch her endless legs out. What was heavenly was the way she looked. And smelled. All the damn time.

Today she was wearing a pair of wide silky white trousers that clung to her legs whenever she moved and a blue top that matched her eyes. She looked fresh and lovely and she was immensely distracting. And even though he ought to be used to it after two weeks of outfit after incredible outfit and enforced proximity, he wasn't, because everything about her seemed to demand attention, whether she was with him or not, which was plain ridiculous.

His decision to give their fake engagement a hundred per cent had undoubtedly been the right one, but that didn't mean it had been easy. Keeping Kate's no kissing, no inappropriate contact condition at the forefront of his mind had required more strength than he could have possibly imagined. Every time he touched her elbow or her back, he wound up wanting to touch a whole lot more and wondering how far he could go before it became unacceptable. And then there was the ring, blinding him at every opportunity it got. With hindsight he should have gone for something smaller but at the time, for some unfathomable reason, he'd wanted there to be no doubt whatsoever that she was his.

All in all, the last fortnight had been a more gruelling experience than he'd expected, and Daniel Bridgeman's invitation could not have come at a better time. Because while he had no intention of ever giving up on his goal, he'd found himself seriously considering his options on more than one occasion, which was disturbing in itself because once he'd embarked on a course of action he never doubted it.

'I'm delighted you approve,' he said, deciding he might as well give up on work and park the perplexing nature of his response to Kate in order to sit back and admire the view.

'It's hard not to. It's very comfortable.'

'How do you usually travel?'

'I don't much.'

Oh? 'I thought it was one of your hobbies.'

Her eyebrows rose. 'Why would you think that?'

'It was on your profile. Along with music and books.'

'Oh. Right. Yes,' she said after a pause. 'I'm surprised you remember.'

'I remember it all,' he said. 'The pictures in particular.'

She flushed and looked away. 'Ah. Yes. Those.'

'They seemed out of character.'

'I was desperate and had had three glasses of wine.' She gave a slight shrug. 'Not a strategy I can currently deploy, unfortunately.'

'Do you need to?' he asked, wondering for a moment whether she was as unsettled by him as he was by her and finding it an oddly pleasing thought.

'No, of course not,' she said dryly. 'What could possibly be stressful about being blackmailed into a fake engagement?' Which, to his mild disappointment, firmly dispelled *that* idea. 'Anyway, my real hobby is numbers.'

'Numbers?'

She nodded. 'That's partly why I became an accountant. Outside work, I love puzzles and brainteasers and things, and don't get me started on calculus. But I couldn't exactly put that in my profile. Numbers are hardly sexy.'

They were when she was talking about them. Her whole

face lit up and her eyes sparkled. 'What do you like about numbers?' he asked with a baffling desire to expand the topic so he could see her light up some more.

'The reliability of them. They're black and white. They never let you down.' The look she shot him then was pointed. 'You know where you are with numbers.'

'Yet they're easy to manipulate.'

She arched an eyebrow. 'And you'd know all about manipulation, wouldn't you?'

He ruthlessly ignored the flaring of his conscience. 'I'm not going to apologise, Kate.'

'I'd be flabbergasted if you did,' she said. 'So what about you? How do you relax?'

'I don't.'

'Don't you have hobbies?'

'I don't have time.'

'All work and no play…'

'Are you suggesting I'm dull?'

She tilted her head and regarded him, her gaze leaving trails of fire in its wake as it ran over him. 'Dull is not the word I would use to describe you.'

'Then what is?'

'Single-minded. Devious. Merciless. Cold. Calculating. Completely lacking in empathy. Oh, and mercenary.'

The adjectives tripping off her tongue so easily were entirely accurate, yet, oddly, her opinion of him stung. 'Please, don't hold back.'

'You did ask.'

And he wouldn't be making that mistake again. He didn't know why he had. Her assessment of him didn't matter. Her attitude, however, well, that *did*. 'We're going to be under scrutiny this weekend, Kate,' he said deliberately flatly. 'It's in everyone's interest to wrap the deal up as soon as possible, so I suggest you lose the prickliness.'

She levelled him a look and let out a sigh. 'Okay, fine,'

she said with a shrug that made her silk shirt ripple enticingly over her chest. 'I can do that. I can play nice. Anything to expedite the goal.'

'Good.'

'So what happens when we land?'

'We drive to the Villa San Michele.'

'And then?'

'Tonight we're having dinner with the Bridgemans. Tomorrow there are meetings, and in the evening is their anniversary party.' Which he could definitely do without.

'Ah, yes. Fifty years,' she said with a trace of wistfulness he'd never understand in a million years. 'Can you imagine?'

No. He couldn't. He wouldn't. 'Unfortunately it can't be avoided.'

'Did you get them a present?'

'No.' He saw little to celebrate about marriage however long it lasted, quite frankly.

'Don't you think you should?'

'This whole weekend is purely about business. Gifts are not required.'

She looked at him for a moment, as if debating whether to push, but then, to his relief, said, 'It's your show,' and she was right. It was. Not that he had any intention of explaining himself to her. 'And on Sunday?'

'Bridgeman doesn't believe in working on Sundays.'

'Extraordinary.'

'Isn't it?' he said, responding to her faint smile with one of his own before he could prevent it. 'The final meetings will take place on Monday.'

'After which you'll know.'

'Precisely.'

'What's so special about this particular company?'

'It's up for sale.'

'But there must be hundreds of companies up for sale.'

'Not of this size.'

'What are you going to do with it if you get it?'

'*When* I get it,' he corrected, 'the majority of it will be absorbed into the Knox Group and the rest will continue to operate independently.'

'Isn't your company big enough already?'

'No,' he said bluntly. 'Not nearly.'

'What can you possibly have left to prove?'

'Everything.'

She seemed to have nothing to say to that but her eyes didn't leave his. They merely narrowed slightly, as if she were pondering some enormous conundrum, which for some reason made him feel as if he were sitting on knives.

'What?' he asked, irritated by the way his body was instinctively reacting to her scrutiny.

'I was just wondering how on earth you and my brother were ever friends.'

He froze, her words cutting right through his discomfort, obliterating the heat and filling him with icy numbness. 'We weren't. We were acquaintances.'

'Oh? I got the impression you were friends. But I guess acquaintances makes more sense.'

'In what way?'

'Well, you're not at all alike. I mean, Mike was ambitious, sure, but you're on another level entirely. He lacked your killer instinct. He had lines. How on earth did you meet?'

'At the boxing club.'

She flashed him a sudden triumphant smile and for a moment he forgot how to breathe. 'Aha! So you *do* have a hobby.'

'I wouldn't call it a hobby,' he said, willing his thundering pulse to slow. 'More a means of keeping in shape.'

'Are you good at it?'

'Yes.' He'd had plenty of practice.

Her smile turned rueful. 'Mike wasn't.'

'No.'

'Did you box each other?'

'Only once.'

'Who won?'

'No one.'

'How come?'

'I collapsed.'

Her eyes widened. 'What happened?'

'I'd taken a blow to the ribs the week before. I hadn't given it any more thought but then when I was in the ring with Mike, my spleen ruptured. He got me to hospital. He saved my life.' Hence the debt that he should not have taken so long to pay back.

'I had no idea.'

'It wasn't something I wanted publicised.' The incident had rendered him weak, vulnerable, and had his competitors got wind of it they would have pounced within minutes.

'Are you all right now?'

'Yes.' Physically, at least.

'So what happened then?'

'Once I'd recovered we went for a drink. It became a regular thing.'

She nodded as if in understanding. 'An escape.'

'Yes. He was under a lot of stress.'

'I meant for you.'

'*I* have nothing to escape from,' he said, ruthlessly blotting out the great neon sign in his head that was flashing the word 'liar' at him.

Her eyebrows lifted. 'Not even work?'

'Not even that.'

'Hmm. So you knew what was going on with him?'

'Some of it.'

'Me, too.' Her cornflower-blue eyes filled with momentary sadness, and his chest tightened. 'I wish I'd known more, though. But he didn't once complain, not even when he had to leave university to come and look after me and Milly, *and* then find the money to move my sister when it became apparent she wasn't being looked after well.'

'What happened?'

'Nothing that awful. It was mainly little things. Cleanliness. The food. The size of the rooms. And then it became apparent that the staff—not exactly the warmest of people—were quick to medicate. Easier to manage the more unpredictable patients that way, I suppose. Fairview is about as different a place as it's possible to imagine. There's more space, outside as well as inside. The staff care. Milly moved just as soon as we could sort it. She's happy there, and well cared for.'

'She will have whatever she needs, Kate.'

'Thank you.' She paused. Then said with a sigh, 'I never appreciated the stress Mike must have been under. He worked day and night. We shared the day-to-day stuff, but financially he bore full responsibility. When he lost his job I wish he'd said something. He didn't have to carry the burden alone. I don't know how I didn't know, especially since he was living with me. I guess I didn't ask. He said he'd resigned to set up his own business and that he'd given up his flat to put the money into it and I just accepted it. But none of that was true.'

Theo frowned. 'No.'

'I feel so guilty.'

'If anyone is to feel guilty,' he said, unable to let her think she was in any way to blame and suddenly burning up with the need to confess and in some small way to atone for what he'd let happen, 'it's me.'

'Why?'

'His death was partly my fault.'

She stared at him in shock. 'What on earth are you talking about? He had an aneurysm. It was sitting there in his brain like a ticking time bomb. How could that possibly have been your fault?'

'I could have done more to help. To remove the stress. I should have insisted.'

'He had his pride. And he was stubborn.'

'That's no excuse.' And it wasn't because hadn't he already discovered what happened if he turned his back on someone who needed his help whether they wanted it or not? Hadn't his mother been enough? How many more people were to suffer before he learned? Whatever she chose to think he'd robbed Kate and her sister of their brother and he'd never forgive himself. 'I'm sorry.'

'There's really nothing to be sorry for,' she said. 'Truly. Did you know about the loans?'

'No.'

'Neither did I.'

'But I could have done,' he said bleakly. 'I should have done.'

'How?'

'A couple of weeks before he died, Mike mentioned he had something he wanted to discuss. I put him off.' He stopped and frowned, remembering how he'd instinctively kept the man at arm's length despite the huge debt he owed him. 'I regret that.'

'You came to the funeral.'

'It was the least I could do.'

She tilted her head, her gaze practically searing into his. 'Do you remember me suggesting a drink afterwards?'

He frowned. 'No.'

'You took it as a come-on.'

'Did I?'

'You did. And you said you weren't interested. But it wasn't an invitation at all. I just wanted to chat to you about my brother.'

'I apologise,' he muttered, now recalling how Kate's

grief had been too great for his guilt to handle and how in response he'd shut down, operating on automatic. 'It was a tough afternoon.'

'You're telling me.'

'How are you dealing with it?'

She bit her lip. 'I'm getting there. Most days I'm okay, but every now and then it hits me like a bolt from the blue. You'd think I'd be used to it by now. The grief, I mean. It's not as if I'm a stranger to it. I've lost more than most people do in a lifetime. Yet it still gets me right here.' She pressed her hand to her heart and rubbed. 'But there's nothing I can do about it. I can't change anything. So I have to just get on with it.' She tilted her head and regarded him thoughtfully. 'I do think, though, that if he'd lived, Mike would have been a good friend to you.'

The vice that had gripped Theo's chest in response to her suffering tightened. What could he say to that? He could hardly admit that he'd never have let things get that far. That the damage caused by his mother's rejection was irreversible and that the traces of it still affected the way he viewed every single person he met. 'Perhaps.'

'What are your other friends like?'

Non-existent. Which was fine with him. He didn't want or need friends. He was better off alone. Always. More importantly, other people were better off if things were that way. And this conversation was over.

'Quiet,' he said bluntly. 'Unobtrusive. They don't ask questions and they let me get on with my work.'

'Ah. Right,' she said with the flash of a grin that hit him square in the gut. 'Point taken. I'll leave you to it.'

They landed at Linate Airport mid-afternoon and the minute she stepped off the plane, Kate felt as if she could once again breathe, despite the thirty-degree heat.

How hard it had been to focus on her book when her

attention kept wandering, her gaze drifting over to where
Theo was sitting, head down, his brow furrowed in concentration as he worked at his laptop. How hard it had been
not to think about the suite at the back of the plane with its
enormous bed just begging to be rumpled. And then there'd
been the urge to strike up the conversation again, which
had been so insistent that her jaw ached with the effort of
keeping her mouth shut.

Truth be told, she found Theo increasingly intriguing.
Now she'd had an unexpected taste of conversation that
went beyond pleasantries, she wanted more because she
had the feeling there was a lot going on behind that cold,
steely facade. She saw it in the occasional flicker in his
eyes and the way his jaw sometimes tightened.

Despite her best intentions to remain aloof and keep
his ruthlessness at the forefront of her mind like some sort
of shield, she could feel her opinion of him beginning to
soften. She might have called him cold and merciless and
lacking in empathy, but that wasn't all he was. His misplaced guilt over Mike's death and the apology for his behaviour at the funeral had been genuine. Then there was
that hint of humour when he'd effectively told her to shut
up, which was all the more attractive because of its rarity.
And now there was the car that was waiting for them on
the tarmac, a gorgeous bright red convertible, low, sleek
and powerful. Was it at all possible that he'd remembered
what she'd once said about always wanting a nippy little
convertible? What would it mean if he had?

Nothing sensible, she thought, if the warm fuzzy feeling
spreading through her at the mere possibility was anything
to go by. And certainly nothing that merited further analy-
sis. She could not afford to let herself get distracted. She
must not seek rainbows where there were none. She had
to keep control of her wayward imagination and her precarious emotions and focus on the reality of her situation.

'Nice wheels,' she said, watching in admiration as Theo hefted their luggage into the boot as if it weighed nothing.

'It was all that was left,' he said and slammed the boot shut before striding round to the passenger door and opening it.

Oh. Right. Well, that cleared that up. Good. And frankly what did it matter how this car had ended up here? She still got to ride in it. So that annoying stab of disappointment could get lost.

'Lucky me,' she said with a bright, slightly forced smile as she walked towards him. 'No chauffeur?'

'I like to drive,' he said, unhooking his sunglasses from the v of his shirt and putting them on. 'Get in.'

By the time Theo pulled off the road an hour and a half later and drove through a pair of giant iron gates, Kate had come to a number of conclusions.

Firstly, the northern Italian countryside in summer was stunning. It had taken a while to get out of Milan, but once they'd left the suburbs there'd been nothing but lush greenery and an abundance of beautiful wild flowers. Secondly, there was something impossibly sexy about a gorgeous man driving a fast car in the sunshine, with his shirt sleeves rolled up to his elbows and sunglasses on. And thirdly, it turned out she had a thing for competence.

The way Theo handled the powerful car was nothing short of masterful. Unlike many of the other road users, he didn't drive recklessly. In the city he kept his cool when everyone else seemed to be yelling and gesticulating wildly, and on the open road that had brought them to the edge of Lake Como, he stuck more or less to the speed limit and didn't overtake on blind bends.

Safe. That was how she felt with him. Everything he did was calculated. Measured. He liked to be in control and he was careful. Maybe that was why he refused to engage with the pregnancy. Maybe it represented a careless moment that he was in denial about. Or maybe he really just didn't care.

Whatever.

It didn't matter.

She was probably overthinking things anyway.

What *did* matter and what she *ought* to be thinking about was that they were here, and it was time to slip into the role of adoring, snark-free fiancée, which thankfully had become easier with practice.

The long wide gravelled drive was lined with soaring cypress trees and the warm late afternoon air was filled with the sweet scent of jasmine and honeysuckle. When the drive split, Theo took the left fork, and a minute later pulled up outside a surprisingly modest house that was ochre in colour, had petrol-blue shutters at the windows and elaborate iron balconies, and exuded old soft warmth.

While Kate smoothed her windswept hair, Theo climbed out of the car and strode to the boot. 'It should be open,' he said. 'Go on in.'

'Can we?' Kate asked in surprise. 'Oughtn't we wait for our hosts?

'It's the guest house. It's all ours.'

Oh.

Oh, dear.

She hadn't anticipated she and Theo being on their own. In fact she hadn't given their accommodation any thought at all. But clearly she should have because this place didn't look big enough to have two bedrooms and what that might mean she didn't like to think.

In some trepidation, she pushed open the door and stepped inside, the sudden drop in temperature scattering goosebumps all over her skin. The flagstone floor was covered with a series of rugs in terracotta and white. The open-plan space was divided into cooking, dining and sitting zones. At the far end to her right was a huge fireplace. In front of it was a long, comfy-looking sofa and a table stacked with magazines. In the middle was a dining table that seated four, and on the left the kitchen. Off that was a utility room and a shower room, and then, up a wide flight of stone steps, the cool white en-suite bedroom.

Singular.

'Ah, Theo?' said Kate, heading back downstairs to where Theo was coming in with their bags and dumping them just inside the front door.

'What?'

'Bit of a problem…'

'What is it?'

'There's only one bedroom.'

His dark brows snapped together in a deep frown. 'Right.'

'I'm happy to take the sofa.'

'*I'll* take the sofa.'

'You're bigger than me.'

'You're pregnant.'

Ah, so he hadn't forgotten… 'Only just,' she said, not wanting to analyse the giddy pleasure and weird relief she felt at the knowledge.

'It's non-negotiable.'

It was ridiculous. 'We could share the bed.'

His jaw clenched. 'No.'

'We could put pillows down the middle or something.'

'No.'

'It *is* huge.'

'Kate,' said Theo tightly, fast running out of patience if his expression was anything to go by, 'the bed could be the size of Italy and it wouldn't be big enough if you were in it.'

Ooh, ouch.

His words landed on her with the sting of a thousand arrows and she had to fight hard to resist the temptation to curl in on herself. 'There's no need to be rude,' she said, feeling herself flush with mortification and searing disappointment that he thought of her like that.

'What?' he snapped, striding towards her and stopping a foot in front of her, his eyes suddenly blazing. 'No. I mean if we occupy the same bed, wherever you are in it, I will find you. And once I do, I can't guarantee there'll be no inappropriate touching.'

Oh.

Oh…

As his confession sank in Kate reeled, her breath catching in her throat and her head swimming. Was he really saying what she thought he was saying? Apparently he was. Which meant that, contrary to what she'd assumed, the attraction wasn't one-sided. He still wanted her. Intensely, judging by the hot, focused way he was looking at her.

Intriguing.

'I see,' she said huskily.

'Do you?' he said, his eyes dark and glinting. 'I'm not sure you do. But believe me, Kate, you do not want us sharing a bed.'

What if she did?

No. She didn't. She couldn't. Sex again with Theo, although no doubt explosive, would serve no purpose whatsoever. Besides, this whole situation was complicated enough and if she had any sense of self-preservation at all, she'd put it right out of her mind.

'Okay, fine,' she said, determined to stamp out the heat and desire pummelling through her and to regain control of her senses. 'Take the sofa.'

'Wise decision. Dinner's at eight.'

'And in the meantime?'

'You can do what you like,' he said, his expression now shuttered and inscrutable. 'I'm going for a swim.'

CHAPTER TEN

EARLIER, THEO HAD swum to the nearest promontory and back. It had taken him two hours at full pace and it should have exhausted him. It should have wiped out the ever-present lust and the increasingly unbearable edginess. But it hadn't. When Kate had emerged from the bedroom half an hour ago in a simple black shift dress, her hair rippling around her shoulders like a blonde wavy waterfall, all he wanted to do was walk her back into the room, tumble her onto the bed and to hell with dinner.

Of course there'd be only one bedroom in the house. Everything about her, to do with her, was designed to torment him, so the less than ideal sleeping arrangements were par for the course.

What *wasn't* par for the course, what had had him scything through the water as though a pair of great whites were snapping at his feet, was Kate's response to his declaration that he still wanted her. He'd had no intention of telling her, hell, he barely admitted it to himself, but when she'd jumped to the wrong conclusion about why they would not be sharing a bed, she'd deflated right in front of him and he hadn't liked it.

She'd certainly perked up when he'd recklessly corrected her misconception. Her eyes had darkened to indigo and her breath had caught, and he had no doubt if she knew what she'd revealed she'd be appalled. He, on the other hand, had experienced a jolt of surprise, inexplicable relief that he wasn't alone in this and, unbelievably, even hotter, more desperate desire, which meant that this was going to be one very long weekend because while the attraction might be mutual there was no way he was going to do anything about it.

'Drink?'

With Herculean effort, Theo switched his gaze from where Kate was chatting to Elaine Bridgeman over by the window of the elegant drawing room to his host, the man he was here to see and to convince. 'Whisky,' he said, ruthlessly blocking out the sound of Kate's laughter and the threat to his peace of mind she presented as he accepted the drink. 'Thank you. And thank you for the invitation this weekend.'

'It was time,' said Daniel gruffly. 'I've been following recent events with interest. Congratulations on your engagement.'

'Thank you.'

'Kate's very striking.'

'She is,' Theo agreed, resisting the monumental temptation to glance over at her.

'How long have you known her?'

'Not long. Seven weeks.'

'A whirlwind romance.'

Inwardly he recoiled, every cell of his body rejecting the idea, but outwardly he barely moved a muscle. 'Something like that,' he replied evenly.

'She used to work for you.'

'She did.'

'But she resigned recently.'

'Yes.'

'And you're okay with that?'

'Absolutely.'

'Has she got another position lined up?'

Theo felt a flicker of annoyance. He could hear the scepticism in Daniel's voice and he didn't like it one little bit. 'Not yet.'

'Pre-nup?'

'No.'

'Is that wise?'

It was irrelevant. Kate wasn't after his money. She wasn't after anything. Which was exactly how he wanted it. 'It's no one's business but mine.'

'Nevertheless—'

'Daniel.'

The older man looked at him shrewdly. 'Interesting. Well. Good. Glad to hear it. Very glad indeed,' he said, nodding and smiling as if he, Theo, had passed some sort of test. 'It may sound trite,' he added with a fond glance in the direction of his wife and sentimentality in his tone, 'but when you know, you know. I knew the second I laid eyes on Elaine that she was the one for me. We were married within eight weeks and I haven't regretted it for a second.'

It was a good thing Daniel didn't appear to expect a response to that because Theo didn't have one. What he did suddenly have was a churning gut, clammy skin and a thundering pulse, because whatever Daniel might be insinuating, Kate wasn't the one for him. She couldn't be. No one ever would be. She was a temporary fiancée, that was all. They barely knew each other. On Monday, with the deal in the bag, they'd go their separate ways. The all-consuming desire and the worrying sense of impending chaos would finally be gone and he couldn't be more looking forward to it.

'Have you set a date?' said Daniel, briefly yanking Theo out of the dark maelstrom of his thoughts.

'Not yet,' he said. Not ever.

'The pregnancy must be an added complication.'

The pregnancy wasn't anything except a means to an end. 'In some respects.'

'You're a lucky man.'

No, he wasn't. He wasn't lucky at all. Nor could he seem to get a grip. Because now not only did he feel as if he were about to pass out, but an image had slammed into his head, the image of a small child with his dark hair and Kate's blue eyes. No matter how hard he tried to wipe it out, the picture wouldn't budge, and suddenly his entire body prickled as if being stabbed with a hundred daggers.

Daniel continued to talk, but about what Theo had no idea. His host's words and his surroundings faded. His vision blurred. All he could see were the images that were whipping around his head, pushing aside everything else, making it pound and his heart race.

Why couldn't he block them out? he wondered, holding himself still through sheer force of will while inside he felt as if he were falling apart. He'd done so successfully so far. He'd hardly noticed the way Kate kept touching and stroking her abdomen. He'd got more than used to the ring blinking at him and tormenting him by making him wish for things he had no right to wish for and could never have. So what was different about tonight?

The pressure. That was what it had to be. Immense and crushing, it was bearing down on him like a thousand-ton weight and exposing hairline cracks in his armour. This weekend was the most important of his life. He couldn't afford any mistakes. Nor could he afford weakness. Ever. He had to plaster over those cracks and bury that weakness. Now. For good.

'Are you all right, Theo?' he heard Daniel ask as, with superhuman effort, he cleared his head of the images, the sense of suffocation and chaos, and refocused his attention.

'Couldn't be better,' he replied smoothly, savagely dismissing the fear that it was a lie.

'Then let's go through to dinner, shall we?'

To hell with playing nice, thought Kate grimly, passing by Theo as he held open the villa's front door after what had to be one of the most excruciating, most stressful evenings of her life.

What was wrong with him?

He'd been tense ever since he'd returned from his marathon swim, the progress of which she'd surreptitiously watched from the bedroom window while admiring the way he powered through the water, but tension was nothing new. It seemed to be embedded in his DNA.

However, the moment they'd gone through to supper, she'd noticed a dramatic change in his demeanour. He'd been even more on edge than usual, his mood black and rippling with swirling undercurrents that luckily it appeared only she had been able to detect. Outwardly he'd engaged, but inwardly he'd been somewhere else entirely and she'd lost count of the number of times she'd had to cover for him. He'd ruined for her a delicious dinner on a terrace that had the most incredible views with interesting and gracious hosts, and she badly wanted to know why.

'Okay,' she said, turning round to face him and crossing her arms over her chest as he closed the door and locked it. 'What's wrong?'

'Nothing's wrong,' he said flatly.

'Was it something I said? Something I did?'

'You were fine,' he muttered, moving round her and fixed himself a drink from the kitchenette. 'Want anything?'

'A glass of water, please.'

He filled a glass with some water and thrust it at her. As she took it from him, their fingers brushed and electricity arced through her, setting fire to her blood and charging the air surrounding them with a crackling sizzle.

'Thank you,' she said, firmly banking down the heat, ignoring the sizzle and getting a grip.

'You're welcome.'

'Well, *something* was up,' she continued, not planning to let it go any time soon despite his reluctance to share because she was done with guesswork and assumption and always getting it wrong. 'You were all right at drinks and then not all right at supper. What happened in between?'

'Nothing happened.'

Right. 'Is there anything you want to talk about?'

His mouth twisted and he took a slug of his drink. 'No.'

'Sure?'

His jaw tightened. 'Leave it, Kate.'

'Because if there's something I can do to help…?'

'Okay, fine,' he snapped, slamming his glass down and shoving his hands through his hair. 'Actually, you *are* what's wrong.'

Oh. That was a blow. 'But I thought you said I did all right,' she said, frowning.

'You did,' he said, stalking towards her with a look in his eye that had her instinctively wanting to retreat. 'Do you want to know what I was thinking at dinner when I should have been paying attention to the conversation?'

Did she? Suddenly she wasn't at all sure. Every drop of intelligence she possessed was telling her that if she had any sense of self-preservation at all she should get far, far away because she sensed he was on the brink of a confession from which there'd be no return. But she'd pushed for this and she wasn't going to back down now, so she ignored the warning voice in her head, and said, 'Of course.'

'I was thinking about you, Kate,' he said, his voice low and rough as he came to a stop just in front of her. 'In that bed upstairs. With me. And no pillows down the middle.'

His eyes blazed into hers with more heat than she could possibly have imagined and her body flamed in response. Her pulse galloped and desire pooled between her legs. 'Well, *that's* not going to happen,' she said a lot more breathlessly than she'd have liked. 'Let's not forget the only reason I'm here, Theo. Because you blackmailed me. I wouldn't sleep with you again if you were the last man on earth.'

'Wouldn't you?'

'No.'

His dark eyes glittered. 'Are you sure about that?'

'I've never been surer of anything.'

'I could prove you wrong.' His gaze dropped to her mouth and her breath caught in her throat. 'Easily.'

And now she did take a step back. 'I would advise against it,' she said with a tiny jut of her chin, even though every inch of her was demanding he get on with it. 'Anyway, I don't believe you.'

His gaze snapped back up, a deep scowl creasing his brow. 'What, exactly, don't you believe?'

'You wouldn't let a little thing like desire get in the way of this deal.'

'It's hardly little.'

'You know what I mean,' she said, refusing to get distracted by thoughts of what exactly he might be referring to. 'This is nothing more than a diversionary tactic. Something else was bothering you. I know it. I know you.'

As if she'd dumped a bucket of cold water over his head, the heat left his gaze and his expression turned stony and forbidding. A chill ran through her and she shivered.

'You know nothing, Kate,' he said icily, 'and you most certainly don't know me.'

'Then talk to me.'

'There's nothing to talk about.'

And quite suddenly Kate had had enough. If Theo couldn't see that this weekend would go a whole lot better if they worked as a team then that was his lookout. What did it matter if he didn't want to tell her what troubled him? They were nothing. She didn't need to know. In fact, it was probably better that she didn't know, because the last thing she wanted was to develop sympathy for him. Or *any* kind of feelings, for that matter.

'Okay, fine,' she said with a shrug as a wave of weariness washed over her. 'It's late. I'm tired. And I give up. Have it your own way. I don't care any more than you care about the fact that I've given up my weekend for this and for you and am therefore missing a visit to my sister for the first time in years. But you really ought to rethink your attitude, because I might have been able to cover for you tonight but I can't keep doing it, and Daniel Bridgeman is no fool.'

Annoyed by the inexplicable disappointment rushing through her and now just wanting to be anywhere he wasn't, Kate turned on her heel to head up the stairs. But as she did so the glass flew from her fingers and smashed into the wall, sending water flying before shattering into a thousand tiny pieces.

For a second she simply stood there staring at the broken glass lying on the floor, the echo of the crash bouncing off the walls, and then she snapped to. 'Terrific,' she muttered beneath her breath, stalking to the kitchen and yanking open cupboards in search of a dustpan and brush. Pregnancy induced clumsiness. Just what she needed.

But as she marched back and began to sweep up the glass, she caught a glimpse of Theo out of the corner of her eye, and something about what she saw made her stop. Straighten. And abandon the clearing up. Because he was utterly rigid. White. A bead of sweat was trickling down his temple and he didn't appear to even notice.

'Theo?' she asked in alarm, her frustration with him suddenly history. 'Are you all right?'

But he didn't answer. He didn't move a muscle. He seemed completely lost in his own world, and for some reason her heart squeezed. Before she could consider the wisdom of it and spurred on by an instinct she didn't understand, she walked over to him, avoiding the remains of the shattered glass, and lifted her hand to touch his face.

And then he reacted.

With lightning-like reflexes he grabbed her wrist and held it. Kate let out a startled gasp and for the briefest of moments they, time, everything, froze. She could hear nothing but the thundering of her heart, could see nothing but his eyes, which burned with myriad emotions she couldn't begin to identify.

And then a split second later the shutters slammed down and he let her go as if scalded and now it was her turn to remain rooted to the spot. She slowly lowered her arm and absently rubbed her wrist, but her entire body trembled and her mind reeled with the sickening suspicion that Theo's reaction had been the instinctive response of someone anticipating a blow. Expecting it. And the unexpected tumult of emotion that rushed through her at the thought stole her breath.

'So. Nothing to talk about, huh?' she said quietly when she could finally speak, her heart hammering and her entire body filling with a sudden and inexplicable burning rage towards whoever was responsible for it.

'Go to bed, Kate.'

As he watched Kate head slowly up the stairs and then disappear into the bedroom, the door closing behind her with a quiet click, Theo felt the icy numbness fade and into its place stormed such revulsion, horror and repugnance that his knees nearly gave way. The room spun around him and he couldn't breathe.

He'd grabbed her wrist, was the thought hammering around his head as his pulse pounded and his gut churned. Not tightly. But definitely firmly. He'd acted on instinct. He'd lost control. Not once in the years since he'd walked out of the squalid flat he'd grown up in had it happened. There'd been triggers, the occasional flash of memory, but he'd handled them. However, not so just now, and if he'd ever doubted the wisdom of his decision to stay away from Kate and the child that doubt was gone for ever. A better man would send her home.

What could she possibly think of what had happened? She had to be horrified. Maybe even terrified of what he might be capable of. At the very least she had to have questions. And since he wasn't a better man and he wasn't going to send her home, he had to give her the answers. He had no option. Despite every cell of his body rejecting the idea, he owed her an explanation. She had a right to know about the genes he carried and he couldn't have her looking at him with apprehension and uncertainty for the next forty-eight hours. He needed to clear the air. He needed to give her reassurance. Now.

Setting his jaw and galvanising into action while his brain shut down everything but the cold bare facts, Theo took the steps two at a time and banged on the door. 'Kate?'

'Come in.'

Bracing himself, although for what he had no idea, he opened the door and went in. Kate was sitting on the edge of the bed, her face pale and her eyes troubled.

'Are you all right?' he said grimly, scouring her expression for signs of pain and fear. He saw none, but he well knew that that didn't mean they weren't there.

'I'm fine.'

'Did I hurt you?'

'No.'

'Are you sure?'

'Yes.'

'Let me look.'

With a tiny sigh, Kate held out her arm and he stalked over to her, taking the wrist he'd grasped and examining it for marks, which thankfully didn't exist.

'You see,' she said softly. 'It's fine.'

He let her go and stepped back, shoving his hands through his hair. 'It's not fine.'

'Really.'

'I owe you an explanation.'

'No, you don't,' she said with a quick shake of her head. 'If anyone owes anyone anything, I owe you an apology.'

Theo frowned. 'What for?'

'Pushing. I had no right.'

'You had every right.' Because she'd been bang on when she'd confronted him on his attitude over dinner. Despite his conviction he'd dealt with it, he hadn't been able to shake the image of that child, and the realisation that his hold on his control wasn't as invincible as he'd assumed had been deeply disturbing and worryingly all-consuming.

'When you dropped the glass,' he said, addressing the part of the evening he understood marginally better and did need to explain, 'it triggered memories. Bad ones.'

She swallowed hard and lifted her shimmering gaze to his. 'Of abuse?'

He ruthlessly ignored those memories clamouring to be let out of the cupboard he kept them locked in and nodded once. 'Yes.'

Her eyes seemed to suddenly blaze. 'Who?'

'My father,' he said, totally in control, his voice utterly devoid of emotion as he relayed the facts. 'I grew up on the roughest estate in west London. We had virtually no money. Dad lost his job as a builder when he fell off a ladder on a construction site just after I was born. He never worked again. My mother was a cleaner. What little she brought in he drank, along with most of the benefits. When he'd had too much he threw things. Plates. Cups. Glasses. Anything he could lay his hands on. And when he'd run out of things to smash he took his frustrations out mainly on her, sometimes on me. Punches and kicks were his speciality.'

For a moment Kate didn't say anything, and Theo could understand her silence. What he'd just told her, the implications of it, was a lot to process. 'Did anyone know?' she asked eventually, her voice oddly gruff.

'No.'

'*Does* anyone know?'

'No.'

'What happened to him?'

'He died,' he said bluntly. 'Five years ago.' As the next of kin, he'd received the call. When he'd heard the news he'd felt nothing.

'And your mother?'

'She had a brain haemorrhage three years before that. Caused by him, I suspect, but the evidence was inconclusive.'

'She stayed with him?'

'Yes.'

'Why?'

His chest tightened for the briefest of moments and memory and emotion flared before he got a grip and shut both down. 'I don't know. Initially I assumed it was because she had no means of escape or subsequent support.' But it hadn't been because she'd refused every one of the many offers he'd made.

'Is your early business success any coincidence?'

'No.'

'You made a lot of money fast.'

'By the time I was sixteen I'd amassed enough to support us both. I had it all set up.'

'What happened?'

'She refused to come with me. She didn't want to leave him.'

She stared at him in growing disbelief. 'So you left on your own?'

'Yes,' he said bluntly, as a familiar dull stab of guilt hit him in the chest. 'I realise I should have stayed.'

'No. I don't mean that,' she said, suddenly so fierce that it sent a shaft of warmth burning through the ice inside him. 'I mean, how could she not have gone with you?'

'I don't know,' he said unflinchingly since he'd learned

to live with the fact that that was a question to which he would never know the answer a long time ago.

'I can't imagine what your childhood must have been like,' she said, her eyes filling with compassion that he neither wanted nor needed.

'I wouldn't ever want you to,' he said. 'I wouldn't want anyone to.'

She went very still. 'Is there any reason why they should?'

'Abuse engenders abuse.'

She stared at him, growing paler, other emotions that he couldn't begin to identify mingling with the compassion. 'Not necessarily.'

'The chances are high.'

'But not inevitable, surely.'

'It's a risk I will never be willing to take.'

'But—'

'No, Kate,' he interrupted, holding up a hand. 'Don't. I don't want to discuss it. I just wanted to explain what happened earlier. And to reassure you that you are in no danger from me. You have nothing to fear. I will make sure of that. There is no need to refer to the subject again. It needn't affect anything. It mustn't. I'll see you in the morning. Goodnight.'

Needn't affect anything? Kate thought, watching Theo walk out and close the door behind him while she tried to process everything he'd just revealed. How could he possibly think that? How could he think *any* of it? Most of all, how could he *ever* believe that she had something to fear from him? She'd experienced many, *many* emotions since she'd met him, but fear hadn't been one of them and never would be.

What he'd told her *did* affect things. Hugely. If he laboured under the heartbreaking impression that he might somehow be capable of harming her and the baby, it was no wonder he'd displayed such a lack of interest in and engagement with her pregnancy. And it certainly threw light on his fierce drive to succeed.

How had he ever got over his mother's rejection? she wondered, her throat tight and her eyes stinging as she struggled to process everything he'd said. Perhaps he hadn't. Did anyone? She'd learned to live without her mother, but her mother hadn't had a choice. His had, and she'd abandoned him. He'd had no siblings. He'd been all alone.

How tough and determined he had to have been in order to survive. How strong and resilient. It would hardly be surprising if that need for self-preservation was still deeply ingrained. She had first-hand experience of how old habits died hard. What had happened clearly continued to affect him. The way he'd presented her with the facts with such little emotion had spoken volumes, and it tugged on her heartstrings.

So where did she go from here? Should she try and make him see that history didn't have to repeat itself? That he posed no threat and that he could absolutely be a part of their child's life? Or should she leave well alone? On the one hand, she owed it to their child to at least try, but on the other, Theo had made it very clear that the subject was closed, and it was far too sensitive an issue for her to bulldoze her way through.

Whatever the options, now was not the time to subject him to her amateur psychology, she knew. This deal he was pursuing might well be wrapped up in his sense of self-worth and the need to prove something, and now she understood a bit more about why, there was nothing she would do to jeopardise it. So no matter how much she thought he needed to talk to someone about the trauma he'd suffered, no matter how much she wished she could help, all she could do was pretend that the last half an hour hadn't happened and carry on as if nothing had changed.

CHAPTER ELEVEN

THE TERRACE OF the Villa San Michele, the venue for the Bridgemans' golden wedding anniversary party, which was in full swing, had been spared no expense. Lights had been strung in and between the trees and around the railings. At one end, a buffet had been set up, the long wide trestle table laden with salads and cold meats and cheeses. A string quartet was playing something light and cheerful at the other, and in between a fountain tinkled with water that shimmered with gold dust. Earlier, boats sped across the lake that sparkled beneath the setting sun, delivering guests whose diamonds sparkled in the softening light and whose languages included English, Italian and who knew how many others. Now, champagne and conversation flowed and joy and sentimentality abounded.

It was absolutely the last place Theo wanted to be.

The noise was giving him a headache and the sense of suffocation that had dogged him all day was intensifying, tightening his collar and covering his skin in a cold sweat. He needed solitude. Time and space to deal with the fallout from last night. Because while he'd had no option but to share with Kate the basic details of his upbringing, he had the stomach-curdling feeling that by giving her a piece of himself he'd put into play something that couldn't be stopped. Look at the plan he'd made for the free day they had tomorrow, which served no practical purpose and was in no way necessary other than to assuage the guilt he felt about the sacrifice she'd had to make this weekend because of him, which should not have bothered him but did.

He had the feeling impending doom was hurtling towards him, and for the first time in over a decade he was in the petrifying position of facing a situation for which he had no strategy.

If only he could block Kate out the way he blocked out anything that threatened his peace of mind. It wasn't as if he hadn't tried. And it wasn't as if he hadn't had enough to focus on today with the intense all-day meetings he'd had with Daniel.

But he couldn't. She invaded his thoughts without warning and he seemed to be constantly tuned to her frequency. Such as earlier this evening when he'd been standing on the terrace of the guest house, looking out over the lake as he waited for her to emerge. He'd left the house at daybreak after a sleepless night and hadn't seen her since, and he'd been brooding about how she would now respond to him. Would she believe that she had nothing to fear from him? Or would she view him with doubt and suspicion?

His entire body had started prickling with awareness, alerting him to her presence behind him, and he'd experienced a rare moment of hesitation before turning. But her gaze had been clear and she'd been wearing a smile that had hit him in the solar plexus, and the relief that she seemed to be all right had been indescribable.

That awareness had not faded. At every second of every minute of the last couple of hours he'd instinctively known where Kate was when she wasn't with him. The magnetic pull of her was irresistible and he was finding it increasingly hard to stop himself clamping her to his side and keeping there.

The way she'd called him darling and wrapped her arm around his waist when they'd been talking to the Bridgemans earlier hadn't helped. Why had she done that? She hadn't before. Didn't she know how close to the edge of losing it he was? How sick and tired he was of fighting the desire he felt for her? How much he wanted another night, two, with her before they went their separate ways?

If she'd had any inkling how close this evening he'd been to grabbing her hand and hauling her back to the guest villa she'd have been shocked. She wouldn't be sipping champagne and laughing as she chatted with an ease he could only envy. She'd be making arrangements to leave just as soon as was humanly possible. And he'd be cheering her on. Because he didn't like the way she made him feel. He didn't like the desire and the need slithering around inside him, rushing through his blood, making a mockery of his reason and battering his defences.

He particularly didn't like the way the guy she was talking to was leaning towards her. Or looking at her, for that matter. As if he was dazzled. Had the man no respect? What the hell was he thinking? Kate was *his* fiancée. His.

And yet Theo couldn't blame him for wanting to get close. She was blinding. The gold silk dress she had on was tight, which emphasised her phenomenal curves, and strapless, which revealed an expanse of sun-kissed skin that he ached to touch. It was knee-length and split to the thigh on one side, which left her lovely long legs exposed, and as for the stilettos she was wearing, well, those had him thinking of her naked beneath him with the spikes digging into his back.

The confidence she exuded tonight surrounded her like some kind of aura. She was enjoying herself, holding herself tall, as if she didn't care any more about her height or what anyone thought of her. She was no longer afraid, he realised with a start. No longer ashamed. Was she aware of the seismic transformation she'd undergone? Did she know how mind-blowingly attractive she was?

He did.

And as she laughed at something the man she was talking to said, everything in Theo's head disappeared beneath a wave of such intense desire it nearly took out his knees. The concern about what Kate might think of him… The terrifying notion that his grip on his control was weakening and that everything he'd spent so long building was about to implode… It all slipped away until all he was left with was a primitive need to claim and possess. And while on one level he realised he was allowing desire to surge and swell to such an extent it overwhelmed more complicated matters, on another he simply no longer cared.

Oh, dear Lord, Theo was coming over.

Up until this point Kate thought she'd been doing really rather well. Although she'd been aware of his gaze on her all evening, burning her up, making her unable to properly follow any of the conversations she'd been having, she'd just about managed to keep her cool.

How, though, she had no idea. She was by no means firing on all cylinders. She hadn't slept well. She'd ached too hard for the boy Theo had been and the man he'd become. When she thought about what he must have suffered… well, she didn't know and she wanted to, so after a few fitful hours she'd fired up her laptop and researched it, which had been a mistake because what she read tore at her heart.

She'd barely registered him leave the villa at dawn— she'd been in too much of a state—but she'd spent the rest of the morning in limbo, the hours dragging while her mind raced. She'd swum and sunbathed, caught up on the news and replied to a few emails, and then had lunch with Mrs Bridgeman, but she hadn't been able to concentrate through any of it, not even her hostess's cross-questioning about how she and Theo had met and her enthusiastic interest in their non-existent wedding plans, which somehow she'd managed to muddle her way through.

She hadn't seen Theo until she'd found him waiting for her on the terrace of their villa earlier this evening. She'd noted the tension in the rigidity of his shoulders and the lines of his tall, powerful frame, and at that moment all she'd wanted to do was hug him. Comfort him. Which was absurd since he didn't need her or anyone and she was supposed to be pretending last night hadn't happened, but there it was.

And when he'd turned round, looking so darkly, smoulderingly handsome in his black dinner jacket and white shirt it had stolen her breath, it hadn't been simple desire that thumped her in the gut. It had been something deeper and more intense. Something that grabbed hold of her heart and squeezed and made her think of that slippery slope she'd been so wary of. The lines that defined their relationship were blurring, and if she wasn't very careful indeed she'd be careering headlong down it.

Assuming she wasn't already, of course.

Worryingly, the fact that Theo had blackmailed her into this whole thing no longer seemed to matter quite as much as it once had. Those feelings she'd been so worried about had smashed through the flimsy dam of her resistance and were flowing through her, hot and fierce. And now he was striding towards her, his expression focused entirely on her, dark and forbidding, and her whole body was alive with anticipation. Shivers ran up and down her spine. Her pulse galloped. And she had the dizzying sinking feeling that she'd been waiting all evening for this moment, the moment he came to claim her.

With a murmured, 'Excuse me,' she moved away from the man she'd been talking to just as Theo came to a stop a foot in front of her. His eyes were dark and glittering with a hint of uncharacteristic wildness, and her mouth went dry.

'Dance with me,' he said, his voice so low and rough it was practically a growl.

Her pulse leapt, the tightly leashed hunger she could hear in his tone sending heat straight to her centre and detonating tiny explosions along her veins. 'I don't think that would be wise,' she murmured, swallowing hard and thinking that quite apart from anything else she never knew what to do with her arms and always worried she'd fall flat on her face.

His gaze darkened. 'I do.'

'Because it would look good?'

'No.'

'Then why?'

'Because I want to.'

Oh.

Well, so did she. Quite desperately. The sultry beat of the music that had replaced the string quartet was thudding through her body. The way he was looking at her was scrambling her senses. To hell with humiliating herself. She wanted to touch him in ways that were wholly inappropriate off the dance floor but entirely acceptable on it and the best thing was, he would never know. 'Then let's dance.'

Theo didn't need telling twice. He held out a hand and she took it and he led her onto the dance floor. And as he drew her into the circle of his arms, nothing at that moment seemed as important as his hands on her back, searing through the fabric of her dress and setting her on fire. Nor did anything seem as necessary as touching him. So she put her hands on his chest, the way his muscles tensed beneath her palms sending heat shooting through her, and slid them up and around his neck.

As they swayed in time to the music, she realised that the worst thing that could happen on a dance floor wasn't falling flat on her face. It was losing her mind. Because she couldn't help responding to the strength and hardness of his body and pressing closer. She couldn't help wishing they were alone so that she could get him naked and touch some more.

So what was to be done?

If the feral look in his eye and the thick, hard length pressing insistently against her were anything to go by he wanted her as much as she wanted him. But ever since that no kissing, no touching condition she'd hit him with he'd been careful about where and how he touched her, which meant that unfortunately it was unlikely he'd simply haul her off to have his wicked way with her.

Did she have the guts to suggest it herself? What would he think if she did? Yes, he obviously wanted her but she'd never met anyone with such control. What if she indicated she'd like a repeat of that evening in his office and he turned her down? Maybe she should steal a kiss, she thought dazedly, staring at his mouth and feeling her lips tingle. He wouldn't be able to reject that, not when they were in the possible presence of the person they were here to fool.

Fevered tension filled what little space there was between them, and the air sizzled and suddenly she couldn't bear it any longer. His mouth was mere centimetres from hers and all she could think about was how it would feel on hers and how desperate she was to find out.

Desire swept through her, drowning out reason and common sense until all that was left was instinct. Helpless to stop herself, she lifted her face and moved her head forward and touched her lips to his and it was dizzying until she realised he'd gone utterly rigid and was not responding and that headiness turned to excoriating mortification.

Flushing with a different kind of heat and feeling like an utter fool, Kate jerked away but she didn't get far because a split second later Theo had yanked her tight against him and crushed his mouth back to hers, kissing her with such heat and intensity that if he hadn't been holding her in his arms she'd have collapsed into a heap on the floor.

After what felt like hours, he broke the kiss, his breathing as ragged as hers, his eyes dark and his face tight with barely suppressed need. 'Enough,' he said roughly.

'Not nearly,' she breathed, staring at his mouth, longing to feel it back on hers.

'We're making a scene.'

'Isn't that the point?'

He tensed and when her gaze flew to his she thought she saw a rare flicker of uncertainty in his eyes. 'Is it?'

And she could lie and say yes, but she didn't want to and, besides, hadn't they gone beyond that? 'No.'

A muscle hammered in his jaw. 'Tell me what you want, Kate,' he said, and she instantly thought that the only answer to that was 'more' because she wanted another night. Possibly two. It wasn't as if she believed things would continue beyond that. She knew perfectly well that once this weekend was over, once the deal was signed, that would be that. But she didn't want to think about what lay ahead for her when she was home—unemployment, single parenthood, reality. She didn't want to think about what Theo had told her and how it made her feel about him. She wanted to lose herself in the heat and the passion that he unleashed in her and just for once live in the moment. 'I want us to go back to the villa,' she said, her heart thundering with anticipation and excitement. 'Together. Now.'

Flames leapt in his dark eyes and his hold on her tightened. 'You do know what will happen if we do, don't you?'

'Well, I know what I'm *hoping* will happen.'

'Then let's go.'

It took two minutes to say their thank-yous and goodbyes. Five to get to the guest villa. One to shove open the front door, hustle Kate in, close it and push her up against it.

For a moment Theo just stared at her, the moonlight flooding in through the window casting pale shadows across her face, losing himself in the depths of her eyes and not caring that she was able to see straight into his, into the empty black hole where his soul should be. With any luck she wouldn't see that. Instead she'd simply see the strength of his need for her and the relief that incredibly she was on the same page.

She was breathing hard. Her eyes were shining and she was shaking with what he hoped to God was excitement, and then she lifted her chin and arched an eyebrow as if asking what he was waiting for, and that was it.

As his control snapped he slammed his mouth down on hers and kissed her as if it had been months instead of minutes. Beneath the onslaught she moaned and opened her mouth and when his tongue met hers, desire instantly flared like a flame to touchpaper. She whipped her arms around his neck and tilted her pelvis to his and it was all the encouragement he needed.

He pulled her closer, devouring her mouth, her jaw, her neck. She pushed her hands beneath the lapels of his jacket, and, without breaking the kiss, he shrugged out of it. She clawed at his shirt, yanking it free while he found the zip of her dress and slid it down. He lifted the hem and she wiggled her hips, and a second later he'd peeled it up over her head and tossed it on the floor.

And then he put his hands to her waist and his mouth to her breast, and when she whimpered, he drew her hard pink nipple between his lips and she whimpered some more.

But it wasn't enough. It had been driving him mad not knowing what she tasted like, so he sank to his knees, and when she gasped and instinctively clamped her legs together, he slid a hand between her knees and eased it up. And when he reached the curls at the juncture of her thighs, he touched her there and stroked her lightly and she gave a soft sigh of surrender as her legs fell apart.

Unable to wait a moment longer, Theo tugged her knickers down and then off. He clamped his hands to her hips and put his mouth on her and then he knew exactly how she tasted. Sweet. Delicious. Irresistible. As he licked and sucked he felt her tremble and he held her more firmly, the desire rocketing through him almost unbearable.

Above him, there came a faint, 'Oh, God,' followed

by the gentle thud of her head against the door, and he increased the pressure, the tempo, while she sobbed and gasped, and then her hands were clutching at his head while she pushed against him and then, with a soft hoarse cry, she shattered.

Tight with the need for release, he kissed his way back up her trembling body until he was upright again. Her eyes were glazed. Her cheeks were pink and he didn't think he'd ever seen anything so beautiful, or anyone so desperate, and something shifted in his chest, something that might have concerned him if the way she was grappling with the button and zip of his trousers hadn't concerned him more.

'Stop,' he grated, summoning up every drop of his control to still her hand.

'Why?'

'I don't have a condom,' he said tautly, every muscle of his body screaming in denial.

Devastation flitted across her face. 'What?' she said dazedly. 'No.'

'Yes.'

'It doesn't matter. It's too late. You can't get me more pregnant. And I trust you, Theo. On this. On everything.'

His chest tightened. 'You shouldn't. Not on everything.'

'I know. But I do.'

Then she was a fool. But she had a point about it being too late. He was granite hard and the need to be inside her was burning through him like wildfire. There was no going back from this. Wild horses wouldn't drag him away from her now. So he crushed his mouth to hers, lifted her leg to open her up to him and thrust into her tight wet heat and it was heaven.

He gave her a moment to accommodate him but he couldn't hold still for long. Beneath his ravenous kisses she moaned and clung onto his shoulders. He began to move, knowing it wasn't going to take much when she matched his every thrust with hot, increasingly frantic demands of her own.

And it didn't. Within moments she was clenching around him again, gasping his name and sobbing and digging her fingers into his shoulders, and that was it. He felt his orgasm building in strength and momentum, and then it was barrelling through him as, with a roar, he thrust fast and hard, burying himself as deep as he could before fiercely and never-endingly spilling into her.

CHAPTER TWELVE

BY THE TIME Kate had recovered from the shuddering effects of two spectacular orgasms, she noticed that, encouragingly, Theo had got himself naked.

'Bedroom,' he muttered, grabbing her hand, his eyes so dark with the promise of more to come that incredibly she wanted him all over again. 'Now.'

But the only thing holding her up was the door, and she had the helpless feeling that if she moved, she might well crumple to the floor. 'I can't,' she said huskily, finally able to run her gaze over him, which only weakened her limbs further. 'Legs. Like noodles.'

So he scooped her up and carried her, all six foot one of her, as if she weighed nothing, and strode up the stairs and into the bedroom. And while he was doing so, it suddenly struck her that she didn't feel self-conscious at all. Moments ago, she'd been upright, bare, and totally exposed to him, and after her initial reservation, she'd loved it. Now her bits were jiggling and she was all squashed up against him, which wasn't exactly flattering, and she didn't even care. In fact, she felt incredible. As if she could do anything. Dance without falling over. Wear heels without towering above the man beside her. Take on the world.

And suddenly she wanted to find out not only how far she'd come but how far she could go. So when Theo took her into the softly lit bedroom and set her down beside the enormous bed, she planted one hand on his chest and pushed.

He landed in the middle of it, and stared at her first in shock and then with a slow smile that robbed her of breath. He lifted himself up onto his elbows and arched an eyebrow, as if daring her to go through with whatever she was planning, and while she didn't have a plan she was more than up for accepting the challenge.

'Where should I start?' she asked, uncertainty nevertheless making her hesitate.

'Wherever you want.'

'What if you don't like it?'

His eyes gleamed. 'I suspect there is nothing you can do that I won't like, Kate.'

Okay, then.

Gathering her courage, she joined him on the bed and let her gaze roam all over him. There was so much of him to explore, so she straddled him, the hard length of him pressing into her in the most delicious way, and ran her hands over his shoulders and then down his arms, feathering her fingertips over the dips and contours of his muscles and delighting in the way they tensed beneath her touch.

And now she wanted to taste him, so, remembering the pleasure she felt when he held her breast and teased her nipple, she bent down and touched her tongue to his and licked. He shuddered and hissed out a breath, so she did it again, the salty tang of his skin making her taste buds dance and sing, and suddenly she wanted to touch him and taste him everywhere. Thoroughly. The way she'd been too afraid to try all those weeks ago.

And though she'd never done anything remotely like it before, and though she was bound to be clumsy and inept, she'd never know if she didn't try. If he laughed she could always make him pay. Somehow.

Shifting herself lower, she ran a hand down his body, over the ridges of his muscled abdomen and the faint trace of a scar, and feeling him shudder. Tentatively she touched the head of his erection and then stroked her fingers along his rock-hard length. His skin there was surprisingly soft and velvety and she was gripped by the need to feel it properly, so she wrapped her hand round him and slid it gently up from base to tip and then down again.

Theo growled and thrust into her hand, which was intriguing. As was the bead of liquid gathered at the tip. She rubbed her thumb over it and his hips jerked. She bent her head and licked, and was about to do it again when he put a hand at the back of her head, his fingers tangling in her hair, and pulled her away.

'You need to stop,' he said, his breathing sketchy and harsh.

Her heart skipped a beat as her stomach plummeted. Oh. Had she been doing it wrong? 'Really?'

'If you don't, this will be over embarrassingly quickly.'

Phew. She hadn't been doing it wrong. And she didn't mind that he'd stopped her, because his rampant need for her and the tight desperation she could hear in his voice were sending shockwaves of desire pulsing through her and if she didn't get him inside her just as soon as she could she might well combust.

She kissed him because it had been too long since her lips had been on his, shifted again and pressed her pelvis into his. Acting on the need drumming away inside her she rubbed herself against him and it sent such sparks of pleasure through her that she did it again and again, until her head was spinning and she couldn't carry on kissing him because she couldn't breathe. She tore her mouth from his, her breath coming in short sharp pants, and all she could think about was racing towards a finishing line that was simultaneously rushing towards her.

'Kate,' he growled and she opened her eyes to see his brows drawn in concentration and his jaw clenched.

'Yes?'

'I know I said you could do what you want but there's a limit to how much of this I can take.'

That went for her as well. She was so close to the edge,

one more rub and she'd have been flying apart around him. But she wanted to come with him inside her again and she wanted it desperately, so she put her hands on his shoulders and pushed herself up. She lifted her hips, her pulse thundering, took him in her hand and angled him so that he was poised at her entrance. Then she lowered herself onto him, slowly, feeling every inch of him, hearing his low groan and shivering when he put his hands on her waist.

'I think I might start moving,' she said hoarsely.

'Don't let me stop you.'

Nothing could stop her. She was being driven by a force that she still didn't fully understand but was all up for going with. She rolled her hips experimentally and Theo moaned, so she did it again a bit harder and this time she moaned. He felt so good. He seemed to be touching her everywhere.

She leaned forwards to kiss him and gasped as the shift in angle meant he hit a spot deep within her and set off a whole new set of explosions. She felt his hands move to her hips, guiding her, moving her, while her breasts rubbed against his hair-roughened chest, the friction rocking her world.

As the delicious pressure inside her grew and everything began to tighten she found herself moving with increasing urgency and less coordination. Her control was history. The desire and need pounding through her was relentless. Unable to help herself, she whimpered against his mouth, she might even have begged. She didn't know. All she knew was that Theo suddenly tilted his hips up and buried himself deep as she ground down, and that was it. White-hot pleasure burst inside her like a firework and lights flashed behind her eyelids and her entire world turned upside down.

Explosive. That was what that had been, thought Theo with the one brain cell capable of functioning. He'd never experienced anything like it. He'd never ceded control in bed.

He'd never even considered it. But perhaps that had been a mistake because he'd just done exactly that and his mind had been blown.

The lack of self-consciousness with which Kate had explored him and the abandoned confidence with which she'd taken what she wanted was breathtaking. *She* was breathtaking. She was also lying naked beside him, uncovered and unashamed, stretching and practically purring with satisfaction, and incredibly he wanted her again.

But giving up control once was more than enough and her allure wasn't that irresistible. To prove it he would make himself wait. He would use conversation as a distraction. He might even try and get the answer to a question that had been bugging him for weeks.

Rolling onto his side, Theo propped himself up on one elbow. 'So what exactly is this?' he asked, trailing the fingers of his other hand over the tattoo at Kate's hip and feeling her shiver beneath his touch.

'It's an upside-down swallow,' she said with a breathlessness that made him briefly wonder why he'd thought it a good idea to wait.

'Why an upside-down swallow?'

'It represents me flipping the bird at the entire male sex. I was twenty and fed up with still not being able to get a date. I wanted to make a point.'

'It's pretty.'

'It's actually pretty pointless.'

'Why?'

'Because looking down on it from up here, it's the right way up, which does rather defeat the object of the exercise. I didn't think of that when I was all fired up and pissed off.'

Unexpectedly, Theo felt a faint smile curve his mouth. 'No, well, who would?'

'Ideally the tattoo artist would have had an inkling,' she said dryly. 'He supposedly had twenty years' experience.

But it's fine. I'm used to it. And now it seems rather irrelevant anyway.'

His smile faded and a ribbon of concern wound through him because he hoped she wasn't referring to them. They weren't dating and they never would. This was a one, maybe two, night thing at most. Which was all it ever could be. And that was fine. The thing stabbing away at him wasn't regret. It was guilt. Because now he came to think about it he'd been remiss earlier and it had been playing on his mind.

'You looked spectacular this evening,' he said, remembering how speechless he'd been when he'd turned and seen her standing there on the balcony.

'Did I?'

'Yes.'

'Thank you. I wasn't sure.'

'The mirror doesn't lie.'

'I wouldn't know.'

'Why not?'

'I don't much like looking at myself in a mirror,' she said, frowning and biting on her lower lip, which gave him all kinds of ideas he intended to put into action later. 'Not a full-length one anyway. There's just so much of me. I went to a hall of mirrors once at a funfair when I was six and was traumatised for weeks.'

'Yet you're now wearing heels.'

'I know,' she said, flashing him a quick grin that did something strange to his chest. 'For the first time in years. Isn't that great?'

Was it? He wasn't so sure. While he was gratified by the improvement in her self-esteem and confidence, he didn't like to think what she might see if she looked him straight in the eye. He liked even less the memory of how as they'd walked to the party, their strides in synch, it had briefly, unacceptably, occurred to him that they somehow matched.

'So come on,' she said, rolling onto her side so that she

faced him and fixing him with exactly the sort of discon-
certingly probing look he feared. 'Your turn.'

'About what?'

'Tell me something about you that no one else knows.'

He tensed and frowned. 'I've already told you something
no one else knows.' Many things, actually.

'Something else.'

'My childhood wasn't enough?'

'It doesn't have to be a big thing. It could be tiny. Humour me.' She shot him a wicked smile and for a second he
marvelled at how quickly she'd gone from virgin to tempt-
ress. 'I'll make it worth your while.'

'All right,' he said, his body hardening all over again
at the mere thought of just how she might go about doing
that. 'I get headaches when I'm stressed. I didn't learn to
read until I was sixteen. And I have a mild allergy to cel-
ery, which makes my tongue go numb.'

'There,' she said, her eyes shimmering with emotions he
didn't want to even try and identify. 'You see? That wasn't
so bad, was it?'

'Depends on what I want to do with my tongue.'

'And what *do* you want to do with your tongue?'

'Why don't you lie back and let me show you?'

Kate was in the kitchen making coffee on Sunday morning
when there was a knock on the door of the villa.

How she'd made it downstairs in the first place she had
no idea. Her entire body felt like jelly. Muscles she never
knew she had ached. By rights, she ought to be exhausted.
She'd only had a couple of hours' sleep. But instead she
felt fabulous, on top of the world, exhilarated. Every sense
was heightened. Colours were bright. Smells were intense.

Last night had been incredible. And not just from a physical point of view. When she and Theo had been able to take
no more, they'd talked. Well, she had at least. His questions

about her life—her upbringing, her job, that second-base bet—had been endless, his interest had been genuine, and she'd basked in the attention. She hadn't managed to get much out of him, apart from a few details about his journey to global domination, but that was okay. She had all day.

Because he was taking her to Florence. More specifically, to the Garden of Archimedes, which apparently was a museum of mathematics. He'd informed her of the plan an hour ago, when she'd suggested spending the entire day in bed, and when she'd heard it and realised that he'd remembered that numbers were her thing, her silly soft heart had melted. The plane was on standby, the finest restaurant in Florence was booked for a late leisurely lunch and she couldn't wait.

Whoever was outside knocked on the door again and Kate jumped. Abandoning the coffee pot and the lovely hot memories of last night, she walked to the door on legs that still felt a bit shaky and opened it.

On the doorstep, to her surprise, stood Daniel Bridgeman.

'*Buongiorno,*' she said, with the wide grin that she just couldn't seem to contain.

'Good morning,' he replied with an answering smile. 'May I come in?'

'Theo's in the shower.'

'No problem,' he said. 'It was you I wanted to speak to anyway.'

Oh? Why?

Kate felt her smile falter for a second and nerves fluttered in her stomach, but she held the door open for him and let him in because what else could she do?

'Would you like some coffee?' she asked, feeling a bit awkward about offering her host his own coffee as she watched him glance around the space as if for some reason checking it out.

Having apparently finished his perusal, he turned to her and shook his head. 'No, thank you.'

'The party last night was wonderful.'

'I'm delighted you enjoyed it.'

'We did.'

'I noticed. Watching you and Theo on the dance floor was revelatory.'

There was a twinkle in his eye and Kate found herself suddenly blushing. 'Yes, well, the music was good.'

'My wife has eclectic tastes.' He looked at her for a moment, his gaze suddenly shrewd, and Kate found that for some reason she was suddenly fighting the urge to squirm. 'Do you know why I invited you and Theo here this weekend, Kate?'

'To discuss the deal?'

'Partly,' he agreed with a nod. 'I wanted to meet you. And see the two of you together.'

'Oh?'

He shook his head and smiled. 'I may be old, but I am far from stupid.'

Her pulse skipped a beat in alarm. 'No, no,' she said, thinking that now would be a really good time for Theo to put in an appearance. 'Quite right.'

'How much do you know about the history of this deal?'

'Some,' she hedged cautiously.

'I had some doubts about Theo.'

'He said.'

Daniel's grey bushy eyebrows lifted. 'Did he?'

'Yes.' She smiled at the memory. 'He was very put out by it.'

'I've spent fifty years building up my business. I'm not going to sell it to just anyone.'

'No. Of course not.'

'One thing that did concern me was your engagement.'

Oh, dear. 'In what way?' she said lightly.

'A suspicious man might question the speed and timing of it.'

'And are you suspicious?'

'On occasion.'

Dammit, what was he trying to say? 'I can understand that.'

'It's a deal that's of huge benefit to both parties. There's a lot at stake. Theo isn't a man to give up easily.'

No, he wasn't. She had first-hand experience of that, although somehow it no longer seemed to bother her. 'He won't let you down.'

'So tell me why I should sell to him.'

What? 'Me?' Kate said, her eyebrows shooting up.

'You.'

'God, I don't know,' she said. 'I actually know very little about the ins and outs of it.'

'But you know him, I assume.'

Did she? She thought she did. A bit. Maybe more than a bit now. Enough to convince Daniel Bridgeman that he had no reason to doubt Theo's integrity, at any rate. 'You're right, I do,' she said, thankfully sounding more certain than she felt. 'And I can promise you won't regret it if you do decide to sell to him. Theo can come across as ruthless, I admit, but he is honourable. He's also incredibly loyal, protective and thoughtful.' Not to mention devastatingly handsome and unbelievable in bed, although she didn't think Mr Bridgeman would appreciate that level of detail. 'You have no idea how hard he's had to work to get where he is,' she said instead. 'He didn't have the advantage of a stellar education or buckets of money to support him. He's grafted his entire adult life and continues to do so.'

'I see,' said the older man, but she hadn't finished.

'And he's an excellent listener,' she said. 'When we met I had a few self-esteem issues but he's given me the confidence to get over them and believe in myself, and that is something I will always be grateful for.'

'Interesting.'

She blushed, suddenly aware that she might have gone a bit far in her defence of him, even if everything she'd said was true. 'Yes, well, he's a decent man.'

'You make a good team,' said Daniel.

'Er…right, yes, absolutely we do.'

'As I told him over drinks on Friday night, with a fiancée like you and a baby on the way, he's a lucky man.'

Oh, dear God. The suggestion must have conjured up his worst nightmare. No wonder he'd been so broodingly distracted at dinner. 'He certainly is,' she said.

Daniel headed towards the door. 'Thank you for sparing me some of your time, Kate, and I hope to see you again soon.'

And even though she and Theo didn't make a good team and she wouldn't be seeing Daniel Bridgeman again, Kate nevertheless fixed a bright smile to her face and said, 'I hope so, too.'

Upstairs in the bathroom, Theo gripped the edge of the basin, his head swimming and his heart thundering while a cold sweat broke out all over his skin despite the icy shower he'd forced himself to take.

He hadn't meant to eavesdrop. When he'd heard Daniel and Kate talking downstairs he'd fully intended to join them, especially when Daniel had revealed his suspicions about the engagement. But then Kate had begun extolling his non-existent virtues and he'd frozen, his body filling with dread and denial and who knew what else. The passion in her voice… The sincerity… It had made his stomach churn and bile rise up his throat, and he just couldn't swallow it down.

In no way did he and Kate make a good team. They

didn't make any kind of team. They would never match. And he'd been wrong when he'd told her there was nothing she could do he wouldn't like. He hadn't liked what she'd said. He didn't want anyone singing his praises. He didn't need anyone on his side. Ever.

One night of spectacular sex. That was all they'd had. He'd assumed she'd been on the same page, but it hadn't sounded as if she was. It had sounded as if she'd become… *involved*. And if he was being brutally honest she wasn't the only one.

When he thought of the uncharacteristic things he'd said and done since meeting her he realised that at some point he'd lost the sense of who he was. Despite blithely assuming he had everything under control, right from the beginning he'd allowed her to get under his skin and invade his thoughts.

Take the way he'd insisted on fixing her issues, issues that theoretically had nothing to do with him, out of some misguided non-existent sense of responsibility. Look at what he'd done with the thank-you note she'd sent him. He'd had no reason to keep it and he should have shredded it. Nevertheless he'd tucked it away in the top drawer of his desk in the office. Why? Who knew?

Then there was the red convertible parked up outside. It hadn't been the only car left. He'd had ample choice. But when he'd been presented with the options he'd recalled the wistful longing in her voice when she'd told him all those weeks ago that she'd always wanted one and he'd simply thought she'd like it. In much the same way he'd thought she might enjoy a visit to the maths museum in Florence.

And then there were the tiny snippets about himself that she'd asked for and he'd given her. She'd only wanted one. He'd given her three. Too many. Too much.

He should never have done any of it, he thought grimly as he pushed himself upright and rubbed his hands over his face. He most definitely shouldn't have slept with her again. However great the pressure of the weekend, however powerful his desire for her, he should have had better control. He'd been careless, weak and self-indulgent and that sense of imminent implosion was expanding with every second. If he didn't want everything he'd striven for to crash and burn, he had to put an end to whatever was or wasn't going on with Kate. Right now.

Shutting down and filling with steely resolve, Theo headed downstairs, and, on seeing that Daniel had gone, after muttering to Kate that he had something to take care of but wouldn't be long, left. And when he returned an hour later, the chaos churning around inside him had been dispelled. Cool, steady calm had returned and nothing, *nothing*, was going to threaten it again.

'Hi,' said Kate, greeting him with a brightness and enthusiasm that bounced straight off his armour and a kiss on the mouth that he didn't even feel. 'Are we off? Did you know that the museum has a section dedicated to Pythagoras? It focuses on puzzles inspired by his theorem and I can't *wait*.'

Too bad. 'Pack up your things.'

'Oh?' she said, staring at him in surprise. 'Why?'

'We're going home.'

Her grin faded and disappointment spread across her lovely face, and it bothered him not one jot. 'But the deal?'

'Signed.'

'So Florence?'

'Cancelled.'

'And…us?'

'Over.'

CHAPTER THIRTEEN

THROUGHOUT THE ENTIRE tautly silent journey back to a grey and wet London, Kate was accompanied by a level of disappointment that she didn't understand. The weekend might have ended abruptly and a day ahead of schedule, but she'd always known that once Theo's deal was signed that would be that. She'd always been more than all right with it, so what was this crushing sense of anticlimax all about? Why did she feel so stunned and so, well, *sad*?

None of it made any sense. Yes, she'd been excited about going to the Garden of Archimedes, but she could easily go on her own another time. She didn't need Theo to make her arrangements for her. And while another night of incredible sex would have been wonderful, it wasn't as if she wouldn't survive without it. In fact, she ought to be glad this ridiculous charade was over and she could get on with the rest of her life, starting with the visit to her sister that she had been prepared to miss.

Yet she wasn't.

Maybe it was the unexpectedness of it that was troubling her. Or the sudden inexplicable change in his mood this morning, which she still couldn't fathom. When she'd left him in the shower, he'd been thoroughly relaxed. She'd made sure of it. Yet, mere moments after the chat she and Daniel had had, he'd stormed off and returned in a very different frame of mind.

What could possibly have happened in the meantime? Had he heard what she'd had to say about him? Since she hadn't exactly been whispering he might well have done, but even if he had, why would that make him react so negatively? She'd only had positive things to say, and she was pretty sure that the false picture she'd painted of their relationship was what had got the deal signed. So really, he ought to be *thanking* her, not blanking her.

She didn't understand it, but when she asked what was wrong all she got in response were grunts and monosyllables, and that hurt because she deserved more. She *wanted* more. She wanted to know what he was thinking and what he was feeling. She wanted to burrow beneath his surface, find out what was going on and fix it. And not just because she found him insanely attractive. She also liked and admired him and cared about him. He was everything she'd told Daniel Bridgeman he was, and so much more. He was complicated and difficult and layered and fascinating. Challenging and annoying and brilliant.

And about to drop her home and drive off out of her life for good.

This really was it, Kate thought, her heart squeezing painfully at the realisation. The fake relationship that somehow no longer felt fake was actually over. Once she got out of the car she'd never see or hear from him again. Why did that hurt so much? Why did she feel as though she were being sliced in two? Was she actually going to be physically sick?

With fingers that were oddly trembling she lowered her window and turned her face towards it. The cool fresh breeze instantly calmed her churning stomach but it did nothing to alleviate the misery now scything through her body. Why had it had to end now? Why couldn't she have had one more day and one more night? Why couldn't she have had for ever?

At that, Kate instantly froze. Time seemed to skid to a halt. Her head emptied of everything but that last bewildering thought.

For ever?

What?

Why would she want that?

Why would she even *think* that?

Theo wasn't for ever.

But she was.

And, oh, dear Lord, she'd fallen in love with him.

As the truth of it landed like a blow to the chest, Kate reeled, her heart pounding, her skin tight and damp. She loved everything about him. He wasn't ruthless; he was dynamic. He wasn't lacking in empathy; he was understandably guarded. He was everything she'd ever dreamed of, plus he was sexy as hell and the father of her child and he'd been planning to take her to a maths museum.

All those feelings that she'd tried to prevent and then deny... The thrill whenever he called... The exhilaration when she was with him... The sympathy and the fury, and the leap of her heart whenever she looked at the ring... They all suddenly made sense. But how had it happened? And when? Only a week ago she'd hated him. What had changed that? Or had she never really hated him in the first place?

The questions spun around her head, tangling with the realisation that she was crazy about him, making her heart thump with hope and bewilderment.

And despair.

Because she couldn't possibly tell him. Love had never been part of the deal. She'd merely be setting herself up for brutal rejection and abject misery. He'd be appalled.

Or would he?

What if his feelings had changed, too? What if the chilly distance he'd put between them emanated from a similar epiphany? What if he too was battling feelings he wasn't sure would be reciprocated?

No. She would not think like that. She mustn't. When it came to speculation about what Theo might or might not be thinking she was always wrong. Besides, he didn't do uncertainty.

And, actually, with regards to one particular aspect of their relationship, neither did she. Because while she still needed time to process how she felt about him and figure out what she was going to do about it, if anything, suddenly she was damned if she was going to let him drop her off and drive away without at least having *tried* to persuade him to change his mind about his involvement with their child. She wasn't going to go back to the Kate of before, afraid and in hiding. She was going to fight.

'So, Theo?' she said, nerves nevertheless tangling in her stomach as he turned a corner and her building hove into view, an indication that time was running out.

His brows snapped together. 'Yes?'

'I was wondering… What are you going to do once the deal's gone through?'

'What do you mean?' he said, shooting her a stony glance that would have had her backing right off had she not strengthened her resolve.

'Well, once you've achieved global domination, what's left?'

'Nothing,' he said. 'I'll be done.'

'Will you?'

'Yes.'

'Are you sure about that?'

'Quite sure.'

She took a deep breath and mentally crossed her fingers. 'Because if you do need another project, there's one cooking away right here.' She indicated her abdomen and watched as his gaze flickered across and down, his jaw tightening in that familiar way.

'That won't be necessary.'

'Why not?'

'You know why not.'

'No. I don't. Not really.'

'Kate.'

'History doesn't have to repeat itself,' she persisted, ignoring the warning note she could hear in his voice because she was in love with him and she had to make him see she was right.

'As I told you before, it's a risk I'm not willing to take.'

'There is no risk.'

'However much I might wish otherwise, you are both better off—and safer—without me.'

At his choice of words, hope flared inside her, spreading through her like wildfire, dizzying her with its intensity. Could it be that he *did* want them but was simply so blinded by fear he believed he didn't deserve them? Could she convince him otherwise? 'You are not your father,' she said, her throat tight and her pulse racing.

'Leave it.'

'No. It's too important.'

'I don't want to talk about it.'

Too bad. He wasn't shutting her down again. Not now. And she'd chosen her battlefield wisely. There was no escape from a moving car. 'But you should,' she said heatedly. 'You need to. You need to see what I see: a man who would go to the ends of the earth to protect and defend those that matter to him. That man would never be a danger to anyone. That man would *never* hit anyone.'

He pulled over suddenly and parked, and then turned to her, his eyes bleak, his face rigid. 'But I did, Kate,' he said bluntly. 'I did.'

She blanched, the words hovering between them, the rain hammering down on the roof of the car. 'What do you mean?'

'Exactly that.'

No. He wouldn't. He couldn't. 'When? Who?'

'My mother. I was sixteen.'

She recoiled with shock, but right down to her marrow she knew that it couldn't be that simple. 'What happened?'

'Nothing happened.'

'I don't believe you. There has to be some explanation.'

'There isn't.'

'Circumstances, then?' she said, because she was not going to let this go and she refused to believe it of him. 'Tell me the circumstances.'

'The day I'd planned to leave,' he said, his voice flat and emotionless in a way that intensified the ache in her chest, 'I told her to grab what she needed. She said no. I begged. My father came home, off his head as usual. She told him what I'd asked her to do and he flew into a rage. He punched me in the stomach and I'd had enough. For the first time in my life I retaliated. My mother went to protect him and my fist caught her on the cheek. She told me to get out. So I did.'

He spoke matter-of-factly, but she could hear the trace of emotion behind what he said, the guilt, betrayal, the rejection, the abandonment. 'It was an accident,' she said, her words catching on the lump in her throat.

'Was it?'

'Yes.'

'That's who I really am, Kate.'

'It isn't. It really isn't.' She took a deep breath and stepped into the terrifying unknown. 'I've fallen in love with you, Theo. I don't know when or how, but I love you and trust you with every cell of my being.'

He barely moved a muscle in response. 'Then you've made a mistake,' he said flatly. 'I can never be the man you want me to be.'

For a moment her heart shattered, pain pummelling through her at the realisation he was adamant in his belief, but then, quite suddenly, anger flared deep inside her, rushing along her veins and setting fire to her nerve-endings. How dared he tell her she'd made a mistake?

How dared he dismiss her feelings? And how dared he continue to reject their child?

'You already are the man I want you to be,' she said fiercely. 'Everything I told Daniel was true. But you are also a coward.'

His eyebrows shot up at that, a chink in the icy facade at last. 'What?'

'You heard,' she said, burning up with frustration and hurt. 'You're a coward. History *doesn't* have to repeat itself. There are choices you can make. There are choices you've *already* made. You are not just your father's son. You're also your mother's. And when it comes to *our* child, you're only half the equation. I have never felt in danger with you, Theo, even when I pushed you and pushed you and you hated it. In fact, I've never felt safer or better protected.'

She stopped, breathing hard, but he didn't say anything. His fingers flexed on the steering wheel, his knuckles white and his face tight, but his simmering anger was nothing compared to hers.

'I think you're scared,' she said hotly. 'I think you're scared of rejection and abandonment and that's why you're not prepared to take a risk on us. And you know what? I get it. I'm scared, too. This pregnancy terrifies me. Everyone I love has a habit of leaving me one way or another. My brother, my father, even my sister. Right now, I miss my mother more than I ever thought possible and it hurts so very much. And then there's the guilt. My God, the guilt. Every time I see Milly, the fact that she will never get the chance to fall in love, have a family, crucifies me.' She shook her head. 'So I don't have a clue what I'm going to do and I'm petrified my anxieties will take over, but I no longer have the luxury of wallowing in my hang-ups. Of being selfish. I have a child to think about. You could, too. And you could have me. Because Daniel was right. We do make a good team. We could make a great one. We could be a family. The one that I want and the one that I know, deep down, you want. And don't you dare give me that "I'm better off alone" rubbish. No one is. Everyone needs someone.'

'I don't.'

'You *do*. Don't you *want* to be happy?' she asked, hearing the faint desperation in her voice but not caring. 'Don't you *want* to let go of the past and look to the future?'

Silence fell and stretched and for the briefest of moments she thought she'd got through to him and hope leapt, but when he spoke it was with an icy calm that splintered her heart and shattered her dreams. 'Why is it so hard to understand, Kate?' he said coldly. 'I don't need happiness and I don't want you.'

'But—'

'What I do want, however, is for you to get out of my car. Now.'

Shaking all over and in agony, Kate closed the door to her flat behind her and sank to the floor, her heart shattering as the sobs she'd held at bay while scrabbling to get out of Theo's car now racked her body.

His brutal rejection of everything she'd offered him was crucifying. Not only had she laid the possibility of a happy future, a happy life on a platter for him, she'd revealed her fears and handed him her heart. And he'd trampled all over it.

Tears streamed down her face and she curled up on the floor, exhaustion and despair descending like a heavy black cloud. She'd given it her best shot and she'd failed. If only she hadn't barged in there with her declaration of love. If only she'd stuck with the plan to keep it to herself for a while. If only she hadn't fallen in love with him in the first place.

She'd been such an idiot. She'd recognised the risk to

her heart he presented and she'd blithely assumed she'd be able to handle it. Why she'd ever thought that when she had zero experience in such matters and the physical and emotional attraction she felt for him was so strong she had no idea. But it was too late for regret because now here she was at the bottom of that slippery slope, and it was just as wretched and miserable as she'd imagined.

Why couldn't he have been willing to give them a chance? Why couldn't he have let her help him? Love him? She had so much to give. What if he just needed time? What if she gave him some space and then tried again?

But no, she told herself with a watery sniff as she angrily brushed away the tears that continued to leak out of the corners of her eyes. She'd be banging her head against a brick wall. She had to stop hoping and imagining and wishing. Theo wasn't going to suddenly and miraculously wake up one morning realising he was in love with her and deciding he *did* want them. He was too damaged. Too entrenched in his beliefs. He was determined to remain alone, an island barricaded from the soaring highs and wretched lows of life.

And however much that hurt, and, oh, how it did, she had to accept it, get up and move on.

CHAPTER FOURTEEN

IN THE DAYS that followed their return to London, Theo was convinced he'd done one hundred per cent the right thing by letting Kate go. He would not tarnish her with his darkness. His actions—and his inaction—brought about the destruction of other people and he would not destroy her, too. Or their child. He didn't deserve happiness and he had no right to take what she had offered. Despite what she believed, he wasn't, and could never be, the man she wanted him to be. And when he thought of the way she'd gone on the attack, which was all the damn time since he couldn't seem to get it out of his head, he was absolutely certain that there was nothing he would have done differently.

He knew he was no coward. She had no idea how much strength and courage it took to stand alone and apart and not seize what deep down he'd always tried to deny he craved. And he was not wallowing or selfish, despite what she might have implied. His concerns were current and real.

So as he'd watched her stumble up the steps to her building he'd told himself that she and her baby would be fine now. He'd driven home and poured himself one drink and then another and then another. The next day he'd gone into the office and thrown himself into work. The deal had been signed. The details were being hammered out. Everything was proceeding smoothly.

But now, two hellish weeks later, he found himself wondering, where was the peace? Where was the sense of achievement? Why was he still so frustratingly restless? And why couldn't he stop pacing?

The sense of impending doom he'd assumed would vanish once he'd dealt with Kate hadn't. Instead, it was larger and darker and more oppressive than ever. And as for order and control that he'd expected to return, he currently felt as if he were hanging on a cliff face by his fingertips. He was popping painkillers like candy and he was snapping at anyone who had the misfortune to cross his path.

What was the matter with him? Why couldn't he concentrate? Why couldn't he eat or sleep? And why hadn't he returned the ring to the jewellers? Kate had returned it to him by courier the day after they'd arrived back. The sight of it had cleaved him in two, but he'd kept it on his desk where it sparkled away at him all sodding day and he had no idea why.

Nor could he work out why he hadn't announced that he and Kate had decided to go their separate ways. The deal was sealed. The contract could not now be broken. A quick press release to announce that their engagement was off would be the easiest thing to do. So why did it feel like the hardest? Why was he still putting it off?

It was all as confusing as hell, but not nearly as confusing as the doubts that had started bothering him a couple of days ago and were now sprouting up all over the place. What if she was right and he was wrong? was the main one, the one that tortured his every waking moment. The minute he crushed it in one place, up it popped somewhere else, churning up his insides and driving him demented.

It couldn't go on.

He couldn't go on.

Not any more.

As the strength suddenly left his body, Theo sank into the sofa, his elbows on his knees, and buried his head in his hands.

He was so damn sick of it. Sick of the torment and the fighting and the bone-crushing loneliness. All his life he'd been alone. He had no siblings and he'd allowed no one to get close. Not even Kate, who'd made him doubt and fear and hope. Who'd pushed her way through his defences and stabbed at where he was weakest and who he might as well admit he adored.

He couldn't do denial any longer. His impenetrability was shot. As the walls around his heart crumbled, pain and regret sliced through him. She'd offered him everything he'd ever wanted and he'd thrown it back in her face. And why? Because she'd been right—he *had* been scared. He'd always been scared.

But, really, what was there to be afraid of? Hadn't he demonstrated time and time again that he had broken the mould? How many times had he been pushed yet stayed in control? He wasn't his father. He never had been. Never would be. Deep down he knew that. So what if that wasn't the real issue? What if he *did* fear rejection and abandonment?

He'd never forget the pain and the guilt, the distress and the trepidation that had gripped every inch of him when he'd shut the door on the flat he'd called home and what little family he'd had. He'd had money and a plan, but that first night he'd spent alone in a cheap nearby hotel had been so cold, so bleak, and the only way he'd been able to move forward was to accept the icy emptiness, adopt it and turn it into armour.

The actions of his mother had cut deep, but it had been fourteen years since she'd looked at him with accusation and disgust. There'd been nothing he could do to save her. He'd given her every opportunity to escape and she'd made her choice and it hadn't been him. There'd been nothing he could have done to save Mike either. Deep down he knew that because he'd done the research and asked the questions.

So he had to forgive himself and let it all go. Because how long was he going to deny himself the future he'd always dreamed of? How long was he going to be able to carry on knowing Kate was out there on her own because of his own blind stupidity?

God, he loved her. She was brave and forthright and confronted whatever life threw at her with her chin up and challenge in her eyes. He wanted her and he wanted their child. And he'd rejected them both.

When he thought of what he'd said to her, and the way he'd said it, he felt sick to his stomach. The ice, the disdain, the cruelty. He could recall every single word and they sliced at him like knives. What the hell had he done? he wondered, shame slamming into him as he broke into a cold sweat. And what the hell could he do to fix it?

The last fortnight for Kate had been something of a roller coaster. One minute she was doing fine, concentrating on putting one foot in front of the other as she got through the days, the next she was dissolving into tears, heartbroken and wishing for what could never be.

A week ago she'd gone to a doctor's appointment and when she'd heard the fluttering whoosh of her baby's heartbeat she'd completely lost it. When she'd visited Milly, who'd grilled her excitedly about the trip to Italy and bombarded her with questions about the non-existent wedding, she'd had to leave before she broke down. Swinging between intense despair and desperate hope that the fact that Theo hadn't issued an announcement about their separation might mean something, she was mostly a wreck and she'd lost count of how many tubs of ice cream she'd consumed.

But while acceptance that he wasn't going to change his mind still shredded her heart it *was* getting easier. Her appetite had returned and she'd stopped waking up in the middle of the night in tears. And look at the way she could now go without thinking about him for a whole five minutes. See how the urge to call him and beg him to give them a chance was gradually diminishing. That was huge progress.

And that wasn't the only area in which she was moving on. The day before yesterday, she'd grabbed a large plastic bag and filled it with the ill-fitting clothes she'd once bought because they made her feel dainty. Then she'd ordered a full-length mirror, which had arrived this morning. If she was going to carry on walking around in her underwear, which she'd taken to doing since everything else was getting tight, she figured she might as well see what she looked like doing it. So what if she was going to become the size of a whale and probably just as cumbersome? Her body was building a baby. It wasn't anything to be ashamed of. It was magnificent. And who cared if she didn't fit in? What was so great about being the same as everyone else anyway?

Besides, she wanted to be able to admire her fabulous new haircut properly. She'd wanted short hair for as long as she could remember but she'd always worried that it would make her look even bigger. And it probably did, but she didn't care, she loved it anyway. Statuesque was how she was going to think of herself from now on. Fearless. And strong.

Because she was all that and more. She'd been wrong about Theo being responsible for the changes she'd undergone. It had been her. All her. She didn't need him. She didn't need anyone. And when she was ready she'd find another man with whom she could wear heels and walk in synch. In Holland, perhaps. Dutch men were the tallest on the planet. They had an average height of one hundred and eighty-two point five centimetres. She knew. She'd looked it up.

In the meantime she had plenty to occupy herself. She had work to find. She had Milly and the baby to focus on. That was more than enough. She didn't need Theo. She didn't need anyone. She was more than capable of doing this on her own. She'd be fine. In fact, she *was* fine.

The buzzer sounded, making her jump and jolting her out of her thoughts. She put down the knife with which she was chopping onions for soup for supper and wiped her streaming eyes. Padding into the hall, she picked up the handset. 'Yes?' she said with a sniff.

'It's Theo.'

At the sound of his voice, the voice that had tormented her dreams and which she'd never ever forget, Kate nearly dropped the handset. Her heart skipped a beat and then began to thunder, the surge of love, need and hope colliding with doubt and wariness. Why was he here? What did he want? And what was she going to do?

The part of her that was still crushed by the way he'd rejected her was tempted to tell him to get lost. Yet him on her doorstep was precisely what she'd been dreaming of, and so even though she was so vulnerable where this man was concerned, even though he had the power to destroy her so completely she might never recover if she wasn't extremely careful, she knew she was no more going to hang up on him than she was going to be a petite size six.

'Come up.'

That was one hurdle cleared, thought Theo grimly, his gut churning with rare nerves as the door buzzed and he pushed his way in. Now for the rest.

As he took to the stairs, it occurred to him that for the first time in decades he had no plan. He had no idea what he was going to say. Once he'd realised how much of a fool he'd been, all he'd focused on was getting here. The only thing he *did* know was that he'd come to fight for the woman he loved and to get her back, whatever it took, whatever the cost, and he wasn't leaving until he'd achieved it.

His throat dry and his pulse racing, he banged on her door and a second later it swung open and there she was, standing there in a dressing gown, her eyes red and shimmering with unshed tears.

'Are you all right?' he asked gruffly, the idea that he could have done that to her, *had* done that to her stabbing him like a dagger in the chest.

'I'm fine,' she replied with a sniff.

Another thought entered his head then, a thought that chilled his blood and for a moment stopped his heart. 'The baby?'

'It's fine, too.'

'Then why are you crying?' he demanded, the indescribable relief flooding through him sharpening his tone.

She blew her nose and gave a shrug. 'Onions.'

He went still. 'What?'

'I've been chopping onions.'

Right. So. Her tears weren't because of him. They were because of onions. That was good. Wasn't it? 'In a dressing gown?'

She lifted her chin a fraction and arched an eyebrow, and he felt a great thud of lust and love slam through him. 'In my underwear, if you must know.'

He'd rather not. The images immediately flashing through his head were immensely distracting and did unsettling things to his equilibrium. Nevertheless, as much as he'd like to pull her into his arms, undo the belt and see exactly what she had on beneath, he kept his eyes up and his hands in his pockets. 'You've had your hair cut.'

'Yes.'

'It suits you.'

'I know,' she said. 'I've also bought a full-length mirror and am considering a move to Holland.'

The ground beneath his feet shifted. What the hell? 'Holland?'

She nodded briefly. 'Holland.'

'Why?'

'Why not?'

He knew of a dozen reasons why not. 'I thought you didn't travel much.'

She shrugged. 'Things change,' she said, and it hit him like a blow to the head that they had. She wasn't sitting at home pining for him. She was getting her hair cut and buying mirrors. She was moving on. Without him. And it was his own damn fault. He yanked his hands out of his pockets and shoved them through his hair, his heart pounding with the very real fear that he'd blown it for good. 'Don't go.'

'You don't get to tell me what to do any more, Theo.'

'I know I don't.'

'Then why are you here?'

'There are so many reasons, I barely know where to start.'

She frowned. 'Is there a problem with the deal?'

'No.'

'Then…?'

'May I come in?'

'No,' she said, folding her arms across her chest and straightening her spine magnificently. 'Whatever you have to say, you can say it out here.'

'All right,' he muttered, beginning to pace in an effort to untangle the jumbled thoughts in his head and calm the panic that he was too late, that he might have already lost her. 'First of all, I wanted to tell you that you were right.'

'About what?'

'Every single point you made in the car. Deep down, I *have* been afraid of rejection and abandonment and it's why I've always kept people at arm's length. But the truth is I ache with loneliness. I want to be happy, Kate, and I want what you offered. You. Our child. The chance to be a family.' He took a deep breath. 'Because I love you.'

She went very still and when she spoke it was almost a whisper. 'What did you say?'

'I love you,' he said, staring at her unwaveringly, unwilling to miss even a flicker of reaction. 'And I need you. You have no idea how much. You are incredible.'

She swallowed hard. 'But you threw me away.'

'Yes,' he said, the memory of his careless brutality skewering him.

'It hurt.'

At the pain in her eyes, his chest tightened as if caught in a vice. 'I know. And I'm sorry. For all of it. For the way I spoke to you in the car. For blackmailing you in the first place. For everything.' He cleared his throat. 'The thing is, Kate, for so long I've believed the world is a safer place if I'm alone and that detachment and distance was the only way to achieve that. It always has been.'

He paused and rubbed his hands over his face as he forced himself to continue. 'My earliest memory is of my father hitting my mother in the face. I can still see her on the floor, him looming over her, huge and angry while she curled up tight. We were terrified every time he came home. I used to wake up to the sounds of crying and shattering glass. I had nightmares. From the youngest age I wanted to protect her, but I couldn't and the sense of failure and hopelessness was all-consuming. I learned to shut down and switch off, and it became so natural I was barely aware I was doing it, or continued to do it. And, yes, I got out, but not before picking up a lot of other damaging belief, especially the "my way or the highway" approach to doing things, which could be attributed to my success or it could just as well be learned. And that's another thing. Success is an easy place to hide, and if no one ever challenges you it becomes even easier.'

He looked at her, willing her to understand and to forgive. 'But you did challenge me, Kate. You *do* challenge me. At first I tried to resist, tried to control it, but that was always going to be a battle I was going to lose. And

I have lost it. Which is fine, because I don't want to hide behind my hang-ups any more. I want to de-programme and learn to live my life with you and our child. You have no idea how badly I want to meet him or her. I can't stop thinking about who they'll look like. I want to be the kind of father I never had. But most of all I want you on my side. By my side. I want everything you have to give and to give you everything you want in return because you deserve to have it.'

He stopped and focused on her, but he couldn't tell what she was thinking and he went cold, his pulse thudding in his ears and dread whipping through him. 'But maybe I'm not what you want any more,' he said, his throat suddenly tight and his voice cracking. 'Maybe I'm too late. Am I?'

All Kate could do was shake her head. The lump the size of Ireland that was lodged in her throat was preventing her from speaking, and her heart was so full she could barely think. Theo loved her. He wanted her. He'd opened up to her, trusting her with his greatest fears and his deepest vulnerabilities and it was everything she'd dreamed of but thought she'd never have.

'You're not too late,' she said, her voice thick with emotion, the need to dispel the uncertainty in his expression and the tension gripping his large, powerful body all-consuming.

His breath caught. His gaze sharpened. A muscle hammered in his jaw. 'No?'

'No.'

'I am still what you want?'

'Yes,' she said with a nod. 'And more. I love you.'

'Thank God for that,' he muttered, striding forward, taking her in his arms and kissing her hard until her head spun and her stomach melted. 'I really thought I'd screwed up beyond salvation.'

'What took you so long?'

'As you may have noticed, I can, on occasion, be rather single-minded.'

She leaned back in his arms and arched an eyebrow. 'On occasion?' she asked with a giddy grin.

'All right. More than on occasion. Once I embark on a course of action I'm not easily derailed. I always know what I'm doing. I always think I'm right. There's safety and security in that. But then I met you and that was shot to hell. I found myself making reckless suggestions and behaving in ways I didn't recognise and it terrified me.' He looked deep into her eyes as if still unable to believe she was there. 'And then somehow you became the plan,' he said in wonder. 'I love you, Kate, and you should know I don't intend to let you go.'

'And you should know,' she said, pressing closer and winding her arms round his neck, 'that however tough things get, I will never walk away. I will always be on your side.'

'Will you marry me?' he asked, his eyes blazing with such love and tenderness that her own began to sting. 'For real?'

And as happiness burst through her like sunshine she tucked her head into his shoulder and sighed, 'I will.'

EPILOGUE

Two and a half years later

'So APPARENTLY,' SAID KATE, sticking two candles into the dinosaur cake she'd spent most of the morning making, 'if you measure a child on its second birthday and double it, that's the height they're going to end up being.'

Theo glanced over from where their toddler son was ripping wrapping paper into shreds, his chest filling with emotion as it never failed to do. 'What's the verdict?'

'Five foot eight.'

His eyebrows shot up. 'Seriously?'

'No, only joking,' she said, with a blinding grin that still stole his breath. 'Six foot four, actually.'

'That's my boy.'

And in three months' time they'd have twin daughters.

Theo didn't like to think how close he'd come to throwing it all away. If Kate hadn't given him another chance... If she hadn't believed in him... But she had and she did. Every single day. The deal had taken a year to finalise, and once it was done, his company was indeed the biggest of its kind. But it wasn't that that had given him peace. It was his family. Daniel Bridgeman had once called him a lucky man. And he was. He was the luckiest man in the world.

* * * * *

COMING SOON!

We really hope you enjoyed reading this book. If you're looking for more romance, be sure to head to the shops when new books are available on

Thursday 16th April

To see which titles are coming soon, please visit

millsandboon.co.uk/nextmonth

MILLS & BOON

Coming next month

THE SECRET KEPT FROM THE KING
Clare Connelly

'No.' He held onto her wrist as though he could tell she was about to run from the room. 'Stop.'

Her eyes lifted to his and she jerked on her wrist so she could lift her fingers to her eyes and brush away her tears. Panic was filling her, panic and disbelief at the mess she found herself in.

'How is this upsetting to you?' he asked more gently, pressing his hands to her shoulders, stroking his thumbs over her collarbone. 'We agreed at the hotel that we could only have two nights together, and you were fine with that. I'm offering you three months, on exactly those same terms, and you're acting as though I've asked you to parade naked through the streets of Shajarah.'

'You're ashamed of me,' she said simply. 'In New York we were two people who wanted to be together. What you're proposing turns me into your possession.'

He stared at her, his eyes narrowed. 'The money I will give you is beside the point.'

More tears sparkled on her lashes. 'Not to me it's not.'

'Then don't take the money,' he said, urgently. 'Come to the RKH and be my lover because you want to be with me.'

'I can't.' Tears fell freely down her face now. 'I need that money. I need it.'

A muscle jerked in his jaw. 'So have both.'

'No, you don't understand.'

She was a live wire of panic but she had to tell him, so that he understood why his offer was so revolting to her.